PENGUIN BOOKS

A PERFECT OBSESSION

Caro Fraser read law at King's College, London. She was called to the bar
in 1979 and worked as a shipping lawyer, and has now been writing full-
time for the last eight years. She has written nine novels, five of which are
part of the highly successful, critically acclaimed Caper Court series, and
Penguin publish *A Little Learning* and *A Perfect Obsession*. She is married
to a solicitor and has four children.

A Perfect Obsession

CARO FRASER

PENGUIN BOOKS

PENGUIN BOOKS

Published by the Penguin Group
Penguin Books Ltd, 80 Strand, London WC2R ORL, England
Penguin Putnam Inc., 375 Hudson Street, New York, New York 10014, USA
Penguin Books Australia Ltd, 250 Camberwell Road,
Camberwell, Victoria 3124, Australia
Penguin Books Canada Ltd, 10 Alcorn Avenue, Toronto, Ontario, Canada M4V 3B2
Penguin Books India (P) Ltd, 11 Community Centre,
Panchsheel Park, New Delhi – 110 017, India
Penguin Books (NZ) Ltd, Cnr Rosedale and Airborne Roads,
Albany, Auckland, New Zealand
Penguin Books (South Africa) (Pty) Ltd, 24 Sturdee Avenue,
Rosebank 2196, South Africa

Penguin Books Ltd, Registered Offices: 80 Strand, London WC2R ORL, England

www.penguin.com

First published by Michael Joseph 2002
Published in Penguin Books 2003

1

Set in Monotype Garamond
Printed in England by Clays Ltd, St Ives plc

For Rosie

January in London. Heavy overnight frost and a twenty-four-hour tube strike. Morning rush-hour traffic standing bumper to bumper along the Hanger Lane gyratory system, the A40, the A2 and the M25. As leaden dawn lightens to pale-grey day, the trains, buses and offices stir into life, the computers hum, the money markets begin to chatter, and the wheels of commerce revolve.

At the centre of this bustling world, in an oasis of apparent antiquity, lies the Temple, a scant square mile of elderly buildings, of lanes and squares and alleyways and courtyards bearing dusty names – King's Bench Walk, Pump Court, Serjeant's Inn, Paper Buildings, Crown Office Row. This sequestered spot, with its fountains and gardens, its flagged courts and cobbled lanes, stands tranquil in the teeming heart of the City of London, and is home to the cream of the English legal system. Here toil the barristers and QCs, their keen minds and well-honed intellects hard at work, delivering views on a multitude of knotty legal questions: on matters of taxation, of banking, of planning, of litigation both civil and criminal, on obscure points of succession and inheritance, on dreary drifts of European directives, on ponderous affairs of international law, on questions which will shape the politics and economic policies of the day, and on smaller matters which will touch the lives of the petty criminal and the humble litigant. They are served and mastered by their clerks, whose job it is to arrange the affairs of chambers, to set dates, exact fees from solicitors, distribute briefs, and to knit seamlessly together the working days of the lawyers. The dignity of the clerks is supreme, their authority unquestioned, and their percentage very healthy.

In the Temple, somewhere between Inner Temple library and Middle Temple Lane, lies Caper Court, a flagged courtyard bounded by handsome buildings, with two trees in its centre and an antique sundial set high up in the wall of one of the buildings. Number 5 Caper Court houses a moderately sized, but élite and marvellously successful set of chambers, where the barristers specialize in commercial and civil litigation, with the odd spot of fraud and shipping thrown in.

Later that same January day, a Wednesday lunchtime, a well-dressed man with sharply handsome features emerged from 5 Caper Court. Hands thrust into the pockets of his navy cashmere overcoat, his prematurely silver hair glinting in the cold sunshine, he strode briskly down King's Bench Walk to where his car was parked. While clerks and office workers thronged the sandwich shops and lawyers and brokers jostled in wine bars, Leo Davies made his way to Highbury to spend a nourishing hour with his therapist.

'It's about sexual orientation.'

'It's about equivocality. I haven't got a sexual orientation.'

Julius Guest looked with bemusement at his patient. He and Leo were old friends – something which, Julius felt, did not perhaps create the best foundation for psychoanalysis – but how little he had known of Leo, he realized, despite those years of friendship. Here was Leo, a man in his mid-forties, looking younger than his years despite his oddly attractive grey hair, fit, good-looking, established in reputation and practice as a QC, in search of solution to some personal problem. What intrigued Julius was to find the problem, rather than the solution.

'Everyone has a sexual orientation.'

'All right, I've got more than one.' He looked at Julius doubtfully. 'Is that too many?'

Julius, a small, intense man of Leo's age, with a neat, pepper-and-salt beard and shoulder-length hair, laughed and spread his hands. 'Have as many as you like. Look, you've told me that you sleep with men as well as women. OK. And I know all about your wife Rachel, about the divorce, and your affair last year with this boy, Joshua. OK, both those relationships made you unhappy –' Julius waved a vague hand '– but let's put them aside for one moment. The question is – this equivocality, call it what you like, does it make you unhappy?'

'Unhappy? Jesus, Julius, that relationship with Joshua . . . When it ended, I thought *I* was ending. I still –'

'No, no. I'm not talking about that. I'm not talking about any specific relationship. That involves dynamics far more complex than mere sexuality. I'm talking here simply, purely –' He leaned forward in his chair, making a compartmentalizing gesture with his hands, '– about you. And sex. Does the fact of your bisexuality upset you? In a general sense.'

There was a silence. 'It troubles me.' Leo spoke slowly. 'That is, it troubles me to think that it's at the root of my problems. But in terms of morality –'

'No, please!' Julius gave an anguished laugh. 'No morals. Facts. Facts.'

Now Leo looked bemused. 'Very well.' He pondered Julius's question again. 'No. No, it doesn't trouble me. My response to any man or woman, in terms of desire, is individual, perfectly genuine. I'm not unhappy with that . . .'

'Well, then?'

Leo sighed. 'I still have this notion that there should be – could be one special person, someone I can share my life with. But relationships – well, they just never go the distance.'

'Maybe *you* don't.'

Leo rubbed a hand across his face. 'I think that's what I meant. I remember saying it to someone once – my ex-wife. It was a kind of warning.'

'Well?'

'It was true then. The relationship with Rachel was never going anywhere. The whole episode was pretty discreditable, if I'm being honest. I shouldn't have married her. Up till then, I'd been more or less happy with the life I led. I never wanted any stability, any commitment or permanence. But since the divorce . . .'

'Since the divorce you've felt lonely. Is that it?'

Leo pondered this. 'Not quite. I think maybe the whole

thing has to do with Oliver, my son. He's only eighteen months old. He's my family. Having him has made me aware of how important it is to have someone in your life – someone to civilize you, keep you from being egotistical and selfish and living only for yourself. I thought Joshua might be the one, the person to share things with. I see now that I was being naïve. He was too young, the balance between us was all wrong.'

'So it had nothing to do with sex. Sex is immaterial. It's about love.'

'I suppose so. I'd hardly say that sex was immaterial.' Leo glanced at his watch. 'Your meter's running out. Come to that, mine probably is, too. I've got to get back to chambers. Got a con at two.' He rose from the comfort of the padded leather chair and slipped on his jacket.

Julius got up. 'Tell me, do you feel these sessions help at all? I've known you for fifteen years, you've been coming to me on and off for six of them, and I sometimes wonder whether you don't need someone more detached, someone who can go more deeply into things. Friendship can throw up certain barriers to effective psychoanalysis, you know.'

Leo smiled. 'I like seeing you. And yes, I think the sessions do me good. Besides, I like keeping you in business. Anyone with five children needs all the help he can get.'

'Your beneficence is mightily appreciated, Leo. Especially when it comes to paying school fees. Not that you know anything about that. Not just yet.' He walked with Leo to the door. 'Still, you're doing all right. Didn't I see your name mentioned in that piece in the *Guardian* the other day about fat-cat lawyers? Fees topping the million-a-year mark, as I recall.'

'I wish. Don't believe everything you read, Julius.' Leo shrugged on his overcoat as Julius opened the door. They walked out together through the receptionist's office.

'By the way,' said Julius, 'when's the opening of this new museum in Shoreditch? I recall you mentioning it last time you were here.'

'Chay had been hoping to have the opening at Christmas, but you can imagine what it's like with renovations, contractors and so forth. It's all fallen a bit behind. Probably some time in February. Why don't you and May come along? I know she likes modern art, even if you don't.'

'A free drink and the chance to schmooze with the likes of Chay Cross is always acceptable.'

'Good. I'll put a couple of invitations in the post.'

Leo went downstairs and out into the cold January air. His car was parked a couple of blocks away. He drove back to chambers through the lunchtime traffic, reflecting on what he had told Julius. It wasn't really true. These monthly sessions with Julius were of little value. Leo knew he used Julius as a sounding board, as much as anything else. He simply talked to him, much as one might to a friend. It went no deeper. In fact, during that dreadful time just after Joshua left him – which was as close to nervous depression as Leo had ever come – it hadn't occurred to Leo to seek help from Julius. He had only told him after the event. Nor, significantly, had he ever told Julius about Anthony. Anthony was a fellow barrister in Leo's chambers at 5 Caper Court, young, good-looking, and bound to Leo by an attachment which neither of them had ever fathomed. Anthony was too important, and the nature of Leo's relationship with him too delicate to touch upon. While it cost him nothing to lay bare to Julius the wretched facts of his brief marriage to Rachel, or to examine the nature of his relationship with Oliver in the light of his own father's departure from his life at an early age, Leo could not bring himself to explore with any other person the complexities of his feelings for Anthony.

He allowed himself to think about Anthony as he sat in the slow crawl of traffic on the Embankment. They were going through one of their periodic phases of discord, characterized by a general aloofness on Anthony's part, and studied indifference on Leo's. Leo thought back to the events of a couple of months ago which had precipitated it. If only Sarah, troublesome as ever, had not chosen that particular evening to call round for a drink. Leo had always found it hard to resist her. He had first met Sarah Colman a few years ago when she was just nineteen, the well-connected daughter of a senior member of the judiciary, blonde, blue-eyed, with a fresh and innocent manner which quite belied her sexual appetite and complete lack of morals. Leo had invited Sarah, plus a young male friend of hers, to his country house at Stanton to share a ménage à trois for a memorable summer. Like all good things, it had come to an end. He and

Sarah saw one another infrequently thereafter. He had been too busy taking silk and shoring up his reputation by making a respectable marriage to have any truck with sweet, scheming Sarah. It didn't escape his attention, however, that she was careful to hover on the edges of his life. She had even gone so far as to have a volatile affair with Anthony, from motives which Leo did not care to examine. And last summer, by a coincidence which Leo could only marvel at, she had started work as a pupil at 5 Caper Court. The propinquity was not one which Leo exactly relished. He liked to keep his private life set well apart from his public one. The kind of sexual intimacy he had shared with Sarah, and the things she knew about him, made her dangerous, particularly given her proclivity for mischief-making. But that evening he had been glad to see her, glad of her cheerful, idle company and the easy warmth of her body, as familiar and pleasurable as ever. He hadn't expected Anthony to call round, just as he'd divested Sarah of her last piece of clothing.

The traffic up ahead suddenly stirred into life, and Leo's thoughts returned to the present. It was already ten past two, and his client – an American cruise operator who had lost several million in an unhappy joint venture – was doubtless already waiting for him, together with the instructing solicitor from Stephenson Harwood. Leo parked his car and hurried into chambers. Henry, the senior clerk, a sad-faced young man in his late twenties, was standing in his braces by the photocopier. He glanced up as Leo came in, and nodded his head in the direction of the waiting-room. Leo nodded in reply and shrugged off his overcoat, smoothing down his hair.

'Ask one of the girls to nip out and fetch me some sandwiches for when this con is over, would you, Henry? I haven't eaten a thing since breakfast.' He headed for the stairs. 'Give me half a minute and then show them up.'

Henry ran a few more documents off and then went to the waiting-room to show the clients up to Leo's room. When he came back down Felicity, a fellow clerk, had just returned from lunch. Henry smiled forlornly at her, in the way that he always did, a smile born out of devotion and hopeless longing. Bright, pretty, energetic, bad-tempered, occasionally foul-mouthed, and with a taste in clothing which ran to the plunging and thigh-revealing, Felicity didn't quite match up to Henry's cherished vision of the ideal woman, but he had been captivated by her ever since she had first come to 5 Caper Court two years before. She was a good clerk, too, quick-witted, practical and hard-working. Henry was proud of the fact that he had trained her to be as capable as she now was, but he nurtured his true feelings for her discreetly. Apart from the impossibility of any relationship between two clerks working side by side, Henry knew for a fact that he wasn't Felicity's type. Felicity went for the well-muscled, good-looking, glib kind, in the shape of a waster called Vince, with whom she had been living for two years. Last October Vince had got into a fight with a couple of youths, one of whom had hit his head on the pavement and subsequently died. At the same time, Felicity had lost the baby she was carrying. All in all, it had been a dreadful time. Vince had been charged with murder, and was still waiting to hear the date for his trial. Henry had no real idea how this had affected Felicity's feelings towards Vince, but, knowing Felicity, he assumed that it had only served to strengthen them. Felicity was loyal and loving, much to Henry's despair.

'Bloody brass monkeys out there,' remarked Felicity, unwinding her scarf and setting her sandwiches and coffee down on the desk. From outside came the clang of scaffolding pipes and the whistling of workmen. Felicity went over to the window and glanced out. 'I wish they'd get a move on and finish the annexe. I can't stand that racket all day long. And the looks you get from those workmen when you cross the court!'

'Can't say I've experienced that problem,' replied Henry. 'Have you seen some papers that came in from Middleton Potts for Simon?'

'Yeah, they're over here,' said Felicity through a mouthful of sandwich.

They both glanced up as Anthony Cross came into the clerks' room. He was a tall, dark-haired young man of twenty-four, with boyish good looks which were losing their softness. Three years of a highly successful practice had polished his manner, which, when he had first arrived at Caper Court, had been somewhat tentative. Unlike most of those at number 5, Anthony had not had the advantages of a public school and Oxbridge background. He had had to exert his exceptional academic capabilities to win scholarships and funding throughout his early legal career. His mother was a primary-school teacher and his father, Chay, at the time that Anthony was growing up, had been a superannuated hippy with artistic pretensions and no money, who had abandoned his family for life in an Islington squat. Just at the time when Anthony gained his much-prized tenancy at 5 Caper Court, Chay Cross's fortunes, too, had taken a sudden and dramatic upturn. His paintings began to sell, and within a year he had become one of the leading lights of the postmodern art movement. Now he was wealthy, with houses in Milan, New York and London, and the kind of celebrity lifestyle which perfectly suited his vanity and pretensions. Success hadn't changed Chay Cross's personality in the least, but Anthony marvelled at the way in which wealth had lent acceptability to its more unattractive aspects. People who would once have run a mile from his boring, rambling dissertations on art and related subjects now listened breathlessly to his utterances, and regurgitated his profundities in the pages of *Modern Painters*. Happy though he was that his father could now hang out with the likes of Damien Hirst and Simon Schama, it bemused Anthony that anyone should achieve such staggering success on the back of what he still considered to be ghastly, derivative pieces of work of no aesthetic quality and questionable integrity.

Anthony dropped some papers on the counter. 'Can you ask Robert to take these documents over to Mr Justice Latham's chambers? They've been revised and they need to be substituted in the judge's bundle. The judge's clerk probably has them. They need to get there this afternoon, as the hearing's tomorrow.'

'Will do,' said Henry. 'By the way, your father rang when you were out at lunch. Sorry I didn't mention it earlier. Asked if you could call him back.'

'Did he say where he was?'

'At his gallery place.'

'Right, thanks.'

Anthony went back upstairs to his room, which was snug and narrow, lined with bookshelves along one side. On the opposite wall stood a low set of shelves stacked with briefs and bundles of papers, and in the fireplace a small gas fire burned against the chill of the January day. Anthony's desk stood by the curtained window, facing into the room, in the centre of which was a polished oval table surrounded by chairs, for conferences. The table, like Anthony's desk, was piled with papers and files, and stacks of cardboard containers full of documents lined the floor beneath the window. On the wall hung pictures, charcoal sketches of the law courts and the Strand. It was not unlike being in a small, comfortable, but faintly austere drawing-room, in which someone had dumped a large quantity of paper and boxes. The only concessions to modernity were Anthony's leather office chair and a state-of-the-art computer, fax and scanner on a side table by his desk. It was an extraordinary contrast to the open-planned and air-conditioned existences of his friends and acquaintances working in banks and solicitors' firms throughout the City, but to Anthony it was all thoroughly normal, and part of the curious blend of past and present which characterized the Temple.

Anthony picked up the phone and rang Chay's mobile.

Chay was totally engrossed these days in a scheme to renovate an enormous derelict brewery in Shoreditch and turn it into a museum of modern art, a task which was near completion. Leo was one of the museum's trustees, and Anthony helped his father with legal aspects of the project.

'It's me,' said Anthony, when Chay answered. 'Henry said you rang earlier.'

'Right, I did. Things are coming together faster than I anticipated and it looks like we could have the opening at the beginning of March if we can get the invitations out. The PR people reckon it would be excellent timing. David Bowie's going to be in London around the seventh, and it would really boost publicity to have him there. I'm hoping Simon Callow and Maggi Hambling will be able to come, possibly Tracey and Damien. Hockney's a long shot, but you never know. Anyway, I'm trying to arrange a meeting of the trustees for tomorrow night.'

'That's rather short notice, isn't it?'

'Yeah, I know, but most of the others should be able to get here. I tried to get hold of Leo at lunchtime, but couldn't track him down. Do you think you could have a word and see if he can manage to be there?'

'All right,' said Anthony.

'And obviously, if you can make it, that would be useful.'

'I'll see what I can do.'

'Catch you later.'

Anthony put the phone down. He sometimes wondered, beyond the setting up of the original trust, what use he was to his father in this project. He seemed to like his presence at these meetings. Maybe it was, as Leo had once suggested, a way of validating himself in his son's eyes, reminding him that he was no longer a failure. Chay was such a child in many ways. Anthony turned to the window and stared out at the building works going on at number 7, diagonally opposite. The top floor was being turned into an annexe to relieve the pressure on the already overcrowded chambers at number 5, and all day the sound of hammering and drilling filled the normally tranquil air.

A figure appeared in the courtyard below, hurrying from number 5 towards Middle Temple Lane, a young woman with chestnut hair, the blue bag containing her wig and gown slung over her shoulder, papers tucked beneath one arm. A pang touched Anthony's heart as he watched her disappear through the archway. It was almost three months since his affair with Camilla Lawrence had ended. He hadn't been out with any other girl regularly since. No doubt there were those, including many members of chambers, who would say that it was just as well, that it wasn't healthy to conduct an intimate relationship with another barrister in the same chambers, but there had been a time when Anthony had thought he was truly in love. He wondered now. Since the relationship had been abruptly terminated by Camilla's discovery that Anthony had had a brief fling with Sarah Colman while Camilla was away in Bermuda on a case, it was reasonable to assume that his feelings couldn't have been as deep as he had supposed. Not that he would have had anything to do with Sarah if she hadn't come on to him in the way she had . . . it was very hard at twenty-four to resist that kind of temptation. She had probably just been making mischief, as usual. Still, she had been the cause of their break-up.

And the cause of his present rift with Leo. He turned away from the window and sat down, moodily winding a length of red tape round his fingers. If she hadn't been there that evening, when he'd gone to see Leo, then there would be none of this wretched animosity. In truth, though, the animosity was on his part, not Leo's. He had gone to Leo that night to tell him – to tell him what, exactly? That he regretted not becoming his lover three years earlier, that he couldn't go on feeling about him as he did . . . That had been the idea. The whisky which Leo had poured for him might have been enough to bring it all out. But it hadn't happened – and no doubt just as well. Sarah had suddenly appeared, wearing nothing but one of Leo's shirts, hair mussed, looking delectable. He had been aware that she and Leo had known one another before she ever came to chambers, but he hadn't realized quite how intimate that friendship was. Embarrassing and humiliating as it had been, it could have been worse. At least she'd come into the room before he'd had the chance to make a fool of himself.

Pointless to think about it now. He could do without all that emotional confusion. He was straight, always had been, and if it hadn't been for Leo and his warped ethical view of the world, his belief that sexuality knew no moral boundaries, Anthony would never have had to worry about all this. Perhaps that wasn't quite fair ... He remembered those long days, sitting as a pupil in Michael Gibbon's room, listening for the sound of Leo's voice on the stair, his whistle, his rapid footstep. How he had held his breath at that last sound, hoping that Leo, as he sometimes did, would look in to have a word with Michael. He had a way of lighting up any room he came into. Anthony had loved him, loved his company, his charm, his looks, the brilliance of his mind and his easy erudition. He loved the fact that Leo, like him, had come up the hard way, from humble beginnings in a dreary Welsh town, to achieve a position as one of the most respected commercial silks in London. He regarded Leo as a kindred spirit. He had worshipped him back then, taken every chance to sit with him in court, watching and learning. He felt he owed much of his own present success to Leo.

Anthony flung the tape aside and sighed. Maybe he shouldn't get so hung up about all this. Sarah could sleep with Leo if she wanted. She'd slept with just about everyone else. The truth was that it was Leo he blamed. He took his pleasure where he pleased and did untold damage. It had been that way with Rachel. No sooner had Anthony set his sights on her than Leo had moved in, seduced her, married her for God knows what selfish reason, all without regard for Anthony's feelings. Not that Rachel had ever cared about Anthony, but still ... The fact was, he had been angry with Leo ever since finding Sarah at Leo's flat that night, and he couldn't seem to get rid of the feeling. Not that it seemed to bother Leo much. He scarcely acknowledged that there was anything wrong. At the bottom of it all, Anthony knew, lay his own jealousy. He was jealous of anyone who took Leo's time and affection. He hated Leo's promiscuity as much as he hated the deep emotional attachments Leo occasionally formed, as he had done with Joshua. In fact, he was thoroughly confused and fed up with caring about Leo. Well, it was finished. He didn't want to become part of Leo's weird world. He'd just have to try and get rid of this feeling of resentment and make something civilized of their relationship. He hadn't spoken properly to Leo for ages. He'd make a start later this afternoon by going to tell Leo about the meeting of the museum trustees tomorrow night.

Leo was gathering up his belongings at six when Anthony knocked on his door and looked in. Leo paused in bemused surprise, then carried on putting papers into his briefcase. That Anthony should come to see him meant nothing. It might simply be about chambers business. Leo closed his briefcase, waiting for Anthony to speak. Anthony glanced round the room, which was quite different from his own, light and modern, the desk of polished ash, clear of clutter, the pictures on the walls expensive abstracts. Its appearance, like Leo's, was of expensive minimalism, giving nothing away.

Anthony came into the room and closed the door, then said diffidently, 'I just came to tell you that Chay rang me earlier.'

'Oh?'

'He couldn't get hold of you. Asked me to tell you that he's holding a meeting of the trustees tomorrow evening. It's short notice, but he's decided to try and bring the opening forward to early March and he wants to discuss arrangements.'

Leo flicked open his diary. 'That's all right. Did he mention a time?'

'No – no, I forgot to ask. I'll speak to him again tomorrow and let you know.'

Leo nodded. He lifted his briefcase off the desk and crossed the room to take his coat from the hanger on the back of the door. Anthony still stood uncertainly in the middle of the room. He was looking for a way to use this opportunity to make peace, Leo realized. Well, let Anthony take the initiative – it had been he, after all, who had created the antagonistic atmosphere of the past few months. He turned to look at him, and was suddenly moved by the uncertain, vulnerable expression on the younger man's face. Anthony might have toughened up a lot over the past few years, but he still found it hard to deal with certain things.

Leo took pity on him. 'Are you going to the meeting tomorrow evening?' he asked.

'Yes – yes, I am. At least, Chay asked me along.'

There was a pause, then Leo relented completely. 'I'll give you a lift, if you like. Assuming the thing's around half-seven, as it usually is, we could go for a drink beforehand.'

Anthony grasped this olive branch gratefully, knowing that by rights he was the one who should have made the first move. He just hadn't known the appropriate thing to say. 'Great. Yes, let's do that.'

Leo was touched by the way Anthony's expression suddenly lightened with relief. He opened the door of his room and they went out together.

'By the way,' remarked Leo as they went downstairs, 'did you see that practice direction about assigning two-judge management teams to longer cases?'

'Yes,' replied Anthony, 'quite a good idea, in some ways.' They carried on chatting for a few minutes on the landing outside Anthony's room.

Anthony felt happier in his heart than he had for some time. He was glad they'd broken the ice. But he was still resolved that he was finished for good with the intense emotional side of their friendship. He wanted no more than a platonic, amicable relationship.

'Right,' said Leo, glancing at his watch. 'I'd better go. I'm meeting someone in ten minutes. See you tomorrow.'

Anthony went back into his room and closed the door, wondering exactly who it was Leo was going to meet, trying to persuade himself he didn't really care.

2

'. . . which brings us, my Lord, to the Brussels Convention, which has the force of law in the United Kingdom by virtue of Section 2 (1) of the Civil Jurisdiction and Judgments Act, 1982. Articles 7 to 11 in Section 3 deal with jurisdiction in matters relating to insurance, but article 12 sets out an exception which I must quote in full . . .' David Liphook had been on his feet for the past forty-five minutes, earnestly addressing the court in the vexed matter of a contractual dispute between three Lloyd's syndicates and a Dutch offshore company, regarding property hired out to a Yugoslav enterprise for purposes connected with the construction of a breakwater in Algeria. Sarah Colman, his pupil, sat next to him, taking notes now and again when she could be bothered – which wasn't often – and discreetly trying to suppress her frequent yawns. She and her flatmate, Lou, had been out clubbing the night before and they hadn't got in until half-three, and Sarah was feeling distinctly ragged. She'd been in such a rush to get into chambers on time that she'd only had time for a cup of coffee, and now, at eleven-thirty, she was famished.

She sat back and glanced up at David. He was a stocky man in his early thirties, moderately attractive, Sarah supposed, but far too much the public-school type for her liking. He was an OE, and in a barrister the Old Etonian blend of ability, arrogance and perfect good manners was a distinct success. High Court judges, like upper-middle-class mothers, loved him. They could say what they liked, thought Sarah, but the class system was alive and thriving at the Bar, and always would be so long as most of the high fliers and judges came from public schools and Oxbridge colleges. Like all tribal animals, they felt most comfortable with their own kind. Sarah reckoned she could spot the products of different public schools a mile off. OEs acted like they owned the place (which more often than not they did), Wykehamists were too brainy for their own good, with a tendency to twitch, Salopians were failed rebels with leftist leanings who held down establishment jobs despite themselves, and Carthusians were snobs, academics, poets or queers, depending on which house they'd been in.

She glanced up at the judge, Mr Justice Stobie, and tried to assess him. He had a sort of pale, Catholic look about him. Ampleforth? Then again, his name sounded Scottish, so possibly Fettes or Glenalmond. She liked assessing the people around her, weighing up their lives. It gave her a heightened sense of detachment. She was with them, but not of them. For instance, Sarah reckoned she knew exactly the kind of wife David Liphook would eventually marry, the kind of children he would have, where they would be schooled, the sort of holidays he would take, the age at which he would take silk, then eventually seek elevation to the High Court ... The predictability of it all was stunning.

'I must interrupt you there, Mr Liphook.' Mr Justice Stobie's mellow tones disturbed Sarah's idle thoughts. 'You appear to be suggesting that the word "interest" is used here in the technical sense to refer to the nature of the title to property held by the person insured. Might there not be an argument for saying that the word is intended in a broader sense, perhaps simply to describe property in connection with which a risk can give rise to loss?'

It's no use, thought Sarah, as she digested this observation and listened in fascination to the speed and enthusiasm with which David replied. Not in a million years could she be a commercial barrister. It wasn't that she didn't understand the law, or couldn't make sense of David's various cases – since her shaky beginnings six months ago she now took a vague pleasure in being able to strip an apparently complex set of instructions down to the essentials. It was simply that she could never care enough. David cared. He was entirely engrossed. Sarah sighed. So what was she doing here? She'd originally taken up law because it was a family thing, and she couldn't think of anything else to do, though her studies at Oxford had been largely peripheral to her social life. After that she'd gone to Bar school because the thought of becoming a solicitor was too awful to contemplate, and when she'd done that she'd sought a pupillage in Leo's chambers because it seemed like an amusing thing to do. Too much ability and absolutely no ambition, that's my problem, thought Sarah, as she half-listened to David droning on about risks and interests. And it was true. She was very bright, but had no real interest in the arduous business of carving out a career at the Bar, or anywhere else, for that matter. On days like these – days when she hadn't had enough sleep, or was hungover, or just bored or dispirited – she sincerely wished that women weren't expected to pursue careers. Not enough to have it all, you had to do it all as well. The curse of Cherie Blair. She and the likes of Nicola Horlick had a lot to answer for. Sarah had recently begun to think that she could quite happily jack it all in, marry someone rich and do nothing at all besides lead a comfortable life, spending someone else's money. She glanced across at Vivienne Lamb, the barrister on the other side. She was formidably bright and had a terrific reputation, which was all very well . . . but it was the prospect of having to work so hard that Sarah couldn't bear. Where was the attraction in slogging away throughout your twenties, trying to get a foothold on a ladder which could be pulled away from under you as soon as you had your first baby, trying to find a marriageable man along with all the other thirty-somethings, biological clocks ticking merrily away? She could see increasing attractions in marrying someone now, and never having to work again. Play your cards right, and your social life needn't suffer. Lovers could be had discreetly, and there were plenty of ways of keeping a lively intellect stimulated.

She yawned and shifted uncomfortably on the hard bench, glancing round the courtroom. Not that she could ever imagine herself becoming a Mrs Liphook, or a Lady Stobie. But what other prospective pool did she have to fish in? Apart from barristers, her male social circle consisted mainly of merchant bankers, chaps in PR and advertising, City types and the odd journalist. Merchant bankers were too boring, PR people were fine to go out with but you'd hardly want to marry one, City types led lives which were financially too precarious, whatever the highs, and journalists – well . . .

Her mind floated back to the reason she was sitting here now. Leo. She had wangled her way into a pupillage at 5 Caper Court because she liked to be part of his life. It had to be admitted that, however casual she pretended her attachment to him was, he had always exercised a fascination for her. One strong enough to make her want to work in the same chambers as he did. Now, didn't that tell her something? She smiled as she doodled in her notebook, amazed that she'd never really given proper thought to the marriageability of Leo. He was perfect – wealthy, and likely to carry on being so, good-looking, excellent company, witty, stimulating . . . and wonderful in bed. There was the minor problem of his proclivity for young men, but since the kind of marriage she had in mind was one of mutual freedom, and as Sarah's own nature was strictly amoral, that was hardly a problem. From a social point of view he was ideal – well-connected, and more than likely to make it right to the top of his profession. He'd make a beautiful law lord when he hit sixty or so. Sir Leo and Lady Davies . . . she could see it now. And life with Leo would never be boring. He was different from other barristers she knew. His path to his present eminent position at the Bar had been far from conventional, his modest beginnings had made life an uphill struggle, one he had won by dint of sheer intellectual ability and brilliance. She liked that. His tastes and interests were eclectic, and his behaviour often unpredictable. She knew enough of that from the summer she and James had spent with him . . . Yes, marrying Leo could be a stroke of genius.

Sarah sighed and glanced at the clock. Almost lunchtime, thank God. The trouble was, Leo wasn't the marrying kind. All right, there had been Rachel, but as Leo himself had once admitted, when his guard was down, he'd only married her to deflect gossip at a time when his private life was under scrutiny, and threatening his prospects of becoming a QC. How ruthless and selfish could you get? Yet for Sarah those aspects of Leo's character held a peculiar attraction. She understood him. They were both cynics, used to using people. Rachel had been beautiful, insipid, an obvious victim. Still, the fact that he hadn't married Rachel for love didn't take things much further. It just made it more likely that Leo would never marry anyone unless there was something to be gained by it. He would be a tough nut to crack. The toughest. It had to be admitted that there was no real reason why Leo, if Sarah really decided to make a serious play for him, should ever consider taking her on. She might be young and attractive, but pretty young things, of whatever gender, weren't hard to come by if you were Leo. Sarah was nothing if not a pragmatist. Still, she had certain advantages, cards which were uniquely hers to play. First of all, he liked her. Secondly, she knew him well, better than most people, and that counted for a good deal. Thirdly, everyone got lonely. Even Leo. And she didn't doubt that forty-six was a vulnerable age for most men, no matter how successful . . .

Sarah suddenly realized that David had finished, and was sitting down. The judge glanced up at the clock. 'Thank you, Mr Liphook. Ladies and gentlemen, this seems like a convenient place to stop. We shall reconvene at two, and hear from Miss Lamb.'

There was a general murmuring and rustling of papers. Sarah closed her counsel's notebook, smiling to herself, amused by her cogitation of the last twenty minutes. She had to spend the next six months at 5 Caper Court, and she relished a challenge. It would be interesting to find out just how much headway one could make in the marital stakes with someone as impossibly eligible and marvellously unattainable as Leo. Regarded in the light of a game, it was as good a way of passing the time as any. She had nothing to lose by trying, and everything to gain.

Later that afternoon, when the court had risen, Sarah and David made their way back across the Strand to the Temple, bearing bundles of paper and books. Coming in through the archway to Caper Court, they met Camilla Lawrence, who smiled and said hello to David, but gave Sarah only a brief, mistrustful glance. Not that Sarah cared in the least. She had always regarded Camilla as something of a wet date. She'd been wet when they'd been at Oxford together, and she'd stayed wet ever since. What Anthony had ever seen in her was beyond Sarah.

Not that that had lasted long. Clearly Camilla still blamed Sarah for seducing poor Anthony away from her. Well, Sarah could live with that. She certainly had no particular interest in Anthony any more. Not at present. He was merely the kind of thing you put by for a rainy day.

The three of them went up the short flight of stone steps and through the portals of Number 5.

'Here,' said David, piling his papers on top of the bundle Sarah was already carrying, 'you go on up with these. I'm just going to have a word with Henry.' He slipped into the clerks' room.

Leo and Anthony were coming downstairs just as Sarah, trying to negotiate the unwieldy bundle of papers and books, dropped the lot at the foot of the stairs. The sight of Leo, so close on the heels of her musings of the day, had startled her.

Leo stopped to help, but Anthony merely stepped over the mess and went into the clerks' room with some papers. Leo glanced after him in surprise. Anthony was normally scrupulously well-mannered. Clearly Sarah, as she so often could, had done something to push Anthony beyond the bounds of polite behaviour.

'Now, what could you have done to make Anthony behave like that?' asked Leo, as he and Sarah gathered up the scattered papers.

'Trespassed on his territory,' replied Sarah with a smile. 'First Camilla, then you.'

'Hmm. I hardly think Anthony assumes proprietorial rights over me.'

'Don't you?'

'Come on, you can't carry this lot up on your own. You take those, and I can manage these.'

They took the papers and books up to David's room.

'So what's all this about Camilla?' asked Leo, who loved gossip. He leaned against the bookcase and folded his arms.

Sarah perched on the edge of her desk. 'Oh, it's old news. Happened last October. Camilla and Anthony were seeing one another – you know, heavy stuff.'

'I do recall something of the kind.'

'Well, she went off to Bermuda on a case for a couple of weeks, I was bored, Anthony was available, and –' She paused, shrugged. 'It was just a casual fling, but Camilla didn't really take it in good part.' Sarah gave a little smile. 'She is *so* principled. Anyway, I can't believe you didn't know. You're usually well abreast of what's going on in chambers.'

'Anthony and I haven't spoken much lately. Besides, it's not a thing one normally gets to hear about. So tell me, how did Camilla find out? Don't tell me Anthony's conscience overwhelmed him.' Leo had learned a while ago from others in chambers that Anthony and Camilla were no longer seeing one another, and for reasons of his own, had not been exactly displeased. The explanation for the break-up, however, was news to him.

'She must have picked it up from someone,' replied Sarah airily. 'Can't imagine who.'

'I think I can.' Leo shook his head, his eyes drawn to Sarah's dark-stockinged legs as she swung them idly. God, this girl was bad news, yet he couldn't help liking her, somehow. Her lack of scruples, her ability to take her pleasure as and when she liked, and damn the rest of them, these were things he could readily relate to.

He looked up, and Sarah's eyes met his. She could almost read his thoughts. She loved the way she could produce this sexual current between them. It was one of the things she was most ready to exploit in her newly hatched campaign. No time like the present.

'Why don't you let me buy you a drink, as a thank-you for helping me with those papers?' Her expression as she said this was one Leo knew of old, suggestive and distinctly inviting. There would be more to the evening than just a few drinks.

'Love to, but I'm afraid Anthony and I have already made plans. We were just on our way out.'

Although her smile didn't slip, this news was not welcome to Sarah. She had always been aware of some special relationship between Leo and Anthony, and its existence galled her. She had taken considerable satisfaction from the events of that evening last autumn, when Anthony had found her there at Leo's flat, particularly since it came close on the heels of the demise of his affair with Camilla. Everyone wanted a little piece of Leo, Sarah knew, but Anthony should learn that he couldn't have everything. It irked her now to learn that whatever rift she had managed to create between Leo and Anthony had apparently healed.

'Why don't I join you?' she suggested, scenting the possibility of mischief.

Leo smiled and eased himself away from the bookcase.

'I don't think so. After what you've just told me, I don't think Anthony would welcome your company, do you?'

'Possibly not.' Sarah sighed and slipped off the desk. 'Have a nice evening, then.'

'Thanks,' said Leo, smiling as he left the room and went back downstairs.

Anthony was waiting for him. 'I wondered where you'd got to.'

'I helped Sarah take those papers up to David's room.' They went out together into the chilly early-evening air. 'Rather churlish of you not to help her as well, if I may say so,' added Leo, as they passed through the cloisters and headed for the foot of King's Bench Walk, where Leo's car was parked.

Anthony flushed slightly. 'The less I have to do with Sarah the better.'

'Yes, I gather she's made something of a nuisance of herself. Still, try not to let your animosity get the better of your good manners.'

Anthony said nothing. Leo gave him a quick sideways glance, wondering whether Sarah, in spite of what Anthony said, still exercised some fascination for him. Clearly Anthony had been prepared to risk his relationship with Camilla just to be able to bed her. Once acquired, Sarah could be a difficult habit to shake off. Maybe Leo had had it all wrong. Maybe when he'd found Sarah at his flat that evening, his jealousy had been directed at Leo. He pondered this as they crossed the cobblestones. He unlocked the car and they got in. Leo put the key in the ignition but didn't start the engine. He turned to Anthony.

'You know, we haven't spoken about that evening, when you came round and Sarah was there.'

Anthony said nothing for a few seconds as he clicked his seat belt into place. Then he glanced up. 'It doesn't matter.'

'Why *did* you come round? I don't think I ever found out.'

Anthony gazed at Leo, at the familiar features etched in the half-darkness. Feelings of love and confusion cut deep into him. It was too long ago now, the moment had passed, and he had already decided that he wasn't going to go down that path. Not again. That was over and done with. It was a friendship, no more. 'I told you – it doesn't matter. I just came to see you. The fact that Sarah was there –' He paused. 'She said something once about how well she knew you, but I didn't realize quite *how* well.'

Leo sighed and turned the key in the ignition. He reversed out of the space and set off towards Middle Temple Lane. 'Look, Sarah and I –' He hesitated, wondering what he had intended to say. He certainly couldn't tell Anthony about Sarah and James and the summer of a couple of years ago. So, what *was* there to say about himself and Sarah? He scarcely knew. He had never given it much thought. She was there, tantalizing, devious, not always when he wanted her, but occasionally when he did. 'Sarah and I have known one another for quite a while. We see one another – well, intermittently.'

'You mean you fuck her now and again?' Anthony's voice was angry and abrupt.

Leo glanced at him in puzzlement. 'Anthony –'

'Sorry. I'm sorry. But it's another way of putting it, isn't it?' He turned to gaze at the lights of the river as they sped along the Embankment. He hadn't meant to get angry. It was just that he could do without being reminded of how easily and indiscriminately Leo took lovers.

Leo decided to let it go. He didn't want any more antagonism between them. 'I suppose you're right,' he replied. 'Let's talk about something else.'

When they reached Shoreditch they parked the car and went for a drink in a pub close to the museum. It was only six o'clock and the meeting wouldn't start for another hour.

'I'll get these,' said Leo. 'What'll you have?'

'Just a pint of bitter, thanks.'

Leo went to the bar, glancing round. The last time he had been in this place was with Melissa Angelicos, a co-trustee of the museum, appointed by Chay by virtue of the fact that she hosted a moderately influential arts programme on Channel 4. God, what a mistake that evening had been. He'd been having problems with Joshua at the time, and had tried to forget about them by passing a drunken few hours with Melissa, after which they'd gone back to her place for coffee. Only it hadn't been coffee that Melissa had in mind. Leo winced as he recalled the subsequent events.

He took the drinks back to the table where Anthony

was sitting, took off his overcoat and sat down. There was silence for a few seconds, indicative of unease on Anthony's part. Leo was aware that the coolness of the last few months could not simply be brushed aside. He'd tried to address it earlier in the car. Perhaps now he should try again.

He drew his chair closer to the table. 'Look, what I said earlier about Sarah –' Anthony glanced at him sharply, but Leo continued, '– I was wondering whether that's the reason you've been so distant of late.' Anthony said nothing. 'I know you had a relationship with Sarah in the past. I thought it was over. I certainly had no wish to hurt you. If you still have feelings for her –'

Anthony interrupted him with a laugh. 'The only feelings I have for Sarah are – well, I don't really think I can decently express them. She is a complete bitch.'

Leo sipped his whisky, and nodded. 'True.'

'What I can't understand, Leo, is why you would waste your time with someone as – as sly and manipulative as she is.' The warmth with which Anthony spoke took Leo a little closer to what he suspected was the truth. But it wasn't something he would touch upon yet.

Leo took a small, silver cigar case from his breast pocket, lit a cigar, then blew out a little cloud of smoke. 'She amuses me.'

'She amuses you? Christ, Leo, don't you look for anything a bit deeper, something with more meaning, in your relationships with people?'

Leo shrugged. 'That invariably produces disappointment. Sarah is intelligent, attractive, and stimulating –

in a rather bizarre way. But above all, she makes no demands.'

'You mean, she simply makes herself available.'

Leo shook his head. 'Actually, one of her most compelling qualities is her elusiveness. Anyway –' He glanced at Anthony, '– why should you concern yourself with Sarah, if she's not the reason for your offhand manner for the past couple of months?'

'It's you, Leo – it's you! Finding Sarah at your place that night – well, it just shows how trivial relationships are to you. I thought you were meant to be heartbroken about Joshua, and yet there you were, not two weeks later, carrying on with her!'

The small pang of pain which touched Leo at the mention of Joshua's name was not betrayed in his expression. 'You know me, Anthony, and yet you don't know me. Don't concern yourself with what goes on between Sarah and myself. It doesn't touch the relationship between you and me, after all.' He paused, glancing up at Anthony. 'Does it?'

Anthony's temper, still simmering, cooled a little at the quiet tone in which Leo spoke. He hesitated before answering. 'I don't know.'

'You made it clear a long time ago that you didn't want our relationship to be anything more than a friendship. I've always understood that to be the case, though there have been times when I've had my doubts.' He paused for a long, reflective moment and looked up at Anthony. 'Or did you come to my flat that night to tell me something different?'

The question hung in the air between them.

Anthony looked away, unable to bear the intensity of Leo's gaze, which threatened to undermine his resolve. 'No,' he replied at last. 'I came round to see how you were. I was still worried about you.'

Leo drew on his cigar, his eyes still fastened on the younger man's face. He felt the force of the moment melt away. He would have to accept the denial at face value. 'I see. In that case, there's no need for any anger.'

Anthony raked his fingers through his hair. 'I just want you to — to care more about the way you behave.'

Leo smiled. 'I love your principles. No — no, truly. I mean it. I wish I could be more the kind of person you want me to be. Still —' He sipped his whisky. 'You'll have to make do with me as I am. Now — can we forget the wretched Miss Colman and try to behave like friends again?'

Anthony relented. When Leo smiled in that way, he couldn't help it. So what if he hadn't been entirely honest in answering Leo? There were lots of different truths, and a person couldn't tell them all. This was the best way. 'Yes. All right. I'm sorry about the way I've been.'

'I should have said something sooner.' Leo glanced at his watch. 'We're due at the brewery in half an hour. Just time for another.'

'Let me get them,' said Anthony, and drained his glass.

So they sat companionably over another drink, immersed in talk of their world, of cases and arbitrations, and Sarah was not mentioned again.

*

The ex-brewery which housed Chay Cross's museum of modern art was a cavernous building in the heart of Shoreditch, in a state of some dilapidation when Chay had taken it over, but now the product of startling changes. The heart of the building was a vast central area, around which ran a gallery at first-floor level, and from which radiated a network of smaller, satellite rooms. When Leo and Anthony arrived, Chay was busy working out which exhibits would be housed in which rooms. Paintings in protective packaging lay stacked against walls in uneven rows, and in the central area a half-finished circular wooden plinth was being erected. Workmen's tools and welding gear littered the floor. Voices echoed, bouncing off the high walls and windows.

Chay came to greet them, a tall, spindly man in his late forties, with grizzled grey hair and designer stubble, dressed in the fashion of an ageing rock star. His manner, which was one of faux-naïf self-deprecation and modesty, masked an ego of considerable proportions and a talent for shameless self-publicity. Having initially managed to seduce the capricious mandarins of the modern art world into accepting his work as brilliant and innovative, Chay was well aware that to keep his stock high depended as much on his personal visibility and the maintenance of a fashionable profile as it did on producing work of any intrinsic merit. To this end he cultivated the great and good from the diverse worlds of art, music and fashion, and was as likely to be found in the front row at Vivienne Westwood's latest collection as to be seen slumming it in a trendy coffee bar in Whitechapel.

'Hi.' Chay transferred his Gauloise to his mouth and shook Leo's hand. 'Good to see you. Come and have a look round before the others get here. Most of the stuff's still in storage, but some of the exhibits arrived today. This –' He pointed to the half-finished plinth, '– is for the Beckman installation. It's going to be enormous. A spiral of metal steps winding round a central bronze column, with video screens at intervals. They'll be showing continuous film of Beckman washing his dog, interspersed with clips of ants gathering grains of rice. And I thought this room at the end here would be ideal for the dematerialists . . .' Leo, who had an interest in modern art and a modest collection of his own, wandered off with Chay. Anthony, who couldn't stand the stuff, his father's work in particular, went through to the office to make himself some coffee.

Two of the other trustees had just arrived – Derek Harvey, the art critic, looking crumpled and weary, sporting his perennial raincoat over a polo-necked sweater and baggy jeans, and Graham Amery, a prominent banker, whose elegant pinstripe suit and shining black shoes contrasted sharply with Derek Harvey's appearance. Amery and Anthony chatted while Derek wandered round the main gallery, morosely examining unwrapped exhibits.

Tony Gear, Labour MP for Parson's Green, arrived five minutes later. He cultivated a deliberately scruffy look, that of a man too busy to be concerned with his appearance, content with an M & S suit and a tie that had seen better days, and battered suede shoes which he fondly imagined were becoming something of a trade-mark. Gear was a man who believed in the profile and the soundbite, and although his interest in modern art was negligible, he had jumped at the chance to become a trustee of Chay's museum. The word in Westminster was that the Prime Minister, keen to deflect recent attacks on the government's arts-funding policy, intended to establish a new Ministry for Artistic and Cultural Development. In the true socialist spirit, Tony Gear was keen for advancement. He longed to hold that ministerial post, yearned to enjoy all the trappings of high office. To be associated with the Shoreditch venture did his reputation no harm in this regard. He raised a swift hand in greeting to Anthony and Amery, and went straight to the office to fetch himself some coffee, his pager already bleeping. Derek pulled a chair up to the makeshift meeting table and sat down, unfolding his copy of the *Evening Standard*.

Just as Chay and Leo returned to the main gallery, Melissa Angelicos arrived, clad in a voluminous coat and a swirl of silken scarves, her capacious bag bulging with papers, her blonde hair loose. From three feet away Anthony could catch the heady drift of her perfume. She dumped her bag on a chair and began to divest herself of coat and scarves, already addressing Derek in a rapid voice about the contents of Brian Sewell's column in the *Standard*.

Leo was careful to sit at the other end of the table from Melissa. She was, as far as he was concerned, bad news. He had seen the jittery, intense creature that lived behind the attractive façade, and mistrusted her. From the very first she had pursued him, and even when he had rejected and humiliated her, she seemed unwilling to give up. Leo was accustomed to the attentions of hungry, single, middle-aged women, but never had he come across one whose passion, he suspected, could turn poisonous and obsessive, if given free rein. He had no intention of allowing that to happen. On the infrequent occasions when he met her now, he was formally, almost frigidly polite. To his relief, she seemed of late to have cooled towards him. Well, he could live with that.

When everyone was seated, the meeting began, with Anthony taking minutes. As usual, apologies were conveyed to the assembly for the absence of the seventh trustee, Lord Stockeld, whose business obligations abroad were of so pressing a nature that he had so far only ever attended one trustee meeting. For forty-five minutes or so they discussed the prospective launch of the gallery, considering the guests, drawing up a list of names which would blend heavyweights from the creative and artistic spheres with a judicious sprinkling of A list celebrities. Everybody had their own suggestions to make, and at one point Melissa and Derek wrangled briefly over two of the names. One was the art critic of an important broadsheet who had previously been a lover of Melissa's, had dumped her, and had been the subject of a vendetta by Melissa ever since. The other was a young female artist shortlisted for last year's Turner Prize, who had poured beer over Derek at an Ellsworth Kelly retrospective and called him a pretentious wanker. When it had been pointed out by the rest of those present that both critic and artist were too important to omit from the guest list, the grumbling subsided and the meeting moved on to the business of fixing an exact date for the opening. This was largely dictated by the availability of the most important guests, which Chay had already ascertained, and they eventually settled on the evening of the first Saturday in March.

'I'll have some invitations designed and let you all see them first. Anything else we need to discuss?' asked Chay, lighting another cigarette and glancing round.

'Just one thing,' said Graham Amery. 'What about that idea that you floated before Christmas, Chay – the one about the restaurant and the cinema? I mean, it would obviously enhance the museum if we could have more than a coffee shop, and although the cinema idea is ambitious, I think it's worth looking at. There's certainly enough space on the site, and it seems a pity not to utilize it.'

'I agree,' said Melissa. 'The coffee shop's all very well, but a decent restaurant would be fantastic. Shoreditch is only beginning to wake up as an area, and it could be just the thing the museum needs. Obviously it would be a long-term project, but I really think we should definitely investigate it. A cinema would be marvellous, too – art-house movies, Basquiat, that kind of thing . . .' She waved a vague hand, then added doubtfully, 'I suppose that would be rather expensive, though.'

'Well, that's the trouble,' said Chay. 'Money. I'm all for the idea in principle, but where would we get the funding?'

Nobody said anything for a few seconds. Everybody

was thinking the same thing. Surely Chay was rolling in the stuff, so why didn't he fund it himself? But as Chay's office staff could have told them, Chay was remarkably tight-fisted. He hated parting with his own money, kept a strict eye on the teabags, and, anyway, he would have argued, he had already expended a considerable amount on refurbishing the brewery. He wasn't about to volunteer to build a restaurant and a cinema with his own money, not if he could find someone else to pay for them.

'There are grants,' said Leo. 'Possibly Lottery money.'

'Why don't I look into it?' said Anthony, scribbling it down with the rest of his notes. He was bored and hungry and wanted to get away. 'Maybe Tony can help with finding out the sort of funding that's available.' He glanced at Tony Gear, who nodded.

'Fine,' said Chay. 'See what you can come up with.'

The meeting broke up. Anthony picked up his coat and went to join Leo. Just as they were leaving, Melissa stopped them at the doorway and touched Leo's arm. He was startled, unaware that she had been anywhere near him, and almost flinched. The musky breath of her perfume enveloped him.

'Leo, I was wondering . . . Are you going in my direction? My car's being serviced, and you know how hard it is to find a cab around here.' Her beseeching smile was too winsome for a woman of her age, and somehow repellent. The last thing Leo wanted was to be alone in a car with this woman. That was how the whole thing had started – by giving her a lift home after that first trustees' meeting. He wasn't going to make the same mistake twice.

He moved his arm from beneath her hand. 'I'm going in the opposite direction, I'm afraid. I'll be happy to ring for a cab, though.'

'Oh, no, don't trouble yourself. I'll see if Derek can give me a lift.' She gave him an arch look and added in a lower voice, 'You're always my first choice, though.' She flicked the end of one of her long scarves over her shoulder and moved away.

'Appalling woman,' murmured Leo, as he and Anthony stepped out into the night air. 'Have you seen any of her recent interview series on Channel 4? Quite abysmal. She should have stuck to the arts-magazine format. At least she could handle it.'

'You know modern art isn't my cup of tea. But I did read a review of her interview with Anthony Caro. Bit of a stinker. What have you got against her personally?'

'A few months ago I made the mistake of going out for a few drinks with her. We finished up at her place.' Leo sighed. 'I'd rather not go into it. Let's just say that I don't particularly want to give her any kind of encouragement.'

Anthony stopped at the brewery gates and stared at Leo. 'Not her as well?'

'What do you mean?'

'Christ, Leo, it's what I was talking about earlier! I mean, don't you know when to stop? Isn't there anyone you won't sleep with?'

Leo was nonplussed by the volatility of Anthony's reaction. In fact, it seemed to him like an over-reaction. What was this new, sensitive area they had touched upon of late? 'I'd hardly put it that way. Nothing happened, and anyway —'

'Oh, forget it, Leo. I don't want a lift.' Anthony turned angrily on his heel and walked off down the cobbled street. Leo gazed after him, bemused, tossing his car keys thoughtfully in his hand. Whatever was eating Anthony, he'd have to work it out by himself. Clearly there wasn't much Leo could do. He heard voices behind him, and turned to see Melissa and Derek Harvey leaving the building. He moved off hastily in the direction of his car.

Twenty minutes later, Derek's car slowed in a queue of traffic at some lights in Bayswater. Turning to glance out of the window, Melissa saw an Aston Martin two cars ahead in the adjoining lane, waiting to turn right. The lights turned to green, and as they passed the Aston Martin still sitting in the filter lane, Melissa saw Leo's profile, the unmistakable glint of his silver hair. She looked away abruptly. Leo had lied. He hadn't wanted to give her a lift, hadn't wanted her company. An insignificant slight, perhaps, but to Melissa, such things could never be insignificant.

3

February the fourteenth. Felicity contemplated the large envelope which had arrived, addressed to her, with the rest of chambers' post. She didn't recognize the handwriting as Vince's. She didn't recognize it as anybody's. Maybe he had got someone else in the remand centre to write it for him. Somehow she couldn't picture Vince doing anything that soft. You'd probably get beaten up, asking someone to do something like that. A valentine. Where would Vince get a valentine while on remand? And the postmark. The postmark was WC2. Not even Vince could manage that, not where he was. Besides, when had Vince ever sent her a valentine? She turned it over thoughtfully, then began to open it.

Henry watched from a discreet distance.

The card was very pretty, in a naff sort of way, very traditional, with lots of flowers, no jokey message. It just said 'with love' in gold letters on the front. She opened it. Inside someone had written: *'From a distance. Always.'* Ah – that was lovely. And a bit sad, sort of enigmatic. Not Vince's style at all. Mind you, considering the mess Vince was in, from a distance was about right. She pondered it, wondering who her remote admirer might be.

'Ooh, somebody loves you. Just the one? I got three,'

remarked Robert, who was the post boy and trainee clerk.

Felicity clipped his head with the card, then slid it back into the envelope, smiling to herself as she did so. Henry saw the smile, and his heart turned over. In a way it was an anti-climax. It was one thing actually to be able to see her open it and read it, but he longed to be able to tell her that it was from him. He watched as she put the card into her desk drawer, then sighed and carried on with the fee note he was drawing up. Leo came into the clerks' room with his robing bag and took a bundle of papers from his pigeon hole. He glanced over Henry's shoulder at the computer screen.

'Henry, you can't charge that – it was only a two-day hearing.'

'It's what the job's worth, Mr D.'

'Well, can't you bring it down a bit?' He pointed to an item on the screen. 'You can waive that, for a start.'

Henry sighed. 'Mr Davies, if I was to let you get away with this, we'd all be in the poorhouse. Go on, then.' Henry tapped at the keyboard.

Robert put his head back round the door of the clerks' room, grinning. 'Come and have a look at this.'

Felicity and Henry went to the door. A messenger from Interflora was struggling through the front entrance from Caper Court with an enormous, heart-shaped basket filled with red roses and swathed in red ribbon. He set it down, and drew out his delivery list. 'You got a Mr Davies here?'

Felicity glanced at Henry, who was smirking. 'Yes,' she answered.

'Good,' said the messenger, and ticked his list. 'This lot's for him.' And he departed.

Henry went back into the clerks' room, where Leo was standing in his overcoat, scanning his diary print-out. 'Someone's just dropped something off for you, Mr D.' Leo glanced up. 'Out there.' Henry nodded in the direction of the hallway. 'Bit big to bring in.'

Leo took off his spectacles and went out to investigate. At that moment David Liphook was coming downstairs. They both looked at the basket.

'Good God,' said David. 'Who's that for?'

Leo stepped forward and gingerly plucked the small, square envelope from among the roses. If this was a practical joke, it was a very elaborate and expensive one. He drew out the card and read, '*From an ardent admirer. M.*'

'Someone really fancies you,' observed David, not without a shade of envy.

Leo was bemused. He must know plenty of people whose name began with M, but off the top of his head he couldn't imagine who would have sent such a thing.

'What the hell am I going to do with them?'

'Don't ask me.' David went through to the clerks' room, with Leo in his wake.

'Felicity,' said Leo, 'would you like a very large basket of roses?'

'No, thanks,' said Felicity with a grin. 'I can't see me managing that lot on the bus tonight.'

Leo sighed. 'Well, I'll just have to leave them there. See if anyone else in chambers wants them, will you,

Henry? Try Jeremy. I'm sure he'd be delighted to be given the chance to impress his wife at no cost to himself. I've got to be in court in ten minutes.' He turned to David. 'Did Sarah tell you she was coming to court with me this morning?'

'Yes, she mentioned it. Said she'd be down in a moment.'

Leo went out and met Sarah coming downstairs. Pausing to pull on her coat and lift her blonde hair from beneath the collar, she glanced at the basket of roses. 'Who on earth are those for?'

'You. From me.'

For the briefest of seconds, Sarah believed him. Or wanted to. 'Oh, sure. That'll be the day.'

'All right, but why don't you have them, anyway?'

'You mean they're yours?'

'Someone's idea of a joke, I suppose. Come on, we're going to be cutting it fine.'

'A very expensive joke,' said Sarah, as they went out together and crossed Caper Court.

'That's what I thought.'

Sarah felt the nibblings of a little worm of jealous curiosity. Of course she wasn't the only woman in London with her eye on Leo. Before he'd married Rachel, his social life had been something else – she remembered all the stiffies gracing the mantel of his place in Stanton, with probably more back in London. No doubt it had picked up again since the divorce. But who on earth would be so blatant as to send him a huge basket of flowers on St Valentine's Day? Very uncool.

47

'Don't you have any idea who sent them?'

'Not really. It would take a bit of pondering and deduction, and I'm afraid I haven't really got time for that.' They reached the top of Middle Temple Lane and crossed the Strand to the Law Courts. 'Now,' said Leo, 'forget about my secret admirer and turn your mind to the Hague-Visby rules and the question of whether or not they're incorporated in our client's charter party by virtue of a clause paramount.'

In her office high over Bishopsgate, Leo's ex-wife, Rachel, sat drinking her first coffee of the morning. She was in her late twenties, slender, with long, dark hair, and dressed in the cool, business-like fashion of a City solicitor. Her appearance was as meticulous as her professional dealings, giving the impression that little could ruffle that composed exterior. This morning, however, she felt distinctly discomposed. On her desk sat the latest bundle of statements in the Lloyd's case. The documentation was unbelievable. Two years ago Fred Fenton, a fellow partner, had handled the first stage of this litigation, and he had hoped then that he had seen the last of the Lloyd's Names. That case, in which Leo had figured prominently, had resulted in a settlement for the Names, who felt aggrieved by the losses they had suffered through their membership of Lloyd's. But in the end there remained certain individuals, a somewhat eccentric and desperate band, who refused to accept the settlement and were now pressing ahead with a fraud claim against Lloyd's. Rachel and Fred had spent the last six months in the preparation of this last-ditch stand. Now the paperwork had reached a point where Rachel and Fred, together with their team of assistants, felt they could hardly cope.

Fred came into Rachel's office and eyed the stack of statements on Rachel's desk. 'Have you spent the weekend with that lot?'

She nodded and sipped her coffee. 'I got through as much as I could. Charles is in Los Angeles at the moment, and Oliver was a real handful at the weekend. I'll have to try to get some more done tonight. It's got to the point where I'm skimming them. I don't know how on earth Grimley is coping.' Conor Grimley, QC, a veteran of the commercial bar, was their leader in the Lloyd's case.

'That's what I came to see you about.' Fred, fair-haired and lanky, settled himself in one of Rachel's office chairs. 'The grant's finally come through from the Legal Aid Board. So all we have to do now is decide on a leader on behalf of the legally aided Names.'

'It's taken them long enough. Did you have anyone special in mind?'

'Well, a few people occurred to me. Edward Fellows, Bob Coulthard, Tim Young ... The thing is, we need someone who's really sharp when it comes to cross-examination. It's vital to this case.' Fred glanced hesitantly at Rachel and added, 'I thought Leo Davies would be the ideal man, if he's free.'

Rachel said nothing for a moment. She set her coffee cup on her desk. It was only a few months since her divorce from Leo had become final. It had been one of the most painful episodes of her life. She was lucky – she had made a new relationship with Charles, something stable and affectionate, and she and Leo had parted on good terms and reached a decent arrangement concerning Oliver. But the fact remained that Leo was the first man she had ever truly loved, and that wasn't something Rachel thought she would ever get over. There had been a brief time last autumn when, if someone had asked her to choose between Charles and Leo, she would have chosen to return to Leo. But it wasn't what he wanted, and she knew that such a move would have been fatally destructive. Fatal. That was the word you could apply to Leo.

Still, that was personal, and this was professional. What Fred said was true – someone whose strength lay in cross-examination was just what they needed, and Leo was very, very good. They were taking an extra leader on at the shortest possible notice, too – the trial would start in just under a month – and whoever they chose would have to be able to get to grips with the essentials of this case in a very short space of time.

'Well,' said Rachel at last, 'he was the leader in the Capstall case, so he has the advantage of experience.'

'Quite,' said Fred quickly. He had been uncertain how Rachel would react to his suggestion of instructing Leo, and he wanted to capitalize on any enthusiasm she showed. He had no doubt that Leo was the best they could hope for. 'Anyone else is going to have to spend twice as long familiarizing themselves with all the details. Most of it will be second nature to Leo.'

Still Rachel hesitated. It would mean working alongside

Leo, talking to him on the phone regularly, seeing him once or twice each week, and then every day when the trial started. It was bad enough when he came to pick up Oliver every other weekend – just the sight of him still made her heart tighten. She had been trying so hard this past year to make a success of what she and Charles had. She had told herself that while she could never hope to replace what she had felt for Leo, at least she could be safe and happy being loved by Charles, and returning that love so far as she was able. Prolonged exposure to Leo could undermine all of that.

But only if she let it. It was ridiculous to be afraid of working professionally with one's ex-husband. Their marriage was over and done with. Life had to go on. After a few moments she looked up. 'Why don't you speak to his clerk and see if he's free?'

Fred smiled and nodded. 'I'll do that. And failing Leo, we can always try Young. He's very good.'

But already Rachel found herself hoping that Leo would be free. Not a good sign.

Leo and Sarah came back from court at lunchtime and met Henry coming out of chambers.

'Oh, Mr Davies, I had Nichols on the phone this morning. They're looking for an extra leader in a three-monther coming up at the end of March. The fraud case against Lloyd's. Seems you could do it, if you wanted to. There's nothing coming up that couldn't be moved or handed over to someone else.'

Leo gave a faint groan. Not the Names again. They

could be some of the most difficult clients on earth – not on account of their individual natures, though that applied in certain cases, but because of their capacity for indecision, in-fighting, and general lack of cohesion. 'It's rather short notice, isn't it?'

Henry shrugged. 'They've spent six months trying to get approval from the Legal Aid Board. They couldn't appoint a second leader till now. They've already got Conor Grimley.'

'Ah, Conor . . .' Leo knew Conor as a lawyer of the old school, a painstaking, maddeningly slow Irishman, infinitely courteous and pleasant but with his own very pedantic way of doing things. Not the easiest person to work alongside, especially since Leo's own way of conducting a case was very different. He thought for a moment. 'OK then. I know most of the background, anyway, so the preparation shouldn't be that hard.'

'Right, I'll put it in.'

'You didn't sound very enthusiastic about that,' remarked Sarah, as they made their way upstairs.

'I'm not. Lloyd's names are a prickly lot. Personalities tend to get in the way of the smooth running of their case. And suing Lloyd's for fraud is an especially difficult number.'

'Why did you take it, then?'

Leo smiled. 'Well, hardly for reasons of sentiment. I suppose I rather like cases where little men pit themselves against big institutions.'

'You mean you think they'll win?'

'Good God, no. While I would never dream of suggesting that our judges are anything less than honourable and strictly impartial, it strikes me as unlikely that one pillar of the establishment – namely the judiciary – would willingly bring about the downfall of another. Then the whole edifice gets a bit rocky. Not that I imagine it will ever come to that.' They reached the door of Leo's room. 'Now, I've got phone calls to make and some papers to read. I'll see you back in court at two.'

Fred strolled along to Rachel's office later that afternoon. 'Right, that's fixed. Leo's taking the case.'

Rachel's face betrayed nothing. She nodded. 'That's good. I'll give him a ring tomorrow and get the papers over to him.' She sighed. 'Several van-loads. Is it my imagination, or is litigation generating more paperwork these days?'

'The changing face of advocacy. At least the judges work a bit harder.'

'Hmm. Anyway, thanks for letting me know.' She smiled. 'I do appreciate these personal visits. Makes a nice change from interminable e-mails.'

'I'm a great believer in keeping the tide of e-mails down,' said Fred. 'See you later.'

When he had gone, Rachel put her face in her hands. When Fred had told her about Leo taking the case, she had felt an instant ripple of pleasure and excitement. She shouldn't let herself feel that way, live in anticipation of seeing him and speaking to him. He was her ex-husband. Their marriage was over. Hadn't he hurt, humiliated and betrayed her? When she was pregnant with Oliver he had been seeing another man, and only last year he had had some teenager to live with him, someone he picked up more or less off the streets. He was abominable, utterly amoral. How could she still love him in the face of all that? But the truth was, she did, and there was nothing she could do about it. It was like a wound that would never heal.

Compared to Leo, Charles was a paragon. Sweet, decent, loving and reliable. What diabolical law ordained that one could love hopelessly without any effort, but find it so hard to return total adoration? It was perverse.

Still, it was no use thinking about it. She was happy with Charles, and there was no way that she and Leo would ever have worked. She must approach Leo's involvement in this Lloyd's case with complete equanimity and professionalism. She would call him tomorrow, and try to take no special pleasure in it.

The court rose at five. By the time Leo had finished discussing the case with his instructing solicitor and reviewing the timetable of events for the following day, it was quarter to six.

'How do you feel it's going?' asked Sarah, as they crossed to the Temple from the Law Courts. Dusk had already fallen, and the twinkling lights of rush-hour traffic stretched the length of the Strand.

'Hard to tell. We should win, but I expect the other side to make a meal out of the fact that our clients' P & I club didn't tell their clients' club that they were going to pursue an indemnity claim against the owners.' He glanced at Sarah. 'What do you think? You've been a pupil for six months now. Should be able to make some sort of an assessment.'

Sarah gave him a cool little smile. 'The trouble is, whenever the great Leo Davies is on his feet and talking, it's hard to see how the other side can possibly win.'

'Do I detect a note of irony? Remember, at my time of life I require flattery to be delivered with some modicum of sincerity.' At the gateway to Middle Temple Lane, Leo stopped. 'Do you know, the last thing I feel like doing is going back to chambers. There'll just be a stack of telephone notes and other things to deal with. Why don't we go for a drink until all the solicitors have safely shut up shop?'

Sarah nodded. 'Suits me.'

They walked back along Fleet Street to Bouverie Street, then down to an out-of-the-way pub at the end of an alleyway, once busy with the rumble of printers' lorries, now, since the defection of the newspapers from Fleet Street, silent and deserted. There were very few people in the pub. Leo bought drinks and they sat at a table tucked away in a corner. Leo stretched out his legs and smothered a yawn.

'Tired?' asked Sarah.

'I'm always tired these days,' sighed Leo. 'Pressure of work. I suppose I'm taking too much on. That's why I didn't particularly feel like going back to chambers to face it all after a day in court.'

'Why do you work so hard? You can't need the money.'

Leo took a sip of his whisky and reflected on this. He

set his glass down. 'If you want the truth, it's probably so that I don't have any time left to reflect on what a fuck-up I've made of my personal life.'

Sarah hadn't been prepared for such candour. While she had already calculated that, in her plan of campaign to marry Leo, it would first be necessary to find her way to the most vulnerable and private part of his being, she hadn't expected an opportunity to present itself so suddenly.

'I thought those things didn't matter to you. Relationships. Feelings. When I first met you, you seemed to have your life nicely sorted out – sex was sex, business was business . . . People were a matter of calculation.'

'I suppose that's how it was, once upon a time.'

'I always liked that way of thinking. Take your pleasure where you can, don't make any emotional investment, don't expect anything in return.'

'Oh, dear – did I teach you that?'

'Somewhat. As a philosophy I've found it's always worked quite well. I hate it when people start wanting things, expecting time and attention.'

'There was a time I thought it could work like that. I think things changed last summer.'

'With that boy?' Jealousy flared in Sarah. 'I'd have thought that would teach you to stick to your philosophy, and not let feelings get in the way of having a good time.'

Leo was silent for a few moments, then asked, 'Have you ever been in love?'

Sarah sipped her wine. 'Of course. Hasn't everyone? How do you think I became the person I am? I won't ever make that mistake again.' Even now her mind shied away from herself at seventeen, that first love, the pain and misery.

'What an odd thing to say. In my experience, it just makes people hungry for more of the same, no matter how miserable the experience. But, as you say, you're a cynical young thing. Maybe it has something to do with age. It's easier to live for yourself when you're young.' Leo gazed reflectively at his glass. 'At my age, love just leaves you feeling more and more vulnerable.'

'Don't tell me you're worried about a lonely old age.'

'Perhaps I am.'

'Come off it, Leo. That summer at Stanton, I didn't know anyone with a busier social life. Look at you now. High-earning silk, unattached, good-looking, all that bullshit – you must still be in heavy demand.'

'Oh, yes – there's all that. Somehow it's lost its appeal. I don't want to go to endless dinner parties and God knows what else. It gets to eleven o'clock and I just want to go to bed.'

'What? With a cup of Horlicks and a good book?'

Leo smiled. 'Something a little more interesting than that, perhaps. But the social circuit leaves me cold. I get tired of the different faces, the talk, the inconsequentiality of it all. The desperation – it's palpable. I can see the attraction of having someone – something ... stable, settled.' He drained his glass. 'Maybe it's all to do with Oliver. Having children changes you.'

'I wouldn't know. And I don't intend to find out.'

'You should. It's worth it.'

'Really?' Sarah regarded him with interest. 'Would you like more children?'

Leo hesitated before replying. 'I might. I don't know. It seems a rather unlikely scenario at the moment.'

'Another?' she asked, picking up his glass.

Leo nodded, reaching into his breast pocket for his cigar case.

When Sarah came back to the table with the drinks, Leo was smoking thoughtfully. 'So tell me,' he said, 'what do you intend to do with your young life? Your pupillage ends in summer. What then?'

'I don't know. I'm afraid my heart really isn't in the commercial bar. Too much like hard work. In fact, anything which involves getting up at half past seven in the morning is a very unattractive prospect. The past six months have been bad enough.'

'If you don't like law, why did you choose it as a career?'

'Oh, I don't mind *law*. As an intellectual discipline it's all right. It's just the idea of getting a job that I don't like.'

'You've got a job. God knows we pay you a small fortune for the privilege of being a pupil. It wasn't that way in my day, I can assure you. Pupils paid their pupilmasters.'

'Leo, you sound positively Dickensian this evening. You're not *that* old, you know.'

'I suppose not.' Leo smoked in silence for a few moments, then said, 'That was the chief problem with Joshua, though. Maybe that's why I harp on it.'

'What – your age?'

'The generation gap. I thought it didn't matter. Of course, it was the reason the whole thing was a non-starter. His interests weren't mine. Music, films – you name it. As for his friends . . .'

'The truth is, no man is ever likely to provide you with the kind of relationship you want. Not of that age, anyway. They're all on the take. If it's stability you're after, stick to women.'

Leo chuckled. 'Like you, you mean?'

'Why not? The generation gap, as you put it, never seems to have troubled us.'

'Hmm.' Leo narrowed his eyes. 'That's very true. But then, our association has been largely physical and occasional.'

'Not always. Take this evening, for example.'

It was hard to deny. He liked her company. She knew so much about him, he never had to be on his guard. One way or another, Sarah had become a part of his life. An irritating one, on occasions, but admittedly a distractingly pretty one. He felt a familiar stirring in his blood, a sexual quickening, as their eyes held one another's.

'Are you trying to tell me something?' Leo blew out a haze of cigar smoke and smiled quizzically at her.

'Not at all. Now, are you going to buy me another drink?' Sarah had a very shrewd idea of the right point at which to turn things and move away.

'Very well,' sighed Leo. 'It'll have to be the last. I ration my intake quite carefully these days.'

When he returned with the drinks, Leo picked up where they had left off. 'Anyway, you didn't finish telling me what you intend to do with your future. If you don't want to stay at the Bar, what else had you in mind?'

'I don't know. Make some suggestions.'

'You could join one of the P & I clubs, I suppose. They like bright young barristers.'

Sarah sighed. 'Nine to five in the City.'

'Can't think of anything else, short of switching over and becoming a solicitor.'

'No thanks.' Sarah drank her wine. 'There must be alternatives to work.'

'Such as?'

She smiled. 'Maybe I'll find a rich man and marry him.'

'Good luck.' Leo knocked back the rest of his Scotch and glanced at his watch. 'Come on, I have to make tracks. I've got some papers at home that I must read before Friday, and I won't get much of a chance tomorrow.'

They walked back up the alleyway in silence, and stopped on the corner. 'Don't you have anything to pick up from chambers?' asked Leo.

Sarah shook her head. 'I took my things over to court. I'll just go straight home from here.'

'Right.' Leo nodded. Sarah thought she knew what was coming next. 'Listen,' added Leo, 'I have to do some work on those papers, but why don't you come back with me, make us both some supper while I read them, and then . . .'

She smiled and lifted a finger to stroke the side of his face, once. 'It's a lovely idea, Leo, but somehow I don't think so – not tonight.'

It wasn't what he had expected, and he felt surprisingly disappointed. Sitting in the pub with her, the prospect of having her company for the rest of the evening, and then the night, had seemed a pleasurable one. He nodded. 'Right. Right, OK . . . Do you need a cab?'

'No, thanks. I'll walk down to Temple tube. Bye.'

She turned and walked away, and after a few seconds she heard the sound of Leo's footsteps dying away in the other direction. She pulled up her collar and snuggled it around her face. That had been just right, she thought. Perfect. It was the first time, ever, that she had said no to Leo. In the past, she'd had nothing to gain by playing hard to get. That had all changed now.

On Wednesday evenings Felicity went to visit Vince in the remand centre at Belmarsh. These were depressing occasions. Felicity always started off trying to be cheerful, but it was impossible to counter the gloom generated by Vince. Not that Felicity could blame him. Even if the police dropped the murder charge to manslaughter when his case came to court, as Vince's solicitor assured him they would, what was the best he was looking at? Four years, possibly five. Vince would be the first to admit that he was no saint, he tended to get into fights and other kinds of bother, but that it should all end like this was to him the most blatant injustice. All right, the guy had died, but he hadn't meant him to. He'd been unlucky. Fallen down and hit his head. How could they put him away for something he'd never meant to do, saying he'd killed a guy when that wasn't the way it had been at all? He hadn't killed him. The bloke had kicked his bike. He'd hit him, and the bloke fell down. He was unlucky. They were both unlucky.

On Felicity's early visits to the remand centre after Vince's arrest, it had been all he could talk about, the unfairness of it, how he hadn't meant to, they couldn't convict him of murder, that wasn't bloody justice . . . until she was weary of hearing it. Then after a couple of weeks his invective against Fate and the police had stopped, and a kind of sullen passivity took its place. Sometimes conversation was hard. There were even occasions when it seemed to Felicity that Vince was deliberately trying to take everything she said the wrong way, so that he could argue with her. She couldn't fathom the growing resentment that she detected in his manner each time she visited. She told herself that she still loved Vince, and that she would see it through with him, but there were times when she wondered if he even wanted her to. The baby she had lost was never mentioned. Felicity told herself that she didn't blame Vince – though if he hadn't been drunk and argumentative, she would never have had that fall . . . She had to convince herself it was for the best, really, otherwise she would have been stuck with a baby, no job, and Vince on remand. Not a happy thought.

That evening she sat at one of the Formica-topped tables in the big room where visits were conducted, and waited for a warder to bring Vince through, hoping he might be in a better frame of mind tonight. But Vince only gave Felicity the bleakest of smiles when he came in. He sat opposite her, hands flat on the table.

'Hi,' said Felicity. 'Happy Valentine's Day.'

'Right.'

'So – how are you doing?'

Vince shrugged. 'Saw my solicitor today. She reckons my case might not come on till June. That didn't exactly do me a lot of good, hearing that.'

'That's another four months!'

'Yeah, I don't need you to tell me that.' He sighed and ran his hands through his shoulder-length dark hair. 'Anyway, tell me what you been up to.'

Felicity talked for a while about chambers, and told him about a film she had been to see the weekend before. She always racked her brains before coming, trying to conjure up interest in her humdrum existence, anything to keep him amused.

'Who did you go to the film with?' asked Vince.

'Maureen.'

'Oh, yeah? Still not got herself a bloke, then?'

'No.'

'Sure it was just you two? No guys?'

Felicity said nothing for a moment. She hated this. 'It was just me and Mo.'

'Yeah, yeah . . .' Vince drummed his fingers on the table. 'Get any valentines, then?'

She felt herself flush instantly. A dead giveaway. Why did he always make her feel like she'd done something

63

wrong, like she had something to hide? Because he was convinced she was seeing someone else while he was on remand, that was why. It was almost like he wanted her to be. She couldn't lie. Vince could read her like a book, and she could feel her cheeks still tingling. She tried to sound diffident. 'Yeah. Just the one. I thought it might have been from you.'

'Like I'd be able to send one, stuck away in here. So who's it from?'

She shrugged, as though the subject bored her. 'Don't know. Don't much care.'

'Don't give us that. Who d'you reckon it was? Who fancies you? One of those barristers you work for?'

'Don't be stupid.' She hesitated for a few seconds, then added, 'It might have been Henry. He's a bit soft like that.'

'Him?'

She nodded, wondering whether it had been such a bright idea to mention Henry. Vince had met him a couple of times, and in Vince's terms, Henry didn't amount to much, so she'd hoped the idea that Henry might have sent the valentine would amuse him more than anything else. But Vince's face was angry and sullen.

'Little bastard. He knows I'm on remand, so he's trying it on with you. He wouldn't dare do that if I was around.'

Felicity laughed in astonishment. 'You really get things out of proportion, don't you? I don't even know if it was him who sent it, and you're getting uptight about it! It's only a valentine, for God's sake.'

'I'll bet it really made your day, though, didn't it? I'll bet you spend half your day giving him the come-on.' One of the guards glanced in their direction, and Vince gave him a surly look in return.

Felicity sighed. 'I didn't come here for an argument, Vince. I'm off, if this is how you're going to be.' She made as if to rise.

Vince stretched out a quick placatory hand. 'All right, all right. Sweetheart, don't go yet. Come on. I'm sorry.' He covered her hands with his. 'It really gets to me, being in here, you out there, getting up to all sorts –'

'Vince! For the last time, I'm not! I went to the pictures with Mo on Saturday, and someone, I don't know who, sent us one rotten valentine! OK?'

'OK, OK . . .'

They didn't return to the subject for the rest of the visit, but spent the remainder of the time going over what Vince's solicitor had said, and weighing up the prospects for the trial. They did this on every visit. It never changed.

Felicity got the bus home, and sat on the top deck gazing out at the dark, depressing sprawl of Thamesmead. There was, she reflected, something completely static about her existence at the moment. With Vince on remand, she couldn't move forward. She thought about the progress of her life up to this point. Three years ago, when she and Vince had got together, she had been a different person. A nineteen-year-old with seven GCSEs (not bad grades) and basic secretarial skills (debatable), living in a pretty squalid flat in Brixton with her brother, moving from one crummy office job to another, with not much hope for anything better in the foreseeable future. Now, thanks to Leo and with the help of Henry – with a bit of effort on her own part as well, of course – she was earning quite a comfortable living at 5 Caper Court, for a girl her age. She could afford a decent flat, the one in which she and Vince lived, and a few nice bits of furniture for it, she didn't have to shop at Top Shop and Etam all the time. Life had turned around. It was as though everything about her existence had changed for the better. Except for Vince. Nothing had changed there. A good-looking charmer on the scrounge, a bit of a boozer who picked up jobs as and when he needed them, fiddled his benefit, lay around the flat watching the racing, with an occasional saunter down to the bookie's or the pub. He had been a natural part of the old life. But now? They were disloyal thoughts, she knew, but sometimes, and especially of late, Vince seemed like a dreadful weight dragging her down. There had been a time a year ago, when he had realized that she was earning real money and he was just wasting his life, when things had improved, when he had begun to study for his Knowledge with ambitions of getting his own black cab. That was dead in the water now. The only future he had to look forward to was prison, for the next few years – of that Felicity had no doubt. And then? And then . . . She would be there when he came out, she supposed. That was what you did if your bloke went inside. So that was her, stuck for however many years, her twenties disappearing, life on hold . . . all for Vince. Felicity supposed she loved him, but did she love him that much?

She thought about this for the rest of the journey, and on the short walk home, and still had no answers.

4

Rachel rang Leo first thing the next day. He was mildly surprised to discover that she was handling the Lloyd's case, along with Fred.

'I thought I mentioned it when you came to pick Oliver up a couple of weeks ago,' said Rachel.

'Did you? I can't have been paying attention.'

'Anyway, I'll try to get the papers over to you later today. The first instalment, that is.'

'So what are this lot like? As batty as the last, I presume.'

'The Names? Oh, they're a mixed bunch. The action's being brought in the name of Lady Norbury, Henrietta, and she's the biggest pain of them all. She must be well over seventy, she's got all her marbles, but a few seem to be rolling about all over the place. She has some personal feud going with the Committee Chairman, Sir Stephen Caradog-Browne, would you believe, and if one of them is in favour of one course of action, the other's sure to be against it. Which makes for slow going.'

'Sounds about par for the course,' sighed Leo. 'In an ideal world, I'd rather never meet any of them, but I suppose I'll have to.'

'They're having a bash at the Guards' Club on Friday, seven-thirty. Sir Stephen's hosting it. You should come along to that.'

'I will,' said Leo, pulling his diary towards him and opening it. 'I was going to call you anyway, to discuss the arrangements for Oliver. How about ten on Saturday?'

'That's fine. By the way, I wouldn't plan on trying to read any of the Lloyd's stuff over the weekend. I made that mistake. I took a pile of statements home on Friday evening, thinking I'd get a chance to read them, but Charles is in the States at the moment, and Oliver's at that stage where he wants you to be totally involved in everything he's doing. I mean, *everything*, from putting his toy farm together to filling and emptying the Duplo box. He's also not keen on taking his nap at the moment. I didn't get much done.'

'You should have rung me. I'd have taken him off your hands for a day. The access arrangement's not set in stone, you know.'

'I didn't want him off my hands,' replied Rachel rather abruptly. 'That's not what I meant. I like spending my weekends with him. The weekends I *have* with him, that is.'

'Don't sound so resentful. I am his father. I do have a right to see him every other week. I was merely suggesting that I could have had him for a few hours.'

'I wasn't suggesting that I wanted to get rid of him. You always misinterpret things I say. I sometimes think you do it deliberately.'

'*I* deliberately misinterpret *you*?' Leo sounded incredulous.

There was a painful silence for a moment. Each of

them was thinking the same thing. Every conversation seemed to descend to this level.

Leo was the first to give way. 'This is pointless. I'll see you on Saturday morning.' He put the phone down before there could be any further acrimony.

At her end, Rachel replaced the receiver slowly. Why, why, did things always end like that? It was pitiful, child-ish, to bicker the way they did. Always over Oliver. Well, if Leo wanted to be with Oliver so badly, he could have behaved like a decent husband and father in the first place. If he had, they might all still be together. But Leo was selfish, too busy satisfying his various appetites to care about his family. Rachel found tears welling in her eyes. She pulled a tissue from her pocket and dabbed them away. Maybe it had been a mistake to let Fred instruct Leo, if she and Leo were incapable of conducting things on a civilized level for longer than five minutes. Still, it was done now, and they would all just have to live with it.

Lady Henrietta Ethel Margaret Norbury possessed a tem-perament admirably suited to membership of the Lloyd's Names Committee. The experiences of a long and colour-ful life had shaped a disposition which made her a natural champion of the dispossessed. A privileged upbringing as the youngest daughter of the 11th Earl of Halstead had equipped her with a marvellous arrogance, so pure as to be well above snobbery, and an assumption of the pre-eminence of her family and class. In her youth she had enjoyed a reputation as a considerable beauty, which had enhanced her sense of self-worth and attracted the first of three husbands, Charles 'Bozzy' Bostick, a dashing American who drove racing cars and had made his fortune in the Chicago meat industry. The marriage, which lasted ten years, left her with an enduring passion for extravagant spending. It was no surprise, therefore, that her subsequent marriage to Monty Smallwood, a handsome good-for-nothing who played second piano in the Ritz Orpheans, ended shortly after Monty had squandered much of his wife's divorce settlement in a variety of unsuccessful business ventures and failed cocktail bars. Monty, a man of immense charm but very weak character, died subsequently of alcohol poisoning. Lady Henrietta's legacy from this union was a son, Gideon, a detestation of impecuniosity and a determination never to allow any subsequent fortune to be frittered away by the improvidence of others. At the age of thirty-nine, with the remnants of her dark-eyed beauty fading, she married Sir Henry Percival Norbury, a Shropshire baronet twenty years her senior, who never gave her a moment's trouble, was fond of Gideon and dutifully attended to his education, who happily indulged his wife's taste for lavish spending, and whose death ten years later left her in possession of a modest fortune, a manor house near Chesterton and an apartment in Belgravia.

That was in 1985. Sir Percy had taken it for granted that membership of Lloyd's befitted a man of his wealth and standing. It was, perhaps, a happy thing for him that he died before he could witness the disaster that was to overtake syndicates 727/418 and 317/661 and see the

71

inherited wealth of three centuries disappear in a matter of years. It was Lady Henrietta who had to watch as, along with thousands of others, she was driven to near ruin by the follies of Messrs Meacock, Outhwaite and Merrett, and nameless others privy to the mismanagement of affairs at Lloyd's of London. The Norbury fortune was all but swallowed up, the manor house and the apartment in Belgravia sold, along with furniture, paintings and jewellery. Small wonder that Lady Henrietta should be driven, if not to the brink of madness, at least to a state of obsessive bitterness. She regarded all men as her enemies now. Stripped of her wealth, she lived in a three-bedroomed flat in Pimlico, surrounded by remnants of the opulent furniture which had graced her former homes, by silver-framed pictures of her youthful self in Hartnell and Schiaparelli ballgowns, and nursed her wrath against Lloyd's. She saw the litigation against Lloyd's as the Armageddon, elevated far above the constant feuds she conducted with landlords and bankers, shopgirls and traffic wardens. This was to the death.

Today she was breakfasting with Gideon, who was staying with her briefly while work was carried out on his own new house in Fulham. As usual, she was rehearsing a litany of complaints against the lawyers engaged on behalf of herself and the other Names.

'It is unnecessary and entirely pointless to instruct an additional leading counsel. A complete waste of money, when we have little enough as it is! And I'm told he's a Welshman — probably another crony of Caradog-Browne's.' Lady Henrietta lifted her coffee cup with a hand that wavered ever so slightly. Her once lovely dark eyes were bright, quick with menace as she brooded on this new grievance. 'The last solicitors' bill alone was sixty thousand pounds. Sixty thousand pounds!'

Smoothing back the pages of his *Telegraph*, Gideon glanced speculatively at his mother. He was slender, of medium height, and the dark good looks which had faded and withered in Lady Henrietta were still vivid and clear in him, albeit touched with the slight pouching and fine lines of early middle age. His brown hair was crisply curled, untouched by grey, and his large, liquid eyes held a glint of something that approached childish mischief. Although his clothes were stylish and impeccable, his conversation and tastes erudite and sophisticated, there was in his smile and mercurial manner and movements something boyish and irresistible. In a man of thirty-six, the effect produced could, on occasion, be somewhat sinister.

'Well, mother, if you want matters progressed and things brought on, you have to pay for it, you know.'

'Yes, but we don't seem to be *getting* anywhere. Nobody listens to me, or pays any attention to the thing that matters *most* about this case.'

'Oh, and what is that?' murmured Gideon. He sipped his coffee, his gaze straying back to the paper.

'The cover-up! The reckless way they behaved! Nobody seems to see it, even though they all admit the existence of the June 1983 letter . . .'

Gideon listened no more. His thoughts drifted to work. Would this be the day that they announced to the press the establishment of the new Ministry? Rumours had been rife for weeks. And if so, would this be his chance for elevation? Gideon felt that the time had come for him to move from the rank of junior secretary to something with greater status, and more money. Money was a constant source of anxiety to Gideon these days. He had grown accustomed to a high standard of living throughout his younger years, and the losses which the family had incurred at Lloyd's had hit him hard. Lady Henrietta had always been generous with her adored only son, and perhaps the extent to which she had been prepared to fund his affluent lifestyle, his bespoke suits, his gambling debts and his passion for good food and wine, had served to underscore the childlike side of his personality. Now, in these dark days, he was dependent on his salary as a grade-six civil servant with the Department of Culture, Media and Sport to keep him afloat. Selling his house in South Kensington and moving to the smaller place (presently undergoing refurbishment to Gideon's exacting standards) had released a certain amount of capital, but Gideon was always hungry for more. It was this hunger that had persuaded him to join his mother and the other Lloyd's Names in their last-ditch attempt at litigation. If they won, the rewards could be great, and Gideon's worries might be at an end. On the other hand . . .

'. . . Gideon, are you listening to me? I need to know if you will come to the reception at the Guards' Club on Friday.'

'No,' replied Gideon firmly. 'That geriatric committee

of yours simply depresses me. I refuse to spend my Friday evening in that dreary club with those dreary people.' He folded his newspaper, rose, buttoned his jacket around his slim figure and drained his coffee cup.

'Don't forget you're a member of the litigation sub-committee. It's your duty to meet this man Davies, make sure he's steered in the right direction from the beginning.'

Gideon sighed. 'Mother, unlike you, I have no desire to go around telling everyone what to do. I'm sure the lawyers know better than we do. Now, I have to get to work.'

As he passed her chair, she reached up a quick hand to grasp his. Her eyes moistened with fondness, beseeching him. 'Darling, do come. I do so love to have you with me at these things. And it won't be for long. Just a few drinks, meet this new QC, and then you'll have lots of time left. Please. For Mummy.'

Gideon couldn't handle much of this special pleading. It would only carry on into the evening, if he didn't capitulate now. 'Oh, very well. If Caradog-Browne is prepared to splash out on champagne for us all, I suppose I might as well drink it. But I won't stay longer than an hour.'

Lady Henrietta smiled a meek and gratified smile. 'Of course, darling, I know how precious your Fridays are to you.'

Lady Henrietta had no clear idea at all what Gideon got up to on Fridays. She only knew, in the short space of time that they had been living together recently, that those evenings were sacrosanct, given over to whatever nameless pleasures Gideon pursued until the very small hours. Saturdays were often the same. She didn't care to think about the kinds of things he did, or the people he consorted with. There was a dark side to Gideon, and she had no wish to explore it. She had long given up any hope that he might find a nice girl with lots of money, and settle down. Not that he was wild. Far from it. Throughout the week he kept regular hours, and seemed to work very diligently at his job. Lady Henrietta had only the very vaguest idea what civil servants did, and beyond wishing that Gideon could have made his way into the higher echelons of the Foreign Office, gave her son's career very little thought.

Gideon bent to bestow a kiss upon his mother's papery cheek. 'See you this evening.'

'Lovely. I'll pop down to Harrods and get us something nice for supper from the food hall.' There were some habits which impoverishment could not break, and although she regarded herself as nearly destitute, Lady Henrietta's lifestyle was still better than most.

Gideon put on his overcoat and his cashmere scarf, then left the flat and set off on the fifteen-minute walk to his office in Whitehall.

The announcement from the Downing Street press office of the establishment of the new Ministry for Artistic and Cultural Development came two days later at eleven o'clock on Friday morning. Tony Gear had been informed by the Prime Minister the previous evening of his elevation to the post of Minister in charge, and rose to greet the day in fine spirits. The hours ahead would be hectic. There would be consultations with senior civil servants, briefings, a press conference at lunchtime, and then a tour of the premises in Whitehall which had been assigned to the new Ministry. He'd have to get moving on arranging redecoration and the installation of suitable furniture for his new office – Tony intended to stamp his personality and authority on this Ministry from the very outset. Tempting fate somewhat, he had dropped into Politicos bookshop a few weeks earlier and discreetly purchased a copy of Gerald Kaufman's *How to Be a Minister*, and had in his spare moments dipped into this invaluable, if somewhat dated instruction manual for aspiring holders of ministerial office. He was keenly aware that the appointment of his private secretary was among the first and most important of his tasks. As the Ministry was a new one, Whitehall couldn't line up their own squad of candidates – the job was in his gift, and Tony thought he knew just the man. For some months now he had observed Gideon Smallwood as he went about his duties as junior secretary in the Department of Culture, Media and Sport, and had been impressed by the man's quick intelligence, discretion and general polish. Polish was something which Tony lacked, and he knew that it would greatly assist him in this new job, where he would be rubbing shoulders with thespians, directors of opera and ballet companies, as well as representatives from the Arts Council, to have by his side someone of Gideon's sophistication. Gideon Smallwood could buff up, so to speak, the rougher aspects of Tony's intellectual and artistic persona. Man was probably queer, but Tony thought he could live with that.

So it was, later that afternoon, that Gideon received a summons from the Government's newest Secretary of State, and was graciously offered, and with alacrity accepted, the post of Principal Private Secretary. The glow of satisfaction which pervaded Gideon's being as he left Tony Gear's office was positively physical. As a PPS he would command a position of power and influence, something he had longed for. He would hold an entire private office under his sway, with secretaries and assistants of his own. As for his new master ... oh, Gideon thought he had the measure of Mr Gear. He had watched him carefully over the last few months, listened to such words as he uttered in the House, studied every television appearance, taking in the clothes, the badly cut hair, the accent, the hungry, furtive eyes and the too-ready, too-loud laugh of a man who longs to be liked and yet jealously guards his own ambitions. Gideon saw a man on the make, someone probably too lightweight for Cabinet office, but who had succeeded through luck and good timing. Mr Gear's tenure of his new office might, Gideon suspected, not be of long standing – the arts-funding brief, after all, was a notoriously tricky one – but Gideon felt he could certainly turn it to his own good use in the time available.

It was with high good humour that he worked his way through the remainder of the afternoon's tasks. The prospect of meeting his mother and the rest of those

Lloyd's bores in a few hours suddenly seemed much more bearable.

Leo and Michael Gibbon sat at tea in the Inner Temple Common Room, Michael idly flicking through an early edition of the *Evening Standard*.

'I see Blair's having another go at appeasing the luvvies on the left,' he remarked. 'A new Ministry for art and culture, no less.'

'Who's the unfortunate being in charge of that?' asked Leo.

'One Anthony Gear, MP for Parson's Green, apparently. Never heard of him.'

'Yes, you have. He's the scruffy one, bit of a Ken Clarke lookalike, only younger. Always banging on about the rebuilding of Wembley Stadium.'

'Oh,' murmured Michael, stroking his moustache with thin fingers, 'that one. Since when did he have the right qualifications to be an Arts Minister?'

'Presumably he's been known to visit the odd gallery now and then. That would do. He's also on the board of trustees of Anthony's father's new museum.'

'You're a trustee of that as well, aren't you?'

'Of the reactive variety.'

Michael laid down the paper and looked at Leo with interest. 'So when will this museum open? I imagine it'll be quite a ritzy event, Chay Cross and other artistic luminaries in attendance.'

'Oh, yes, he's got them all lined up – Bowie, Damien Hirst, Hockney . . .'

'Really? Quite something.'

Leo glanced across as David, cup of tea in hand, came to join them. 'How is life in the House of Lords these days?' asked Leo, as David pulled up a chair.

David gave him a weary glance. 'We finished this morning. I rather suspect we're in for a right royal judicial kicking. Anyway, just as I was looking forward to a quiet life for a few weeks, Henry has arranged for me to spend five weeks in South America taking depositions on a ship-building case, as of the end of next week.'

'Weather will be nice.'

'I could do without it, frankly.'

'The curse of fluent Spanish. If you will advertise your specialisms . . .'

'What am I going to do about Sarah for that length of time? I can't just leave the girl kicking her heels.'

'Oh, someone will find her things to do,' remarked Michael. 'Jeremy, for instance.'

'Spare her that,' said Leo. 'If you want Sarah kept busy while you're away, she can help me to prepare for this Lloyd's case.'

David rubbed his chin. 'Yes. She might enjoy that.'

'Well, I wouldn't put it quite like that, but she could be useful.'

'Who's your junior?'

'I rather think it's going to be Camilla.'

Michael glanced at his watch. 'I'd better be getting back.'

Leo drained his cup. 'I'll join you.'

They walked back through the cloisters. 'So what's this

bunch of Lloyd's Names like?' Michael asked Leo. 'As much fun as the last lot?'

'I don't know yet. I'll find out tonight. The committee chairman is hosting a reception at the Guard's Club, and I'm going along.'

'Have you time for a quick game of squash beforehand?' asked Michael.

'Absolutely. I've got a con in ten minutes, but it shouldn't last long. Book a court for five.'

Leo passed Sarah on the stairs. 'By the way, I just spoke to David at tea. Apparently he's going abroad for a few weeks, so out of the goodness of my heart I said I'd take you under my wing while he's away. You can help Camilla and me to prepare for the Lloyd's case.'

Sarah's initial pleasure faded. 'Camilla?'

'She's my junior. Some problem?'

'No,' muttered Sarah, and passed on into the clerks' room. The idea of being Camilla's dogsbody for a few weeks was singularly unattractive. Still, at least it meant being around Leo on a full-time basis, and that might present all kinds of useful opportunities.

After a few games of squash with Michael, Leo drove home to his flat in Belgravia. The red light was winking on his answerphone. Dropping his coat on a chair, Leo pressed the button and let the tape wind back, which it did, at length, indicating that there were quite a few messages. He poured himself a drink and loosened his tie.

At first he didn't recognize the breathy female voice.

'Leo darling, I hope you liked the roses . . .' He turned cold. Melissa. The basket of flowers which had turned up the other day in chambers. Melissa had sent that thing. The voice went on. 'Wasn't I naughty? But I can never resist Valentine's Day, not if there's someone special. And you are *very* special. I wanted to show you that I'm prepared to put things behind us and make a new start. Do you think we can do that? I could tell at the meeting the other night that there's still that chemistry between us. I'll be waiting to hear from you.' Click. The message ended.

Leo sat, slightly stunned. The next three messages, from his stockbroker, a bookshop and his mother respectively, played, but Leo wasn't listening properly. What had got into that woman? He'd made it perfectly clear he wasn't in the slightest bit interested. In fact, he'd been pretty sure she'd seen him at the traffic lights after he'd declined to give her a lift at the last trustees' meeting, which must have told her that he'd lie rather than spend time with her. Yet here she was, cooing down the phone like Fenella Fielding, telling him she was waiting to hear from her. Barking. That was the only logical explanation. Oh well, best just to ignore it and hope she would go away. He showered and changed, then took a cab to St James's to offer himself up for inspection by the Committee of Lloyd's Names.

It was Gideon's policy to arrive late at most functions – not so late as to imply discourtesy, but allowing sufficient time to have elapsed to enable him to scan the room, assess the company, swiftly decide whom to bother with and whom to avoid, and work the room in the most expedient manner. He entered the dreary portals of the Guards' Club at half past seven and was directed to the room where the Lloyd's Names were holding their bash. He stood to one side of the doorway and surveyed the room. There were one or two faces he knew, elderly Lloyd's Names and acquaintances of his mother's, but for the most part he reckoned them to be geriatric nonentities. Hardly anyone seemed to be under fifty. He stepped forward and took a glass of champagne from a tray – one sip told him it was inferior and insufficiently chilled – and went to greet his mother, vowing as he did so that he would be clear of this place in twenty minutes, if not less.

'Gideon, darling!' His mother was bright-eyed with pride and affection as she clasped his arm and proffered her cheek for his kiss. 'You know Verity Eames, and her husband Charlie? And this is Harold Bessemer – Harold, may I introduce my son, Gideon . . . ?' Gideon smiled into the rheumy eyes and shook the bony, liver-spotted hands, recalling from childhood the sensation of being offered like some tender morsel to the hungry yearnings of the elderly. How they liked young people, how they looked to them eagerly for some sustenance, for news of the vital world of which they were no longer part. Gideon, as he sipped his champagne and made charming, bright conversation, squirmed inwardly. The only good thing to be said of a gathering such as this was that it dispelled any sense of one's own incipient middle age. To be thirty-six felt positively juvenile.

On the other side of the room, Leo had been cornered by Sir Caradog-Browne and his cohorts and was being closely quizzed as to his view of the case, their chances of success and his intended strategy. Conor Grimley, the elderly Irish leader already instructed in the case, stood by, sipping his champagne and feeling faintly huffy. He was put out by the fact that Leo had been brought into the case, being of the view that he could conduct the cross-examination of the Lloyd's witnesses perfectly well. Of course, he knew Leo's style, and it was a modern approach which he did not care for. Leo was too easy and friendly with judges and witnesses, he didn't keep the kind of reserved distance which QCs of the old school did. On the other hand, he could be acerbic and cutting to a point which Conor regarded as rude. Conor had been on the other side from Leo in a couple of cases, and knew that Leo regarded the lengthy case conferences which Conor himself thought necessary to the proper prep- aration of a case to be time-wasting. He was determined that Leo's legendary energy and briskness would not force him beyond the customary leisurely pace at which he liked to conduct things. It might put him in conflict with Leo, but that would just be too bad. He'd been instructed first, anyway.

Leo stood, his champagne untasted, nodding and listening with every evidence of keen interest to the detailed litany of complaint from the Names surrounding him. Their grumblings fell upon his ears with a numbing familiarity. He knew what lay ahead. It was all a matter of patience and reassurance, of apparently complying with their mad suggestions and schemes, their crafty plans to scupper the other side, and of gently distracting their fevered minds while trying to conduct the case as one saw fit. Fortunately, Rachel and Fred would take most of the flak if the committee got stroppy, as he knew they would. No doubt Conor Grimley had been happily going along with everything they'd said up to this point, allowing factions to develop. Conor would do most things for a quiet life. Leo had already taken on board the fact that two opposing camps existed in terms of tactics. He glanced across to where Lady Smallwood and friends formed their own huddle and wondered whether there was some way of smoothing out the tensions which clearly existed. Division between the Names would only make things very difficult as the case got underway. He noticed that a younger man had joined the group and regarded him with interest for several seconds. Very attractive. Wasn't there something familiar about him? At that moment the man looked across, and as their eyes met Leo knew that he had encountered him before. But where? He couldn't think.

On the other side of the room, Gideon knocked back the remains of his champagne and smiled. 'You didn't tell me the new leader was Leo Davies, Mother.'

Lady Henrietta glanced up at her son and then across at Leo. 'I told you his name. I'm absolutely sure I did. Why – have you heard of him? That *is* a good sign.'

'I haven't just heard of him – I know him. From some time ago. He was my sponsor when I was at Bar school.'

'Your what, darling?' Lady Henrietta, after three glasses of champagne, looked sweetly baffled.

'Sponsor. It's when an older barrister is nominated by his Inn to look after a younger one. You dine with them, have the odd drink, then after a while they get bored, and the whole thing rather fades away. I was Leo's spondee.'

'Isn't that something to do with dactyls? Or so I always thought. How very quaint.' Lady Henrietta looked across at Leo again, this time more searchingly. 'He's very good-looking.'

'Hmm. Always was. Gone grey a bit early, though.' Gideon was rather proud of the fact that his own hair was still dark and lustrous.

'Well, why don't you bring him over? I think Caradog-Browne has monopolized him for quite long enough. We have a few important points to put to him, haven't we, Harold?'

Gideon set down his glass and sauntered across the room. Leo glanced round and saw Gideon approaching. Damn it, the man was smiling at him. He clearly remembered Leo, but Leo for the life of him couldn't place the fellow.

Gideon stretched out a hand. 'I don't expect you recall me,' said Gideon, with uncharacteristic modesty, as Leo shook his hand. 'Gideon Smallwood. I was your spondee at one time. No doubt one of many, so I would hardly expect you to remember me.' This was quite untrue. Gideon always expected to be remembered, but he was prepared to forgive Leo. It had been fifteen years, after all.

'Good heavens, of course I remember you, Gideon – how are you?'

'Very well, thanks. I'm one of your clients, as a matter of fact. My mother, Lady Norbury, is over there by the window. She's a member of the committee and she'd very much like to meet you.'

Gideon introduced Leo to Lady Henrietta and friends, and Leo sat for a good half-hour having roughly the same conversation as he had had with the other lot. This time his concentration was disturbed by the surprise of meeting up with Gideon Smallwood again. The Gideon of fifteen years ago had been a slight, rather effeminate youth, with beautiful eyes and an unsettling manner, and an ageless quality about him. He had been a fixture in the Inner Temple Common Room for several months, playing endless games of bridge with his friends. A fiendishly excellent bridge player, Leo recalled. But at the time they knew one another, Gideon was already unenthusiastic about the practice of law, and when eventually his dapper presence was no longer to be seen in the Common Room and around the Inns of Court, Leo for one was not surprised.

He glanced at Gideon, who was leaning by the window, half-listening to the conversation, bored, Leo could instantly tell, out of his wits. At a glance he took in the details of Gideon's expensive clothing, his air of utter assurance, and wondered what Gideon had made of the world, and the world of Gideon, over these fifteen years. Gideon's fine-boned face had filled out slightly, and the lovely eyes had a weary air, but he still looked dashing and youthful. Leo was aware that Gideon was exactly, in a superficial sense, the kind of man he usually found sexually attractive, but, looking at him now, he felt no direct response, but rather a sense of unease. Gideon, bored and restless, eyeing the room, was an enigma.

Gideon's own thoughts were calm and measured, and entirely his own. He allowed himself another glass of champagne, and waited. He glanced at Leo a couple of times, careful to do so only when Leo's attention was otherwise engaged, and each time he looked, he smiled to himself. There was only one disturbing moment, when a slim woman with long, dark hair came into the room, breathless with apologies for her lateness. Leo rose, kissed her, spoke briefly to her, then crossed the room with her to speak to some other Names.

Gideon leaned swiftly down and murmured to his mother, 'Who's that woman?'

'Gideon, you really must get more *involved*. It's your litigation too, you know. That's our solicitor, Rachel Dean.' She leaned confidentially towards Gideon's ear and added, 'She was married to Leo Davies, as I understand it, but they divorced.'

By nine, the evening was losing momentum and people were drifting off. Gideon was still leaning by the window when Leo approached him.

'So – what have you been doing with yourself for all these years?'

'Oh, this and that,' replied Gideon. He smiled. 'Tell you what – if you're not in a hurry, I thought we might have dinner somewhere and catch up.'

'That sounds like an excellent idea. I'll just say a few farewells first.'

Ten minutes later they were strolling up St James's. 'What about the Criterion Brasserie?' suggested Gideon. 'Simply can't bear club food.'

'Fine,' said Leo.

Dinner lasted two hours. During that time they covered Leo's fortunes at the Bar and Gideon's career in the Civil Service. Leo found Gideon very amusing, his apparently louche manner masking a bright wit and bizarrely diverting turn of thought.

'It's hard to imagine you in such a staid profession,' said Leo with a smile. 'When I heard you'd left the Bar, I rather imagined you'd decided to go into the theatre, or advertising. Something faintly glamorous.'

'How kind of you to say so. Actually, the Civil Service suits me very well. I enjoy its intellectual discipline and the restraints of protocol. It means that one's energies and appetites out of hours are so very much more *alive*, so to speak. Do you know what I mean? The work itself can be – well ... *exciting* is perhaps the wrong word. Intriguing, shall we say? As a matter of fact, I'm moving to a new department within the next couple of weeks. I'm to be PPS to Tony Gear, the new Minister for Artistic and Cultural Development.'

'Really? Congratulations. That's something of a coincidence – he's an acquaintance of mine. We're both trustees of a new museum of modern art which is opening next month.'

'How interesting.' Gideon leaned forward over his

coffee. 'I don't know terribly much about my new boss,' he lied. 'I'd be fascinated to hear what you make of him. It could be rather a help.'

Two brandies later, Leo was feeling distinctly mellow. The waiter brought the bill, which Leo insisted on paying. Gideon made only a token gesture of demurral. 'I suppose,' said Leo, glancing at his watch, 'that I'd better ask the waiter to call a cab.'

'Nonsense. It's only half-eleven. There's the rest of the night still ahead.'

'Perhaps for you, Gideon, but I have to pick up my son tomorrow morning . . .'

Gideon pushed his chair back and stood up. 'I refuse to let you desert me now. I'm enjoying myself far too much. Come on.'

Ten minutes later, Leo found himself heading with Gideon to the Ritz Club. Feeling light-headed after the wine and brandy, Leo decided that it was rather enjoyable to surrender oneself to somebody else's whims.

The next few hours were such as Leo had not passed in some years. At the Ritz Club Gideon ordered Kirs, and then proceeded to lose a couple of thousand pounds at the gaming tables. Leo watched in amusement, with no desire to play himself. He had grown out of that long ago. This was followed by a quick visit to Annabel's, where Gideon was greeted by friends, and embraced by a brunette at the bar, with whom he proceeded to have a long and intimate conversation. Leo met, to his surprise, several people whom he knew, and drank two large whiskies while chatting to them.

When they emerged into the dark night air, Leo knew he was tired, but the alcohol had given him something of a second wind. Gideon looked fresh, bright-eyed, and clearly still hungry for amusement.

'Come on,' he said. 'Let's give it some real Wellington boot. What about Aspinall's?'

'Gideon, it's three in the morning.'

'So? Gaming doesn't stop till four. Look – there's a cab – come on.'

So they made their way to Curzon Street, where Gideon ordered champagne and gambled until the tables closed. All the time, as at the Ritz Club, he kept up a flow of fast, amusing conversation. Everyone who passed seemed to know him, stopping to exchange a bright piece of banter with him.

Leaving the club shortly after four, Leo realized he felt extremely ragged. He would have to try to get in a few hours' sleep before going to pick up Oliver. Gideon, on the other hand, gave every appearance of being relaxed and refreshed by the night's doings. Leo watched as he took a little leather notebook from his pocket and scribbled some hurried calculations.

'How much did you lose?' Leo asked.

'More than I meant to. I've rather been pushing the Coutt's card of late. Still –' He slipped it back into his pocket, '– what are Friday nights for?'

'It's been quite an experience.' Leo yawned hugely and hailed a cruising cab. 'Thank you very much.'

'We must do it again sometime. I'll give you a ring at chambers.'

'Do that,' replied Leo.

In the cab he leaned back and closed his eyes. Shattered though he was, and rather drunk, Leo thought he hadn't enjoyed himself so much in ages. An odd fellow, Gideon. That angel's face, and those dark, wicked eyes. There was something very compelling about him. Leo very much hoped he would call – it wasn't every day that one made a new friend.

Gideon, sitting in the cab which was taking him across town to fresher, darker adventures, was thinking something along similar lines.

5

Charles Beecham surprised himself by sleeping late on Saturday morning. When he opened his eyes he saw from the bedside clock that it was nearly half-ten. His flight from California had got in at lunchtime the day before, and Charles had expected to be jet-lagged and up early this morning, brain fizzing. As it was, he felt much better than usual. He rolled on to his back and lay listening to the sounds of the house. He could hear voices in the kitchen below, Rachel's low murmur and Oliver's bubbling, bright baby responses, their words indistinct. Thank God the child slept through the night now – well, by and large – and even bigger thanks to God for the fact that Leo was coming this morning to take him for the weekend. Charles loved Oliver, but there was no question that having Rachel to himself, without interruption or distraction, was what he liked best of all. And there was little enough of that, the way things were at the moment. This was the second trip he had made to LA in three months, and it looked like there would be more in the offing, particularly if the deal his American agent was trying to put together ever came to anything. Charles had decided not to mention it to Rachel yet. No point in agitating her – it might all fall through. Besides, she was taken up with this Lloyd's case, and that would have to

93

finish before any plans could be made. He rubbed his eyes and got out of bed, and went to shower and dress.

Rachel heard Charles moving around upstairs and put on some fresh coffee.

'Come on, Oliver, take the train into the living-room. We don't want Charles falling over it.' She scooped up Oliver and his train and wrinkled her nose. 'And let's get that nappy changed before Daddy comes. He'll be here any moment.'

It was what she had been saying to herself for the past hour. Leo usually came no later than half-nine when it was his weekend to have Oliver, and she found herself glancing at the clock at ten-minute intervals, the knot in her stomach growing ever tighter. She shouldn't care so much about seeing him, but she did.

She changed Oliver's nappy and took it out to the bin, and the crunching sound of wheels on the gravel made her turn in expectation. But it was only the post-office van, with a parcel of books for Charles. She took them in and put them on the kitchen table.

Charles pulled on some jeans and a faded-blue sweatshirt, and gave himself a searching look in the mirror. He thought he looked pretty good for a guy in his mid-forties. All right, the blond hair was going rather grey, and his face looked a bit weather-beaten, particularly after the West Coast sunshine, but the *Radio Times* were putting him on their front cover for his new series this spring, so that was worth something. The Charlie Dimmock of historical documentary, that's what I am, thought Charles.

He went downstairs to the kitchen, humming, where he embraced Rachel with jocular passion and poured himself some coffee. Oliver had made his way back in from the living-room, pushing his train on his hands and knees. Charles reached down and ruffled his silky hair.

'Leo not here yet?' He noticed the parcel of books on the table and picked up the bread knife to open it.

It was a mild enough enquiry, but something about its redundancy irritated Rachel. 'I don't know where he's got to,' she replied. 'I saw him last night but he didn't say anything about being late. Charles, do you *have* to use the knife? It's so dangerous. Here, use the scissors.'

Charles, who didn't see why it mattered if he used the bread knife, obediently put it down and took the scissors. He was used to these domestic reproofs and took them with his customary good humour. Rachel always got a bit edgy when Oliver was going off for the weekend.

'That must be Leo now,' said Rachel, glancing up at the sound of a car, something like relief clearing her features. She was unaware that her expression, and the speed with which she moved to open the door and go to greet Leo, told Charles certain things he would rather she had kept hidden. Charles wanted so much to fill the space which Leo had left in her life, wanted Rachel to be as much in love with him as she had been with Leo. But he knew that Leo, despite all the pain he had caused Rachel, or perhaps because of it, was still very special to her. Charles stood at the kitchen window, the scissors motionless in his hand, watching as Leo got out of the car and

Rachel moved forward, tentative as a girl in love, to greet him. A raw sense of pain and jealousy filled his heart. Absurd, he told himself. He knew he had nothing to fear from Leo. He was her past. Oliver was what they had in common, but Rachel lived here now. She was his, and tonight he would have her all to himself.

'You're late,' said Rachel, lifting her hand to shade her eyes from the watery sun. Immediately she knew it sounded like a rebuke. She hadn't meant to be that way. She would like to have been able to say how glad she was to see him. But that was the way things came out when she was with Leo. 'I meant I was worried – you know, in case something had happened.'

Leo closed the car door and stepped forward to kiss her cheek, a perfunctory, sexless kiss. The very faint scent of his expensive cologne was achingly familiar.

'I met an old friend at that do at the Guards' Club last night, and I'm afraid we made rather a night of it. I had to catch up on some sleep.'

'Coffee?' asked Rachel, leading the way into the kitchen.

'Yes, please – I'd love some. Morning, Charles.'

Charles raised a hand in greeting and poured them both some coffee while Rachel went to fetch Oliver's things. Leo sat at the kitchen table and glanced at the half-opened parcel of books.

'What's this?' he asked, as Charles set down the mugs of coffee.

'Copies of my new book. I don't know why my publishers send me so many.'

'So that you can distribute them to your loved ones

and to your extensive circle of admiring acquaintances. Let's have a look.'

Charles hacked through the rest of the packaging with the bread knife and handed one to Leo.

Leo surveyed the cover, which consisted of a full-length shot of Charles in weather-stained khakis, squinting handsomely at the camera from a barren, brown landscape. Lawrence of Arabia, the boyish Englishman abroad, thought Leo. He had found himself briefly in love with Charles Beecham not so long ago. It had been a disappointment to discover that Charles was rampantly heterosexual, to say nothing of the fact that he was in love with Leo's ex-wife. Leo put the book down and sighed.

'Your doting female readers are going to love it.'

'What d'you think of the title?' asked Charles.

'*From an Antique Land*? Very good, if people catch the reference. Otherwise there's a danger of you sounding more like Hugh Scully than Shelley's traveller.'

Rachel came into the kitchen carrying Oliver, who stretched his small arms out at the sight of Leo.

'Come here, king of kings.' Leo took Oliver from Rachel and sat him on his lap and kissed him. 'My, you're getting heavy.' He glanced up at the rucksack in Rachel's hand. 'He can't need that much. It's only till tomorrow night.'

Rachel flushed slightly. 'It's just some of his favourite toys and books. And some spare nappies.'

'Rachel, I've got plenty of nappies. And anyway, he doesn't need to bring toys or books. There are lots at the flat, and at Stanton. You know that.'

She shrugged and set the rucksack down. 'What had you planned to do over the weekend?'

'I don't know. The usual things that dispossessed fathers do. If the weather holds out, we might go to London Zoo. Or we may head down to Stanton this evening and have a peaceful Sunday in the country. What about you two?'

'Enjoy the peace and quiet,' murmured Charles. 'Sorry,' he added, catching Rachel's glance. 'Just a mild pleasantry. I've actually booked a table at an extremely new and expensive restaurant for tonight, so while you and Oliver are eating scrambled eggs, or whatever, we will be –'

'Charles,' interrupted Rachel suddenly, 'would you mind getting Oliver's buggy from the hall and folding it up?'

'Sure.' He rose and left the room.

There was silence for a few seconds. Leo, still jiggling Oliver on his knee, picked up a copy of the book and inspected the cover again.

'Oh, by the way,' he said, glancing up at Rachel, 'when do you think we'll have the last of the statements?'

'By the end of next week, I hope. Fred has to go up to Scotland to take two, and I have to go back to see some woman in Swanage.' Leo nodded. 'What did you make of the Names you met last night?'

Leo put down the book. 'Much the same as the last lot, but I see what you mean about factions having developed. That's going to be a pain unless we can sort them out.'

Charles came back into the kitchen with the buggy. 'What's this about factions?'

'Oh, we were just discussing the latest Lloyd's case. Rachel has very kindly instructed me.'

'Really?' Charles glanced at Rachel. 'You didn't mention it.'

'You've been in the States for a fortnight. Leo only came into the case last week.'

'Oh, I see.'

Leo stood up, setting Oliver gently down on the floor. 'We'd better make tracks, then.'

Charles brought the buggy out to the car, while Leo strapped Oliver into his car seat and loaded the rest of his belongings. Rachel stood on the driveway and waved until the car was out of sight.

She went back into the kitchen, arms folded, her expression thoughtful.

'That's going to be cosy,' remarked Charles. 'Working on a case with your ex-husband.' He picked up the mugs and took them to the dishwasher.

Rachel was surprised at the tone of his voice, which was as close to chilly as Charles' voice ever got. 'I instructed Leo because he happens to be a very good lawyer,' she replied. 'One of the best.'

'Is that all it is?' Charles leaned against the sink, regarding her.

'Of course it is! What on earth are you getting at? Leo and I got divorced last year – remember?'

He held out his arms and she moved towards him and into his embrace. 'Sorry.' He kissed the side of her head, stroking her hair. 'I love you so much. So much. I want it to be the same for you. I don't want you to think about Leo – ever.'

'I don't,' she lied. 'Not in that way. He's Oliver's father – that's all.' She drew back a little and looked into Charles' eyes. 'I do love you. I wouldn't be here with you if I didn't. You know that.' It was true. How could she not love someone who was so honest and open and affectionate? All the things that Leo wasn't.

'Good. That's all I need to know.' He hugged her again, wondered if this was the moment to mention the American thing. No, he decided – best leave it for now.

Sarah woke late. The flat was empty. Lou, her flatmate, had gone to Amsterdam for the weekend. Everything was in a mess, no one had cleaned the bathroom for a week, and Sarah couldn't be bothered to do it now. She sat by the window in the kitchen with a mug of coffee and last night's copy of *ES*, and wondered what to do with her Saturday. Certainly not clean this place up. That could wait till Lou got back. She could ring up friends and see if anyone felt like lunch and shopping, but she'd been spending too much recently. Time to rein things in till next payday.

Her mind drifted to Leo. She found herself thinking about him more than usual these days, which was hardly surprising, given what she had in mind. That last time they'd had a drink together, she'd judiciously played it cool. Perhaps it was time to warm things up a little. Then she remembered – she'd overheard him mentioning to Michael that Oliver was going to be staying with him this weekend. Oh, well . . .

She gazed down at the quiet street and pondered this. If he was on his own with Oliver, might it not be a clever move to drop in on them, get to know the kid, do a bit of sunny, big-sister stuff? Leo, so far as she knew, regarded her in no light other than the sexual and practical. If she wanted to make a husband of him, then he would have to see that there was another dimension to her. With a smile, Sarah finished her coffee and went to shower and dress.

At the flat in Belgravia, Leo gave Oliver lunch, then took him, plus a ball, down to the communal garden in the middle of the quiet square. The air was still chilly, but the sun was out, and the high plane trees which bordered the garden were in bud. Leo and Oliver kicked the ball around for a few minutes, then Leo sat on a bench, flicking through the Saturday *Times*, while Oliver squatted on the path and made a careful pile of gravel and twigs, murmuring to himself under his breath as he did so. Every so often Leo would lean down to listen, smiling, but not interrupting. They were perfectly happy.

The sun went behind a cloud. Leo was just wondering whether he should put Oliver's coat on when a voice interrupted his thoughts.

'What a very touching pair you make, father and son together.' He turned and saw Sarah leaning over the railings, wisps of her blonde hair blowing around her face. She smiled. 'I've just been to your flat, found you weren't in, then saw you in here on the way back to my car.'

'Come and join us.'

Sarah came through the gate and sat down next to Leo on the bench. 'So this is Oliver.' Oliver looked up from his gravel mound at the sound of his name and scrutinized the new arrival. 'Gosh, isn't he like you! Same eyes.'

'Mmm. Cold and calculating. Look, he's weighing you up.'

Oliver resumed work on the gravel mound.

'Clearly finds me very boring.' The sun appeared from behind the clouds again and Sarah leaned back and lifted her face towards it, closing her eyes.

'So what brings you out to see me on a Saturday? You should be out cruising Bond Street and Harvey Nicks, spending the excessive amounts of money we pay you for doing very little.'

'I came to see you because I had nothing to do, and thought it would be nice to go and have lunch down on the river. Putney, say. Or Kew.'

'Nothing to do? I would have thought you, of all people, would have several men in tow at the weekends.'

'I haven't, as it happens. Not at present.' Sarah opened her eyes and looked at Leo. 'What about you?'

Leo hesitated before replying, 'No. Not just at the moment.'

'Come and have lunch with me, then. Both of you.'

'I had been thinking of going down to Stanton with Oliver this afternoon, and staying overnight.' Sarah said nothing to this, merely waited. Leo hesitated, wondering whether it was a good idea to let Sarah any further into his personal life. She was a potentially dangerous young woman, as he had found out in the past. But time with a toddler, even one as beloved as Oliver, could pass slowly, and there was always the prospect of Sarah's compliant body later in the evening. On the last occasion they had spent time together, she had turned him down, which had irked him. So he added, 'Why don't you come down, too?'

She smiled into his eyes, thinking rapidly. It would mean jettisoning Hugo's party, and the possibility of Hugo, whom she'd been lusting after for some time. But so what? Long-term strategy was far more important. She delayed replying for some seconds, as though weighing the proposition up. 'I'd like that,' she replied at last. 'I haven't been to Stanton for a long time.'

'Good,' said Leo. 'Why don't we set off now? We'll stop off at a pub on the way there, and you can buy me lunch, as promised. Oliver's already had his.' Leo called to Oliver, who bumbled across on chubby legs, allowing himself to be scooped up by his father. 'Shall we all go in my car?'

'No, I'll follow you down. I like my independence.'

'Fine. I'll be spared your taste in in-car musical entertainment, which is probably execrable.'

They went back to Leo's flat, where Leo put together a few belongings, then went to their respective cars. 'Keep an eye-out for the turning to Bamford once we get off the motorway,' said Leo. 'There's a pub there with a garden.'

*

An hour later, Sarah and Leo were sitting in the deserted garden of a village pub, eating shepherd's pie and watching as Oliver poked at two mournful rabbits through the wire netting of their cage.

'God, it's freezing out here,' said Sarah, pulling her hands up into the sleeves of her denim jacket.

'I have to admit it's better in summer. I found the place last August, when Oliver had just started to walk. At least the animals keep him busy.' Leo sipped his beer and gave Sarah a speculative glance. 'I can't believe you would really choose to spend your Saturday this way. What's the hidden agenda?'

It was a close touch. She smiled. 'How typical of you. Always ready to read a motive. I told you — it just so happens I was bored. And you're fairly amusing company.'

'Enough to keep you away from your dinner parties and clubs? I think not. And young Oliver's not exactly the average young woman's idea of fun. It's hard work keeping an eighteen-month-old boy and his father amused. He still wakes in the night, sometimes, so you needn't expect an unbroken sleep, either.'

'I think I have enough resources to amuse you both,' replied Sarah. 'Besides — a good night's sleep wasn't exactly what I had in mind.'

Leo raised his eyebrows. 'Come on, we'd better get going.'

Twenty minutes later, both cars pulled into the gravel driveway of Leo's country house. Stepping out of her car,

Sarah breathed in the clear, chilly air and surveyed her surroundings. The house, of warm, reddish brick, was built in a sprawling L-shape and was surrounded by an acre and a half of lawned garden, fringed with trees. She had always liked it, and the air of tranquillity which the place exuded. It was as though it held the key to some other, hidden part of Leo's character. Here things were haphazard and comfortable, unlike Leo's flat or his room in chambers, which were both elegant and uncluttered, almost severe in their aspect. Even though Leo came here barely once a month, the house had a welcoming, lived-in feeling.

Sarah followed Leo into the low-beamed hallway. Leo set Oliver down, and the boy toddled ahead into the living-room, babbling and shouting.

'I'll build a fire,' said Leo. 'Why don't you go and make some tea?'

When she came back into the living-room, Leo had managed to get the fire to catch, and Oliver was distributing the contents of a large chest of toys across the rug. Sarah sank into one of the large, comfortable sofas and sipped her tea.

Leo picked up his own tea and sat near the fire in an armchair. She understood entirely why it would not occur to Leo to sit with her, or touch her, or behave with any warmth or affection. Their relationship was one of convenience. If they chose to have sex, it was always a dispassionate, physical affair, their minds and pleasure separate. That was the basis on which Leo had first brought her to this house, her and James. They had been his playthings. He never thought of her in any other way, and assumed she treated him in like fashion. They simply amused one another, but it meant nothing more. He was probably quite glad to have her here this weekend, as a means of relieving the tedium of coping with a toddler, and as someone to sleep with. Sarah knew that it didn't matter to Leo whether it was with her, or some other person, even some man. It was that, she knew, that she would have to change. His whole mind-set would have to be turned around, so that he came to regard her in quite a different way.

No mean task, thought Sarah, given the functional basis on which their relationship had existed up until now.

'I don't know what you thought you were going to live on,' remarked Sarah. 'There's absolutely no food in the cupboards, not even of the tinned variety.'

Leo leaned back, suddenly weary from the drive and lack of sleep. He smothered a yawn. 'I'll go down to the village shop in a while, see what it has to offer.'

'That place is useless, unless it's very much changed since I was last here.'

'I haven't got the energy to think about it right now. I had rather a late night last night. Or rather, morning. I didn't get to bed until half-four.'

'Really? That's pushing it a bit, at your great age. What on earth were you doing till that hour? Or is it best I don't know?'

'It was all very innocent. I found myself being taken to a few gaming clubs – by a rather amusing man, as it happens.' Leo gave a tired, reflective smile. 'An old acquaintance.'

Sarah wasn't in the mood to hear about it. She set down her tea. 'Well, if you're so worn out, I'll drive into Oxford and get some stuff from the supermarket.'

Leo yawned again. 'Fine. But keep it simple. I don't feel like cooking much tonight.'

'Don't worry, you won't have to. I'll see to that.'

When she got back to the house in the late afternoon, dusk had fallen, and the room was gently bathed in the light from lamps around the room. Leo was lying on the sofa, watching the football results on television, while Oliver was rolling the contents of the log basket out on to the floor and filling it with his toys.

'Thank God you're back,' said Leo. 'I've been fighting to stay awake for the last half-hour.'

A log fell on Oliver's small fingers and he set up a shrill wail. Leo groaned. Sarah reached down and picked him up. 'Why don't you catch up on some sleep while I give Oliver tea?'

'God bless you,' murmured Leo, and closed his eyes. It was a good thing she'd come down with them, he realized. He'd have to be careful in future when it was his weekend to have Oliver. Late nights and childcare didn't mix.

In the kitchen, Sarah had to wrestle for some moments with Oliver's high chair before she could unfold it. Then she sat him in it and kissed his hot, wet face. The sobs subsided in the small chest as Sarah tore off the end of a French loaf and handed it to him. 'Here, keep going with that till I can make you something more substantial.' She put groceries into the fridge and cupboards. She hadn't bought much – just some pasta and salad, and the makings of a carbonara sauce. Leo always had a stash of wine around the place, but she'd bought a couple of extra bottles just in case, and some bread and fruit.

She made Oliver a boiled egg and helped him to eat it, and gave him a cup of milk, the contents of which he poured on to the table of his high chair, casually dropping the cup on the floor afterwards. He ate the better part of a banana, squashing the rest between his fingers and kneading it into crevices in his high chair, and leaning down to smear some of it affectionately into Sarah's hair as she knelt to clean up the milk. Sarah rinsed out the cloth and leaned against the sink, fishing bits of banana from her hair. Jesus, toddlers were hard work, and she'd only been on her own with this one for twenty minutes. She scrutinized Oliver, who gazed back at her with bold, intelligent eyes. He would come with the package, reflected Sarah. It was all very well to regard the pursuit of Leo as an amusing game, but what if she were to succeed? What if Leo were to be persuaded that she would be as good a constant companion as any, and actually take her on? Then it would be less of a game. It would involve this little being, for a start, and all the complications of being someone's stepmother. This was going to take some thought.

Since Oliver was becoming restive in his high chair, she plucked him out and took him through to the living-room, where Leo lay fast asleep on the sofa, and set him down on the rug with his toys. They played together for half an hour or so, after which time Sarah grew bored of building up brick towers for Oliver to scatter. She found a small selection of videos in a cupboard by the television, and sat Oliver in front of the Teletubbies, while she took at random a book from the shelves and curled up in an armchair. After another half-hour, Oliver began to rub his nose and look generally sleepy. Sarah went upstairs to his bedroom and found some pyjamas in a drawer, and took them back downstairs.

'Lord, I suppose I'd better change your nappy first,' she muttered. Oliver gave her a baleful, tired look. Sarah went to hunt down the nappies, and when she came back she found Oliver standing by the sofa, gently patting Leo's face. She watched them for a few moments, father and son, and felt something like jealousy at the realization that Oliver was, and always would be, the most precious being in Leo's life, the one person he loved. No one else came close. Oliver began patting with greater force, in an attempt to wake Leo, who merely shifted on to his side. Sarah scooped Oliver up to find a convenient surface on which to change him, Oliver trailing a shrill cry of 'Daddeee!' as he went.

When he was changed, Sarah carried him upstairs, rather enjoying the warmth of the small, compact body against hers, hoping that his relative inertness signalled that he would go straight to sleep. She laid him in his cot and tucked his quilt around him, pulled the curtains, and switched on the night light in the corner of the room. She tiptoed to the cot and looked down. Oliver stared back at her, then smiled, startling her with his likeness to Leo. She bent and kissed him lightly, then left the room quietly, praying that the silence would continue. It did.

Downstairs Leo was still asleep. Kneeling on the rug to pick up Oliver's wooden bricks, Sarah glanced at his sleeping face. She was suddenly touched by the vulnerability of his tired features, which frowned slightly, then cleared, like a child's. A feeling such as she had not experienced in some years swept through her, and she found herself thinking – no, not that, not that, ever again. Loving someone was one thing, but she never wanted to find herself in love again. Leo stirred, and gradually opened his eyes. He saw Sarah kneeling on the rug by the sofa, watching him. He blinked and stretched his arms above his head.

'God, how long have I been asleep?'

'A couple of hours.'

He ran his fingers through his hair and yawned, then after a moment he turned to glance at Sarah. Her expression was unusually reflective. In fact, all day she had been unlike herself, less barbed and provocative. 'You look very pensive. What are you thinking about?'

Sarah smiled. 'I was thinking about the time you were in court and you didn't have your glasses.'

'One of my increasingly frequent senior moments. What, for heaven's sake, made you think about that?'

'I don't know. It made you vulnerable. Like now, when you were sleeping.'

'Hmm.' Leo clasped his hands behind his head. 'I don't

know if I like you feeling sorry for me. Go and make us both a drink.'

'Yes, sir – when I've tidied up these toys.'

'I've just realized how quiet it is. That's probably what woke me up. Where's Oliver?'

'Upstairs, asleep. I gave him tea, then we played for a bit, then he got tired.'

'Did you give him a bath?'

'God, no! It was bad enough changing him and getting him into his pyjamas.'

'Rachel likes him to have a bath every evening.' Leo stooped down from the sofa to pick up some of the toys.

'Does she now? Too bad.' Sarah stood up. 'If you'll put the rest of those away, I'll make us that drink. Scotch?'

They sat companionably by the fire with their drinks, and Sarah listened as Leo explained the Lloyd's case to her. When he had finished, he added, 'I'm afraid it's not going to be the most exciting case. Most of your work will consist of trawling through documents, checking references, making sure things are in the right order.'

'It's what I do most of the time.' She uncurled herself from her armchair and stood up. 'I'll make us some supper.'

'Want a hand?'

'No, I'm fine, thanks. You never used to help, anyway.'

'Ah, that was way back then. That was when you were paid to do it.'

Sarah stood looking down at Leo. 'That's right – I just cooked your food and let you screw me, didn't I?'

There was a pause before Leo spoke. 'That, as I recall it, was the general arrangement.'

'So what's changed now?' Sarah wondered why she felt a sudden spurt of anger. She was momentarily confused.

'Nothing, if that's what you want out of this weekend. You don't get paid, that's all,' replied Leo quietly. The note of indifference in his voice chilled her. She tended to forget what a bastard he could be. It was something she would have to bear in mind.

'In that case,' she said with a smile, 'you can help. Come on.'

They ate at the big wooden table in the kitchen. At the end of the meal, Leo tipped the last of the wine into their glasses and reached across to touch Sarah's hair, surprising her with the apparent affection of the gesture. But he was merely taking something out of it. 'What on earth is this?'

'Banana,' replied Sarah. 'Your son thought I needed some.' She picked up the plates and carried them to the dishwasher. 'I'm going to take a shower.'

'I'll join you upstairs in a while,' said Leo. She turned and met his eye. His expression was fathomless.

He wants me, thought Sarah, as she showered. He always has. Or rather, he wants sex. I'm good at it. I know what he likes, I'll do anything that he turns his mind to, and he needs that. He needs to let go. That's why he likes to sleep with me. But there has to be more to it than that. I have to make it more than that, so that he starts to think about me in a different way. As she stepped out of the shower and began to dry herself, Sarah had to admit that she didn't have a clue how to do this.

Leo was already there when she came through, sitting up in the huge bed that was big enough for more than two people, if necessary. She and Leo and James had shared it for a while. Sarah wondered, fleetingly, where James was now. Jacking up with a load of other junkies, probably. Not that Leo cared. Leo had never cared.

He was reading a magazine. Sarah lifted it gently from his hands and glanced at the cover, then burst out laughing.

'*Arbitrations and Disputes Resolution Law Journal*? Is this to get you turned on, or something?'

'I don't need turning on,' said Leo. 'Come here.'

She knelt, naked, on the edge of the bed, and he kissed her breasts, drawing her towards him, immediately aroused. His touch was electric, sending waves of desire through her limbs. She lay next to him.

'Now . . .' said Leo softly. He kissed her fiercely, and she closed her eyes.

After a moment she said, 'I want to ask you something.'

'What?' His hands caressed her body.

'Do you think of this –' She hesitated. 'Do you think of this as just sex, or as making love?'

'If there's a difference,' replied Leo, 'then this is sex. Of the very best kind, I might add. Bringing love into it is quite another thing. That implies closeness. And closeness is not something I'm very good at. Nor are you, if everything you say is true.'

'No . . . I'm not. Oh, God, that's so good . . .' She

closed her eyes as he moved his hand. 'Could you just . . .'

'What?'

'Could you just . . . pretend? As a game. Just to make it more erotic.' She smiled, kissed him, her tongue against his. 'Pretend that it's more than just sex. That you love me, you've never wanted anyone as much, that this is something passionate, some huge romance. It's something we've never done before.'

Leo chuckled. 'You strange girl. Anything, whatever. I'll even pretend it's the first time, if you like. I enjoy games, especially with you.' And he kissed her tenderly, lovingly, murmuring to her like a lover, and Sarah had a heart-aching longing for it to be real. Not just a game. One day, she promised, as she gave her body to him, she would make it real. And even as she thought this thought, she knew she was slipping into dangerous waters.

Rachel was cooking breakfast the next morning when she remembered. Her hand went to her mouth.

'I forgot to tell Leo.'

'What?' Charles looked up from the Sunday papers.

'That we wouldn't be back until seven. Remember, we're going over to Nick's for lunch, and then we said we'd drive over to that antiques auction. There's no way we'll be back for six.'

'Well, give him a ring.'

Rachel dialled Leo's London number and got his answerphone, and guessed he must have gone to Stanton. She rang that number.

Sarah was lying in bed, drowsy from early-morning

sex. For someone over forty-six, she reflected, Leo had extraordinary energy. And inventiveness. She listened to Oliver wailing in his bedroom and was glad that it was Leo, and not she, who had to attend to him. When the phone rang, she stretched out a lazy hand.

'Hello?'

Rachel was taken aback by the sound of a woman's voice. 'Is Leo there?' she asked, her voice sharp.

Sarah yawned. 'I'm sorry . . . he's rather busy at the moment. Can I ask who's calling?'

'Rachel,' came the tight reply.

'Oh, Rachel, hi! This is Sarah.' She smiled, delighted by the situation. 'We met at a party a while ago – remember? Can I help?'

'I'd really like to speak to Leo, please.'

'I think he's changing the baby . . . Hold on, I'll just see if he's finished.' She put her hand over the receiver and called out to Leo, who came in in his boxer shorts, carrying Oliver. She held the phone out to him, mouthing Rachel's name, and Leo took it.

'Rachel. Hello.' He sat down on the bed, Oliver on his knee.

'I rang to say that Charles and I won't be back till seven tonight. We promised to go to an auction with Charles' son after lunch. I forgot to mention it yesterday.' Her voice was cold.

'Right. Well . . . I'll bring him back around half-past. How's that?'

'Fine.' There was a strained pause. Rachel wanted to say something about Sarah, wanted to give vent to her irrational displeasure that Leo should have some woman with him when he was meant to be giving his full attention to Oliver, but of course she couldn't.

'So,' said Leo, reading the silence, feeling the familiar depression that Rachel's unspoken reproaches always brought, 'see you tonight. Bye.'

He put the phone down and glanced at Sarah, who was leaning back against the pillows and smiling wickedly. 'Oh dear, Leo – she wasn't pleased.'

'No, she wasn't. My ex-wife can be remarkably censorious. Doubtless thinks you're a moral danger to Oliver.'

'She's probably still in love with you. I don't think I ever saw anyone as besotted with anyone as she was with you. Remember Sir Basil's party?'

'Don't think I haven't forgotten your little performance on that occasion,' remarked Leo dryly. 'Come on,' he said to Oliver, 'let's get you some breakfast.'

'What's up?' asked Charles, glancing at Rachel's face as she put the phone down.

'He's at Stanton. With some girl.'

'Leo? Well, he's entitled to a bit of fun, isn't he?'

'You'd think he might choose some time other than the weekend that he's meant to be looking after Oliver.'

'Yes, well . . .' Charles sighed and scratched his head, sympathizing with Leo. Two days on the trot with Oliver without any other adults around would test anyone. 'Maybe he just wanted some company. Chaps do.'

'I happen to have met this particular creature he's sharing his weekend with. She's part of his more sordid past. A few years ago she spent a summer at Stanton, she and some young man, some boyfriend of Leo's. God alone knows what they got up to. I can just imagine.'

Charles absorbed this with interest. 'What? You don't mean they –? Really? Well, well . . . The more the merrier with Leo, eh? You've got to admire him for it.'

Rachel shot Charles a glance. 'I don't particularly like that kind of girl around my son.'

Or in your ex-husband's bed, thought Charles. That's what really gets you. He stared bleakly back at his newspaper.

Leo was making Oliver's breakfast when Sarah appeared, dressed, swinging her car keys.

'Not staying for breakfast?'

'Things to do. I have to get back to London.'

'Not even a cup of coffee?'

'Not even a cup of coffee.' She approached Oliver's high chair and dropped a kiss on the silky head. 'Thank you both for a very stimulating few hours.' She didn't kiss Leo, but gave him a brief smile as she opened the back door. 'Bye.'

'Bye. See you in chambers tomorrow.'

Leo was only mildly surprised by her sudden departure. It was part of her unpredictability, and therefore her charm. Yet as he set Oliver's bowl of cereal before him, he was aware of a feeling of loss. She was good to have around. Sunday would be less fun without her.

6

Henry was feeling distinctly stressed. His phone hadn't stopped ringing all day, he had so many e-mails he couldn't answer them all, and the volume of work was increasing to the point where he was definitely going to have to raise the matter of bringing in another clerk. On top of all that, he couldn't get hold of Felicity, because she'd gone down to the House of Lords and hadn't switched her mobile on. He sighed in exasperation as the phone rang again.

'Answer that, will you, Robert?' Henry tapped at his keyboard and stared at the screen. 'Who was it?' he asked, as Robert put the phone down.

'Richard Crouch at More Fisher Brown. Needs someone to do an application for summary judgment tomorrow. Wants a fluent French speaker, someone no more than two years call. I said I'd try Simon.'

'Right.' Henry glanced up as Anthony came into the clerks' room in his shirt-sleeves. He looked as harassed as Henry felt.

'Henry, can I have a print-out of my diary for this week? I've got a feeling there's a hearing on Thursday on that judicial review.'

'Printer's on the blink,' remarked Robert in passing.

'Oh, brilliant!'

'Don't,' said Henry, putting his hands to his temples. 'Someone's coming round in half an hour to have a look at it. Hold on, let's have a look on the screen . . . No, you're all right. The Crown Office somehow got the date wrong. The actual hearing's been set for March the fifth.'

'That's a relief.'

Michael Gibbon, who had once been Anthony's pupilmaster, came in and took some mail from his pigeon hole. He glanced at Anthony. 'I'm just off for lunch. Want to come? If we go now, we can hit the Devereux before the teeming hordes descend.'

Anthony looked at his watch. After the morning he'd had, he could do with a drink. Normally he didn't drink at lunchtime, but today he would make an exception. 'Just give me five minutes. I'll see you there.'

By the time Anthony got to the pub, Michael had found a table and bought a couple of half pints. Anthony sat down and took a grateful sip. 'Shall I order us some lunch before it gets busy?'

'Good idea. I'll have the shepherd's pie.'

As Anthony paid for the food, he heard someone call his name and turned. A cheerful, florid face, surmounted by a shock of flaxen hair smiled back at him.

'Edward! Good to see you.' He and Edward shook hands. Edward Choke and he had once been rivals at 5 Caper Court, both vying for the same tenancy. Anthony had had the brains, but Edward had had the distinct advantage of being the nephew of the then head of chambers, Sir Basil Bunting. In the end, Anthony had been successful, much to the chagrin of Sir Basil, but to the secret relief of Edward, whose intellectual powers had been severely taxed by the work which had come his way during his pupillage at Caper Court. 'Haven't seen you in months. Michael and I are just having a quick spot of lunch. Why don't you join us?'

'Thanks – I'll just get myself a drink and order some food.'

Eventually Edward emerged from the scrum at the bar and sat down with his drink, demanding to know all the gossip from Caper Court. Anthony and Michael were happy to oblige.

'So,' said Anthony, halfway through his shepherd's pie, 'how are things going at Morgan Grenfell?'

'Oh, I packed that in a year ago,' said Edward airily. 'Not really my scene, you know.'

'So, whose gain is the financial world's loss?' asked Michael with a smile.

Edward took a few seconds to unravel this. He blinked and took a sip of his beer. 'Oh, I see what you mean. Well, as a matter of fact, I've joined the Civil Service.' He lowered his head to scrape up the remains of his hotpot, and Michael and Anthony exchanged the briefest of smiling glances.

'Not fast-tracking, are you?'

'God, no. Just wanted something decent that wasn't too much like hard work and didn't interfere with my social life. I come into my trust fund next year, when I'm twenty-five, so money's not a problem, but a chap's got to have something to do.'

'So what's your job, exactly?' asked Anthony.

Edward scratched his head. 'Well, I'm an officer attached to the old culture set-up. Only it's not old – it's the new thing, the Ministry for Artistic and Cultural Development. I'm not quite sure what I do half the time. Field applications from people wanting money, mostly. Everyone wants money for some project or another. I'm in charge of East London bids, but since there's not a lot of culture in East London, it makes my life a fairly easy one.'

Anthony put his knife and fork together and stared at Edward. 'That's astonishing. You're just the man I need.' Edward looked blank. 'My father, Chay Cross, has set up a museum of modern art in Shoreditch, and the trustees are looking for additional funding.'

Edward waved a hand. 'Stick in a bid. I'm sure I can use a bit of influence with a junior minister to help things along.'

'Tell you what,' went on Anthony, sensing that Edward could be more than a little useful here, 'the museum launch party is taking place in a couple of weeks. Why don't you come along?'

'Love to. In the meantime, I'll dig out some forms for you to fill in. I think I've got some somewhere.' Edward drained his glass. 'Fancy another, you two?'

'Can't, I'm afraid,' said Michael. 'I have to be getting back to chambers.'

'Me, too,' said Anthony. 'But look, I'll put a couple of invitations in the post. You still living in the same place?'

'Still in Onslow Gardens.'

'Right. I'll be in touch. Good to see you.'

Michael and Anthony walked back across Fountain Court to chambers. Michael chuckled and shook his head. 'How long do you suppose he's going to last at the Civil Service?'

'Long enough to help us with our grant for funding, I hope,' said Anthony. 'Sounds as though he won't need a job after his next birthday. Wish someone would set up a trust fund for me. Lucky beggar.'

She'd seen him on the way in. Now, as she left the House of Lords and set off for Westminster tube to hop the couple of stops to Temple, Felicity noticed him again. She couldn't help taking a second glance. He was very good-looking. Early thirties? Slim, not as tall as Vince, not as big as Vince . . . brown hair with blond streaks that might have come out of a bottle, or might be the product of the same sun that had given him his nice tan. He looked like he fancied himself, but Felicity could hardly blame him. She walked up to the lights to cross Parliament Square, and was aware that he had come in the same direction and was standing next to her. She glanced at him, and their eyes met. He smiled.

'You're from 5 Caper Court, aren't you?'

Felicity was startled. 'Yes.'

'I'm a clerk at 3 Wessex Street. Peter Weir.'

'Oh . . . hi. I'm Felicity Waller.'

'I know.' Suddenly he took her elbow and steered her. 'Quick, make a dash now.'

Felicity allowed herself to be propelled through the traffic.

'Where are you headed?' Peter Weir took his hand from her elbow as they reached the other side, and Felicity was instantly conscious of the loss of contact. God, he was gorgeous.

'Back to chambers. How do you know my name?'

'I asked back there.' Peter jerked his head in the direction of the House of Lords. They paused on the pavement. 'D'you have to go straight back? Or do you have time for lunch?'

She hesitated, surprised by the directness of this. 'Why?'

For a moment he looked blank. 'Because you look like a wonderful, warm human being with whom I would like to share my lunch hour.'

She laughed and shrugged. It wasn't every day some amazing stranger asked you out to lunch. And those eyes, all warm and crinkly. He looked a little older than she'd thought at first. 'OK. Why not?'

It was just a quick sandwich and a cup of coffee, but by the end of their conversation Felicity felt as though she'd known Peter Weir far longer than half an hour. It was certainly a change to be treated with such charm and candid admiration. He could teach Vince a thing or two. He had a confiding, easy manner, he was funny, but a little acerbic and cynical about the members of his chambers, and Felicity guessed that he thought himself a cut above most clerks. That was the only thing about him – he really rated himself, a thing Felicity generally didn't care for. Still, maybe it was just his way of chatting someone up.

At last Felicity glanced reluctantly at her watch. She'd left Henry up to his eyes in it, and she really should be getting back. 'I have to go,' she said.

'Come on, we can get a cab back together and I'll drop you off.'

'I was going to get the tube.'

'I'm not one for public transport. Share my cab.'

'OK,' said Felicity, though she suspected she'd be faster taking the tube. It would be nice to prolong this new acquaintance. If there was one thing she'd found out during their brief lunch, she liked looking at him. A lot.

As Felicity got out in Middle Temple Lane, Peter leaned across. 'Busy tonight?'

Blimey, thought Felicity, this one didn't hang about. She felt flattered, and quite ridiculously pleased. But there was Vince, and besides, tonight she had to go to Belmarsh to see him.

'Afraid so.' What would she have said, she wondered, if in fact she hadn't been busy?

'Pity. Give us your number.' Felicity watched as he keyed it into his mobile. 'Nice meeting you, Felicity,' Peter said, and grinned.

'You too.' The cab door closed and he was gone.

A little dazed, and disproportionately excited by the events of the last hour, Felicity went back to chambers. Things seemed to have quietened down since the morning, and the printer was up and running once again.

Henry glanced up as she came in. 'You're looking pleased with yourself.'

Felicity suddenly realized that, quite unconsciously, she had been smiling to herself. 'Life could be worse,' she replied jauntily, and hung her coat up. She was sure he'd call. What was she going to say when he did? She couldn't two-time Vince . . . Well, she'd worry about that if and when he called. She felt a little flutter of excitement in her stomach at the mere thought of it.

Leo came into the clerks' room on his way back from lunch and Henry buttonholed him.

'Mr Davies, I've been meaning to have a word. It seems I can never get hold of Mr Hayter. It's about the amount of work being generated. Felicity and Robert and I can just about cope, but I'm worried about what's going to happen when the annexe is finished. Are we going to be taking more tenants? Because if we are, I don't see how the three of us are going to manage. Things are bad enough as it is.'

'Actually, I've been giving it some thought. The original idea was simply to create more space for the present number of tenants, but the whole of that floor gives us much more room than we'd realized. Expansion is always a possibility.'

'Well, in that case, I think we'll have to look seriously at bringing in another clerk. Not necessarily a junior, either.'

'Yes, I take your point.' Leo gave a sigh. 'Look, I'll bring it up at the next chambers meeting.'

'I'd be grateful.'

Leo went up to his room, and on the way knocked on Camilla's door. They had arranged to spend the afternoon going through statements and bundles in the Lloyd's Names case. 'Ready when you are,' said Leo.

'I'll just finish this and be up in five minutes,' said Camilla.

The afternoon was spent reading through statements, documents and letters. It was wearisome work. Towards half past four there was a knock at the door and Anthony looked in. He seemed a little startled and embarrassed by the presence of Camilla, who gave him a chilly glance and carried on with her reading.

'I wondered if I could borrow your copy of Scrutton,' said Anthony, his voice and manner distant.

Leo lowered his half-moon spectacles and inspected his bookshelves. After a few seconds he stretched up to pluck a volume from the shelf. The way his muscles moved beneath his shirt touched Anthony suddenly and unexpectedly with a rush of feeling. Leo handed him the book.

'Thanks.' It was spoken grudgingly.

'Any time,' said Leo, with a bemused smile. Anthony's touchiness, his ability to nourish antagonism, was quite remarkable. But then, he was very young.

When Anthony had gone, Leo remarked to Camilla, 'You two barely seem to acknowledge one another these days.'

Camilla looked up at him in surprise. 'I haven't a great deal to say to him. No more than to any other person who might drop into your room for a book.'

'I don't mean just now. I mean generally. I don't think it's very good for the morale of chambers.'

'Leo, as I recall, it was only a year or so ago that you delicately hinted to me that having too close a relationship with Anthony might jeopardize my chances of a tenancy. Of course it has crossed my mind since then that perhaps you were just trying to scare me off Anthony for reasons of your own.' She paused. 'Very personal ones.' Leo turned abruptly and walked to the window. Camilla could tell this had hit home. 'So naturally I don't take very kindly to any suggestions from you as to how I should conduct relationships with other people in chambers.'

Leo was forcibly struck, not just by her perspicacity, but by the calm and deadly manner in which this little speech was uttered. She certainly knew how to deliver. When, after a few seconds, Leo had regained his composure, he turned to face her with a smile, leaning against the window-sill with his hands in his pockets.

'You're quite formidable, Miss Lawrence. I apologize for my impertinence.'

Something in his eyes made Camilla colour slightly and look away. It had taken more nerve than Leo knew to say what she had said. Added to which, she now spent much time smothering the feelings which she harboured for Leo, and which had grown in her, despite her own emotional resistance, over the last year or so. She almost despised herself for the weakness of it. It was as though no one was able to escape his fatal charm. She turned her attention to the papers before her.

Leo considered her, the soft abundance of her reddish hair, the paleness of her skin. Pretty girl. He wondered what she was like in bed, what kind of lover Anthony had found her to be ... no, he decided. Better not. Too unprofessional, with the case coming up. She wasn't really his type. He knew enough by now to realize that it was probably just the spark of her hostility which had faintly aroused him. Nothing more.

They carried on working as though no interruption had occurred. By the time six o'clock came, Camilla showed no signs of flagging. It occurred to Leo that she would probably work all evening if he asked her to. She had the makings of success. Intelligence, dedication, and, as he had discovered this afternoon, a steady fearlessness that would stand her in good stead when it came to dealing with some of the more temperamental bastards on the Commercial bench. But there was something a little sad about such steeliness in someone so young. It certainly hadn't been there a year ago. Leo reflected that the break-up with Anthony, being hurt and betrayed like that, had probably affected her badly. He had seen it before. People throwing themselves into their work to escape from the unhappiness of some love affair, and never quite recovering. Staying that way, hardening, not letting the bitterness go. Surely she was too young for that.

He was leaning back in his chair, hands clasped behind his head, and it was only when Camilla looked up that Leo realized he had been staring at her, quite unintentionally.

'I was thinking,' he said, breaking the silence, 'that you take work too seriously.'

'Is that possible?'

'Oh, yes.' Leo stifled a yawn. 'I'll bet you take briefs home with you.'

'Doesn't everyone?'

'Not every night.' He saw that he had hit a raw nerve. Poor kid. She was probably lonely as hell, with nothing but chambers business to occupy her. 'You need a social life, too, you know.'

Camilla flushed. 'You seem amazingly preoccupied with my private life, if you don't mind me saying so.'

'I don't mind at all. Try not to use these redundancies in speech. They're infelicitous in a good barrister.' She was about to make some retort, then realized that he was joking. 'Come on, lighten up,' said Leo. 'What say we work another hour or two and then you let me buy you dinner?'

A little wave of fear and pleasure shook her.

'You don't have to, you know.'

'I know that,' replied Leo patiently. Oh, the young. So resistant, so graceless. 'But I should like to.'

'Thank you.'

Five minutes later, the phone rang.

'Leo! Coming out to play tonight?' For a moment Leo couldn't place the voice, jaunty and smooth at the same time.

'Gideon?'

'The very same. I've just spent the most *gruelling* day with our esteemed Minister and a delegation from the Board of South-Western Arts, and wondered if you might be free for a drink. Or two. Or three. Or more.'

If he hadn't just invited Camilla to dine with him, Leo would have been tempted. However, given Gideon's idea of a pleasant night out, it was probably just as well he couldn't accept. Particularly since he had to be in chambers early tomorrow morning to carry on with the rest of these documents. 'I'm afraid I can't. I've just arranged to do something else.' For a moment Camilla's eyes met his, then she looked back down at her work. Leo was briefly distracted. What faint flicker had he detected in that glance?

'Well, that's a pity.'

'But, look, why don't you come to the Temple for a drink one evening next week – say, Tuesday? Revisit old haunts.' He liked the idea of spending another evening with Gideon – the man was amusing, a novelty. Though this time he'd have to make sure it ended before midnight.

'Tuesday, Tuesday . . .' Gideon scanned his diary. 'Yes, I can do that. I'll come to chambers from work. Around sevenish?'

'Fine.'

'By the bye,' said Gideon, 'when's our case due to start?'

'In a couple of weeks. March the eleventh.'

'Good. That'll keep mother quiet on one point, at least. She liked you *very* much, I might add. Says she found you most reassuring.'

'Good. Perhaps there won't be quite so much in-fighting from now on. As it happens, I'm slaving away in your cause right at this moment.'

'In which case, I won't keep you. Bye.'

Gideon put the phone down and sat back in his chair, glancing round the largely deserted office. The only people still remaining were Gideon's own secretaries, a couple of ambitious high fliers in their early twenties, whom Gideon, for his personal amusement and satisfaction, worked tremendously hard. Gideon's desk stood just outside the portals of Tony Gear's private inner sanctum, the last bastion; no one could see the Minister without Gideon's express authorization. Gideon was already working assiduously to foster in his new master a sense of complete dependence on his private secretary. He had sown the seeds swiftly and cleverly in their first few days together, and by a combination of subtle flattery and gentle manipulation had generated in Tony Gear a feeling of admiring gratefulness that he had so able an assistant. Gideon had been careful, however, to keep Tony's ego well bolstered at all times, to make him feel that he was in complete control. Which, of course, he was. Who could doubt that?

The door to Tony Gear's private office opened, and a young woman in her mid-twenties emerged, Tony Gear's diary secretary. She interested Gideon not a little. Her name was Kelly, which Gideon found risible enough, and she was blonde and attractive in a fashion which Gideon thought tiresomely predictable. Sensible skirt, nothing too flashy, but figure-hugging little tops which showed off an ample bust, and heels just high enough to let her strut across the office. Gideon watched her as she went back to her desk. It had been very interesting to discover that Kelly and Tony Gear were already acquainted, and that there was every possibility that her appointment as his diary secretary had been carefully engineered. The happily married Mr Gear, as the official word had it. Gideon knew a little more about it than that.

Caper Court was deserted and silent when Leo and Camilla left at eight o'clock. Leo drove to Leicester Square and took Camilla to a small Italian restaurant tucked away in a courtyard off St Martin's Lane, where Leo was greeted warmly, and seemed well known. Camilla listened as Leo chatted in Italian to the owner, reflecting that it was impossible not to be impressed by everything about Leo. Even the darker aspects of his personality, and the flaws in his character, such as his occasional volatility and impatience with stupidity, merely served to sharpen his points of brilliance. The rumours about his bisexuality, which had at first shocked her, now faintly excited her, adding to the mystique surrounding him. Camilla credited herself with considerable good sense and the ability not to be swayed by irrational feeling. She knew all the reasons why someone like Leo was out of her league. In her own case, apart from anything else, he was probably too old for her. Yet all the reason and clarity in the world came to nothing in the face of one smile from him, or a glance from those blue eyes.

The conversation over dinner, mainly about cases and people in chambers, was easy enough, but Leo was aware of the reserve in Camilla's manner. She'd always been a rather staid girl, to his way of thinking, and even though she'd lost her former gaucheness, she still had about her an air of one who knew too little of the world. Leo, as he sipped his coffee, reflected that it was in some ways rather charming. He eyed her thoughtfully as she expounded on some case of a few days ago, taking in her clothes, the nondescript white shirt she wore beneath the boring black jacket. The standard gear for women at the Bar, and difficult to make interesting. He wondered what she would look like dressed in something else, something that showed off her neck and shoulders, and with her hair loose, shining. She needed someone to make her smile a little more, to bring warmth and genuine pleasure to her eyes.

Camilla saw that Leo's mind was elsewhere and paused, smiling apologetically. 'I'm sorry. I'm being boring.'

'No – not at all,' replied Leo, still distracted. 'I was just trying to picture you –' He stopped.

Camilla sat, lips parted, astonished, her eyes fastened on Leo's. A little blush mounted to her face at the thought that he had been sitting thinking about her as she talked.

He leaned his elbow on the table and tapped his fingers against his lips, as though musing. He had her; she was caught. How easy. Too easy. He gave a smile, as though faintly embarrassed. 'I shouldn't have said that. It doesn't matter. I'll get the bill.'

She was entirely silent as he went through the motions of paying, caught within the web he had woven with his few careless words.

They walked down Goodwins Court into St Martin's Lane. Camilla stopped on the pavement and turned to Leo.

'Thank you for dinner. It was lovely.'

'I'm glad you enjoyed it.'

She hesitated for a moment, then said, 'I'd better go and get my train.'

'Where do you live?' asked Leo.

'Clapham.'

'I'll drive you,' said Leo.

'No, really – you don't have to.'

Leo lowered his head and said in a gently mocking way, 'Do you *always* have to say that when men are trying to be helpful, or gallant, or just want to spend some time with you?' The casual intimacy of the words utterly transfixed Camilla.

'No. Right. Sorry,' she stammered. Leo began to walk in the direction of the NCP car park where he had left his car, and Camilla followed.

Camilla experienced a childish pleasure riding in Leo's car. It was warm and leathery, clearly ridiculously expensive, and utterly in keeping with Leo, she thought, as she leaned back and enjoyed the sensation of gliding through the traffic, listening to the quiet music from the CD player.

As they drove down Wandsworth Road, Leo broke the spell. 'You'll have to tell me which way to go from here.'

Camilla directed him, and after a few minutes they pulled up outside a large, shabby, semi-detached house. Camilla ducked her head and glanced up at the first floor. No lights on. 'Jane must still be out. She's in a criminal set in Hare Court. She put an advertisement up on the

noticeboard in Inner Temple Common Room for someone to share, and that's how we met. I was very lucky,
really –' Camilla stopped. 'Anyway, thanks for the lift.'

As she turned to glance at Leo, he was instantly struck
by the open, soft expression in her eyes. In the half-light
from the street lamp, the skin of her cheek was pale,
framed by hair which had come loose. He was not often
touched, but he was at this moment.

They sat looking at one another, and then he chuckled
softly.

'What?' asked Camilla. She felt anxious, mildly
offended, wishing she could handle situations like this
with ease and maturity. Perhaps she should just say thanks
again and get out of the car.

Leo laughed again, then said in a gentle voice, 'I've
never in my life seen anyone who wanted to be kissed so
much.' He waited with interest to see how she would
react.

She looked, as he expected, indignant and astonished
both at once, and entirely lost for words.

'Come here,' said Leo. She did nothing, said nothing,
and he put out an arm and drew her towards him, and
kissed her.

Camilla wanted the moment to go on and on for
ever. The feeling in the pit of her stomach, the melting,
dissolving sensation, was so wonderful that he could do
anything with her that he wanted. She knew that. He
knew that.

'There,' murmured Leo, when it had ended.

'What?' asked Camilla. She felt dizzy.

'Wasn't it what you wanted?'

Camilla struggled for words, and for poise. Both were hard to find. 'Not – not necessarily.'

Leo smiled. 'Ah, well. My mistake. I'll know better another time.' She looked so totally open and pliable, body and soul, that Leo knew that if he were to turn around now, drive her back to his place and take her to bed, she wouldn't resist for one second. He sighed. 'Go on – get to bed. I need you bright and fresh tomorrow morning.'

Camilla couldn't tell whether she minded being spoken to like a child, or not. Her thoughts were too confused. She didn't want to go, but she had not the words or self-possession to turn the situation. So she opened the door and got out.

'See you in the morning,' called Leo.

When she let herself into the empty flat, Camilla could tell that Jane hadn't been in all evening, had probably gone out straight from work. She could have invited him in, she could have made him coffee, he would have kissed her again, and then – She stared around the living-room, and thought of the jumble of clothes and books that littered her own bedroom. God, there were at least two old coffee mugs on her bedside table. What was she thinking of? Leo, here?

She went quickly to bed and lay in the darkness, reliving the kiss, and then the whole evening. She thought of what he had said, his soft laugh in the half-darkness of the car. He was so arrogant. He could do what he liked with people, and he knew it. She closed her eyes and squeezed

136

tight fistfuls of the duvet in self-reproach and embarrassment. She had made herself so easy for him. And yet,
when she remembered his mouth on hers, and the hunger,
the instant desire that his very touch invoked . . . She
thought suddenly of Anthony, and their lovemaking, and
knew immediately that to be with Leo would be a wholly
different experience. She thrust Anthony from her mind,
for there had been an innocence and affection there that
was not in keeping with thoughts of Leo.

She turned on her side, pulling the covers around
her. It was just a kiss. He had done it merely to amuse
himself, just as he had taken her to dinner because there
was nothing else with which to fill the evening. She was
intelligent enough to understand that much. Yet it was
hard not to hope that there might be more to it than that.
After all, she had worked enough with Leo to know
that he was nothing if not thorough. When Leo began a
thing, he always liked to finish it.

Leo drove back through the thin, late-night traffic,
reflecting absently on the events of the evening. Perhaps
kissing Camilla had not been clever. She clearly had
some kind of a crush on him, and Leo liked his sexual
adventures with women to be conducted without the
mess of sentiment and emotion. Yet, when it came to the
point, she really had been rather irresistible. All that dewy
innocence, probably no more than one or two youthful
love affairs behind her, and, as he had been able to detect
even through the layers of coat and sensible clothing, a
wonderfully firm and voluptuous young body. She was a

standing invitation. He sighed. She would want too much. Like Rachel, she would invest an affair with significance. No, it really wasn't worth the trouble. Pity. A little imagination and encouragement, and that girlish reserve could be coaxed into something much more interesting. He turned into the mews and parked his car in the garage. Just as he was about to walk away, someone stepped out of the shadows in front of him, startling him.

'Hello, Leo.'

It took him a couple of seconds to recognize her. He stopped dead, the adrenalin still pumping, filled with unease at the sight of Melissa standing before him, clutching her long coat round her, blonde, straggly hair lifting in the cold air.

'Melissa . . . What are you doing round here?' He spoke evenly, his mind racing to assess the situation, trying to work out why this woman should suddenly appear here, in a deserted Belgravia mews, with no apparent motive other than to accost him. He had long suspected her of being unstable, but he hadn't been prepared for this.

'You didn't answer my phone call. I knew if I left another, you'd ignore that, too. I had to come and see you.'

He stood looking at her in the eerie halogen glow of the street lights, trying to read her eyes, but failing. She might be entirely off her head, so this had to be handled carefully. 'I didn't ask you to call me, Melissa. I had no reason to ring you back. I'm sorry if you were offended.'

'Leo, I'm not offended. Only sad. I just want us to be

friends.' She laid a hand on his arm. The pressure of those fingers. She kept her hand there, the fingers tightening and relaxing, tightening, relaxing.

Leo tried to draw his arm away. 'Melissa –'

But before he could say any more, her arms were around him, pinioning him, and her face was close against his, her mouth groping for his. 'Please, Leo, just tonight. Let me be with you tonight. You can't start something and not finish it. You don't know what you do to me. I know we could be good together.' Between her gasping words she was trying to kiss him, to embrace him feverishly. With a struggle Leo pulled away from her and grabbed her wrists, holding her fast, feeling her resistance. Jesus, she was strong.

'Listen,' he muttered furiously, as she moaned and mouthed at him. 'Understand this. I don't even like you. I don't want you anywhere near me. I wish to God I'd never met you!' Leo could feel himself trembling with rage and revulsion, and something like fear. He hated to lose control, and this woman had brought him to it. It was vile to have to use the amount of force he was exerting just to keep her hands away from him, and her body from his. 'Now get out of here, leave me entirely alone, or I'll call the police.'

He felt her suddenly relax, and saw her eyes spilling over suddenly with huge, mad tears. Her body sagged a little. 'Oh, I'm so sorry!' She gave a little shuddering wail and he loosened his grasp and let her hands drop. He watched, appalled, as her face contorted with misery and she wept like a child. It was embarrassing, and more terrifying still. 'I just love you so! I can't help it! I waited all evening! I hoped you'd be . . .' The rest was lost in sobbing and wailing so loud that Leo feared its wracking echoes in the mews would wake people up. He glanced around, expecting lights to come on.

Through gritted teeth he tried to soothe her, calm her, his mind working on ways to get rid of her. It was all he wanted. At last he managed to find out that she had driven here earlier, that she was parked nearby, and he led her stumbling and sobbing across the cobbles to her car. He could detect no smell of drink about her, so presumably she would be all right to drive. On the other hand, it was more than a little alarming to know that she could do this kind of thing sober. As they walked she kept telling him between sobs how sorry she was, and how much she loved him, and he answered by saying it was fine and he quite saw the problem. It didn't matter what he said. By the time they reached her car she had calmed down a little, though tears were still pouring down her cheeks, unstoppable. She stood by the car, drawing quavering breaths.

'Go home, Melissa, and don't ever come here again,' said Leo. 'I mean it. And get rid of any ideas about me. I don't think this is healthy.'

She fumbled for her keys and got into the car. He closed the door firmly and walked away. At the corner he turned to watch. He couldn't feel entirely unconcerned about leaving her here, but he was damned if he was going to do anything else. He could see her profile as she sat there in the car, staring straight ahead. He waited, hoping she would start the engine and drive away. When she didn't, he turned on his heel and walked across the deserted square.

In his flat, he poured himself a drink and drew the curtains, resisting the temptation to peer across the square to see if her car was still there. He couldn't afford to care. The light on his answering machine was blinking, but he didn't dare press it, in case she might have left some demented message. He couldn't take any more of that this evening. Damn the woman! He wrenched off his tie, drained the remains of his whisky, and went to get ready for bed. There he lay for a long time, reflecting. It was his own fault. That was what could happen if you made a move on some infatuated female. Being pissed was no excuse. And he'd just done it again, that very evening, only hours before. Stupid, stupid . . . He wondered exactly what hideous kind of trouble he had stored up for himself. He should steer clear of women. The last disquieting image he had, before he fell asleep, was of Melissa still sitting out there in the darkness in her car, waiting.

7

A week later, Anthony was sitting in the Admiralty Court, gazing down at his papers and listening dispiritedly as the judge threw out each and every one of his clients' claims. He had known from the start that this case was doomed, but it was no fun to hear it spelled out.

'The next item,' intoned Mr Justice Stubbs, turning to the next page of his judgment, 'is in respect of fuel, bonded stores and paint. As regards the fuel, this is put forward at twenty-one thousand pounds for two hundred tonnes of gas oil. This strikes me as a most unlikely quantity for a vessel following completion of the ballast passage . . .'

Anthony knew that it wasn't just losing this case that was making him feel so dejected. He felt generally fed up these days. It seemed that everything outside chambers bored him, even going to the cinema or theatre, or to dinner with friends, or to parties such as the one he had been to last Saturday. A year ago, having someone like the nubile young Serena Williams coming on to him in such a blatant way would have kept him happy for a week. But he hadn't been able to muster enthusiasm for her, much to her clear annoyance. Even that he'd failed to find flattering.

'. . . the material before me being so very limited, I

cannot accept that the plaintiffs' claim of twenty-six thousand seven hundred pounds has been proved. Next there is a claim for wages and NAT from July to December in the sum of forty-five thousand pounds. I cannot see why the full period is claimed —' the judge shook his head, '— since the crew were repatriated in September . . .'

Ever since the end of his affair with Camilla last year, he had been determined to avoid serious relationships. They just ended up as disasters. But the idea of occasional flings or one-night stands didn't seem to work either. There was something shallow and pointless about that kind of trivial relationship, with whatever available girl happened along. Lots of his friends seemed to exist happily in that way, but Anthony knew it would never be enough for him. He wondered gloomily whether this was the consequence of coming from a dysfunctional family. He needed real companionship, someone like-minded, someone to complete him. But after his previous encounters with women, he wasn't about to start looking again. He sighed and tried to stretch his long legs, which were cramped from sitting in the narrow benches. Even the female element in chambers seemed set against him. Though that was mainly his own fault. Camilla behaved as though he barely existed, and Sarah, when they met, usually gave him no more than a cool smile and a knowing look. Bewildered by the way she could lure him into bed one minute then switch off entirely the next, Anthony had come, slowly and suspiciously, to the conclusion that Sarah regarded him as someone she could pick up and drop at will, depending on how bored she was. Probably just when Leo wasn't available. Anthony squirmed at the very idea of being regarded in such a light by any girl. Sarah was a prize bitch if ever he'd known one, but she seemed to possess something which amused and captivated Leo, and Anthony resented that.

'Lastly,' said the judge, to his own evident relief and that of the court, 'we come to the claim for loss of profits on voyages that would have been made during the period of arrest. Despite Mr Cross's submissions, I don't find it necessary to look beyond the performance of the vessel prior to arrest . . .'

Leo. Even though Anthony's thoughts about him over the past months had swarmed with antagonism and petty jealousy, he always carried about with him the belief that Leo was his friend. Having said that, it was difficult to work out where he stood on Leo's list of priorities. Time was, when Leo would have sooner been with Anthony than anyone else in the world. At the sudden memory of that summer's night when Leo had sought to make him his lover, he felt his heart turn over. It always did, at that recollection. That moment had passed, and the friendship remained, but it seemed to have been subsumed by layers of other things, people and events. Despite everything that Leo had said on the last occasion they had been together, in the pub just before the trustees' meeting, Anthony couldn't help feeling that Leo would rather spend time with Sarah than with him. It might just be sex, or it might be something more. Anthony had no way of telling. He only knew that they had lost the intimacy which he had once so much treasured. It came to Anthony, with sudden clarity, that this was the real source of his present unhappiness. He needed Leo, but Leo was not his. So many people seemed to have come between them over the past couple of years – Rachel, Sarah, and, most importantly, Oliver, Leo's son. Anthony sighed, confused, miserable.

'I have tried to deal with all the issues, and trust that none have been overlooked –' Anthony glanced up, realizing that Mr Justice Stubbs was speaking directly to him and to the barrister on the other side. 'In any event, I will need Counsel's assistance in putting together the appropriate order.'

Counsel for the defendants rose and began to make dutiful noises, and Anthony tried to bring his concentration to bear on the events in hand. Whatever else he did, he must try to rationalize his feelings for Leo, decide what he wanted. But even when he had decided, where did he go from there?

'Look, Sarah, it's not as though it's difficult. When the documents come down from Nichols, they're already referenced and paginated. All you have to do is interleave them in the bundles in the right places. Frankly, this is a complete mess.' Camilla flipped closed the bundle of papers before her, sat back in her seat and sighed. Sarah stood at the other side of Camilla's desk, arms crossed, sullen and enraged. How dare Camilla try to boss her about like this? It had always, always been tacitly accepted – not just between them, but by everyone else around them – that Camilla was pretty much beneath Sarah in everything. During their time together at Oxford, even though she'd been in the year below Camilla, Sarah had felt superior to Camilla in every way, in terms of looks, clothes, money, the schools she'd been to, the people she knew . . . OK, Camilla had been very bright and slogged away at her studies, but that, frankly, hadn't been much of an asset in most people's eyes. And fine, Camilla was a tenant at 5 Caper Court, while she, Sarah, was still a mere pupil, but that didn't give Camilla the right to push her around. At that moment, Sarah heartily wished that she'd never taken this pupillage, and, in particular, that Leo hadn't tried to do her a good turn by taking her on while David was away. If she'd known that Camilla was going to be Leo's junior in this stupid case, and that as Leo's pupil she would have to be doing work for her, she'd never have let it happen.

'Well, frankly, Camilla, if it's so important to you, I suggest you sort the documents out yourself.'

'Sarah, I have enough to do, drafting cross-examination plans for Leo, without having to worry about updating bundles. That's a pupil's job.'

'Oh, you mean it's beneath you? Of course, you're *far* too important. Well, do you know what I think, Camilla? I think that you still can't get over the fact that darling Anthony, instead of doing the faithful puppy-dog act while you were away last year, was more than happy to sleep with me, and lie about it to you. That's why you sick all this dreary, irrelevant work on me, as your way of getting back at me.'

Camilla flushed, and retorted angrily, 'That's not true!

It has nothing to do with anything. I asked you to do a simple task that even –'

Camilla broke off as Leo came into the room. 'What on earth is going on in here? I can hear you from the stairs.'

Unable to control her temper, Sarah burst out, 'Camilla seems to have a personal grudge against me – we all know why. So she's decided to take it out on me by giving me the most menial tasks possible and then criticizing everything I do.'

Camilla picked up the bundle and held it out to Sarah. 'I can assure you that this has nothing to do with anything apart from the fact that I asked you to update this bundle, and you haven't done it properly. I'd be grateful if you'd take it away and do it again.'

Sarah wished immediately that she'd held her tongue. Grudgingly she took the papers from Camilla, trying to think of something to say to redeem her position. Before she could, Leo said, 'I'd like a word with you in my room, Sarah, if you don't mind.'

Leo closed Camilla's door and Sarah followed him across the landing to his room. Once there, Leo sat down behind his desk and regarded her coldly for a few seconds.

'We are two weeks away from a trial. The documentation is vitally important, and I don't intend to stand floundering around in front of Mr Justice Olby simply because you can't do the things you're asked to.'

'Oh, come on, Leo. We all know what Camilla's problem is. She can't stand the fact that –'

'When Camilla says there is nothing personal,' cut in Leo, 'I believe her. Above all, she is far too professional and competent a lawyer to allow anything of that kind to interfere with the smooth running of a case. That's why I chose her as my junior. I think very highly of her. Which is more than I do of you, at this moment. That petulant little outburst –'

'Oh, stow it,' murmured Sarah, strolling across the room, past Leo, standing behind him and staring down through the window. She knew how to change an atmosphere in an instant. The trick with Leo was not to take him seriously, even when he wanted you to. She heard him swivel round in his seat, and she turned so that they were facing one another.

She could tell from the faintly grim expression on his face that he wasn't going to let it go. 'Sarah, as long as there's work to be done –' She put a gentle hand against his mouth, and he pulled it away impatiently. 'Look, I meant what I said –' He stopped, watching as she hitched herself up, pushing papers aside, and sat on the window-sill, pulling her skirt up around her thighs, spreading them ever so slightly.

'Leo, just think,' she murmured, taking his hand and moving it between her legs, over the tops of her stockings and up towards her crotch, 'if someone were to come in right now . . .'

Despite his annoyance, he felt immediately aroused. Damn it, she was so provocative . . . She leaned down and he let her kiss him for a long moment. He had a sudden, delirious vision of what it would be like to have her here and now, in his room. Probably not something that had happened between the walls of 5 Caper Court before. Though one never knew. He took his hand away, and his mouth from hers. 'Go on – take that wretched bundle and get back to work.' He turned round in his chair and slipped on his half-moon spectacles in a matter-of-fact way. Sarah slid from the window-sill, smoothing down her skirt, her face a little pink from the brief pleasure and excitement. She loved being able to turn him on so quickly.

As she came round the other side of the desk, she said, 'Let's call that unfinished business. Why don't I see you after work?'

He glanced up at her. 'Not tonight, I'm afraid. I'm having a drink with an old friend.' There was a pause as he regarded her. 'For Christ's sake, behave from now on. And do what Camilla says, no matter how little you like it. That's what you're paid for.'

Sarah smiled, picked up the bundle, and left the room.

'Nice lunch?' asked Henry. He could tell, just from the brightness of Felicity's eyes and her little smile, that she'd been to lunch with the same man again. He'd seen the way she'd looked when she'd taken the call from him that morning, pleased and all caught up in herself.

'Yes, as it happens.'

'Anyone I know?'

'Possibly. Possibly not.' Her careless, happy smile cut Henry to the quick. How little she realized what it did to him, knowing she was seeing someone new. He'd even thought of reproaching her with a mention of Vince, but that wouldn't be fair.

Felicity hung up her coat and sat down at her desk. This was the fourth time she and Peter Weir had met for lunch, and today was the first time she'd agreed to see him one evening next week. So far, everything had been merely friendly, but Felicity knew that was probably about to change. Did she want it to? Yes, she couldn't deny it. He was pretty practised, she suspected, the smooth way he came on, the little touches, the lingering eye contact, drawing things out until now. She should feel guilty, she knew. It wasn't fair, with Vince stuck in Belmarsh, to fancy someone else. But she did. There was no escaping it. And anyway, she was only twenty-two. What was she meant to do – live like a bloody nun? It would be nice to be taken out for a change. Vince had never bought her a meal. He never had any money. If ever she and Vince went out, it was generally she who paid. The contrast didn't do Vince any favours. Peter was a lot of things Vince wasn't. Gainfully employed for a start, smartly dressed, charming as all get out, and he possessed a conversational range that extended beyond motorbikes and the highlights from *Men Behaving Badly*.

Henry's phone rang. As he answered it he glanced up and caught Felicity's eye, then looked quickly away. Felicity had known for a long time that Henry had a soft spot for her. She couldn't help knowing it. If it hadn't been for that, she'd have been on at Henry to give her the low-down on Peter Weir. Henry had been a clerk for ages, so he probably knew a bit about him, whatever there was to be known. But the new man in her life wasn't exactly a subject she could raise with Henry. He'd just go all morose on her, and then she'd feel even *more* guilty. Besides, she suspected that Henry wouldn't entirely approve of her seeing someone else while Vince was banged up, and she didn't want Henry thinking badly of her. Most of the time she couldn't care less about other people's opinions, but with Henry, for some reason, it was different.

Michael Gibbon came into the clerks' room and dropped some papers on Henry's desk.

'Oh, Mr Gibbon,' said Felicity, 'this came in for you earlier.'

Michael took the envelope from Felicity and scanned the contents. 'Good . . . By the way, has Bernard Harrison's chambers sent round that list of authorities?'

'No. They say they're still waiting for ours.'

'Oh, for heaven's sake!' muttered Michael in exasperation. As he turned away, he caught sight of Leo. 'Ah, Leo. Have you got a minute?'

'Certainly,' replied Leo, taking his mail from his pigeon hole. He and Michael walked out of the clerks' room into the reception area.

'I saw Francis Lake at lunchtime, and he told me something very interesting,' said Michael. 'Great ructions, apparently, at Maurice Faber's chambers. Faber had a huge row with Andrew Peters, said he wasn't being clerked properly, the clerk had to go, Peters said over his dead body . . . You know the kind of thing. Anyway, two opposing camps appear to have formed, and Marcus

Jacobs, Ann Halliday and Roger Fry are all backing Faber.'

'That's an interesting little caucus.'

'Quite. Of course, it may all die down, but there's always the possibility that Faber will decide to leave.'

'Taking the others with him?'

'Can't say. Anyway, leaving aside Faber, who's a difficult man at the best of times, the others are all excellent juniors.'

'Are you suggesting we make an approach?'

Michael shrugged. 'We're up for some rapid expansion as soon as the annexe is finished, and that's just two months away.'

'The trouble is, you never know how reliable information is, coming from Francis Lake. I suggest we see what happens over the next few weeks. You have to tread very delicately with these things.'

'I agree. Interesting, though, isn't it?'

'Very. Maurice Faber's a hell of an ego, though. Imagine taking that on board.' Leo glanced up as Camilla came downstairs with her coat on. 'Don't forget we've got a con in ten minutes on the Names case.'

'I haven't forgotten. I'm just going out to the bank.'

The queue at the bank was frustratingly slow, and by the time Camilla got back, hurrying upstairs, Rachel Dean and Fred Fenton were already seated in Leo's room round the long conference table, papers spread out. Sarah gave Camilla, who was pink and slightly breathless, a smug smile.

Camilla ignored her and greeted Fred and Rachel. 'Sorry to keep you waiting.' She had met Fred before, had been instructed by him on a couple of cases since taking up her tenancy at Caper Court, but this was the first time she had met Rachel. As the meeting got underway, Camilla gave Rachel a covert, curious glance. She was struck by how lovely Rachel was, and how sophisticated she looked. She was very slender, dressed in a dark-grey suit and a cream silk blouse, her dark, shining hair drawn back from her face. There was a coolness about her which Camilla found a little unnerving. What was there about her which had caused Leo to fall in love with her? He must have, to have married her. But in the atmosphere between them now, Camilla could detect nothing, absolutely nothing, to suggest the slightest warmth, or any hint of previous intimacy.

'. . . Fred's still in the process of preparing a definitive list of the Outhwaite run-off contracts, because the judge is likely to ask for one . . .' Rachel was talking directly to Leo, but he didn't so much as glance up at her, merely nodded as he listened. Camilla's gaze strayed from Rachel to Leo, who was sitting back in his chair, the ankle of one leg resting on the knee of his other, balancing his papers, running the fingers of one hand restlessly through his silver hair. She felt the familiar little tightening of her heart. For someone in his forties, he looked a lot better than most men of his age in chambers. He didn't have the slack, flabby look of Stephen Bishop, or the middle-aged heaviness of Jeremy Vane. He looked spare and muscular, and his face, though a little lined and careworn, still young. Especially when he laughed, as he did now at some remark of Fred's. The way he had of glancing up, blue eyes bright with amusement . . . Camilla watched, lost and infatuated, as he leaned forward to fish among the documents on his desk, his smile relaxing, his face growing thoughtful. He said something, but she was hardly listening.

'Which bundle is the list of action groups in?'

Camilla jumped, as she suddenly realized he was speaking to her, though not looking at her, still searching through his documents.

'Oh, sorry. The action groups list . . .' Camilla scanned her own papers. 'It's part of an exhibit to John Pointer's affidavit.'

'Oh, that explains it.' Leo leaned back and nodded at Rachel. 'Go on with what you were saying.'

Camilla was intrigued by Leo's manner towards his ex-wife. He didn't smile. He didn't even address her by name. He seemed utterly indifferent to her. She, however, looked at him with expressive directness. There were some things people couldn't hide. Camilla would have loved to know more about their marriage, what had brought them together, how it had fallen apart. She was filled with the insatiable curiosity of the infatuated. She wanted to savour every detail of Leo's life, especially its most intimate aspects. She felt a sudden stab of jealousy at the thought of the ways in which Rachel had known Leo, the things they had shared . . . She sighed inwardly as she glanced again at Rachel. If that was Leo's ideal, she could never hope to aspire to it. Rachel, she guessed, could be only a few years older than she was, but she was a proper grown-up, something Camilla never felt. Rachel had the kind of chillingly lovely poise which Camilla could never hope to achieve. Then again, maybe she should try to cultivate it. Camilla lifted her chin slightly, and sat up in her chair. No, that just made her chest stick out. Anthony had always thought her breasts rather wonderful, but Leo obviously preferred the boyish, skinny type.

Oh, give it up, she told herself morosely. It was getting to the point where she couldn't even concentrate on an important case conference. With an effort, she fixed her attention on what Rachel was saying, reminding herself that Leo prized efficiency above anything else, so she might as well make an effort on that front.

Camilla had been totally oblivious of the watchful Sarah, sitting a few feet away. Sarah had observed Camilla's scrutiny of Rachel, and the way in which her gaze had shifted a few moments later to Leo, then lingered there. Sarah had seen, too, the empathetic, scarcely perceptible little smile which crossed Camilla's lips when Leo laughed, and knew in that instant that Camilla had a major crush on Leo. All the signs were there. She was practically eating him up with her eyes. So that was the way the land lay, was it? Sarah smiled to herself. Hardly surprising. Everyone fell prey to Leo's charm at some point. Not that Sarah had anything to fear from Camilla, who was hardly a woman of the world and not likely to interest Leo in the slightest. Still, it was amusing, and there might be a bit of fun to be had out of it all. She would have to wait and see.

The conference lasted two and a half hours, in which time they managed to cover a good deal of ground.

'It's amazing how much we can get through when our dear clients are absent,' observed Fred to Rachel, as they packed their papers away. 'No in-fighting, no obsession with bogus lines of argument, no petty disputes about whose point is the most important . . .'

'I know,' said Rachel. 'It's a relief to be able to concentrate on the practicalities. Just think how much time we'd have wasted today if we'd had Caradog-Browne or Lady Norbury hectoring us with their pet theories. I can't wait to see the back of this case.'

She glanced across at Leo, who was still deep in conversation with Camilla about the documents. When the case was over, there would no longer be the bitter-sweet pleasure of coming into contact with Leo on an almost daily basis. Although she looked forward – too much, she knew – to every meeting, it was always painful and difficult. Leo himself always appeared perfectly indifferent, and she had no way of telling if this was studied or not. She suspected it wasn't. He had recovered quickly from the emotional turbulence of their marriage, but for Rachel it would take much, much longer to get over it. If she ever did. It would probably be for the best when she no longer had to see him so often.

'Fred, I just want to have a quick word with Leo.'

Fred closed his briefcase. 'OK. I'll see you downstairs.'

Rachel went over to where Leo and Camilla were still talking. 'Leo, can you spare a minute?'

'Of course. We'll finish talking about this later,' he added to Camilla.

Rachel waited for a few seconds until everyone had

left the room. 'Just a couple of things to do with Oliver. What time will you be picking him up on Friday evening?'

'Damn!' exclaimed Leo. 'It's the museum launch party on Friday. I meant to ask you ages ago if we could move the weekends around, and I completely forgot about it. Sorry. Could I pick him up on Saturday morning?'

'Just as well he's too young to look forward to things,' replied Rachel. 'Still, I suppose he'll have plenty of disappointments to come.' Instantly she wished she'd said neither of those things.

'Oh, for Christ's sake, Rachel . . . I haven't the energy for this. Shall I pick him up on Saturday morning or not?'

'If you don't think it will interfere too much with your social life –'

'Rachel,' said Leo warningly, 'don't push it.'

There was a brief silence. 'I'm sorry,' she said stiffly. 'I'm just a bit overtired at the moment. This case is getting me down. Pick him up on Saturday – before eleven, if you can, as I have to go out.'

'Right,' said Leo. 'That's settled. I'll see you on Saturday around ten-thirty.' He moved back behind his desk and began to pick up papers. There was nothing left to say. Rachel went downstairs to find Fred, feeling even lower than she had before.

Melissa Angelicos sat on the edge of her bed, fingering the object in her hand. It was a tie clasp of smooth, eighteen-carat gold. It had cost a great deal of money. She stared at it for a long time, turning it over, then took a tissue from a box and gently polished it. Then she slipped the clasp into its little leather pouch. This, too, she admired for a brief moment, before setting it down on the squares of tissue paper already laid out on the bed, and carefully wrapping it up. Of course, she could have left it in the neat package which the Harrods assistant had made, but she had wanted to look at her gift, to dwell on it, to imagine Leo receiving it. From the bedside table she picked up the pages of the letter she had written half an hour before. There were seven of them, both sides of each covered in her somewhat large, expressive handwriting. They smelt of her scent, a few drops of which she had carefully tipped on to each page before writing. She had had to wait for the drops to dry before she could take up her pen again. She sniffed the pages, then scanned them for the twentieth time, smiling. At last she folded them, slipped them into a matching envelope of pale blue, and wrote Leo's name on the front. She didn't add the address. She was going to deliver this personally.

At seven o'clock she drove to Leo's home in Belgravia, and rang his bell. She rang and rang. She refused to believe he was out. With one long-nailed finger she stabbed again and again at the buzzer. Only the sound of footsteps behind her finally interrupted her.

'Can I help you?' The quavering, faintly imperious voice caused Melissa to turn round. She stared blankly at the old woman who stood there, cradling a small dog in her arms, its leash trailing. Mrs Gresham, Leo's neighbour from the ground floor flat, had been walking her Tibetan terrier on the other side of the square, and had seen the strange woman constantly ringing one of the building's entrance bells. 'Were you looking for someone?' Mrs Gresham didn't altogether care for the look of this woman; she had an unhinged, fraught air about her.

'I was trying to deliver a parcel,' said Melissa at last. 'To Leo Davies.' Her eyes did not connect with Mrs Gresham; they ranged past her, round the empty square.

'Well, as you can see, he must still be out. Mr Davies often doesn't get home till quite late in the evening.' Melissa gave Mrs Gresham a brief, impatient glance. After a pause of a few seconds, Mrs Gresham added, 'Perhaps you would like me to take the parcel and give it to Mr Davies when he gets in?' She had no great wish to assist this peculiar-looking woman in any way, but she didn't much relish the idea that she might stand on the doorstep for the rest of the evening, pressing Leo's bell.

Melissa glanced down at her package. She was tempted to wait until he came home, so that she might see him, put the package into his hands herself. He might ask her in. But then her mind plunged downwards, back to the last time. 'No, no,' she murmured to herself, deflecting, ignoring, steeling herself against the recollection of that horrid recent encounter.

'I'm sorry?' Mrs Gresham spoke sharply. She wanted to be done with this, to get rid of this woman and get into her own flat and make tea. Mr Davies did seem to keep odd company – there had been that young man last year, and all his rowdy friends . . . Suddenly Melissa thrust the package into Mrs Gresham's hands, almost causing her to drop her dog.

'Very well. You give it to him.'

With that, Melissa hurried down the steps and across the square to her car. Mrs Gresham, clutching her dog and Melissa's parcel, stared after her. Then she unlocked the door and went inside, closing the street door carefully behind her.

Melissa drove around for a little while, then, as dusk fell, parked again on the other side of the square, and settled down to wait.

'I thought of looking round here when I was trying to find a new place,' observed Gideon, as he and Leo walked through the Belgravia square to Leo's flat an hour later. It was true. He had inspected a cubby-hole of a flat near Sloane Square, with a diminutive leasehold, which had been on offer for some extortionate price the year before. The Lloyd's losses which his mother had suffered had put paid to the possibility of anything larger. But even for Gideon the price of a fashionable postcode had been too high, especially in exchange for such cramped quarters, so he had looked elsewhere.

'It's rather impersonal,' replied Leo. 'I took the place more or less without thinking, after my wife and I split up. It's not exactly ideal when my son comes to stay. I may look for something else, once the summer's over – somewhere with a garden. Anyway,' said Leo, putting his key in the lock, 'come up and have a nightcap.'

Melissa watched from the shadows. A man. Leo was taking a man back to his flat. They had walked past her car a few moments before, and even in the darkness she could see he was young, good-looking in a very feminine kind of way. It could be mere coincidence. But there had been that boy last year, the beautiful boy whom Leo had brought to the gallery. She had heard rumours. She sank her upper teeth into her lower lip and bit hard, pressing painfully against the flesh until the pain was horrid and sublime. Then she stopped, exhaling a low breath. It would explain everything. It would explain that night when he had come back to her place after they had been drinking together, and he had humiliated her, leading her on and then making a fool of her, laughing at her need, her degradation. He must have meant to do it. He must be one of those homosexuals who liked to debase women, through some kind of bitterness and spite. She hated him. She wanted to hurt him, cut him, spit at him. Oh, but how much she loved him and wanted him! The mixture of pain and longing and hatred and love was so exquisitely powerful. She must find some way to reach him, to fix his gaze and keep it there, on her. It could be done, little by little. It was a question of time, and love, and attention . . . In a few moments he would receive the parcel from that old neighbour of his. Would it be now? Was it happening at this moment? Her heart dipped in tenderness and apprehension as she thought of it, and in the next moment she seethed bitterly at the thought of Leo and his lover up there, behind the curtains which she could see being drawn. She sat and watched.

Gideon settled himself in an armchair in Leo's drawing-room and sipped his drink, glancing around. Then he rose suddenly from his chair and paced round the room.

The series of movements instantly reminded Leo of Joshua on his first visit here. But Gideon was nothing like Joshua. Where Joshua had been young, awkward and fresh, Gideon was practised, assured, and possessed of all the charm of a latter-day Dorian Gray. Leo did not find him in the least bit sexually attractive. There was something sybaritic and dark about Gideon, repulsive yet intriguing. He had a personality which people found hard to resist, and Leo was no exception. In a world where many pleasures had gone stale, a companion as amusing and quirky as Gideon was hard to come by. He watched Gideon closely as the younger man ranged round the room, gazing at the many pictures, fingering a sculpture here and there, an enigmatic smile touching his sensuous mouth.

'You do go in for Lehrman in a big way, don't you?'

Gideon had paused in front of a smallish canvas, discreetly framed, depicting a pair of closed eyelids against a background of grey fading to deep amethyst. It was entitled *The Sleeping Mind*.

Leo made a wry face and strolled up next to Gideon to study the picture, sipping his Scotch. 'He was an early fad of mine. When I started to earn money at the Bar, I'd buy a picture after each case I won. A kind of reward. Lehrman wasn't much in vogue then, but I liked his stuff and picked it up wherever I could.'

'Worth a tidy fortune now,' observed Gideon, glancing around at the other examples of the painter's work which dotted the walls.

'I imagine so. It's all well insured. The trouble is, I

don't much care for it now. It's rather like literature. One's taste moves on. The things one loved in one's twenties don't have the same appeal a couple of decades later. I'd really like to move a lot of it, make way for some newer pieces I've acquired, but I haven't the heart.'

'Sell it.' Gideon waved an airy hand. 'All of it. All your Lehrmans. Pocket the proceeds and buy things you really like. That's what I'd do.'

'You're not a sentimentalist, are you, Gideon?' Leo settled himself in a chair.

'Good God, no. When I tire of something or someone, I dispense with them. Out they go. Life's really too short, old thing.'

Leo knocked back the remains of his Scotch. 'Perhaps you're right. It used to be my code for survival, and certainly life was less complicated when I lived it that way.'

'No use being stuck with things you don't like, pictures or people.'

Suddenly Leo's front-door bell rang, and he went to answer it. It was Mrs Gresham.

'Someone called earlier and left this package for you, Mr Davies. A woman.'

Leo took the parcel from Mrs Gresham, and glanced at it with a certain sense of misgiving. 'A woman?'

'A blonde woman. Middle aged. She seemed a little agitated. Anyway,' she turned to go back downstairs, 'I've done my duty, Mr Davies. Goodnight.'

'Goodnight, Mrs Gresham. Thank you.' Leo closed the door. He stared at the package, neatly wrapped, his name printed on the front in handwriting he did not recognize, but whose author he could guess. Slowly he opened it and stared at the contents. He unfolded the letter, saw the number of sheets and glanced only at the first and last pages before folding it up again and dropping it on the hall table. He set the gift down next to it and sighed, passing his hand over his face.

Gideon came through from the drawing-room. 'Something up?' His quick glance scanned Leo's face intently, then settled into mildness as Leo turned to him.

'No, nothing. Just some damn pest of a woman.'

'Oh, I'm sure you must be used to that . . .' Before Leo could stop him, Gideon had picked up the unwrapped leather pouch from the hall table. He slid the tie pin into his hand and admired it. 'How very lovely. I wish some woman would pester me with trinkets.' He raised his eyes to Leo's. 'Only in my case, you know, that's rather unlikely to happen.'

His gaze remained fixed on Leo's, searching there for some clue. Leo had talked about his ex-wife, and his child, but Gideon was not convinced. He had a sixth sense for these things, could usually spot someone's sexual orientation at twenty paces. Leo, however, was an enigma. For the briefest of seconds, Gideon's sharp senses detected a momentary unease in the atmosphere. No, whatever the truth about Leo might be, Gideon could tell when someone was attracted to him. There was nothing there. They were standing close together, yet even at this proximity there was no flicker of a muscle, no glance of the eye, not the slightest response. This would have been the moment, if Leo cared to take the hint. Gideon had given him the opening, with his last utterance.

His gaze slid away from Leo's and he dropped the pin back in its leather pouch. Then he turned and walked back into the drawing-room. Leo stood for a moment in the hall, the hairs on the back of his neck prickling. It had been a most odd, almost uncomfortable moment. He walked to the drawing-room, where Gideon was finishing his drink.

'Would you care for another?' Leo asked. Without quite knowing why, he hoped Gideon wouldn't.

'No, thanks. I have to be going. It's been a pleasant evening, though. I enjoyed strolling round the Temple, revisiting the pubs.' He went past Leo into the hall and slipped on his overcoat. His manner and movements were assured, but slightly distant.

Leo felt himself to be at some peculiar disadvantage, as though some discourtesy had occurred for which he should apologize. A significant balance had subtly shifted between himself and Gideon. He couldn't put his finger on the reason why, but was suddenly moved, as though to make up for whatever had happened, to say, 'By the way, I was wondering whether you'd be interested in coming to the opening of Chay Cross's new modern-art museum in Shoreditch on Friday evening. Since you seem interested in my own modest collection.'

'*Far* from modest,' replied Gideon, turning up the collar of his coat. 'That's very kind of you. I should like to come.'

'Good,' said Leo. 'I'll put a couple of invitations in the post.' He picked up a pen from the hall table. 'What's your address?'

'Oh, best send them to my mother's place. I'll be there for some time yet, until my place is finished.' Preparing to depart, Gideon stretched out a hand and patted Leo's shoulder. 'You must come to dinner and meet some of my friends when I move in. I'm sure you'd like them.'

Leo smiled. 'Thank you.' He wondered in that instant, though, whether he wanted to be drawn into any further intimacy with Gideon. The man was good company, but something lurked behind those smiling, mischievous eyes . . . He opened the door to let Gideon out. 'There's a cab rank just up by Sloane Square. Should be plenty of taxis at this time of the evening. It's still early.'

'Oh, no trouble – I'll walk. Thanks for the drink.' And he was gone, feet noiseless on the carpeted stair. The front door closed. Leo went back into his flat and stared at Melissa's gift and her letter. With a muttered curse he folded up the unread pages of the letter and put them on the table with the tie pin. Something about the events of the last ten minutes had left an unpleasant taste in his mouth, and he couldn't for the life of him tell whether it was to do with Gideon or the wretched Angelicos woman. He went back into the drawing-room, turned on some music, poured himself another drink, and wished he were not alone. The thought of Camilla, and her sweet, uncomplicated nature, came suddenly unbidden to his mind, and he allowed it to rest there, soothing him, letting it evolve into musings of an altogether more voluptuous nature. Thinking how pleasant it would be to have her here, in every sense, he closed his eyes.

8

Leo brooded over the business of Melissa on his way into work. The basket of roses on Valentine's Day – that he could have dismissed as the silly expression of an over-the-top infatuation. He'd known those before. Even the gift which she'd left with Mrs Gresham yesterday, tiresome though it was, could be dealt with somehow. Throw into the equation the fact that the woman had lain in wait for him late at night in an unbalanced, emotional state . . . well, the whole thing became more sinister. Apart from anything else, what seemed to Leo most unsettling was the fact that Melissa Angelicos, far from having any grounds for showering him with gifts and protestations of affection, had every reason to dislike him intensely. He had rebuffed every advance she'd made – apart from that drunken evening when he'd inadvertently humiliated her – and had been positively rude to her. If, as seemed to be the case, she had developed some kind of obsession with him, there was every chance that it could manifest itself in unpleasant ways, too.

He strode from Temple station and up through Fountain Court, wondering how best to deal with it. Presumably he would have to see her on Friday evening, at the museum opening, which wasn't a prospect he relished. Then again, she was hardly likely to embarrass them both in public – was she? – and it would afford an opportunity in which to return her gift and letter, and spell out to her, in the most civilized terms, that unless she desisted from writing to him or visiting him, or sending him gifts, or communicating with him in any way at all, except at the trustee meetings which they both had to attend, he would take legal steps against her. That should be enough. If he acted firmly, he could stop this nonsense before it went any further.

Anthony, on his way down Middle Temple Lane, saw Leo coming through Fountain Court. The sight of the familiar figure, silver head bent in thought, hands in the pockets of his dark cashmere coat, gave Anthony a start of pleasure. He and Leo had scarcely spoken since the trustees' meeting, and the effort of remaining aloof was tiresome. Anthony was glad of the opportunity to accost him with some good news. He waited for Leo at the entrance to Caper Court. Looking up from his reverie, Leo saw Anthony and smiled. They fell into step together, and Anthony pulled a letter from his pocket and handed it to Leo, who unfolded it.

'Remember Edward Choke?' asked Anthony.

'Basil's nephew?'

'The same. Well, I bumped into him in the Devereux a couple of weeks ago, and he told me he was working in the new Ministry for Artistic and Cultural Development. I asked if he might be able to help out with funding for the museum, and I got this letter from him this morning. Believe it or not, he's actually an officer with responsibility for handling East London bids for arts funding, and he reckons he might be able to pull a few strings. He's sent some forms.'

Leo scanned the letter. 'So he's working for Tony Gear?' He wondered if Edward was acquainted with Gideon Smallwood. It seemed very probable.

'I imagine he's fairly low down the ladder. When we met him, he wasn't exactly talking about this job as a long-term thing. He comes into his trust fund next year.'

'Well, that's probably a blessing for Her Majesty's Civil Service. Have you told Chay?'

'No, I'll tell him on Friday at the opening.'

Leo handed the letter back to Anthony. 'I do foresee problems, you know. Now that Tony Gear is the Minister for the Arts, I don't know how it would look if his department starts handing out grants to a museum of which he's a trustee.'

'I hadn't thought of that.' They mounted the steps to the doorway of 5 Caper Court. 'Surely he'll have to step down from the trusteeship of the museum?'

'I imagine he will.'

'In which case, we can appoint another trustee and go ahead with the funding application.'

'Possibly. I think it might be worth talking to Chay and Tony Gear about it on Friday evening.'

In his room, Leo hung up his coat and commenced the endless task of studying the documentation in the Lloyd's case. He glanced at the empty table and chair in the corner which Sarah was temporarily occupying, now that David was in Bermuda. Half past nine, and she still wasn't in. Not exactly committed and industrious.

Recalling their conversation in the pub, Leo reflected that marrying a rich man was probably the best option for Sarah. She was never going to hack it at the commercial bar at this rate.

Shortly after ten o'clock, Sarah arrived and set down a cup of coffee on Leo's desk and one on her own. She yawned and sat down. 'OK, put me to work.'

'Those came over from Nichols last night.' Leo pointed to two large cardboard boxes of documents by the door. 'Go through everything and make sure it's all properly paginated and in date order.'

'God, that's going to take days. How boring.'

Leo was beginning heartily to regret suggesting that Sarah help out on the Lloyd's case. The relationship between them was such that it was easy for Sarah to treat him, and everything to do with the case, too casually. What he really needed was someone scurrying around in mortal fear of him, carrying out orders instantly and with meticulous care.

He leaned back in his chair. 'I'd suggest, too, that from now on you get in on time. Start taking this case seriously.'

She sipped her coffee nonchalantly. 'OK, OK. Why don't I spend more nights with you? That way you could make sure I was in bright and early.'

Leo sighed. 'Don't presume too much on what's gone on between us in the past, Sarah – this is work, you know.'

'All right, don't get stressy. I had a late night. Sorry.' She opened the top box and began to haul out Lever Arch files.

'Maybe you should give up late nights for the duration of this case. Take a leaf out of Camilla's book, put work before your social life.'

Sarah snorted. 'That's not exactly hard for Camilla. She hasn't *got* a social life. Never has had, unless you count Anthony.' She bent her head over the pages of a file.

Leo didn't bother to reply to this, and they worked on throughout the morning in relative silence, interrupted only by the occasional phone call and by the sounds of the workmen in the annexe. When he glanced across at Sarah she seemed to be working diligently enough, and Leo hoped he would find everything in order when the hearing started. You never knew with Sarah.

Melissa woke late, slightly hungover from a party the night before. She lay back, massaging her aching temples with her fingers, thinking about the evening. It hadn't been her kind of thing at all, a desperate re-launch of a fashion magazine by a friend who was old enough to know better. The place had seemed to be jammed to the hilt with impossibly young people, the women all interchangeably pretty. Melissa hated their fresh faces, their perfect smiles, their silky hair and gym-slip bodies. Everybody seemed to be bloody young these days. It had happened overnight. One minute her world – the world of television, art and fashion – had been populated by people of her own age, and the next it was apparently run by children. How horribly significant the slipping of the years became. In two months she would reach her forty-eighth birthday, and then fifty loomed menacingly close. She sat up and fished a cigarette from the packet on her bedside table, lit it, and lay back again. She had given up six years ago, but recently pressures had got to her . . .

She glanced at the clock. Ten past eleven. Her commissioning editor had arranged lunch today. Twelve-thirty at the Ivy. Her mind shied away from the possible reasons why he might want to talk to her, buying an expensive lunch to cushion her against – what? She didn't want to think about it. Everything these days felt precarious. One newspaper had recently axed her weekly arts diary. She told herself she didn't care. There was enough work on the journalistic side, even though she hated the deadlines. It was more the empty spaces. The ones in her life and in her head, which she tried to fill up. Things had changed subtly over the last year or so. The life that had once seemed busy and bright had become arid and threatening. Anxieties which she had once coped with now obsessed her, thoughts of dying, or loneliness, or the point of waking up to face life. Sometimes there were pauses in the day when her mind would fill with frightening thoughts, and she would try to talk herself out of the fear. Literally. Sit and talk, make it go away. Her own voice in her ears.

There was always one escape. There was one place of feathery fantasy, as mentally comforting as eiderdown, to which she could go. She rose from her bed and crossed the room, and took from her underwear drawer a buff folder. She carried it back to bed with her and opened it, drawing out the contents one by one. Not many, admittedly. Photos of Leo were hard to come by. She had managed to cull these few from the photo library of one of the newspapers she wrote for, some attached to brief articles about important cases in his career, one from a piece in *The Times* of two years ago about top earners in the legal world, and two which formed part of a long piece printed in the *Evening Standard* a year ago, devoted entirely to Leo. This she treasured. She re-read the piece over and over, dwelling on the tantalizing little clues, the paragraph about his divorce, the speculation about the loneliness of so successful a figure . . .

Melissa stroked long fingers over the newsprint picture of Leo striding into the Law Courts. He must be lonely. She felt he was. She knew him. She had been close to him for a few hours, and they could be close again. Properly. It was a matter of persistence. He would see. Poor, lonely Leo. They were made for one another. He would see. The gift would help, soften him. She could find many more of those. Little kindnesses, reminders that she cared for him. She might have to keep reminding him. Or else there were other ways to make sure he paid attention.

Melissa rose from the bed, put the folder back in the drawer and went to shower. She felt pliant, easier in her mind after looking at the photos. They were the next best thing to seeing Leo in the flesh. Which she would on Friday. That evening held many possibilities. It could be wonderful – they could be wonderful to one another. It only took a little sense on Leo's part to see that it was better for him, for everyone, if she was happy. It was up to Leo to make sure, to be careful not to make her angry. It was all up to him.

Mark Ashton sat at the table in the Ivy, sipping his spritzer, waiting for Melissa. He was a fresh-faced, chubby man in his late thirties, sporting youthful clothes, shoes and hair-cut, as befitted the head of a television production company. He glanced at his watch. Quarter to one. The Melissas of this world always made a point of being late. He tapped his fingers nervously on the table, working over in his mind how he was going to play this lunch. He wasn't good at this kind of thing – hated it, in fact. But the interview series was proving to be little short of a disaster, and someone had to tell her they were pulling it after this first run. How would she react? Apart from knowing she had a reputation for being mildly eccentric, he had also heard she could be a complete banshee on occasions. He glanced round the restaurant, hoping she wasn't likely to make a scene.

At that moment he caught sight of her coming through the door and raised a hand in greeting, smiling automatically. They double-kissed one another as though long-lost friends, their expressions conveying delight at seeing one another, their eyes wary. For the first hour or so, Mark made cosy, chatty conversation. He specialized in putting people at their ease, keeping things light. They gossiped, talked about Mark's children, and then the property in Italy which Melissa had inherited the previous year – the Italian theme kept them going for a good twenty minutes.

Mark wasn't sure whether or not it was a good thing that Melissa was knocking back the Chablis in a businesslike fashion – probably good, he decided. Hoped. As he thought of what he had to say, he felt a flash of pity for her. She had clearly been something of a beauty fifteen years or so ago, but it had all faded and grown hard. The quirky enthusiasm and offbeat charm, which had made her such a good presenter when she had started in the late eighties, seemed to have dried up, coarsened somehow. Would there be much more work for her after this? He doubted it. She'd probably had her day. By the time they had finished the main course, he could put it off no longer – the tension was too palpable.

'So, tell me –' said Mark, leaning back in his chair, 'how do you think the series is going?'

Melissa took some time to light a cigarette. 'Hard to judge, really – we're only halfway.' A little knot of suspicion and fear tightened inside her.

Mark nodded thoughtfully, gravely. 'True. But we're not getting good feedback. I'm sure you're aware of that . . .'

It took five minutes. He watched the anger growing steadily in her, but carried on with what he had to tell her.

'I see,' said Melissa.

'Naturally, you're disappointed. We all –'

'Of course I'm fucking disappointed!' flashed Melissa, crushing out her cigarette. She kept her voice low, to his relief. 'I put everything into this series, and now you pull it from under me! God . . .' She looked away, blinking.

He prayed she wasn't going to cry. Not yet, at any rate. He hadn't finished. He leaned forward, about to carry on. But she had started talking. Talking in a low, breathless voice about something he couldn't at first understand. Then he realized that she was talking about love, about how everybody needed one special person in their life. She was making sense, but it had nothing to do with anything. Not that he could see. The expression on Melissa's face was wild and soft, and she kept her eyes fixed earnestly on the tablecloth as she talked. At first Mark made sympathetic noises, nodding from time to time. Then he grew faintly alarmed. She didn't seem to be with it at all. He laid a hand on her arm, and she stopped, quite abruptly, and looked up at him. Something which seemed to have fled from her eyes returned in that moment.

There was silence for a few seconds, in which space of time Mark decided to pretend nothing untoward had happened. He also decided to shelve the other piece of bad news for the moment, that the magazine programme which she'd hosted for ten years was going to get the chop, too. That could go in a letter. There was something a little wrong here, and he didn't want to upset her further.

'So . . . you do understand?' He had to make sure she'd taken it on board.

She lifted her chin and gave him a brief, hard look. 'Yes. Yes, of course I do. I suppose you have to pretty it up with lunch, and so forth . . .' She picked up her bag. 'I have things to do. There really isn't any point in making small talk over the coffee. I'll be speaking to my agent about this.'

Mark said nothing. He didn't like to tell her he had already discussed it very fully with her agent. He let her go. She was furious, and he couldn't blame her. But the series was no good. She couldn't cut it any more. Even dear old Sir Anthony Caro hadn't been able to salvage much from his interview, hard though he'd tried. Mark sat back in his chair, glad it was over. It could have been a hell of a sight worse. He allowed himself another twenty seconds or so to feel sorry for the poor old bat, then asked for the bill.

Camilla had had a hearing all day, and returned to chambers at five. She went to Leo's room, where he and Sarah were still working in industrious silence.

Leo glanced up. 'Just the woman. Have you got a couple of hours? Freshfields have sent over the agreed list of issues. We'll have to spend some time going through it this evening, I'm afraid. I'd like to be able to talk to Fred and Rachel about it first thing tomorrow.'

'Fine,' said Camilla. 'I'll just get myself a coffee. Anyone else want one?'

Leo shook his head and carried on writing.

Sarah glanced up and gave Camilla a smile. 'No thanks. I've done my stint for today.' She looked at her watch. 'Another twenty minutes and I'm off. Meeting some friends for a drink.' She leaned her chin on one hand. 'Don't you find that all the work you do is seriously interfering with your social life? I mean, isn't there a balance to be struck in these things?'

'If there is, it's a balance you haven't exactly got right yet,' remarked Leo, seeing the defensive look on Camilla's face.

Sarah shrugged and turned back to the documents. When Camilla had left the room, Leo added, 'Lay off Camilla. She's having to work bloody hard at the moment.'

'Just as well. She's got nothing else to do.'

Leo sighed. 'Why don't you make an early start for the wine bar? Leave me in peace.'

Sarah was happy to agree. As she was putting on her coat, she remarked, 'If you feel like some company later on, I'll be home around eight.'

'Don't you think we've had enough of one another for one day?'

'Oh, I don't think of myself as having had you in any way at all. In fact, it's been a long while . . . A fortnight, at least.' She came round his desk, leaned down and kissed him briefly, lifting his hand to her breast.

Leo stroked his thumb over her stiffening nipple. 'You are –' He stopped, pushing her gently away.

'What?'

'I don't know.' He shook his head and picked up his pen again. 'Impossible. Stop doing this in my room. It's very distracting.'

She went back to her desk and picked up her bag. She could hear Camilla approaching the room, and as she came in bearing a file of papers and a cup of coffee, Sarah, as though she hadn't seen her, glanced across at Leo and said, casually, intimately, 'See you later, then.'

She gave Camilla a little smile as she passed her. 'Night-night.'

Camilla and Leo pored over the list of issues to be agreed between both sides in the Lloyd's case until well after seven. Leo was grateful for the intelligence and incisiveness of Camilla's approach to every aspect of the case. He'd harboured certain doubts about taking her as his junior at the beginning, but he had none now. The work she'd done so far on the skeleton argument was as good as anything Anthony could produce. As they were shuffling papers back into order, Leo glanced across his desk at her. She looked tired and slightly dejected. He thought about what Sarah had said about her, how all she had in her life was work, and felt mild stirrings of guilt. He might be appreciative of the amount of time she was putting in on the case, but she should have other things in her life.

'Tell me,' said Leo, on a sudden whim, 'what are you doing tomorrow night?'

She looked across at him in surprise. 'Why? Do you need me to work late again?'

'God, no. Not on a Friday night. I wondered whether you were busy.'

'I'm going to a dinner party with some friends.'

Leo wondered why on earth he'd been so convinced that what Sarah had said was true. How stupid. You only had to look at Camilla to realize that she must have plenty of friends, and a normal, London social life. What did Sarah know about it? Why had he formed some image of Camilla as a lonely young thing, spending the evenings and weekends alone? It was ludicrous, really. But he was also aware of a sense of disappointment, one which prompted him to ask, unguardedly, 'Can you cancel it?'

Instantly she wanted to say yes, yes, that anything he wanted, she would do. While she hesitated, Leo went on, 'You see, I'm a trustee of a museum of modern art in Shoreditch. It's having its opening-night party tomorrow, quite an up-market affair, if you like celebrities and endless supplies of champagne. I thought it would do my image good to have a pretty young thing like you on my arm.'

It was badly put. Gathering her courage, Camilla replied, 'I'm not really into massaging egos, I'm afraid. I'm sure you can find someone else. Sarah, perhaps. Besides, I don't want to let my friends down.' She had astonished even herself. She wanted more than anything to spend an evening with Leo, but some instinct told her this was the right thing to do.

Baffled, Leo leaned back and folded his hands behind his head. 'Sorry – maybe I didn't put that very well. I don't want my ego massaged. That wasn't why I asked you. I quite understand that you'd rather not cancel the dinner party. But what on earth has Sarah to do with it?'

'I happened to hear her parting remark to you this evening.'

Leo frowned. 'Which was?'

'Something to the effect that she would see you later. I took that to mean tonight.'

She didn't want to believe that Leo was just another of those randy old QCs, chasing every skirt in chambers, but if she had read Sarah correctly, that was what he was.

She had to fight to keep a sense of proportion in the face of her feelings for him.

Leo regarded her thoughtfully, then rose and came round from behind his desk. He put his hands in his pockets, leaning against the desk, close to her. He found the remote, defensive look on her face rather sweet, quite a turn-on, in fact. Camilla couldn't take her eyes from his, waiting for what he had to say.

Leo put his fingers gently beneath her chin, and said softly, 'She was saying goodnight, that's all. It's just a turn of phrase.' He leaned forward to kiss her.

Camilla drew back. 'Don't.' There was silence for a few seconds. 'I really don't think this is a good idea at all, Leo. I'm your junior on an important case. This kind of thing could be –'

'What?' Leo felt disturbed, slightly annoyed. He knew she wanted him, he felt it. So what was all this about?

'Damaging. You should realize that.'

She turned away and began to put papers into her briefcase. Then she picked up her jacket from the back of a chair and put it on.

'Look,' said Leo, disliking the position he found himself in, 'if this is simply about Sarah, let me assure you that you have entirely the wrong idea. I asked you to come tomorrow night because I want your company. And I wanted to kiss you because . . .' He paused. She looked up and met his eyes. He took his cue and smiled, a sensual but kind smile, one that made Camilla's insides melt. 'Because you are extremely pretty and because it's hard being near you without wanting to kiss you.'

Camilla fought against her feelings. 'Then maybe you'd better find another junior. One of us has to be professional about things.' She looked away again, picking up her belongings. 'Anyway, I'll see you tomorrow. Goodnight.' And she was gone.

Leo stood leaning against the desk, examining his feelings. He had just come close to making an utter fool of himself – and what for? What he had told her was true. Spending this much time with her, he had developed feelings for her which he couldn't define; the easiest thing was to translate them into simple terms of desire. It was more complicated than that, he knew, something to do with the respect he had for her mind and her abilities, and little ways she had of doing and saying things . . . Putting it plainly, he wanted her. And the way she had rebuffed him made him want her even more. He felt angry with himself, and with her. That high-handed line about professionalism. The trouble was, he knew she was right.

He moved back around his desk and sat down. The arousal he had felt as he leaned to kiss her was still there. He glanced down at his papers. He couldn't work any more tonight. After a few seconds' thought he reached out for the phone. There was one easy way to relieve his feelings.

At the other end, Sarah picked up the phone.

'I'll be with you in half an hour,' said Leo.

Half an hour before the museum opening party, Chay was into his twenty-second Gauloise of the day. He had been there all afternoon, pacing anxiously from gallery to gallery, reviewing the installations, making last-minute switches and adjustments. In the central gallery, waiters in black tie hovered behind white-linen-draped tables laden with food and champagne. On a table in the foyer, copies of the museum's catalogue stood in pristine, glistening heaps for the guests. In the smaller, offshoot galleries, assistants were making final lighting adjustments and fretting over the video installations. The atmosphere was buoyant and buzzing.

Leo and Anthony arrived together, having changed in chambers. It occurred to Anthony that he was quite glad Edward Choke was coming. He doubted whether, apart from the trustees and his father, he would know anyone else. One by one the trustees arrived, Derek Harvey in newly washed and pressed denims for the occasion, Tony Gear looking self-important, with a couple of political underlings in tow, and Melissa, scented, carefully made-up, her blonde hair loosely pinned up, dressed in a dazzling blue creation in silk and chiffon and looking ten years younger than usual. Graham Amery and Lord Stockeld, with their middle-aged wives dressed in safely staid evening attire, represented the affluent and dignified world of commerce.

Guests began to drift in, and as the minutes passed and the museum filled, the air grew brighter and shriller with conversation. Cigarette smoke drifted high into the gallery, around the massive central installation, and below, little groups of people moved through the various rooms, behaving as though interested in the exhibits, while keeping an eye out for photographers and fellow celebrities.

Anthony kept himself amused simply spotting famous faces. Every time a new A-list figure arrived, a little tide of excitement rippled through the sea of guests. Although Chay behaved with no more than casual mateyness when Mick Jagger turned up, Anthony could tell that it was the crowning glory of his evening. He had them all there, glittering figures from the world of fashion, rock and pop, art and letters, to say nothing of daytime television and popular journalism. The evening smelt of success. People lavished praise on the exhibits and the layout of the gallery, and Chay was generally fêted and admired.

Leo moved around the gallery alone, drink in hand, greeting people, but not stopping to chat. Before he began to socialize, he wanted to find out how the gallery and its contents were being received by those who weren't just there to drink Chay's champagne and be photographed for *Hello!* magazine. He was intrigued by some of the exchanges he overheard.

At one end of the main gallery, he heard Chay explaining to the art critic from the *New York Journal of Modern Art* that the aim of the gallery was to get away from traditional forms of display. 'I'm totally against the imposition of anything like a master narrative,' Chay declaimed.

The critic nodded sagely. 'I guess you feel that any narrative is an interpretation.'

It was tacitly understood between both conversationalists that nothing either said had to make any sense, so long as the words made beautiful patterns of apparent authenticity.

'Exactly so,' replied Chay. 'I take a Jacques Derrida view of art. I eschew the linear approach.'

'So we could say that what you're trying to achieve here is a collection that avoids being taxonomic?'

'Of course. I think we have to move away from the canonical narrative that privileges some works of art above others. That's not to say that we don't recognize the centrality of artists such as Picasso and Matisse . . .'

Leo smiled and moved discreetly away. At the other end of the same gallery he came across Derek Harvey explaining to the *Guardian* art critic that the new museum respected orthodox presentation and was at pains to identify, either by chronology or by reference to particular 'isms', the distinct movements which had influenced the progress of modern art through the twentieth century. 'We have a chronological narrative,' he heard Derek explaining, 'which is something the Tate Modern definitely doesn't have. I mean, where is the *raison d'être*? It's simply curated chaos, a Braque hung next to a piece by Craig Martin simply because both works are in glass. It won't do. Here at the Shoreditch the approach is linear, whereas the Tate Modern is a mass of undeveloped themes.'

Bemused, Leo wandered away, wondering if Derek and Chay realized that each assumed the museum fulfilled a function exactly the opposite of what the other supposed. From the corner of his eye he caught sight of Melissa, resplendent in blue chiffon, talking and laughing loudly with a group of people. He moved quickly away, anxious to avoid her. Twice this evening he had glimpsed her coming towards him, and on both occasions he had evaded her. He had resolved to return her gift and speak a few words to her, but intended to do so only when he was leaving, and not before. He caught sight of Gideon Smallwood lounging elegantly next to an Opdahl land-scape, talking to Tony Gear. He wondered whether Gideon had chosen to stand next to that particular paint-ing, knowing that it toned perfectly with his beautifully cut evening jacket of taupe velvet. Probably. He went over and greeted both men, aware that since Melissa detested Tony Gear, she was unlikely to come and join them.

Anthony let the waiter fill his champagne glass for the sixth time. He was beginning to feel pretty drunk, and he didn't care. He had spent the last forty-five minutes with Edward, his friend Tristram, and an excitable bevy of young women who all seemed to know Edward and Tristram from somewhere, and their mood of hilarity had failed to infect him. The girls were all very pretty, all apparently unattached, and he suspected that he could have picked up any one of them if he'd wanted to. The fact was, he didn't. For the hundredth time his eye sought out Leo. He had seen him moving round the gallery throughout the evening, clearly bound up in his own thoughts. On the one occasion when Anthony had approached him to talk, he had stopped for only a moment before excusing himself and moving on. Nursing a feeling of rejection, Anthony had watched him obsess-ively ever since. Why did it always come down to Leo? Why couldn't he just ignore the man and concentrate on enjoying himself? He could see Leo now, standing with Tony Gear and some dark-haired man, extremely good-looking and slightly effeminate. Anthony watched the way the man's lazy, amused gaze rested closely on Leo's features as Leo talked. He liked Leo, that much Anthony could tell. He looked gay, too – probably wanted him. Would probably have him, if Leo's track record was anything to go by. Just the thing to round off Leo's evening. Anthony knocked back his champagne, hating his own train of thought, trying to define the emotion that filled him.

Jealousy, that was what it was. He stared morosely at his empty glass. Christ, I'm a mess, he thought.

'Cheer up, Tony – you're a boring bugger this evening,' remarked Edward. 'We were all just thinking of going off for a spot of clubbing. What do you say? That might liven you up a bit.'

Anthony glanced at Edward, then at the girls. 'No, I won't come, thanks. It's Dad's big evening, so I'd better stay.'

Edward shrugged. 'OK. Come on, girls, let's get going. Where's Tristram? He's got my car keys . . .' Edward wandered off, girls in tow.

Ten minutes later, Tony Gear was whisked away by his minions for an important vote in the House, leaving Leo and Gideon together.

'Is that Chay Cross?' asked Gideon, as Chay passed them, leading Ronnie Wood towards the video instal-lations. 'Perhaps you should introduce us. Maybe we could have a useful chat about that funding he's after.'

'Certainly,' said Leo.

They followed Chay through, and Leo introduced Gideon. After a few moments, Leo saw Melissa in the offing and excused himself. Gideon set to work on Chay in his most accomplished fashion, and soon Chay, flattered and beguiled, was taking Gideon on a tour of the museum.

Gideon paused in one of the smaller side rooms, hung with only eight exhibits by mediocre contemporary artists, on loosely connected themes. 'I suppose you find this kind of space rather harder to fill,' he remarked.

'You're right,' agreed Chay. 'Proportion is a problem. Most of our exhibits are too large for these rooms. Of course, this is just temporary . . .'

Gideon gazed around reflectively. 'What would be ideal in a room like this would be works by an artist such as Lehrman – you know, someone who worked to a small format.'

'Oh, he'd be perfect. We have one of his works in another room, and two sculptures. I'd love to have a room devoted to his work. The trouble is, he didn't produce a lot, and he's hard to come by.'

Gideon smiled, rested an elbow on one hand, and tapped his chin thoughtfully. 'The reason I mention his name is that I have a friend, a dealer, who tells me that a number of Lehrmans may be coming on to the market soon. Would the museum be interested in acquiring them, do you think? My friend would take a commission, of course.'

'More than interested,' replied Chay, returning Gideon's smile. He understood that Gideon, somewhere along the line, would have to make something on the deal, no doubt in return for expediting the matter of the extra funding. If it meant that the museum would acquire enough Lehrmans to fill one of the smaller rooms, Chay was happy to go along.

'Good,' said Gideon. Now it was just a matter of bringing Leo round, and then the fun would follow.

It was well past midnight when Leo decided to leave. He realized then, with a sinking heart, that it might have been more sensible to speak to Melissa earlier, before she'd started knocking back the champagne. She seemed pretty tight, which increased the chances of a scene. He hesitated. Damn the woman – why did he feel he had to speak to her personally? He would put the thing in the post along with a terse letter on chambers paper. The less contact he had with her the better.

He said goodnight to Chay; they congratulated one another mutually on the success of the evening. 'I just hope the paying public like it as much,' said Chay.

'Marvellous hang, Chay, darling!' exclaimed a departing woman, blowing him a kiss. Chay blew one in return.

'I think the critics like it, from what I could overhear,' said Leo.

'D'you think so?' Chay blinked anxiously behind his glasses.

'Yes, I do. See you soon. Well done.'

Leo went through the foyer, letting a small crowd of

guests go out ahead of him, while he paused to light a cigar. He stepped out into the cold night air, and smoked for a few seconds.

The hand on his arm was gentle, then instantly forceful. He smelt her scent before her breathy voice murmured in his ear, 'I've been trying to get you alone all evening, Leo.'

Leo turned, trying to ease her hand from his arm. 'I made it clear that I don't want anything to do with you,' he said evenly. He reached into his breast pocket and drew out the tie pin in its loose wrapping, and her letter. 'And I certainly don't want this kind of thing. Take it back and don't pester me any more.'

Melissa merely smiled and shook her head. 'Darling, I know you don't mean that. Don't be embarrassed. I want you to have it. It means so much to me. You just have to give these things time. It will happen between us. I know it will. It nearly did, after all . . .'

'Get this clear. I don't want you. I don't like you. I don't want you anywhere near me –'

'Nonsense, Leo.' Her voice grew suddenly hard. 'You're not listening. You just don't listen, do you? It's going to happen! You have no choice. It's such a mistake to make me angry. Why can't you see that?' Her tone became wheedling. 'Why not be nice about it?'

She brought her face so close to his that he could see the glitter of her eyes and smell the stale champagne on her breath. She held both his arms in her hands, and he tried to push her away. But, letting go of his arms, she suddenly grasped both his hands between hers and squeezed. He could feel her nails digging into his flesh, and gasped aloud at the pain. She pressed harder, astonishing him by her strength, and clamped her mouth against his, kissing him as though she would suck the life from him.

With a violent effort he pulled her hands apart with his own, and slapped her swiftly, once, across the face. The blow was light, but effective enough to stop her.

'I'm sorry,' said Leo, grasping her by one wrist and turning her towards the entrance to the museum. 'I'm sorry. But you have to understand, this stops now. If I ever hear from you again, if you ever speak to me, I shall go to the police.' He thrust her into the foyer and she staggered forward a little. People were making their way out. Melissa glanced round at him, her expression one of uncertainty mixed with pure venom, then moved through the foyer and back into the museum. Leo leaned against the wall in relief. He glanced down at his hands, at the stinging, red indentations where her nails had dug into his flesh. Another twenty seconds of that and she'd have drawn blood. Mad bitch. This couldn't go on. He realized that anything he said to her was probably ineffectual. She was unhinged. That was the only explanation. Well, he'd just have to deal with it as it went along. If it meant involving the police, he had no qualms.

Standing in the foyer, he caught sight of Anthony coming through from the gallery. He looked as though he'd had rather too much to drink. Leo put out a hand to touch his shoulder as he passed.

'How are you getting home?' he asked.

Anthony shrugged. 'Find a taxi, I suppose.'

'That's not going to be easy at this time of night. I'll give you a lift.'

They walked together through the gate and into the darkened street. After a short interval, Anthony turned to Leo. 'Aren't you taking your boyfriend home?'

Leo realized Anthony was more than a little drunk. He sighed. 'What are you talking about?'

'That man I saw you with earlier. Very cosy. Is he your type, then?'

They reached Leo's car. Leo unlocked it and gestured to Anthony to get in. Anthony did so, clumsily, wearily.

Leo got in and put the key in the ignition. 'Why don't you come back to my place and have some coffee, and get it all off your mind?'

Anthony gave a careless, tipsy shrug. He said nothing for the rest of the journey, as Leo drove through the quiet streets to Belgravia.

In the flat, Leo snapped on lights and went into the kitchen to make Anthony some coffee. Anthony leaned against the sink and watched him, his dark eyes cloudy, his hair rumpled. Leo handed him a mug of black coffee. 'D'you want to go through to the drawing-room?' he asked.

Anthony shook his head. 'I'm fine here.'

'At least sit down.'

Anthony shook his head again. Leo couldn't fathom his resentment. He went through to pour himself a small Scotch, then came back to the kitchen and sat down at the table.

'So, what's up? What on earth were you talking about before we got in the car?'

Anthony swallowed some of his coffee. It was some seconds before he spoke. He felt less drunk now. The ride back had helped to sober him up. He wasn't sure if he should say any of this. But if he didn't do it now, the thing would just go on and on. 'That man you were talking to for half the evening. The good-looking one. I saw the way you were together.'

'What conclusion did you reach?'

Anthony shrugged. 'I guessed it was some kind of pick-up. I mean, the way you usually carry on, it's a fair assumption, isn't it?'

'Not really, no.' Leo was bemused by the patent hostility. He had his own idea of what lay behind it, but it was something Anthony was going to have to face up to on his own. 'I do have normal friendships, involving ordinary conversations.'

'I know that!' burst out Anthony. 'Of course I bloody know that! It's stupid, isn't it, imagining that every man you talk to is some potential lover? But I can't help it! God, it doesn't just have to be men either, does it? I mean it could be anyone!' He spread his arms out, slopping coffee on to the floor.

'What on earth are you so angry about?'

'I'm angry because —' Anthony closed his eyes for a brief second, then spoke with an effort. 'Because I'm jealous. Because I don't want anyone to be that close to you.'

Leo rose from his chair and came over to Anthony.

Time to lay this demon to rest. It was four years now, after all. 'Look at me,' he said. Anthony's eyes met his. 'You know I love you. I've told you that before. I love you as a friend, and I could love you in every other way, if that were possible. It's entirely up to you.'

Anthony felt a tremble of desire shake him, then fear. He put out his arms and held Leo, feeling him move against him, his body warm and close. He felt a peaceful longing – for what, he didn't know. For an end to this uncertainty, a salve for his unhappiness.

'Let me stay,' he asked.

'Of course,' said Leo. The flame of promise had flickered into life at last, but even at that moment Leo's mind ranged around the problems, finding no answers. Time enough for that, he decided, and kissed Anthony on the mouth with gentle finality.

9

Anthony lay in Leo's bed, listening to the sounds of the morning, his mind moving over the last few hours. He had no sense of transgression, of having moved from one sphere of sexuality to another. He could see now how easy it was for Leo to be as he was. Well, if not easy, at any rate explicable. The limits of desire were non-existent. That was the theory. For himself, he thought he had come as far as he wanted, and need go no further. Leo was all he needed.

Leo came through from the shower, a large towel knotted round his waist, hair slick and wet. He opened the long closet at the end of the room and began to pull out clothes for the day. He glanced at Anthony, who had rolled on to his back and was stretching his arms.

'There's coffee in the kitchen, if you want some.'

Anthony clasped his hands behind his head and watched as Leo dressed. 'I'll get up in a minute.'

'Don't leave it too long. I have to pick up Oliver in an hour.'

Anthony's disappointment was sudden and acute. 'I didn't realize. I'd hoped we could spend the day together.'

'I'm afraid this is where my life gets complicated.' Leo sat on the end of the bed and put on his shoes.

'It doesn't have to be complicated. I'm happy to help with Oliver. I'd just like to be with you.'

Leo said nothing for a moment. 'Anthony, it doesn't work like that. Oliver is a separate part of my life, one I don't intend to mix up with lovers.' Even as he said this, Leo was well aware of the hypocrisy of it. After all, hadn't Sarah spent a weekend at Stanton with him and Oliver? So what was the difference? It was too subtle for him to articulate. It was to do with the knowledge that while Rachel would not – could not – object to women friends, she would draw the line at Oliver being exposed to any men in Leo's life. The access arrangements which existed in relation to Oliver were a concession on her part. There had been a time when, during their arguments over access, she had been prepared to expose Leo's lifestyle in court. She had relented, it had never gone to court, but Leo couldn't afford to jeopardize things by having male lovers on the scene. The time he spent with Oliver was too precious to risk.

'It makes that much difference?' asked Anthony. Leo nodded. He was about to stand up when Anthony laid a hand on his arm. 'You make me feel like all this means nothing to you.'

Leo put a hand over Anthony's. 'That's not true. It's just that I have to leave in half an hour.' He hesitated, wondering if he'd been wise to allow Anthony to stay last night. He saw that Anthony was ready to invest a great deal in this new development in their relationship. That was not necessarily a good thing for either of them. The pleasures of the moment were so easy to take, but he should have given greater thought to the consequences. 'This kind of involvement isn't straightforward, you know. You haven't thought it through. I don't think I had, really,' Leo sighed.

'You sound as though you regret it.' Leo said nothing, and Anthony added, 'What about the boy you were living with a year ago? How is it different from that?' There was a resentful edge to his voice.

'It's different in all kinds of ways. You and I work together. There's a status quo we have to respect, professionally. Besides,' He turned and met Anthony's gaze directly, 'I'm not asking you to move in with me.'

'I know that. That's not what I meant. But I feel as though I'm being treated like a one-night stand.'

Leo rose, exasperated. 'Look, last night was your idea as much as mine. I don't think I understand what it is you expect all of a sudden. I have a great deal of affection for you –'

'Last night it was love.'

'Fine. OK. Call it what you like. But you can't expect me to start building my life around you. It's very complex, this kind of thing.'

'So you keep saying. I just had the idea that I was important to you. That we were important. Or could be.'

'Maybe we can,' said Leo patiently. 'Unfortunately, the disparate aspects of my life don't all necessarily fit together easily at the moment.'

'So it's a question of priorities.'

'If you like. And at the moment, Oliver is my priority. Please try and understand.' He glanced at his watch. 'I'll have to go. Make yourself breakfast, whatever you like. Set the alarm on the way out. Here's the code.' Leo scribbled a number down on the pad by the bed. He took a jacket from the closet. 'Oh, and don't forget to switch the coffee off before you go. I'll see you on Monday.'

Anthony lay in Leo's bed, letting the silence of the flat settle around him. So this was what it was like to be one of Leo's acquisitions. Important, needed, desired one moment, then dispensed with the next. He should have seen the pattern. No one was ever important to Leo for long. Not even Rachel, his wife. She'd simply been discarded as soon as she'd served her function of shoring up his ramshackle sexual reputation to enable Leo to become a QC. Anthony had known for a long time that, all things being equal, he was someone Leo desired. He'd just never let it happen. Now that it had, could he really be sure that the love he'd always imagined existed between himself and Leo was of any substance at all?

He lay back on the pillows, tormented. He'd thought this would seal everything, make sense of his life. If anything, he felt more confused than before. How did anyone gain Leo's love and attention? What had that boy Joshua done to reduce Leo to a state of dependence? He had been indifferent. Maybe that was the secret. Leo didn't want to be needed. Reflecting on this, he could see that the conversation Leo and he had just had was a mistake. If there was to be any hope of keeping Leo in his life and heart, he must not betray himself. Game-playing. All love affairs seemed to be about that. Very well, if it meant hardening his spirit and affecting not to care, then he would do it. He would do anything to hold on to Leo.

On the other side of the city, Felicity was waking to her own misgivings. She lay in bed for a few moments, assessing the situation, thinking guiltily of Vince. Not that Vince was the only problem. What if it had been a huge mistake to let Peter stay over on the first night they'd gone out together? What if he'd only wanted to get her into bed, and that would be the end of it? Her heart dipped painfully at the thought of it. She liked him so much, that smile of his that dissolved her insides, the sophistication of him compared to Vince, the way he took an interest in her, understood her life. They shared things. Last night had been wonderful. Not just the sex, which was great, but the whole evening. Vince would never have taken her to that trendy bar, and then to dinner at Nobu. He wouldn't know those places existed. She knew it was unfair to think that way, because Vince never had any money when he was on the outside, so what could she expect? Mind you, she didn't really go much for Japanese food. But that hadn't been the point. She had felt special, someone wanted to impress her, to see she enjoyed herself. She'd never had that from any bloke before.

She snuggled further under the covers, yawning. Peter came into the bedroom, a mug of tea in hand. He was already dressed.

'You don't have to go yet, do you?' asked Felicity, hastily smoothing down her rumpled curls and hoping she didn't look too godawful without make-up.

Peter sat on the edge of the bed and kissed her. 'I do, I'm afraid. I play football on Saturday mornings, and we've got a league match at ten. Can't let the side down.'

Felicity sipped the tea, then put it on the bedside table. She'd have to tell him she took it with sugar. 'Can I come and watch you?'

'You don't want to waste your morning doing that. Besides, it's way over in Morden, and I've got to pick a mate up in Wimbledon. In fact, I'd better get going.'

Felicity longed to ask when she'd see him next, but she knew that wasn't the cool thing to do. In fact, asking if she could go and watch him play football had been distinctly uncool, she realized. She watched as he tied his tie, her gaze moving admiringly across his features. She still couldn't decide whether the blond streaks in his hair were natural.

'By the way,' said Peter, 'I hope you don't mind, but I borrowed the shaving stuff in the bathroom.'

Felicity shook her head. She'd told him about Vince, but it didn't seem to worry him. In fact, she wished it had bothered him more. So why did she feel so small when he obliquely brought up the subject? Guilt, guilt. She had nothing to feel guilty about.

He came to the bedside and kissed her again. 'Are you glad you stayed last night?' Felicity couldn't help asking.

'What a daft question. Of course.' He straightened up. 'Lunch some time next week?' The slight uncertainty within her died away and happiness blossomed. She nodded. 'OK. I'll give you a call. Bye.'

She heard the front door close and lay back on the

pillow. He wanted to see her again. They were lovers now. Everything had changed. While they were just friends, spending the occasional lunchtime together, there had been no issues to face up to, no decisions to be made. Now it was different. Vince would be on remand for another couple of months, and even after his trial, she knew in her heart of hearts that he was going to get a custodial sentence. That was inevitable. So what was she to do? Tell him now, make his life even worse than it already was, take away any hope for the future? That would be the honest, cruel thing to do. The alternative was to say nothing. Just carry on seeing Peter, knowing that Vince would be none the wiser, and let events take their course. That was dishonest, but it was less painful for everyone.

Anyway, wasn't she jumping the gun a bit here? She and Peter had slept together once; OK, he said he wanted to see her again, but what if it was all going nowhere? What if two weeks from now, he dumped her? Or she might dump him . . . No chance of that, thought Felicity ruefully. She wasn't in love with the guy, but she was quite smitten. He was too good to be true. Anyway, the point was, in a few weeks' time there might be nothing that Vince need know about. Who could say? Even so, she knew already that she and Vince were drifting apart. It wasn't just Peter. It was the culmination of weeks of thinking. No present, no future. There would come a time when Vince would have to face up to the fact that her life had to move on without him. But not yet. No point in hurting him yet.

She got out of bed, picked up her mug of tea, and went through to the kitchen to add some sugar, satisfied that she had salved her conscience for the present, at least.

As he drove to Bath, Leo went over in his mind that parting conversation with Anthony. He hadn't meant to be dismissive or unfeeling. It was simply that he'd woken late, and he'd been in a hurry to pick up Oliver . . .

No, that was only part of the truth. The rest was more complicated. There had been a time, a few years ago, when Anthony had first arrived in chambers, when the spark between them could have engendered all kinds of possibilities. At that time, Leo himself was a different being, entirely without ties or responsibilities. He had wanted Anthony, not just as a lover, but as part of his life. But that was once upon a time. The years had changed things, even though Anthony might not be able to see it. Last night had happened because it had all gone on too long, something needed to be resolved. If Leo was being completely honest, he had taken advantage of the confusion of Anthony's feelings to satisfy himself. So now what was he left with?

The traffic up ahead slowed, as cones appeared on the road, blocking off a lane. Leo glanced at the dashboard clock and swore under his breath. He picked up his train of thought again. It was clear from Anthony's tone and attitude that he expected something from their altered relationship. Of course he did. The step he had taken was probably monumental, for someone of his ambivalence. Not that Anthony had any clear definition of what his expectations were – yet. Exclusivity would be part of it. Leo tapped the wheel impatiently, glancing again at the clock. The kind of relationship he and Anthony had already established made it impossible for Anthony to view what had happened in terms of a casual encounter, yet Leo knew that he himself wanted it to be no more than that. For him it was merely the selfish satisfaction of a long-held desire. Things had changed much in the years since that desire had first been born. He had married, he had had a child, his ambitions as a lawyer were gradually being realized, though there was still much further to go. His experiences with Joshua last year had shown him the dangers a hedonistic and uncontrolled lifestyle could pose to his professional existence. And mental stability.

The traffic began to speed up, and Leo sighed in relief. The Aston Martin moved smoothly forward. There was a time when he would willingly have taken Anthony as his live-in lover. That had been at the very beginning. Anthony hadn't yet been made a tenant at 5 Caper Court. That had been crucial. If it had got about – as it would have – that Leo Davies had as his lover a junior tenant in the same chambers, he would have been finished. Or at any rate, stalled in the professional doldrums for all time. He had even gone so far as to weight the chambers' vote against Anthony and in favour of his rival for the tenancy, Edward Choke, to achieve his desires. As it turned out, it hadn't happened. Nothing had happened – until last night. But the fact was, there were things he cared about more than having Anthony in his life. That was the personal and professional truth. And he had no idea how he was going to make this apparent to Anthony without causing him pain.

He pulled off the motorway on to the spur road, and resolved to think no more about it. He would simply have to play it by ear, and hope Anthony's good sense and professional judgement would prevail.

Melissa had sat in her car on the other side of the square where Leo lived for two hours, waiting for him to appear. She would have waited all morning, if necessary. Not that she had any real idea of what it was she intended to do. When he emerged from the door of the building, she felt galvanized, as though electricity were threading through her veins. She watched alertly as he went round the corner, fishing keys from the pocket of the battered leather jacket he wore. He must be going to fetch his car from the garage. She waited. After a few moments she saw the sleek shape of the silver Aston Martin emerge from the mews, and pull out to the left. Her fingers shaking with excitement, she turned the ignition and drove round the square until she was following some way behind. She let a car waiting at a junction slip ahead of her into the queue of traffic, so that she would not be directly behind Leo's car, then followed him carefully through the streets of Knightsbridge, heading in a westerly direction.

There had been heart-stopping moments. Once, she'd got stuck as a refuse van backed slowly out into the street. The length of time it took the van to reverse, straighten up again, then lumber off, seemed endless, but when she sped past it she could see Leo's car still up ahead at traffic lights. She'd had to put her foot down to get across before they changed. Two lines of traffic merging at roadworks on the M4 had left her many cars behind, but she had been able to keep the Aston Martin in her sights and catch up with it at a discreet distance later on. Later, when he had turned off the motorway on to an A road, she thought everything was going smoothly, until the car in front of her, two behind Leo's, decided to let a tractor out of a farm gateway. By the time the tractor turned off further up the road, Leo's car had disappeared. Glancing left and right at the junction of the road, Melissa had no means of knowing which direction he had taken. She turned left, hoping, and put her foot down. A few bends further up, she was rewarded by the sight of the Aston Martin ahead of her. She slowed, followed for another mile, and then the Aston Martin indicated right and turned through a gateway and up a driveway to a house set a hundred yards back from the road. Melissa drove slowly past, parked in a gateway further up, and walked gingerly back to the edge of the stone wall which bounded the garden. With shrubbery for cover, she peeped over the wall. She could see nothing at first, just Leo's car parked by the house. He must have gone in. She waited, standing in her long raincoat, hair unkempt about her shoulders, eyes fixed on the house.

At last Leo came out, and he was holding in his arms a toddler, a little boy. Some nameless emotion filled Melissa. This must be his son, the one he had talked about that drunken evening. The humiliating evening which had contained the dark beginnings of her present obsession. She watched greedily. A young woman with long, dark hair handed him a few things. Leo put the boy in the car and, after a few moments' conversation with the woman, he got in. Melissa hurried back to her car. She imagined Leo was now going back to London, but she couldn't be sure. She would have to carry on, keep her distance, and see where he went. This was all beginning to seem very promising.

On Monday morning, first thing, Leo went to Camilla's room. She had been in since half-eight, and was bent industriously over a bundle of documents. Simon, with whom she shared the room, wasn't yet in. Leo closed the door. In the moment before she raised her head to look at him, Leo found himself oddly touched by the sight of her, working away. She looked very young and alone in the big, dark room filled with briefs and books.

After a few seconds he said, 'I came to apologize. You were quite right to behave as you did on Friday evening, and I was entirely wrong.'

Camilla blushed, disconcerted by the idea of Leo coming to her room to apologize for anything. 'It doesn't matter.'

'Well, you worried me when you suggested that perhaps I ought to find another junior. I've no wish to do that. So far you've been invaluable.'

Camilla made an effort not to betray the pleasure his words gave her. 'I wasn't being serious when I said that.'

'In any event, I wanted to let you know –' He sat down

in a chair opposite her desk and crossed his legs, '– that from now on my behaviour will be entirely professional.'

A faint sense of panic struck her. What if he thought she wasn't interested in him at all? She hadn't meant that – only that the conduct of the case might suffer. What if he never came near her again?

'Why on earth are you gazing at me like a frightened rabbit?' asked Leo in bemusement.

'I wasn't. Sorry. OK, whatever,' she babbled.

'My conduct will be entirely circumspect for the dur-ation of this case.' He changed the subject, indicating the papers on her desk. 'What's that you're reading?'

'The Selikoff report on asbestosis. I got it last week and I've nearly finished it.'

'That thing by the American Surgeon General? Good God. You must be the only person on the planet who's ever read it all the way through. Apart from Dr Selikoff himself, that is. Everybody kept referring to it in the last Lloyd's case in tones of great authority, but it turned out no one had a copy. Where did you get it?'

'I got someone from one of the American Names groups to send it over. I thought I might be able to dig up some useful material from it.'

Leo nodded thoughtfully. The girl was a thorough grafter. 'And?'

'I've got quite a lot of figures and helpful quotes.'

'Good. I'll have a look at them when you've finished.' Leo eased himself out of his chair. 'See you later.'

When he was gone, Camilla exhaled a long breath and sat back in her chair. *For the duration of this case . . .* That's what he'd said. What if he'd lost interest by then? What if several weeks of working together in platonic harmony dispelled any ideas of ever kissing her again? That would probably happen. She guessed she was of momentary interest to him, and that it would pass. Well, that would be the price she'd have to pay for rebuffing him now. At least it spared her any pain in the long run. She gazed sorrowfully at the seven-hundred-page report on her desk, then, with a sigh, resumed her reading.

At lunchtime, Leo chanced to meet Anthony in the clerks' room, but beyond saying hello and exchanging a few comments about work, the encounter held no significance. To Leo's relief, Anthony's manner was entirely normal. He seemed to expect nothing more from Leo – that, Leo suspected, was just for the moment. At some time soon, Anthony would want to talk, and Leo had no real idea of how he would handle it.

That evening Leo got home feeling tired and jaded. He still had an entire evening's work ahead of him, reading and re-reading statements. When this case was over, he told himself, he would take a holiday. He hadn't had one in a long time, and the events of the last eighteen months had been gruelling, one way or another. He poured himself a drink and stabbed at the 'play' button on the answerphone. The sound of Melissa's voice made him groan. Without listening to what she had to say, he fast-forwarded to the next message. The one after that was Melissa again. And the next. Jesus, he thought angrily, the woman was out of control. He wiped the tape.

As he was changing in his bedroom, the phone rang. He found himself hesitating before he picked it up.

'Hello?'

'Leo, did you get my messages? I thought you might ring back –'

He hung up.

He wasn't surprised when the phone rang again a few seconds later. He picked it up, slammed it down, then took it off the hook. After fifteen minutes he replaced it. He couldn't leave the phone off the hook all evening. The case began next week, and all kinds of people would be trying to contact him. He stared at the phone, willing it to remain silent, but it began to ring, gently, persistently. He left it unanswered. He knew it was her. What was he to do? It might not be her, and he couldn't just let the damn thing ring all evening. In that case he might as well just leave it off.

But the fact that the phone rang at two-minute intervals for the next hour told him it had to be Melissa. He tried to eat supper and ignore it. He tried to work and ignore it. The persistency of it was maddening. And, though he didn't like to admit it, frightening. After a while he could stand no more. He sat at his desk in his study and stared at the phone as it began to ring again. Almost beside himself, he picked up the receiver and snarled, 'Listen, you mad –'

Before he could get the word 'bitch' out, he was aware of Conor Grimley's cultivated Irish tones saying 'Hello?' in bewilderment.

Leo took a deep breath. 'Conor. Sorry. I had no

idea. I've been getting nuisance calls. I just – anyway . . . Sorry.'

'Nuisance calls? Dear me, that's very distressing. It happened to my sister-in-law. I suggest you get your number changed.' He paused sympathetically for a second or two. 'Actually, I wanted a word with you about my opening statement. Have you got a moment?'

'Yes, of course,' said Leo, and sat back in his chair. At least while he was talking to Conor, he had some respite from that lunatic woman.

When he'd finished talking to Conor, Leo put down the phone and tried to resume his work. But the silence seemed threatening, poised and expectant. It was almost a relief when the ringing began again. Leo reached below his desk and disconnected the plug from the socket. Anyone who wanted to talk to him, apart from the madwoman of Kensington, would have to call him in chambers. He went through to the drawing-room and disconnected the phone there. The ringing ceased. Silence settled, and Leo felt the tension in him ease. Tomorrow he'd see about getting his number changed. That wouldn't be the end of it, he suspected. It was probably only just the beginning. It was intolerable to think that this woman could so insidiously affect his existence, forcing him to the inconvenience of changing his number, then informing friends and colleagues, changing his personal notepaper, and so forth. He would have to see his solicitor, to find out just what steps he could take, before she really began to wreck his life in earnest.

*

A week later, the case between Sir Stephen Geldard Caradog-Browne and the Society of Lloyd's opened before the Honourable Mr Justice Olby in Court Seven, Chichester Rents, Chancery Lane. The court itself was a large, low-ceilinged, windowless room of a most depressing aspect. The barristers and solicitors were seated on either side of it at ranks of long, functional tables. All round the room, shelves were filled to the ceiling with documents, which Sarah and many of her kind had spent long hours paginating, marking and filing in endless Lever Arch files. Yet more boxes of documents stood stacked beside the lawyers' tables. Rows of chairs were provided at the back of the room for those Names who cared to follow the day-to-day proceedings, and to the side for the press and public. Not that anyone anticipated public interest. The opening of the case was reported only in *The Times*, the *Telegraph*, and the *Financial Times*, and each devoted only a couple of paragraphs to it. It was generally felt that the Lloyd's scandal had burnt itself out, and that this action for fraud was something of a no-hoper.

The mood amongst the attendant Names, however, was tense and hopeful – at least, to begin with. They thronged the rows of chairs in the courtroom, and hung avidly on Conor Grimley's words as he embarked upon his opening statement, listening intently as he set forth their grievances and expounded the iniquitous behaviour of Lloyd's of London over a twenty-year period. Any hope that the joint satisfaction of hearing their case put at last might improve relations between Lady Henrietta and Sir Stephen Caradog-Browne remained unrealized. If anything, now that the action had begun, their separate factions focused more closely than ever on tactical matters and each day, after the court proceedings had ended, they conducted long and wearisome meetings about disputed points with Rachel and Fred in the offices of Nichols and Co.

Conor Grimley's opening address lasted throughout the entire first week, and well into the second. The initial tension generated in the first couple of days amongst clients and lawyers alike rapidly died away. By the time Paul Rollason, counsel for Lloyd's, rose to make his opening address, things had become positively soporiferous. Leo and Camilla attended for the first two days, and then absented themselves to attend to more important aspects of the case.

The end of March came, the first buds began to break on the trees in Fountain Court and the gardens of the Inns of Court, and in Court Seven a steady procession of witnesses took the stand, day after day, to be examined by Conor in his patient Irish brogue. Leo took over the examination of a particular few, whose acerbic and indignant tendencies he could best keep in check, but by and large he busied himself with the preparation of his cross-examination. For him, involvement in a case of this kind was like being buried in some grey half-world, where the sights and sounds were those of the sombre courtroom in Chichester Rents and his room in chambers, his preoccupations exclusively those of minimum percentage reserves, stop loss insurance, and reinsurances to close.

Since he had had his number changed, Melissa had ceased to pester him in that way, but she had taken instead to writing him endless letters. These were instantly recognizable, and at first Leo dealt with them by consigning them to the wastepaper basket, unread. He was determined that they should bother him as little as junk mail. Then he realized that if this were to go on, and he found himself obliged to take legal steps against her, he would need the letters as evidence. So he kept them. Similarly with the long, rambling e-mails she sent him in chambers. It would have been as easy to delete these as to swat flies, but he saved them. If the persistence of her harassment troubled him, he tried not to admit it to himself. Just so long as the woman kept her distance. Surely even she would begin to get bored eventually.

Over the weeks, Leo and Camilla had developed a certain camaraderie, finding common areas of amusement in the case, developing a shorthand of eye-contact and body language which each could read more and more easily as time passed. She was growing familiar to him, but in a pleasurable, tantalizing way which was novel to Leo. He had never in his life desired someone and been unable to make them his lover within a matter of days – a couple of weeks at the outside. Spending so much time in close proximity to her was becoming immensely frustrating.

In the meantime, Sarah provided the perfect occasional diversion – emotionally undemanding, sexually obliging and inventive, and happy in the notion that she had something Camilla wanted, but was never likely to have.

Being able to spend the night with Leo now and again made her feel she was getting back at Camilla in some sweet way for having to run around at Camilla's beck and call during the case, photocopying, looking up cases, and being treated like a general dogsbody. She could tell from Camilla's manner in Leo's company that she still had a crush on him, but it appeared to Sarah that Leo didn't return her interest in the slightest.

During the third week of the case, when Leo had returned to chambers after a tiresome day spent examining an elderly ex-broker with hearing problems, Anthony came to his room. Leo had just hung up his robing bag and was taking off his coat. One glance at Anthony's face told him what he wanted to discuss.

'I know you've been busy with the Lloyd's case,' Anthony said, closing the door, 'but I really need to talk to you.'

There was silence for a few seconds. Leo nodded. 'I know.' He glanced at his watch. 'Sit down.'

'I don't want to talk here.'

'Right. Let's go for a drink.'

They went to the same quiet pub that Leo and Sarah had gone to weeks before. At five o'clock, it was still deserted.

Anthony bought a double Scotch for Leo and a pint for himself, and brought them to a corner table where Leo was sitting, tapping a beer mat thoughtfully. As Anthony approached, Leo glanced up and smiled, and the unmistakable warmth of it made Anthony's heart rise. Perhaps he had been mistaken about the silence of the past few weeks. Leo had been busy with the case, after all. He pulled up a chair.

Anthony was about to ask how the case was going, but stopped himself. It wasn't what he had come here to talk about. He drank some of his beer and said, 'I had the idea we might have seen more of one another before now.'

'I've been busy with this case. You know how it is.'

'It's more than that.' He waited, but Leo said nothing, merely sipped his drink. 'Don't you think I deserve better than that kind of evasion?'

'It's not evasion, Anthony.' Leo passed a weary hand over his face.

Anthony shook his head slowly, uncomprehendingly. 'Amn't I more important than one of your casual pick-ups?'

Leo tilted his glass reflectively. 'What do you want me to say? Of course you are. You're very dear to me, in every way.' He looked up at Anthony, his gaze intent. 'There was a time when I thought our relationship could be the single most significant thing in my life. But both our situations are altered now.' He paused for a few long seconds. 'Do you remember, the morning after, you said to me that I sounded as though I regretted what had happened? Well, in a sense I do. Because you want it to alter your life, or the way things are between us. It can't.'

'Don't say it can't,' said Anthony in a low voice. 'For me it already has. It's changed everything.'

216

'It's only sex, Anthony.' Leo gave a shrug and pulled out his cigar case.

Anthony stared at him, appalled and bewildered. He hadn't ever truly believed that Leo was as utterly amoral as he professed to be, but perhaps he was. Yet could he be so callous as to detach all emotion from what had happened between them?

'Do you think only about yourself? Only about the significance of things in relation to yourself?'

'I'm afraid so – yes. One of my many faults.' Leo lit a cigar and blew out a small cloud of smoke. 'I don't want you to think I don't care for you, that I don't want you as a lover – you can be, any time that's convenient. But I haven't room in my life for what I suspect you want.'

'And that is?'

'Time. Attention. Exclusivity.' With each word Leo gave his cigar a little tap against the ashtray. He raised his gaze and looked steadily at Anthony. 'Am I not right?'

For a moment Anthony could say nothing. He felt almost choked by hopelessness, and his sense of rage at Leo's cruelty. When he spoke, his voice was a little hoarse. 'Didn't you know all that before you let me stay? Didn't you know how everything that happened between us would affect me? How important it was?' He gazed at Leo, searching for some trace in his eyes of guilt and shame. Leo looked away. Anthony went on, his voice stronger, 'People are not like you, Leo. I see now that I'm not. For me love means warmth. Closeness. It means trust.'

Leo lifted his cigar to his lips. 'Like screwing Sarah while Camilla was away?'

'You bastard,' said Anthony slowly.

'I'm just trying to root out the hypocrisy,' said Leo. 'I'm not the only one who can divorce sex from love, you see. Love means whatever you choose it to mean. Perhaps my variety is a little more free and easy than you'd like, but you can take it or leave it. It's always there if you want it. I'm always there if you want me.' His gaze, as he said this, was frankly sensuous, and Anthony felt helpless stirrings of desire, adding to his bewilderment.

'Do you mean it's that simple for you?'

Leo shrugged. 'It can be for you, too. Now, if you like. This evening. I'm not busy.'

'My God – you sound like . . .' Anthony shook his head. 'I can't reduce things to your terms. I don't understand you. Maybe I'm glad I don't.' He rose and picked up his coat. 'I'm sorry I bothered trying to talk it through. I just had the idea it meant something more to you.'

'Not really,' sighed Leo. He watched as Anthony left the pub, then went to the bar to buy himself another drink. He sat down again, wondering if Anthony would come back, hoping he wouldn't. It had gone against his true feelings to behave so brutally, but in the long run it was probably best for both of them.

Outside, Anthony stood on the cold pavement for some moments, wishing he could bring himself to accept Leo's casual invitation, to submit to his terms. But he knew in his heart that it would be the beginning of a degradation from which he would never recover. Whatever Leo might think, there had to be love. Slowly he walked back to chambers.

IO

It was a balmy Thursday morning in mid-April, and Gideon had spent an hour drinking coffee at his desk and trawling through the papers for stories which might be of moment to the Ministry for Artistic and Cultural Development. Thursday mornings, when Tony Gear attended Cabinet meetings, were always something of a welcome break. Glancing at the diary, he saw that his lord and master was lunching that day with the political editors of both the *Independent* and *The Times*. Tony, unlike many in his party, was a politician who enjoyed food, drink, and the company of journalists. He wouldn't be back in his office until well into the afternoon. Time, thought Gideon, to slope off and attend to a little business of his own.

Twenty minutes later, in the aftermath of a light shower of spring rain, Gideon was stepping from a taxi in Curzon Street. He cut a debonair figure as he sauntered up through the streets of Mayfair, side-stepping puddles, admiring the breaking buds on the trees in Berkeley Square, pausing occasionally to glance in the windows of shops and galleries. When he reached a particular gallery in Hay Mews, he stopped, pressed the bell, and was admitted. Half an hour later he emerged, his business satisfactorily completed. He had negotiated a price for the seven works by Germano Lehrman which he had seen at Leo's flat, and whose titles he had, with quick assiduity, committed to memory and shortly thereafter to paper. It was a price which Leo, given his admitted disenchantment with the Lehrman works in his possession, would undoubtedly jump at. He would realize enough from the sale to buy himself one or two larger works much better suited to his present tastes – say, some Mapplethorpe photographs, or a Nadelman sculpture. If this all went smoothly, and Chay's museum then bought the paintings from Gideon's gallery-owning acquaintance (a friend of long-standing from their years together at Eton), Gideon stood to make a healthy little percentage from the deal, of which Leo would naturally know nothing. Not for a while. But that small profit was only the beginning – it was as nothing compared to that which Gideon hoped would eventually come his way.

Gideon took a taxi back to Whitehall, and there spent the rest of the morning dealing with various junior officials anxious to know if Tony Gear had signed their letters and documents. When these and other routine matters had been disposed of, Gideon called Leo in chambers. Told he was engaged on a case, Gideon left a message to say that he would call on Leo in chambers at half-six that evening.

The afternoon passed and, true to form, the Minister for Artistic and Cultural Development returned to his office a little after three, slightly flushed, with the air of one who has dealt masterfully with the press. Gideon glided into the inner sanctum to remind the Minister that he had a meeting at half past with the Chief Secretary to the Treasury to discuss next year's funding for regional ballet, and watched as Tony went into a ten-minute fluster and bluster, casting about for figures and memoranda. Gideon didn't know why he bothered. They both knew that it was Gideon who would steer the meeting on Tony's behalf, allowing it to appear to the Chief Secretary that it was, of course, the Minister who was master of all the relevant facts and figures, while Gideon merely murmured on the sidelines. It was an elegant deception practised by both of them with many a delegation and policy forum, and Gideon often felt that he had elevated his own role in these little pieces of theatre to something approaching high art.

When the meeting ended, Gideon departed with the notes he had taken in his fastidious hand, to be written up later, and set about the daily task of making up the Minister's box with the correspondence clerk. From the corner of his eye he saw Kelly, Tony Gear's diary secretary, enter the Minister's office. He glanced at his watch. She emerged three-quarters of an hour later, after the other staff in the office had gone home, and just as Gideon was putting the final letters for signing into the box. Forty-five minutes was far longer than was strictly necessary to inform the Minister of his next day's movements. Gideon gave her a smirk, which Kelly tried to return with an airy smile. Gideon thought he could read those smiles of Kelly's very well. They had been a touch nervous in the early days, but now they had a trace of hauteur about them. She didn't like Gideon. She was a little afraid of him. Gideon knew this, and was well content.

When Gary, Tony Gear's driver, arrived to take the red box, Gideon was careful to have a friendly chat with him. For all that he had bought Gerald Kaufman's book, Tony Gear had failed to read past Chapter One, and so had never taken on board the salutary advice that *a Minister should, if he is sensible, do a great deal to please his driver.* From the very beginning, Tony Gear had made the fatal error of rubbing Gary up the wrong way. Gideon had divined this, and had every intention of profiting from the Minister's mistake. There was much that Gary knew, and was prepared to tell – to the right person.

Gideon bade the Minister goodnight, put on his coat, and left the office. A warm, rainy spell had set in, and the early evening air in Whitehall was damp and pleasantly fresh. Gideon decided to walk all the way to the Temple.

He reached Caper Court a little before six, just as Henry was about to leave. Henry buzzed Leo and showed Gideon up to his room. There Gideon found Leo in his shirt-sleeves, desk stacked with documents, going through papers. They greeted one another, Leo fetched a bottle of claret from the case standing by his door, opened it, and poured them both a glass. They sat there, the room lit only by the glow from Leo's desk lamp, and discussed the case briefly. Gideon knew most of what had happened so far, since Lady Norbury was in attendance at Chichester Rents most days and regaled Gideon with the details every evening. After a little while, Gideon made casual mention of his friend who ran the Mayfair gallery, and who happened to be interested in acquiring works by Germano Lehrman. He mentioned the typical price his friend was offering. Would Leo be interested in selling the few he had? Leo said he certainly would, reckoning up in his own mind the profit he would make since he had first acquired the paintings in the early eighties. It was too good an offer to refuse, and he didn't care for the things any more. He supposed Gideon, acting on his friend's behalf, stood to take a cut of some kind, but that was hardly Leo's business. They toasted the deal, and arranged a time when the gallery could collect the pictures and settle up. Far easier, Leo observed, than putting them up for auction. Gideon, with a smile, agreed.

When the bottle of claret was empty, Leo suggested dinner at his club. Gideon regretfully declined, saying that he had work to attend to. He left Caper Court and took a taxi to a busy, but discreetly tucked-away restaurant in Islington whose name Gary had mentioned to him earlier. As he came in, Gideon saw the bar was crowded, and that he could stand there safely unobserved from the restaurant. He ordered a drink, and from a discreet distance scrutinized the tables and the diners. He picked them out quickly at a table at the far end of the room. Although Tony Gear had his back to him, Gideon recognized Kelly, deep in intimate conversation with the Minister. Not, thought Gideon, that there was anything wrong with that. Tony Gear could dine with whom he pleased. Of course he could. Gideon finished his drink, and took a taxi back to his mother's house in Pimlico. There, as his mother watched *Newsnight* and dozed, Gideon made a telephone call to Chay, who had given Gideon his

London number on the evening of the museum launch. Chay happened to be in New York, but Gideon left a message to the effect that eight works by Germano Lehrman were available for purchase, if Chay and the museum were interested. He didn't mention a price. That would come later, when Chay called back, as Gideon knew he would.

Because of the routine, dragging nature of the Lloyd's case, the time Leo spent with Sarah had settled into something of a pattern. He thought little of it, regarded it as nothing more than a useful release of sexual energy and a way of having someone cook dinner for him two or three times a week. Sarah, however, attached greater significance to it than that. She felt she could read something into Leo's behaviour. He was getting older, work tired him, he liked having her around, he liked making love to her. Surely it was just a matter of time before Leo realized that the pattern was a comfortable one, that they were good for one another – in short, that he might as well marry her and have done with it. Then she could forget all about the boring slog of being a barrister – or of ever having to work again. She could have a comfortable, secure life, and do exactly as she pleased while Leo earned ridiculously large fees and took them both further up the social ladder. It was the marrying bit that was tricky. Even Sarah could see no immediate reason why Leo should alter the status quo and actually bother marrying her. She toyed with the idea of getting pregnant, but decided that not even Leo was worth that sacrifice. No, she might want Leo and his money and everything else that marriage to him might usefully bring, but she wanted her freedom, too. Otherwise there was no point. It was something she would have to talk him into eventually, in a roundabout way. She was pretty sure she could. It was just a question of time, letting the pattern develop until she was a fixture in his life – that meant every part of his life, including the time he spent with Oliver. She might not care much for small children, but Sarah knew that that was an area where she had to make her mark. She would have to start sacrificing a few weekends.

The opportunity to show her nurturing side came in late April. On one of the routine evenings spent at Leo's, as they ate the dinner she had cooked, Leo mentioned that he would be going to Stanton with Oliver that weekend.

'Given the stage this case has got to, it means trying to divide my attention between Oliver and a large pile of work. The other side are going to start calling their witnesses next week, and that means I have to prepare my cross-examination.'

'Why don't you hire my services for the weekend?' said Sarah. 'I'm moderately child-friendly, as you know, and my rates are very reasonable. Just a warm bed, regular meals, and the odd glass of wine.'

Leo eyed Sarah speculatively. There must be some hidden agenda, one that went with the routine she had established lately, the meals she cooked, her easy availability. It wasn't like the Sarah of old. That Sarah had a price for everything, and a reason.

'You've become very domesticated, all of a sudden. What's happened to your late nights, your hedonistic weekend lifestyle?'

'I'm simply offering to help out. I do like the occasional weekend away from London, you know.'

'Well, your offer is very kindly accepted.' He poured her another glass of wine. 'Do you think you could throw in a spot of gardening as well? The place could do with tidying up.'

Sarah gave a weak smile and took a gulp of wine. Child-minding *and* gardening, not to mention other attendant chores that a weekend at Stanton would bring. She sincerely hoped this was going to pay off in the long run.

By the time the weekend came, the frequent showers which had dogged the early part of the month had disappeared, and the weather was warm and sunny. Sarah drove to Stanton in fairly good humour, despite the fact that she had had to turn down a last-minute dinner invitation from Hugo. Still, plenty of time for amusements like that once she had achieved her aim. Being the wife of Leo Davies would bring money and enough spare time to indulge any number of fancies. When she finally reached Leo's house, she had painted a delightful picture of her future life, one in which she and Leo lived free lives and in which Oliver didn't figure too prominently.

By the time Saturday evening came, Sarah would cheerfully have obliterated Oliver from the picture altogether. She'd spent all day with him, while Leo worked on the case, and had discovered that keeping a lively toddler amused was an exhausting business. At half past six, when Leo abandoned work and gave Oliver a bath, Sarah slumped in an armchair with a drink. She thought regretfully of Hugo, and hoped he would keep. Was this all going to be worth it? There was no guarantee at the end of the day that it would pay off, and she couldn't spend too many Saturdays like this. She felt so tired she didn't think she could be bothered with sex later on. Besides, even with the ever-inventive and energetic Leo, it had become somewhat routine of late.

Leo came down with a clean and sweet-smelling Oliver in his arms, and found Sarah brooding over her gin and tonic. 'You look exhausted. I'll cook supper tonight.' Sarah gave him a weary and grateful look, then hastily set her drink down as Leo put Oliver on her knee. 'Just read to him for twenty minutes or so while I start cooking. He should be ready for bed soon.' Leo turned as he reached the kitchen door. 'Thanks for making a start on the garden. I've done most of what I need to do, so I should be able to help you tomorrow.'

Tomorrow, thought Sarah, as she turned the first pages of *Thomas and the Magic Railway*. She could hardly wait. Gardening, and looking after Oliver. Things at Stanton had certainly changed since that first wild summer she had spent here with Leo, James, and whatever like-minded friends Leo had cared to invite for weekend parties. Perhaps that was what parenthood did for you. In which case, Sarah decided, she was having none of it. She began to read aloud to Oliver, wondering what the crowd at the

Met Bar were talking about right at that moment, and where they were going afterwards.

The following day was better, because Leo took Oliver for a walk to see some horses in a nearby field, leaving Sarah to read the Sunday papers for an hour or so. Then they had lunch at a pub in the village. It was only when they got back to the house that Leo discovered that Oliver's supply of nappies had run out.

'I'll have to go to the supermarket in Oxford,' he said. 'The village shop will be closed by now.'

'What about the nearest petrol station? They usually have things like that.'

'Good idea. I won't be long.'

When Leo had driven off, Sarah fetched a rug from the house, spread it out on the lawn, and plonked Oliver on it with some of his toys. The weather was gentle and warm. She stretched out and began to read A. A. Gill.

Melissa drove slowly up to the house and parked. No sign of Leo's Aston Martin, just a small, red Fiat in the driveway. Perhaps she had the wrong weekend. But she had been watching his movements regularly, knew the pattern now. This was his weekend with his son, surely it was. Her heart began to thud thickly. The idea that he wouldn't be here, that this would end in failure, was torment. She needed to feel that her planning and calculation were perfect, effective. She needed that sense of control. Above all, she needed, after all this time, to see him close to, in the flesh. It was like a physical hunger.

She got out of the car, went up to the house, and pressed the bell.

Sarah heard it from the garden, and got up, surprised that anyone should call. She ambled through the house, opened the door and saw a tall, middle-aged blonde woman, dressed in an immaculately tailored suit, with expensive accessories and abundant jewellery, standing on the doorstep. Sarah absorbed these details rapidly, noticing at the same time that the expression on the woman's face was faintly wild and apprehensive. Melissa stared back in silence at the girl in T-shirt and jeans who had answered Leo's door. Her mind raced with possibilities, and she had to will herself to calmness. This person was no one of significance. She couldn't be. Not to Leo. She was just a child. She was no one.

Melissa's manner became instantly poised and warm as she smiled at Sarah. 'Hello – I'm a friend of Leo's. I was in the neighbourhood and I thought I'd call. Is he in?'

'No. He's just popped out for a moment.' She looked uncertainly at the woman, who seemed familiar. Should she invite her in? 'Don't I know you?'

'Melissa Angelicos.' She was gratified by the instant flash of recognition in the girl's eyes. 'May I wait, if he won't be long?'

'Of course,' responded Sarah, sufficiently impressed by Melissa's sophisticated bearing and media status. If she was a friend of Leo's, she couldn't leave her on the doorstep. She ushered Melissa into the house. 'Come through to the garden. Oliver's playing out there.'

'Are you the nanny?' asked Melissa with lofty kindness, as they crossed the lawn.

'That's right.' Sarah replied without hesitation, and smiled. There was something about this expensively dressed, carefully made-up woman that told Sarah it would be better all round if she remained under this delusion.

'So this is darling Oliver!' Melissa knelt gingerly on the rug, high heels splayed out behind her, bracelets clinking, and stretched out her hands towards Oliver. Oliver regarded her thoughtfully, then put out his hand to touch the bracelets. Melissa slipped a couple off and gave them to him. Oliver turned them round in his small hands, then put them to his mouth, staring at Melissa once again. 'I've seen him before, of course, but this is the first time I've met him. Isn't he like his father?'

'Mmm.' Sarah rumpled her hair with her hands and sighed inwardly. She hoped Leo would get back soon. For some reason, she didn't much care for Ms Angelicos. 'Would you like some tea or coffee?' she asked Melissa.

'Tea would be lovely. Do you have any Earl Grey?'

'I'll have a look,' said Sarah, and went to the kitchen. As she reached the door, she glanced back at Melissa, who was now sitting on the rug, as comfortably as her tight Chanel skirt would allow, and trying to entice Oliver on to her lap. As Sarah poked around in the cupboards for tea, she heard the sound of the front door opening and closing. Leo came into the kitchen.

'Whose car is that?' he asked, his voice tense. Sarah glanced at him in surprise.

'A friend of yours – that TV presenter, Melissa whatsit. Said she was passing and thought she'd drop in. Do we *have* any Earl Grey tea?'

But Leo was striding out into the garden with a face like thunder. Sarah went to the kitchen door. When he reached the rug, Leo leaned swiftly down and grabbed Oliver from Melissa's arms. Oliver began to wail and the bracelets he had been holding dropped from his hands on to the rug. Over Oliver's crying, Sarah could hear Leo tearing into the Angelicos woman like a man possessed. She actually flinched as she caught his words, and then her mouth dropped in horror as she saw Melissa, still kneeling on the rug, catch Leo round his legs in a beseeching rugby tackle. He backed off with Oliver in his arms, almost falling over, and at this, Sarah ran out into the garden to help. By this time Melissa was weeping as well as Oliver, scrabbling frantically at Leo as she tried to get up from the ground. Sarah took Oliver from Leo and watched as Leo, grabbing Melissa by the arm, pulled her up and marched her round the side of the house. He reappeared a few moments later, and was crossing the lawn towards Sarah and Oliver when Melissa, too, reappeared round the side of the house. The thing looked farcical. With a roar, Leo turned on Melissa. This time, when he marched her back round to the front of the house, he succeeded in getting her into her car. Sarah carried Oliver, whose sobs had subsided, through the house and watched the rest of the pantomime from the drawing-room window. Melissa was sitting in her car, wiping her face with a tissue.

'Go on, leave!' Leo shouted.

Melissa sat weeping in her car.

'Will you for Christ's sake get out? Go!'

Minutes passed, but Melissa just sat there in her car. In exasperation, Leo slammed into the house and went to the phone.

'What are you doing?' asked Sarah.

'I'm ringing the police. What on earth possessed you to let that bloody woman into my house? Don't you know she's a lunatic?'

'Of course I don't know! She said she was a friend!' replied Sarah indignantly.

'Right, so every stranger who turns up at my house claiming to be my friend, you'll invite them in – is that it?'

'Of course not! I knew who she was, she seemed all right. Why are you blaming me?'

'Because –' Leo broke off as the phone was answered at the other end. Sarah listened as Leo explained the ludicrous situation, striving to maintain his temper. 'Well, no, she's not doing anything threatening. She's just sitting there. But I want her off my property. The woman's been stalking me for the last two months, for God's sake . . . Right . . . right. Thank you.' He put the phone down. 'They'll send someone round.' He ran his fingers through his hair. 'The point is, Sarah, that woman is potentially dangerous. And you left her alone with Oliver.'

Sarah handed Oliver to Leo. 'I've had about enough. I've been skivvying for you all weekend, and I get blamed for a situation which has nothing at all to do with me. Do you think it's reasonable to expect me to know which of your friends is mad? I think I'll head back to London now, if you don't mind.'

She left the room, watched by Oliver and Leo. Leo sat down, feeling the trembling of spent anger in his limbs, holding Oliver close against him, kissing his soft hair. Something in the urgency of his embrace caused Oliver to look up at his father in wonder. Leo met his eyes and smiled, amazed by the force of emotion he felt as they looked at one another. If only all love could be as unquestioning, so entirely pure, he thought. The devotion he felt for his son was the most perfect and enduring he had ever known. The idea that any harm should ever come to him was worse than anything he had ever contemplated in his life. Leo sat cradling his son, his eyes fixed on Melissa's car, still in the driveway.

Next day in chambers, Leo recounted the episode to Michael Gibbon. Michael had known from the very beginning about Melissa's harassment, and Leo found it a relief to confide in someone about the latest events.

'So what happened in the end?'

'Oh, eventually they persuaded her to put the window down, then they just talked to her for a while, and she drove off.'

'The whole thing's gone a bit too far, if you ask me. What are you going to do about it?'

'Well, up till now I've been reluctant to do anything drastic. We do have a certain business relationship, with the trusteeship of Chay Cross's museum, and taking out an injunction hasn't really seemed appropriate. But I think that's what I'm going to have to do.'

'I don't see that you have any alternative, now that it's gone beyond letters and e-mails.' Michael moved away from the bookcase in Leo's room where he had been leaning and glanced at his watch. 'I'd better let you get ready for court.'

There was a light knock at the door, and Camilla looked in. 'Ready for the fray?'

Leo rose from his chair and picked up his robing bag. 'As I'll ever be. Let's go and do battle with the deputy chairman of Lloyd's.'

In the clerks' room two days later, Henry was watching Felicity out of the corner of his eye as she talked on the phone. He could tell from the way she swivelled her chair away from the rest of the room that it was personal, and he could tell from the glimpse he caught of her smile that it was this new man of hers. She'd never mentioned him – she didn't have to. Henry knew Felicity well enough to read all the signs. Out every other lunchtime, humming happily when she worked, and that particular light in her eye . . . He was gut-churningly jealous. He tried not to be, but he couldn't help it. And what about Vince? Poor bloke probably didn't have a clue that he was being two-timed, hanging about in prison, waiting for his trial date. Henry had never thought he'd feel sorry for Vince, but he did now. But this was what women were like. Henry told himself he was probably lucky he'd never got involved with someone like Felicity, if this was what she did. He tried to console himself with this thought, but it wasn't much help in the face of Felicity's patent infatuation with whoever-it-was.

Felicity put the phone down and glanced at her watch. Two hours till lunchtime, when she would see Peter. The way she felt about him was still a marvel and a revelation. Even the prospect of seeing him for a snatched, one-hour lunch was enough to make her day. Well, not quite. Tonight was her night for visiting Vince, and with each week that passed she dreaded the visits more and more. A few weeks ago, when she had realized that her feelings for Peter were really serious, that it wasn't just a passing fling, she had resolved to tell Vince. But when she had gone to the remand centre that evening, he had just heard that his mother was in hospital after a heart attack, and he seemed so low, and so much in need of her, that she couldn't say anything. It had gone on like that. Each time she went, the guilt got worse, and so did her sense of emotional detachment. She felt nothing much for Vince any more. Not just because the situation he was in seemed so pathetic and hopeless – she still felt intensely sorry for him – but because what she felt for Peter was so different, so much more romantic than anything she and Vince had ever had. Peter seemed to care about her in a way in which Vince never had. Not only that, he had opened her eyes to possibilities in life which she hadn't appreciated before. He took her to places, clubs and expensive restaurants that she never knew existed. She liked being shown how to spend money well. Particularly now that she had plenty of it. The amount she was earning now was fantastic for a girl of her age. Peter had recently suggested to Felicity that she should look for a bigger flat in a better part of London. He even pointed out clothes and shoes in magazines and suggested she buy them, change her image. In the time she'd known Peter, Felicity had begun to form a new concept of herself, and her worth. At the end of the day, the kind of person she now wanted to become, and the lifestyle she had begun to adopt, were as remote from Vince and his ideas of life as Belmarsh was from Notting Hill. Which, it so happened, was where Felicity was thinking of buying a new flat.

But tonight had to be faced. She wondered how many more visits she would be making in the future. On the last visit, Vince had told her his trial date had been fixed for the 27th of May. Felicity had thought this news might focus and energize him, bringing as it did some prospect of hope and change, but it just seemed to make him more dispirited. She would make no decision about how and when to tell Vince about Peter until the trial was over. Whichever way it went, whether he was acquitted or found guilty, she had to tell him. Of course she hoped, for Vince's sake, that he would be acquitted. But she had to acknowledge to herself that it was a possibility she dreaded. That was the worst and most selfish thing of all.

Robert's voice interrupted her thoughts, calling over to her that he had someone on the phone who wanted to know when Jeremy Vane would be back in chambers.

'I think his plane gets in midday on Monday, but whether or not he'll come in that day, I don't know. Hold on, I'll check in his diary.' She tapped away at the keyboard, and cheered herself with the thought that she would see Peter in just a couple of hours' time.

All that week and the following week, as April turned to May, Lloyd's introduced one witness after the other, and Leo cross-examined them. The case was not one which called for theatricality or devastating displays of advocacy. The pace was leisurely and the atmosphere almost stultifyingly polite. Even so, thought Camilla, as she watched Leo put a former deputy chairman of Lloyd's through his paces, Leo knew how to turn the screws. Gerald Ruddick, a plump, prosperous man now in comfortable retirement, had been sworn in that morning and had seemed affable and confident at the beginning of his cross-examination. Now, mid-afternoon, his smile had long since faded, and he seemed flustered and ill at ease. He had made much play of searching through the papers before him for information with which to reply to Leo's questions, but now gave up and answered them baldly.

'Let's go back to 1981,' said Leo, 'where sometime in the future it was within possible contemplation that there might be thirty thousand asbestos claims. What would bring home the risk of that range to me, as a person, a prospective Name, applying to join?'

'Well,' replied Ruddick, 'only, I suppose, if your members' agent had knowledge about it and decided he was going to inform you.'

'So if my members' agent either didn't inform me or had no such knowledge, as a prospective Name I just wouldn't know. Is that right?'

'No, you wouldn't know, but then you wouldn't know exactly what your exposure to earthquake was either. All you would be told was that joining Lloyd's was a risky business.'

'Indeed. But there's a distinction between an earthquake and asbestosis, isn't there? Unless an earthquake had happened, it would only be a contingency, wouldn't it?' Leo gave Ruddick the most charming of smiles, leaning forward a little as he spoke. I love him when he does that, thought Camilla, her eyes fixed on Leo's face. She could watch him for hours.

'Well, it's a contingent exposure . . .' Ruddick shifted in his seat, glancing across at his solicitors and then back at Leo.

'It's a contingent exposure to risk, one that might happen or might not.'

'Yes.'

'But asbestosis had happened, Mr Ruddick, hadn't it? It was known within Lloyd's that huge numbers had been exposed to that risk. Is that not so?'

'Well, I don't know the precise numbers . . . I don't know the years in which potential numbers were known to be greater than they were thought to be earlier.'

'That wasn't my question, Mr Ruddick. Let's look at it again. It was known within Lloyd's that in the past huge numbers had been exposed, hadn't they? My question didn't contain a quantification, it contained the adjective "huge". Do you quarrel with that as knowledge within Lloyd's?'

Ruddick fiddled with the papers in the bundle before

him. 'I'm not sure. It's a long time ago and my recollection . . . Well, I think I thought that early on the losses would come from the major manufacturers, you know, who were mining . . .'

At that moment, the courtroom door to one side swung gently open, and someone came in and took a seat in the rows of chairs set aside for the public and press. It was the case that Names, solicitors, court officers and clerks constantly came and went throughout the day, as noiselessly as possible, and generally no one paid any attention. But for some reason, as Ruddick was waffling on, Leo glanced across at the newcomer. Camilla, accustomed by now to being closely attuned to Leo during the proceedings, felt his attention shift, his body freeze momentarily. She glanced in the direction in which he was looking and saw a blonde woman arranging herself, plus bags, coat and scarf, in a seat at the end of the row. The woman smiled at Leo, who looked away instantly, flicking through the papers in front of him to recapture his train of thought. Whoever she was, Camilla could tell her presence had entirely thrown Leo.

'. . . I mean, I think we knew that firms like that, whose employees had been very heavily exposed, would be severely damaged, but I don't think that I personally understood how wide – I mean, we, that is to say I, may have failed to appreciate that larger numbers of firms working with asbestos in a more minor way, might have workers with claims . . .' Ruddick came to a drifting halt, but it was a couple of seconds before Leo could capitalize on his inadequate testimony.

'A fatal misapprehension, Mr Ruddick.' But the momentum was already lost. Leo looked down again at the papers and paused for several long seconds. 'So, let us think about this date, the beginning of March 1982 . . .'

An hour later the court adjourned. Camilla saw that the woman who had caused Leo to lose his concentration was still sitting in her chair, eyes fixed on Leo as he and the other lawyers packed away their papers.

'Who is she?' asked Camilla in an undertone.

Leo gave a grimace. 'She's a woman with some kind of fixation on me. She bombards me with letters and e-mails. We know one another socially, and on a couple of occasions she's been physically aggressive. A while ago she came to my house in the country. I had Oliver for the weekend –' He stopped. It wouldn't do for any mention to be made of Sarah. He certainly wouldn't make any headway with Camilla at the end of this case if she knew he was regularly bedding Sarah. She wasn't the type of girl to accept an explanation that one was only doing it to keep one's hand in, so to speak. 'Anyway, to cut a long story short, I had to call the police, and they had a little warning word with her. She knows now that if she comes near me again I'll have her up for assault, or at any rate take out an injunction against her. But in the meantime –' Leo sighed and glanced across to see if Melissa had left yet, '– there's not much I can do about her.'

Camilla and Leo finished packing away their belongings and left the courtroom together. Melissa still sat in her chair in the almost empty room, following Leo with her eyes, smiling. He ignored her. They and a few others took the lift down to the lobby, where Leo paused to speak to Fred Fenton and Rachel. As they stood there, Melissa emerged from the following lift. From her bag she produced a camera, spoke Leo's name, causing him to turn his head, and took two photographs in quick succession. She put the camera back in her bag, smiled at the speechless group, and left the building.

'Who on earth was that?' asked Rachel.

'Some journalist, probably,' replied Leo, shooting Camilla a glance. He certainly didn't want Rachel to know he was being stalked by some obsessed woman, and especially not that the scope of her harassment had recently come to include Oliver. His access to Oliver was fragile enough, resting solely on Rachel's goodwill, and everything could quickly change if Rachel had any reason to fear for Oliver's safety.

As they walked back to chambers, Camilla brooded on the matter of the woman so obsessed with Leo. Things like that didn't come out of the blue. What had he done to the woman – or with her – that had left her stranded with a mounting obsession? She knew that Leo had his dark sides, had caught little shreds of rumour concerning his sexuality, his past, his treatment of his ex-wife. She had chosen to ignore these. They were alien to her infatuation, which she wanted to preserve unsullied, romantically intact. But here was evidence that she knew nothing about him, really, or the way he treated people. Reason told her that the feelings she had for Leo were entirely misguided, possibly even dangerous. She had let herself think he could care for her in some way, when in fact he probably just saw her as another unconquered and convenient possibility. He had only taken her out to dinner that night to amuse himself, because he had nothing better to do. It had been the same with that kiss. It must be easy to find someone like her amusing. But the damage was done. Just by turning to look at her with his blue eyes, as he did now, he reduced all her careful rationalization of his character to a mere nothing.

'What are you thinking about?'

'That woman,' replied Camilla.

'Forget her. She's a complete and utter bitch,' said Leo. He scanned the traffic as they prepared to cross the road. 'I wish I'd never met her.'

Camilla wondered how many people Leo had said that about, and whether she might be added to the list at some time in the future.

11

Sarah had sulked for an entire week, hoping that Leo would notice and apologize. After all, he'd had no business blaming her for what had happened that Sunday. But Leo was far too preoccupied with the Lloyd's litigation to pay her any attention. Besides, since David had returned from his second and final South American trip three weeks ago, and had reclaimed Sarah as his pupil, she was no longer involved in the Lloyd's case and scarcely saw Leo in chambers. She realized, with some dissatisfaction, that it had been she who had initiated and established the cosy little routine of supper and sex two or three times a week, and unless she took the initiative and made the first overture, which was not something she relished doing, she would have to wait for him to reinstate things.

Leo knew he had been unreasonable in suggesting that Sarah had been in any way to blame for Melissa's visit that Sunday, but he rather welcomed the break in the pattern of their relationship, brought about by her flouncing back to London. He decided to let Sarah cool her heels for a bit, while he would enter a temporary and cleansing state of chastity, until the case was finished.

Melissa continued to haunt him, through letters, and by occasional appearances in the courtroom. She didn't repeat her trick with the camera, and Leo was just learning to try to ignore her once more when Rachel rang him one morning in chambers, an hour before he was due in court.

'Leo, do you happen to know Melissa Angelicos, the television presenter? Because she sent some presents to Oliver on Saturday. A whole train set, a load of books . . . I've never met her in my life, and neither has Oliver – so far as I know. Do you know what's going on? It's not even his birthday yet.'

Leo took a deep breath. Not only had Melissa been devious enough to find out the address of his house in the country, she had obviously gone to some lengths to find out where Rachel and Oliver lived. This was becoming intolerable, and more worrying than ever. As long as Melissa targeted him alone, Leo felt he could just about handle it, but when she started spreading her net wider to include his family . . .

'She's one of the trustees of Chay Cross's museum. That's how I know her.' He paused, wondering how best to explain the situation without unduly alarming Rachel. Given Rachel's nature, that was probably impossible. 'She's become something of a pest recently. She writes me letters, sends me presents. All very harmless stuff, but annoying.' Even as he tried to downplay it, he knew it wouldn't work.

'What on earth has that to do with Oliver? Why is she sending him things?'

'I don't know. Perhaps –'

'More to the point, how on earth did she find out where we live? You didn't tell her, did you?'

'Of course not. The trouble is, she's developed something of an obsession about me. I spoke to Julius about it, when it began to get out of hand, and he said that people like that are often very resourceful. They become fixated on someone, and they find out as much as they can about them.'

'Oh, that's just great. Are you telling me some unbalanced woman is snooping around our lives, simply because she's got a crush on you? Wonderful. What if it doesn't just stop at presents, Leo? What if she's really deranged, and tries to harm him?'

'Rachel, I don't think it will come to that. She knows better than that. The warning the police gave her two weekends ago –'

'What warning?' cut in Rachel, her voice rising. 'Two weekends ago Oliver was with you at Stanton!'

If he had made such a slip in forensic circumstances, Leo would have been appalled. He could hardly believe he had done it now. His mind floundered, seeking a means of redressing the error.

'Are you telling me this woman was at Stanton, when Oliver was there? I don't believe this.'

'There's nothing to get alarmed about. I told you, she's perfectly harmless. She just called to see me –'

'I see – a harmless visit ended up with the police coming round and giving her a warning. Leo, how can you keep this kind of thing from me? If some crackpot with an obsession about you is trying to get at my child, don't you think I have a right to know?' Rachel's voice now had the hysterical edge which Leo knew well.

'It was nothing. Don't get so alarmed. Don't you think I would tell you, if I thought she presented any danger to Oliver?'

'I don't know, Leo. With you, I never know.' There was a long pause. 'I'm not sure I want Oliver staying with you at the weekends while this kind of thing is going on.'

'Oh, come off it. She may have sent him some presents, but that's harmless enough –'

'Don't try to play this down! What else is she going to do? How long is it going to go on for? I don't want this kind of intrusion in our lives, Leo. Until you sort out your problem with this creature, Oliver's not staying with you. And make sure she doesn't send anything to our house again.'

The phone went down. Leo held the receiver for a few seconds, then replaced it, and buried his face in his hands. If he could find out a way of taking out a contract on this Angelicos woman, he would cheerfully do it. He knew Rachel meant what she said. The prospect of not seeing Oliver for weeks was appalling. It was up to him to do something. But what?

Mid-May brought an unexpected upturn in the weather, and conditions in the low ceilinged courtroom at Chich ester Rents became stifling. Mr Justice Olby allowed counsel to dispense with their wigs and had fans installed around the courtroom. These, however, whirred so noisily that, even with the microphones, witnesses had trouble making themselves heard at the back of the courtroom and in the press gallery.

In these circumstances, the proceedings seemed more tedious than ever. Junior counsel on both sides had opened a book on how long Grimley's closing submissions would take, to the closest hour, but it was still some weeks until that event. Even standard diversions, such as Paul Rollason betting Leo that he couldn't introduce the word 'armadillo' into his cross-examination, failed to enliven things much, though Leo unintentionally created his own brief diversion, during his cross-examination of a former underwriter.

'Now, Mr Grace, in 1982 you remained the active underwriter *de jure*, but it was Mr Knightley who undertook the responsibilities *de facto*. Am I correct?' Leo asked.

But before the witness could reply, Mr Justice Olby intervened, addressing Leo with an arch smile. 'Mr Davies, I'm sure you must be aware of the Lord Chancellor's edict, not so long ago, against the use of legal Latin in our proceedings. I cannot say I favour his views, but none the less, *pacta sunt servanda*, eh?'

Leo paused for the briefest of moments before replying, 'My Lord, I assumed *in limine* that my witness, Mr Grace, and my learned colleagues, were all far from being members of the *profanum vulgus*, and would readily understand the references.'

Paul Rollason rose gracefully to his feet. 'My Lord, *de minimis non curat lex*. We do not trouble ourselves about small matters either. We are *in omnia paratus*.'

Much delighted by these sallies, Mr Justice Olby riposted, 'Indeed, Mr Rollason, indeed. It is, after all, *lex non scripta*, and one might well ask – *quo iure*?'

Mr Rollason nodded gravely. 'Quite, my Lord. I am sure Mr Davies had no intention of creating a *scandalum magnatum.'*

'Far from it,' said Leo with a smile. 'However, I apologize to the court for the lapse. *Tempora mutantur, nos et mutamur in illis.'*

'As usual, Mr Davies, *rem acu tetigisti,'* concluded Mr Justice Olby, who, having enjoyed this little interlude thoroughly, intended to have the last word. *'Cadit quaestio.* Please do continue with your cross-examination.'

Later, when the court had risen for the day, Camilla asked, 'What was that all about, with the Latin?'

'Old Olby loves his Latin. Used to use it whenever he could, before that oaf Derry Irvine came down on it. I suppose it was rather malicious, really – Olby's way of sorting out the educated from the uneducated. Paul Rollason and I know it of old. It was just a little game.'

'But how did you know all that? I couldn't understand half of it.'

'Ah,' said Leo, 'therein lies the value of good grammar-school education, you see.'

Just for a moment, as he smiled at her over the tops of his half-moon spectacles, he seemed not Leo, but someone impossibly removed from her in age and experience. Leo, as he regarded her, had thoughts roughly along the same lines. The idea made him feel sad and middle-aged. Yet he caught, too, the connective expression in her eyes, and was moved by it. She was, he thought, not like other girls of her age. He looked away.

'Come on, let's get back to chambers and prepare for

Sawbridge tomorrow.' Sir Arnold Sawbridge was ex-chairman of Lloyd's, and probably the most important witness Leo would cross-examine in the proceedings.

They worked until long after everyone else had left chambers, Leo on one side of his desk, Camilla on the other.

'Let's have a glass of wine,' said Leo, some time after eight. He stood up, stretching the stiffness from his legs, fetched a bottle from the case by the door, and poured out two glasses.

'I'm going to miss you when this case is finished,' he remarked. 'We're a good team – all things considered.'

'And what might those things be?'

'Well . . .' Leo pushed back his chair and put his feet up comfortably on his desk. 'There's the age difference. You're by far the youngest junior I've ever used. Mind you, you're a sight better than many people twice your age. And a lot prettier. Certainly having you around has made this case less of a chore than it might have been.'

'Thank you,' said Camilla. 'That's a nice thing to say. You know, when I'm with you, it doesn't feel like you're twenty-five years older than I am.'

Leo put his head back and roared with laughter. 'What a way with words you have.' He poured her some more wine.

Camilla drank it, summoning up her courage to say the thing she wanted to. It was probably entirely mad. She didn't care. She let the glow of the wine spread through her.

'I want to say something,' she said, after a brief silence.

'This sounds very serious.'

'Not really. Well, that depends . . .' She stared at her wine glass. 'Do you remember when you came to my room and apologized to me?'

'Mmm. For making an unwelcome pass at you.'

'You said that your conduct would be entirely professional for the duration of the case.'

'Hasn't it been?'

'Yes. That's just it. I wish this case was over. Oh, Leo, I wish it was.' There was a pause as she held his gaze. 'I want to know what happens, you see.'

'What happens?'

'When you start behaving unprofessionally.'

Leo stared at her. He had no idea all this had been going on in her mind. 'If you want to, you can always find out,' he replied slowly.

'Can I?' Camilla could feel her pulse beating hard. Just a glass or two of wine, and she had precipitated this.

'Come here.' He waited, watching, as she rose from her chair and came round to him. He got to his feet, and she came into his arms. He kissed her at some length, with all the pent-up desire of several weeks, then said, 'Look, I have no idea what you expect from me. I simply want you. Every day spent sitting next to you in that bloody courtroom makes me want you more. That's all I can tell you.'

'That's enough,' replied Camilla, and put her mouth to his again. 'Will you take me home?' she whispered at last. Her legs felt a little shaky.

'No,' said Leo softly. 'I have no intention of letting

you go. Not now. I'm going to take you back to my flat and make love to you.'

'That's what I meant.'

As they entered Leo's flat, he went ahead, switching on lights. Camilla looked around, taking in the lush, expensive silence of the place, the pictures and sculptures, the long sofas and fine furniture. Panic rose in her throat. It was as though the place was a metaphor for Leo himself – suave, elegant, expressive of taste and experience. How could she possibly let him take her to bed? She felt gauche and a little lost.

'Don't look so worried,' said Leo, smiling at her as he took off her coat. 'Drink?'

She shook her head, looking like a stricken child.

'What's wrong?'

Camilla forced a smile. 'I just don't think I'm the kind of person you're used to making love to.'

Leo stroked her hair back from her face with both hands, looking into her anxious eyes. 'I'm certainly not used to making love to you – yet. We shall remedy that.' When he drew her against him and kissed her, it was as though he wanted to transmit every fibre of his own urgent desire, to reassure her, and the sense of being so wanted by someone she loved melted away her apprehension.

He took her to his bed and undressed her. She lay watching him, utterly unselfconscious, waiting. When he lay next to her, kissed her, touched her, she closed her eyes against the astonishing delight of it. If she had felt afraid, she knew now that Leo was too expert, too assured, to allow her anything but the purest enjoyment.

Later in the evening, he said, 'I want you to stay, but I'll take you home, if you'd like.'

Camilla shook her head. 'I spend all my time being conscientious about work. No one will miss me in chambers for an hour tomorrow morning, if I go home to have a shower and change. We don't have to be in court till ten.' She snuggled against him. 'I like being here with you. I feel safe.'

Leo stroked her shoulder and gazed at the ceiling. He wished she hadn't said that. Making people safe was not his speciality. Yet, of all the people he knew, apart from Oliver, he felt he would rather not fail her than anyone else.

The next morning, Leo, David and Michael stood in the clerks' room discussing the progress of the annexe. Anthony came in to fetch papers and post from his pigeon hole. He glanced briefly at the others and murmured a greeting, then disappeared abruptly.

'Anthony's looking a bit hollow-eyed lately,' remarked Michael.

'I gather he's playing the social scene rather hectically these days,' said David. 'One girl after another, parties, drinking every evening.'

'I seem to recall you were a bit like that yourself, not too long ago.'

'Ah, that was in my youth,' sighed David, 'my callow

youth. At least I knew when to slow down. Anthony doesn't seem to. He overslept the other morning and missed a case-management conference.'

Leo listened, absorbing this. The thought that Anthony's behaviour might be a reaction to what had passed between them some weeks ago disturbed him. But there was nothing he could do about it. It was something Anthony would have to deal with himself. Leo felt he could hardly be blamed for Anthony's failure to accept the reality of the situation between them.

'Well, anyway,' he said, reverting to the original topic of conversation, 'the completion of the annexe is something we'll all have to discuss at the chambers meeting next Friday. The best we can do for now is to get Henry to chivvy the builders.'

Henry happened to overhear this. 'Mr Davies, I've been on to that lot a million times. Every excuse under the sun. The weather, supply problems, men off sick . . . No use you asking me to chivvy them.'

'I'm sure you do your best, Henry,' sighed Leo.

Passing through the reception area, Leo met Sarah. She shot him a morose look.

'Still sulking?' asked Leo.

'No,' replied Sarah. 'I'm fed up. I didn't think anything could be worse than working on that Lloyd's case, but the arbitration David's got on at the moment is killing me.'

'Looks like you chose the wrong career.'

'Something like that.' She paused, while Leo set down his bundle and robing bag to put on his overcoat, then added quietly, 'I think I've forgiven you sufficiently to come round one evening this week, if you like.'

'Sorry,' said Leo. 'I'm rather busy for the foreseeable future. Pressure of work, you know.' He smiled at her as he picked up his papers. 'Thanks for the offer, though.'

Bastard, thought Sarah, as she watched him go out and down the steps. She'd made a tactical error in going off in a huff that Sunday, even though she'd been quite within her rights to be upset. How on earth was she going to make any headway with him now? She would simply have to lie low for a while and work something out. Leo hadn't suddenly stopped being marriageable. The way she felt right now about a career in the law – or anything else, for that matter – the option was still definitely worth pursuing. She wasn't the kind of person to let one little upset defeat her.

Leo arrived at Chichester Rents at the last minute. Rachel came to speak to him as he was sorting out his papers. 'Leo, she's sent more things to Oliver.'

'Oh, Christ,' muttered Leo.

'Aren't you going to do anything about this? Don't you want to see Oliver?'

'Look, I'm dealing with it. I'm seeing my solicitor this afternoon about taking out an injunction against her. In the meantime, don't throw away anything she sends. Just put it away somewhere. We may need it.' He glanced up as Mr Justice Olby entered the courtroom. 'We can't talk now. I'll see you at lunchtime.'

Camilla, who had been talking to Fred Fenton when Leo came in, overheard the tail end of the exchange and was aware of a flicker of curiosity and jealousy. She sat down next to Leo at the counsel's table, feeling a rush from his mere proximity and from the thought of making love with him the night before. Leo gave her a brief, preoccupied smile, but the absence of expression in his eyes caused her an agony of disappointment. Nothing tender, nothing special. She barely listened as Rollason called Sawbridge and went through the rote of details about his written statement. This morning, before she'd left his flat, Leo had seemed distracted, the atmosphere quite different from the previous evening. As she made her way home to have a quick shower and change, she'd been able to dwell on the details of the night before, and reassure herself with these. Now, she felt beset by new doubts. Was it going to go on like this? What if it wasn't going to go on at all? She was aware of Rollason sitting down and Leo rising to his feet.

'Sir Arnold, if at any time during my cross-examination you feel you need a break, please say so.'

Arnold Sawbridge, an elderly man, not in the best of health, leaned towards the microphone and threw Leo a gruff 'thank you'. It came out rather loudly, and he moved the microphone away a little.

'Please could you explain to me how your statements are constructed? Do they represent your own dictated words?' Leo asked.

'A combination, sir. There are my written words, then parts are dictated and then corrected and confirmed, summarized from what I have said. They end up as my words.'

'Very well. So you accept the fullest responsibility, do you, for what goes in and what stays out?'

Camilla smiled, catching the heightened Welsh inflection as Leo geared himself up for confrontation.

'Yes.'

'A few moments ago you took an oath which included the words "The truth, the whole truth, and nothing but the truth". You have that firmly in mind, Sir Arnold?'

As Sir Arnold again barked 'yes' into the microphone, and settled himself for what was to come, Camilla picked up her pen and endeavoured to concentrate.

When the lunchtime adjournment came, Leo immediately went off to speak to Rachel, without saying a word to Camilla. She picked up the papers she needed and set off back to chambers to get on with routine tasks, telling herself that there was no reason why she should feel so leaden-hearted. It was entirely irrational. Of course he wasn't ignoring her. Unless, of course, he was regretting what had happened.

When court resumed in the afternoon, Leo found Camilla already seated at the table, going over her notes on the morning's proceedings, her face solemn.

'Cheer up,' murmured Leo. 'I'm going to give Sir Arnold a roasting this afternoon about asbestosis. You'll enjoy that. Most of it was your work.'

Camilla gave him a grateful smile, and reflected once more on what a horrible roller-coaster being in love with

Leo might prove to be. With Anthony, everything had been so steady and assured. Leo was utterly different. If every chance slight or cheerful remark was going to have this effect on her, life was going to be hell.

Leo spent the afternoon putting the elderly Sir Arnold through a meticulous grilling, though he was at pains to remain courteous at all times. Camilla looked up when Melissa Angelicos, as she now did on most days, entered the courtroom by the side door, but Leo paid no attention.

When it was approaching four-thirty, Leo said to Mr Justice Olby, 'My Lord, I was going to move from G14 to the next period of Sir Arnold's evidence, which is volume G15, but I wonder in view of the hour whether . . . ?'

'How much longer are you going to be, Mr Davies?'

'My Lord, I am more than halfway through.'

'You will finish tomorrow?'

'I hope so. It's difficult to estimate with a long cross-examination, but I would aim to.'

'It would be useful if it could be completed before the weekend. Very well, we shall continue with Sir Arnold's evidence in the morning. Now, I believe there are certain housekeeping matters which Mr Rollason wishes to raise . . .'

Camilla contemplated the brief walk which she and Leo would shortly take back to chambers. He must do or say something then to settle this awful turmoil in her mind. She had had no idea that anyone could suffer such dreadful uncertainty. Nor did she know what kind of certainty it was she wanted or expected. He'd only slept with her, after all. Maybe he did that with women all the time, and then just discarded them. Why should she be special?

When Rollason's points had been sorted out and everyone was packing up for the day, Leo turned to Camilla. 'You'd better go back to chambers without me. I have some things to attend to. See you in the morning.'

So that was that. Numb in heart and mind, Camilla put her things together and left.

As usual, Melissa stayed seated at the back of the public gallery until most people had left. Leo lingered over his papers. She sat there, smiling fixedly at him. Soon, apart from the court usher rearranging chairs and switching off fans, they were the only two people left. Against every instinct, Leo approached her. He had spent much time thinking about her, and had come to the conclusion that, unless she was truly deranged, which he didn't necessarily believe her to be, she might remain open to something that went a little way beyond reason. He could only try.

'I want to talk to you.'

'I knew you would.' She was still smiling. Her eyes looked wild and soft.

'Come outside.'

They stood together on the deserted landing by the lifts.

'I've let you push this game as far as it will go,' said Leo, his voice low and even. 'I should tell you that I intend to take out an injunction against you, preventing you from writing to me, or contacting me in any way, or coming to my place of work.' Leo paused. Melissa said nothing, merely raised her eyebrows a little. 'I can see that that doesn't impress you much. Perhaps this will. You may think of me as a decent, fairly conventional human being, Melissa. I may move in what you perceive to be upstanding, professional circles, but take it from me, I number amongst my acquaintance some seriously unpleasant people. They will do most things for money. I may decide to introduce them into your life, just as you've introduced yourself into my son's life. I can assure you, they can make themselves much more unwelcome than you could ever hope to.' Melissa stared into his cold, blue eyes, and realized with horrid certainty that he meant what he said. He was that kind of person. She simply knew it, beyond doubt. Leo caught a gratifying flicker of fear as her expression faltered.

'Leo –' She put out a gloved hand, then stopped a little short of his shoulder. 'This is all so silly. There's only one thing I want. Give me that, and I'll leave you alone. I promise.'

This was unexpected. 'What?'

'Love. Just to have you. Make love to me – once, that's all. That's all I want.' Her voice was breathless, beseeching.

Leo stared at her. Every instinct in him recoiled, and yet, for one lunatic instant, he thought, why not? If it was that easy, if she would stop, if that would satisfy her, surely he could bring himself to it. He had prostituted himself in worse ways before, though few knew it. The thought lasted a fraction of a second, before sense took over. Even if he could bring himself to it, even if he were to degrade himself to such blackmail, it would never end there. It would go on, probably worse than before.

'Why should I resort to anything so disgusting?' replied Leo. 'I've already spelt it out for you. I don't like to think of any woman being put in fear, or in the way of physical harm, but if you carry on disrupting my private life, or that of my family, I won't hesitate to do whatever it takes to stop you.' He pressed the lift button. 'The lift will be here in a moment.' He walked past her to the stairs and went down to the lobby and out into the street. To his relief, a cab was passing, and he jumped in, directing it to the offices of his solicitor in Gray's Inn, where he had a five o'clock appointment.

There he spent three-quarters of an hour with Alison, his solicitor, discussing the business of taking an ex parte injunction out against Melissa.

'Seems to me we've plenty of evidence to make out a good case,' said Alison.

'And the scope of the order will include my child and ex-wife?'

Alison nodded. 'Certainly. You know, Leo, you could have sought this injunction weeks ago. Why did you leave it till now?'

'I suppose I hoped it would stop. That she would get tired of it. Besides, there is a sort of business connection – we're co-trustees of a museum, and I had the idea that an injunction would just complicate that position. Since I'm going to resign my trusteeship, that no longer presents a problem. It was when she started trying to make con- tact with my son that I realized I had to do something concrete.' Leo sighed. 'Though I'm well aware that an injunction isn't always the answer.'

'Not when someone's utterly obsessed, no,' agreed Alison. 'Still, we'll lodge the application and take it from there.'

Leo thanked Alison and left her office. On the way out of the building, he heard someone call his name and turned. Coming down the steps behind him, beaming broadly, was one Caspar H. Delaney III, a West Coast lawyer whom Leo had first met at Bar School, and with whom he had kept in regular contact over the years. They had been able to help one another out on more than one occasion with legal problems in their respective jurisdictions.

'Caspar! How are you? Why didn't you tell me you were coming to London?'

Caspar, a tall, beaky Californian with thick dark hair and a diffident manner, replied, 'Last-minute business. Only knew myself last night. Or rather this morning. I'm dog-tired. I just flew in. Had to come straight here for a meeting with Barry Sullivan. You know him?'

'By name. He's a colleague of my solicitor, Alison Fairchild. I've just been to see her on some personal business. Look, how about a drink?'

Caspar shook his head. 'Can't right now. Got another meeting across town, then I got to catch up with some sleep. Tell you what – I'm in town for three weeks or so. How about I give you a call and we get together for drinks and a meal one evening? Maybe in a coupla weeks?'

'Do that. You've got my chambers number.'

They parted. Leo found he was still smiling as he scanned the evening traffic for a taxi. Caspar always had an uplifting effect on him. He would look forward to his phone call. An evening with Caspar was just the thing he needed to take him out of the foggy world of the Names and their dreadful litigation.

After supper, Leo rang Chay, who was still riding high on the critical acclaim which the Shoreditch Museum had received since its opening.

'By the way, I haven't thanked you for introducing me to that chap, Gideon Smallwood,' said Chay. 'He's been very helpful with the business of extra funding for the museum. He seems to think we might even get a bit of Lottery money. Something called the Designation Challenge Fund. Got to meet all kinds of bureaucratic criteria, but Gideon seems to think we can swing it. Of course, Tony Gear's had to resign from the trusteeship of the museum, and we'll have to have a bit of a time lag for the sake of appearances, but I'm optimistic. Anyway, it's something to be discussed at the next trustees' meeting.'

'That's what I wanted to talk about. I'm afraid I'll be resigning from the trust, too.'

'I see . . . well, that's a disappointment. Why?'

Leo's mind hovered over the possibility of fobbing Chay off with some excuse about the museum taking up too much time, given his other commitments, but he knew it wouldn't wash. The fact was, the museum was very little trouble to him. Might as well just give him the truth. 'To be honest, it's to do with personal problems between myself and Melissa Angelicos. She's become something of a thorn in my side. So much so that I'm having to take legal steps. This is strictly between ourselves, you understand. Anyway, the upshot is that I simply can't continue to have any kind of contact with her. So I'm afraid I have to give up being a trustee. I'm sorry to have to do it because I've enjoyed being associated with the museum. I really have.'

'Well, if it's a serious problem, and it sounds like it is, I appreciate your position. That Melissa is an odd woman, isn't she? I believe she's been having a few problems lately. That new arts interview series of hers isn't going to be repeated – mind you, it was a bit of a disaster. And I gather *Open Space* may have breathed its last. I suppose the format had become dated. That leaves her with just the odd bit of journalism to fall back on. I can't see her being given another arts programme at her age. It must be pretty awful suddenly to turn into yesterday's news. But that's television for you.'

'I didn't know any of that,' said Leo. No doubt it had all contributed to the way she'd been behaving. If he wasn't her victim, Leo might even have felt sorry for her. 'Anyway, as I say, I'm sorry to have to give it up, but it can't be helped. Anthony will sort out all the necessary details. I'll still take a very active interest in the museum's progress, though.'

'Good. Things are going from strength to strength. You'll have to drop in and have a look at some of our new acquisitions. They're very exciting.'

'I'll do that,' said Leo. 'Perhaps in a couple of weeks.' He thought of Caspar. One of their mutual interests had always been modern art. 'I have an American friend who's in town on business for a while, and I'd very much like him to see the museum.'

'Let me know when you're coming, and I'll try to be there.'

When the call was ended, Leo sat back in his chair and stretched his arms. He thought suddenly about Camilla, and with a touch of guilt. What with one thing and another, he'd hardly spoken more than a few words to her all day. After last night, it wasn't very good form, he knew. She was very young, after all, and young women, in his experience, could be made to feel very insecure if a new sexual romance wasn't bolstered by copious attention and emotional reassurance. He dwelled for a few minutes on the pleasures of the previous evening, recalling most vividly of all the extraordinary rush of tenderness he had felt making love to her. Perhaps it had been because she was so very young, so vulnerable and uncertain. He had found intense pleasure in making her surrender all her modesty, her sense of inhibition. That had been delightful. Dwelling on the sensuousness of it, Leo's hand moved to the phone. Should he call her? It wasn't too late for her to take a taxi over. His glance strayed to the papers before him and he sighed. No. The final leg of his cross-examination tomorrow of Sir Arnold was too important. Camilla would keep. He switched on the desk lamp and began to work.

Camilla sat on the sofa in her flat, feet tucked up beneath her, watching a repeat of *Friends* and paying hardly any attention. She felt as though some hollow space existed where her heart and stomach should be. She couldn't eat. She couldn't think of anything but the fact that he had virtually ignored her all day. The few words he had spoken to her no longer contained any comfort. They were swallowed up by the obvious and overwhelming fact – Leo had no real feelings for her at all. Like an idiot, she had gone out of her way to make herself available – so what did she expect? He'd had what he wanted, and she was left miserable and humiliated. She hadn't really known, at the start of the day, what she had expected his behaviour to be. Anything but this.

Suddenly the television became a mocking distraction to her misery. She reached for the remote and switched it off. Then she picked up a cushion, buried her face in it and wept. She was glad Jane was out, so that she could give vent to her unhappiness. After a while, when she had cried enough, she put the cushion down and turned the television back on. There was still a chance he might phone. It was only nine-twenty. She sat there until quite late, hoping.

12

The next morning in chambers, Camilla waited for Leo
to come to her room, which he usually did, for a brief
discussion of the day ahead. By twenty to ten he still
hadn't appeared, and she picked up her papers and robing
bag and went to the clerks' room.

'Isn't Felicity in yet?' she asked Robert. 'I wanted to
find out what the Listing Officer said about that judicial
review.'

'She won't be in today, nor most of next week. Her
boyfriend's case is being heard at the Old Bailey.'

'Oh, I see.' Poor Felicity. Other people had problems
far worse than hers, she supposed. Picking up her robing
bag, she set off for court.

Leo was already there in court, arranging his papers
and running briskly through the points he intended to
put to Sir Arnold that day. He glanced up and smiled at
Camilla, but before he could say anything to her, Fred
Fenton came over with Lady Henrietta to badger him
about tactics.

Mr Justice Olby came in, Fred spirited Lady Henrietta
away, and the day's proceedings began. Camilla concen-
trated furiously, allowing herself no pause to think about
herself and Leo. She even tried not to glance up at him,
because he was so painfully wonderful to look at.

When the court adjourned for lunch, Fred, Lady Henrietta and, this time, Sir Stephen Caradog-Browne swooped on Leo and Camilla immediately and commenced a wrangling discussion, which was only halted when Fred proposed a swift meeting at the offices of Nichols & Co to sort things out. Camilla and Leo shared a taxi with Fred; Lady Henrietta and Sir Stephen refused to share a cab, and so went separately with their respective Committee cronies. As the meeting got underway, Camilla reflected that Leo was probably glad he didn't have to be alone with her. There was probably nothing to be said. But how much she had hoped she could have talked to him, just in case.

At the end of the afternoon, when Leo had finished his cross-examination of Sir Arnold, Camilla waited with bated breath to see if someone was going to come and claim Leo's attention or whether, as on the previous day, he would just make some excuse and leave. But neither of these things happened. They packed up their papers, and Leo said, 'Thank God that's over. As it's Friday, I propose we go and have a drink somewhere before we go back to chambers. What do you say?'

'You mean with Fred and the others?'

'Certainly not. Just you and me. I haven't had a chance to talk to you since the other night.'

Camilla's wild sense of thankfulness didn't last long. As they went down in the lift with a handful of other people, it suddenly occurred to her that his words could mean anything. It could be that he'd been thinking things over and wanted to let her down gently. She felt such an agony of nervousness that she could only make monosyllabic replies to Leo's general remarks about the weather and the traffic as they crossed Chancery Lane to the wine bar.

Once there, Leo found them a snug booth and ordered a bottle of wine.

'Congratulations. You did a very good job on Sir Arnold,' said Camilla, as the waitress set down two glasses and opened the bottle. In a way, she thought she would be happier if they simply talked about the case.

'Thanks,' said Leo.

'What do you think the chances are that the Names will win?' she asked. She already had a good idea of Leo's views, but she wanted to keep the conversation general. At least, she thought she did.

Leo swallowed some of his wine. 'At the end of the day, I think Olby will come to the conclusion that Lloyd's were staggeringly incompetent and that the market was extremely badly run, but not that there was any fraud.' He sighed. 'I never like the prospect of losing a case, but this one was pretty hopeless from the outset. Still, I think we're giving them a run for their money. Conor, of course, seems to be in no doubt that we'll win. But that's Conor for you, ever the optimistic Irishman, whereas I am a Welsh pragmatist.' Camilla smiled and sipped her wine, her heart in her mouth. 'However,' went on Leo, 'I have had enough of that bloody case for now. It wasn't what I came here to talk about.'

She glanced at him, her expression gently questioning and a little afraid. Leo was forcibly struck by her defencelessness. I should have called her last night, he thought. I should have said something yesterday, even a quiet word earlier on today. 'Don't look like that,' he said.

'I don't mean to look like anything. Why do you sound so sad?' She felt her fear blossom and grow. If that was pity in his eyes, she thought she would die.

'I'm not sad,' replied Leo quietly. 'I'm very happy. I'm happy I've found you.'

She wondered if the exhilaration which spread through her showed in her face. She felt flooded with it, as though it would spill from her eyes and the corners of her mouth. She had to smile. Not too much. But she had to. 'I wasn't sure what you were thinking. All yesterday, and today. I had the idea you regretted it all.'

Leo put out a hand and touched her cheek. 'Not for one minute. How could you think that? It's been even more difficult for me, being in court next to you, after Wednesday. I thought about you a great deal last night, you know.'

'Why didn't you ring me?'

'I should have. I'm sorry. Work got in the way. But now all we have to look forward to is Rollason's re-examination of Sir Arnold, and the closing submissions, which are Conor's problem. So every evening is at your disposal.'

'This evening?' As soon as she'd spoken, she regretted her impulsiveness. It sounded so eager, so uncool.

He hesitated. 'Not this evening, no. I'm afraid I'm busy – something I arranged some weeks ago.' Only dinner with Gideon, but he could hardly call off at the last moment. She nodded, her face stiff, and took a sip of her wine. 'But if you're not busy tomorrow night, I'd like to see you. In fact, I must.'

It didn't even occur to her to prevaricate, to try to make herself more desirable by being unattainable for a few days, as Sarah might have done. She simply smiled and nodded.

'Good,' said Leo. 'What would you like to do?'

'I don't mind. Anything. Whatever you like.'

'Right. Let me think about it. I'll pick you up around eight. I think I can remember the way. I made a point of memorizing your address.'

There were some compliments, thought Camilla, that were quite beautiful in their transparency.

When Leo got back to chambers, Michael stopped him on the stairs. 'I had lunch with Maurice Faber yesterday. He and the others are definitely leaving 3 Wessex Street, and there's more than a strong hint that they'd be interested in joining us.'

'Well, I know Maurice Faber isn't everyone's favourite QC, but that's a very strong body of talent he'd be bringing with him. We really need to expand our field of expertise. Mind you, if we're going to do anything about it, we'll have to move fast,' observed Leo. 'We won't be the only chambers interested, and nobody's particularly gentlemanly about these things nowadays.'

'That's why I'm on my way to speak to Roderick about it now.'

*

When he got home early that evening, Leo ran himself a bath, poured a drink, and rang Rachel.

'I saw my solicitor yesterday. You weren't in court today, so I couldn't tell you. I've taken out an injunction against Melissa Angelicos. I should have it by next week.'

'I see. Well, that's a start.'

'What do you mean, a start? Perhaps now you'll let me see my son. I thought I might take him out on Sunday.'

'I'm afraid not. Apart from anything else, we're going to Charles's sister's for lunch that day.'

'What does "apart from anything else" mean?'

'It means, Leo, that I won't be happy until you can demonstrate that this injunction is going to have some effect, that she intends to stop pestering us. Charles got a letter from her this morning. Eight pages of lunatic drivel.'

'Well, Charles is welcome to her.'

'That's not funny. You started this –'

'*I* started this?'

'She's your friend, acquaintance, whatever you want to call it. Until this nonsense ceases, I don't want Oliver to come to you.'

'Then at least let me come to see him – to visit, not to take him away.'

Rachel hesitated. 'Not this Sunday. I told you – we're going to be out.'

'Next weekend?'

He could hear her sigh at the other end. 'I suppose so. I'll talk to you about it next week. By the way,' she added, 'well done with Sir Arnold.'

'Thanks. I don't imagine it's going to do much good at the end of the day.'

Why, Leo wondered, as he put the phone down, was she so reluctant to let him visit the boy? The only answer, he presumed, as he put his drink on the side of the bath, undressed and got in, was that she was a flint-hearted bitch. He sighed, leaned back, and closed his eyes. With this problem, too, he would reach a solution.

After she had put the phone down, Rachel sat motionless for a few minutes in her chair. Over the past weeks she had grown accustomed to seeing Leo day after day in court, though his potent effect on her would always remain. What she didn't want was to have him here, for a few hours perhaps, being with Oliver, seeing them together. It would just reinforce the pain she felt at knowing that they – Leo, herself and Oliver – could never be the family she had wanted them to be. Had been, once, for a brief time. And she didn't want any situation in which Charles was marginalized, for she had to sustain the belief that she loved Charles. And she did, she truly did. Only not in the way that she went on loving Leo. And hating him.

Gideon had arranged to meet Leo at nine, and had booked a table for two at Tante Claire. Flawlessly dressed in a Richard James suit and a silk Gucci shirt, his dark, curling hair newly cut, enhancing his faun-like appearance, Gideon was in sparkling form. Leo, mentally fatigued after a week spent on his feet in court, was happy to spend most of the evening listening to Gideon's tales of life in the Ministry for Artistic and Cultural Development, which sounded, by Gideon's account, like something from an Evelyn Waugh novel. He did wonder why Gideon had dressed himself so beautifully, and took such pains to amuse him, to scintillate and win approval. Perhaps it was mere habit. Yet Leo couldn't help thinking something lay behind it, something he couldn't yet identify.

'I hear you've been inflicting a good deal of damage on the other side's witnesses over the past few weeks,' remarked Gideon, as he ordered another bottle of Château Palmer 1983. Whatever losses he and his mother might have suffered on Lloyd's, thought Leo, Gideon certainly believed in living expensively. Still, if Gideon could afford it, he certainly could. 'Mother has been marvelling at your skills, though of course she would have liked to cross-examine the entire bunch of reprobates herself.'

'Really? She was complaining at lunchtime yesterday that I wasn't "going for the jugular", as she put it. Not that it's going to make much difference, I'm afraid.'

'What do you mean?' Gideon gave Leo a searching glance. 'Mother seems quite confident of success. I understand Conor Grimley is as well.' He motioned to the waiter to replenish their glasses. 'I must say I am.'

'Really?' Although he and Gideon had never discussed the litigation in depth, Gideon's words surprised him. He had imagined that Gideon lived on a more pragmatic plane than Lady Henrietta and the other Names, and had never supposed that Gideon entertained sanguine hopes of success.

'Well,' laughed Gideon, 'it seems perfectly self-evident that the entire business was a deliberate conspiracy, a clear case of fraudulent misrepresentation of the asbestosis situation. Just look at the annual accounts!'

'Oh, I have, believe me,' murmured Leo.

This clearly irritated Gideon. 'Don't sound so cynical. After all, you're one of our leading counsel. You must believe we'll win.'

'You seem to have forgotten your legal training, Gideon. I simply do my job, put your case as advantage-ously as I can, do my best to destroy that of the other side. Whether I believe you're right or not is another matter. No – I put that badly. Whether or not Mr Justice Olby thinks you're right is another matter.'

Gideon drank off the remains of his wine. His eyes glittered. 'Are you saying you don't think we'll win?'

Leo was disconcerted by Gideon's abrupt change of mood. He lit one of his small cigars, pausing before speaking. 'You might. Anything is possible. I do like to win the cases I take on.'

'That's what you're fucking well paid for.'

There was a pause. 'My clerk would certainly regard those as apt words to describe my remuneration,' replied Leo coolly. 'But to return to your question about the outcome of the case, you really have to ask yourself why most of the other Names, after the Capstall litigation, settled with Lloyd's, instead of tackling the very risky business of accusing Lloyd's of fraud.'

Gideon's features in repose, and after an immoderate amount of alcohol, were dark and sullen, his eyes a little vicious. 'You backed us.'

'I?' laughed Leo. 'I was instructed on behalf of the Names. I took the case because that is my job, and I thought I could do it well. I hope I have. Your mother and the rest of the Committee have always been utterly convinced of the justice of their case. Their conviction, and yours, is guarantee of nothing.'

'If we don't win this case,' said Gideon, 'the state of my personal finances will be nothing short of disastrous. Do you realize that?'

'I'm sorry to hear it.'

'The average losses,' went on Gideon bitterly, 'may be in the region of half a million. I haven't got half a million.'

'You could have settled for sixty-four thousand,' Leo reminded him. Gideon said nothing, just stared at his wine glass. 'Oh, cheer up, man,' said Leo at last. 'Nobody knows how things will turn out.'

Gideon met Leo's eye, and he gave a thoughtful smile. 'How true. How very true.' With that, he changed the subject and returned, gradually, to his earlier, cheerful mood.

When the time came to pay the bill, Gideon tendered his card for his half. Leo wondered whether Gideon hoped that he, Leo, would insist on paying for both of them, after Gideon's remarks about his potentially parlous financial state. But Leo had no intention of doing so. He had seen Gideon at the gaming tables, and had decided that this young man could dispose of his own money as he saw fit.

They moved on to the Clermont Club for Calvados and espressos, and Leo watched without surprise as Gideon threw away a couple of thousand at the roulette table. After all, anyone who would take on as big a gamble as suing Lloyd's for fraud was bound to think nothing of throwing away money he couldn't afford.

'And now,' said Gideon, drinking back another Calvados, apparently unperturbed by his losses, 'I'm going to take you somewhere I think you'll rather like.' His smile was one of impish debauchery, at once repellent and strangely attractive.

Leo shrugged. 'Whatever you say.' It was only a little after midnight, and he was intrigued to see what novel forms of entertainment Gideon might come up with.

Leo didn't catch the address which Gideon gave the cab driver, but was mildly surprised when they left the lights of Mayfair behind and travelled up through Holland Park and into the seedier reaches of Notting Hill. They stopped in a crescent in front of a large, shabby, Victorian villa.

Gideon led the way up the steps and pressed a bell, then murmured something into the intercom. After a few seconds a buzzer sounded, and Gideon pushed the door open. They were in a small vestibule, beyond which lay a second, glass-panelled door, and when they passed through this they were in a long, dimly lit hallway painted dark red, a velvet chaise longue on one side, a series of framed prints on the wall above, and an ornate, narrow table running the length of the opposite wall. From the staircase ahead there drifted the scent of incense, instantly evocative, to Leo, of student days, and a little sickening. Despite the connection with his youth, the word 'brothel' came to his mind. He glanced at Gideon, who gave him a rakish smile.

'Come and see what pleasures await,' said Gideon, and mounted the stairs ahead. There were several doors on the first landing, some closed, some slightly ajar. Gideon went through the one which lay straight ahead and Leo found himself in a large, opulently furnished room, even more dimly lit than the hallway below, with lamps casting a muted pink glow on the proceedings. Sofas and chairs were positioned about the room, which seemed to be busy with people, although the entire scene had an air of slow-motion about it. There were no women there, only men, mostly of middle age, some elderly, some in lounge suits, some in evening dress, but all more or less formally attired, and among them, or coupled with them, Leo saw boys. As he and Gideon threaded their way through the room, some of the boys smiled at them, and he saw that some wore subtle make-up, so that their features were enchanting, beguiling. Some of them were clad in jeans and singlets, some were stripped to the waist. All of them moved with self-conscious sensuality, like well-muscled girls. Leo could tell instantly that a few of them were high on some drug or other, for the curve of their smiles was senseless, and the light in their eyes luminous and blurry.

There was no sexual activity of any kind. Some of the boys had an arm intertwined with that of an older man, and some were seated on middle-aged laps, but nothing more. Gideon led Leo to a small bar at the back of the room, where he helped himself to Scotch.

'Have a drink,' he said to Leo, 'and take your pick. This part of the evening's on me.'

Leo declined the drink, and turned and surveyed the room. 'Jesus, Gideon,' he muttered, 'most of them are just children.'

Gideon shrugged. 'I thought you liked young men, Leo. Or perhaps my sources aren't as reliable as I thought they were.' He smiled at Leo over his drink, and Leo found himself disliking the expression in those dark eyes very much. What had Gideon found out about him, and how? 'Besides,' went on Gideon, 'soon it'll all be above board, and you can have as many sixteen-year-olds as you want, perfectly legally. Until then –' A boy passed them, one who seemed to know Gideon, and he squirmed and smiled as Gideon lightly smacked him, '– feel free to enjoy yourself. Charlie –' He beckoned the boy back, '– say hello to my friend, Leo.' Charlie took Leo by surprise by reaching up with one hand and kissing him gently, full on the mouth. 'There are rooms down the hallway, and on the floors above,' added Gideon.

Leo let Charlie drift away. He glanced round the room again and suddenly, with a shock that was instant and physical, caught sight of one boy with curling, reddish hair combed back from his face, bending to whisper something in the ear of a fat, eager man in his sixties sitting on a sofa. *Joshua*, he thought. Please don't let it be, he prayed. The boy turned his head slightly to catch the fat man's reply, and to Leo's utter relief and extraordinary disappointment, his profile was nothing like Joshua's, with none of its beauty and strength. It was just the insipid face of a painted child, playing a part. Something in Leo stalled, bringing him to earth.

'I can't stay,' he said abruptly.

'Why, Leo,' said Gideon, 'don't tell me you've suddenly found some scruples? From what I've heard, I didn't think they were part of the package.'

Leo didn't know whether he was more angry with Gideon for his insinuations and presumptions, or with the fact that the man seemed to know parts of his background which he'd hoped were hidden – or with himself, for being helplessly aroused by the sight of some of these youths as they cavorted and simpered with their customers. He looked at the faces of the various middle-aged men, the lechery, cynicism and tired dissolution etched into their features. *By the time he is fifty, each man has the face he deserves.* Orwell was right. If I don't stop, thought Leo, I'll become like them. It was a wild and horrible truth, and it hit home hard.

'I'm leaving. I wish you hadn't brought me here.'

Leo made his way through the room to the door, and as he went quickly down the stairs to the hallway, he thought he could hear the sound of Gideon's laughter, like that of some devil, even though he knew no such sound could carry that far.

The crescent was deserted, and Leo walked back in the direction from which the cab had brought them. He could hear the roar of traffic on the Westway not far off, and knew he would come to a main road and the lights of taxis in a few minutes. As he walked he tried to make sense of his feelings about the villa and its human contents. Why had his reaction been one of such revulsion, when for years he had led his own life of carefully controlled debauchery? Because, he knew, something had happened to him since the birth of Oliver, something slow and inevitable. He could no longer look on the world as it was, or on worlds such as the one he had just visited, and pretend that people could behave just as their wills and appetites directed, and no harm come of it. For whatever he wanted Oliver to be, it was not the kind of person he was, or had been, that much he knew.

He reached a main road, and scanned the cars for a taxi. He thought back to that revelatory moment of fifteen minutes ago, when he had looked at the faces of the men around him and faced certainty. For Oliver's sake, he never wanted to be like that. He thought suddenly of Camilla, and it was like a swift, yet gentle descent into something safe and uncorrupted, something he suspected he did not deserve. When at last a cab drew to a halt, Leo gave him Camilla's address, and got in.

Jane had gone to bed early with a headache, but Camilla was still up, wearing tartan pyjamas and watching a late film with the sound turned low so that it wouldn't disturb Jane. She kept thinking of Leo, touching her happiness to check it was real, telling herself that she should go to bed and get some sleep so she wouldn't look washed out for him tomorrow.

The sound of the doorbell startled her, but the sound of Leo's voice on the intercom startled her even more.

'Of course. Come up,' she said, delighted, yet horrified. She gazed around wildly, wondering if she should tidy up, wishing the place looked a little more elegant. It was decently furnished and cosy enough, but pretty basic compared to Leo's fabulous flat. They didn't even have any drink in the house and – oh God, she was wearing these awful pyjamas! Too late to change. She grabbed a hairbrush and pulled it a few times through her hair, then went to answer the gentle knock at the door.

Leo came in, kissed her briefly, then flopped down on the sofa as though he had been here often before. He didn't even glance at his surroundings, just leaned his head back and closed his eyes. After a moment he opened them and looked at Camilla.

'Thank God you're still up. I was afraid you might have gone to bed.'

She came and sat next to him, and he drew her into the crook of his arm and kissed her forehead. He smelled of brandy and cigars, scents which were to her, at twenty-two, evocative of sophisticated and masculine pleasures.

'Where have you been?' she asked.

'Dining with a friend. That is to say, a man I know. A man I'm beginning to wish I didn't know.'

'It's very late to have dinner.'

'We went on to a couple of places afterwards. One of them wasn't quite my scene.' He looked at Camilla from head to foot and smiled. 'Is that what you always wear to bed?'

'Don't. Don't look at my pyjamas.'

'I have to, if I want to look at you. Which I do.' He marvelled at her expression, at its openness and beauty, and at the young softness of her skin, the shine of her hair. So perfect and familiar. He buried his face in the nape of her neck and drank in the smell of her, unbuttoning her pyjamas, running his hand over her breasts and enjoying the shudder that passed through her. 'I'll tell you what,' murmured Leo. 'Take your pyjamas off now, and tomorrow I'll take you shopping and buy you some wonderful and expensive things to wear to bed.'

'It's a deal,' sighed Camilla, giddy with desire. 'Only not in here, in case we wake up Jane.'

Leo wondered, with an inward sigh, how he came to be back in a world of flatmates and pyjamas. He hoped to God she didn't sleep in a single bed.

Camilla, as she led Leo through to her room and closed the door, wondered what Jane would make of Leo when they met in the morning. And her parents – what about her parents, if they were ever to meet him? But at that moment Leo was slipping her legs out of her pyjama bottoms and laying her down upon the pillows, and her thoughts moved somewhere else entirely.

Gideon did not stay long after Leo's abrupt departure. He left the Notting Hill house and took a cab to a club in Ealing. From there, two hours later, he and a companion took another taxi, this time to a flat not far away, on the fourth floor of a nondescript building, with two bedrooms and views of a sorting office and a dairy yard. No one knew about this flat, not Gideon's friends, nor Lady Henrietta. It amused Gideon to think of it as his weekend retreat.

Leo left the next morning very early, before either Camilla or Jane was awake, and went back to Belgravia to shave and shower. He had slept badly, missing the comfort of his own custom-made bed, and his back was playing up. Moreover, he had no wish to make the acquaintance of Camilla's flatmate over her Saturday-morning cornflakes. He sensed the lack of dignity in a forty-six-year-old man emerging at breakfast in the flat of two twenty-something girls.

He had scribbled a note on a piece of paper and left it lying on Camilla's bedside table, telling her he would call for her at twelve. She would enjoy lunch at San Lorenzo, where Leo was well-known enough to be sure of getting a table, and then he would take her shopping, as promised. He wondered whether women of her age minded having money spent on them, whether it offended their feminist principles. Rachel had never disliked it, he recalled.

When Camilla woke up and found Leo gone, she felt utterly bereft – until she saw the note. Then she spent the rest of the morning in a frenzy of indecision over what to wear. In the end, she opted for her standard weekend wear of jeans and a Gap top, on the basis that Leo had to take her as she was. She was relieved, when he came round, to see that he was similarly casually dressed. Only on Leo, any clothes, old or new, casual or smart, always looked expensive and wonderful.

For Camilla, the day was perfect. They had lunch at San Lorenzo – just another Italian place, as far as Camilla was concerned, so Leo realized he had scored no points there, which was something he rather liked. Then he took her to Harvey Nichols and chose simple, but ridiculously beautiful and very expensive, silk pyjamas for her. Camilla made only a mild protest when Leo insisted on paying for them, her main objection being that they had to be hand-washed. She refused to allow Leo to buy anything else for her, though he wanted to. Dressing women had long been one of his pleasures. It became clear to him, however, as they went around the shop, that she was too young, that he wouldn't have known what to buy for her. She was not, like Rachel, a classically feminine dresser.

'What now?' asked Leo at four o'clock, when they had exhausted the pleasures of the Knightsbridge shops. He was feeling distinctly jaded.

'Let's go to a film,' said Camilla.

At Leo's suggestion they took a cab to the Curzon cinema, where they watched a long and over-produced adaptation of yet another Edith Wharton novel. Or rather, Camilla watched, while Leo slept through most of it. When she asked Leo afterwards why he'd chosen that film, he had to confess the film had had nothing to do with it. 'I happen to know that, of all London cinemas, it has the comfiest seats. I felt like a nap.'

'That's so middle-aged.'

'It is, isn't it? Let's go home and do more middle-aged things.'

While Camilla, at Leo's request, put on her silk pyjamas,

Leo took a bottle of champagne from the stock in the fridge and brought it to bed with two glasses.

'This is like a film,' said Camilla.

Leo handed her a glass of champagne, which she drank, and then poured her another. 'Two glasses – the perfect aphrodisiac,' remarked Leo.

'I don't need one,' replied Camilla. 'Do you like me in my pyjamas?'

'I love you in them, but probably more so out of them . . .' Leo leaned across and kissed her, and for some time all sensible conversation ceased.

'Don't you think you're being a bit unreasonable?' Charles asked Rachel. They were sprawled together on the high-backed sofa in the drawing-room of Charles's house, discussing the sudden intrusion of Melissa Angelicos into their lives. Oliver was fast asleep upstairs.

'In what way?'

'Not allowing Leo to see Oliver. He adores the kid. It must be pretty hard for him.'

'Charles, until I'm sure that this dreadful woman is definitely going to stay away from my son, and stop sending him things, I want him here, where I know he's safe.'

'Well, she knows where Leo lives, obviously, and she knows where *we* live, so I don't see why Oliver's in any greater danger with Leo than he is here. Besides,' pointed out Charles, 'he's taken out an injunction against her.'

'He's gone as far as instructing his solicitor. He hasn't got the injunction yet.'

'Fair enough. But I really think you should let Leo see as much of Oliver as possible in the coming months – let him come here to see him, if necessary.'

'I *am* going to. We've already discussed it. Only this weekend's not convenient, as you know.' Rachel turned to give Charles a quizzical stare. 'What d'you mean – in the coming months? I don't get it.'

'The thing is – I wasn't going to tell you till it was all in the bag –' Charles huffed and puffed for a moment, brooding on whether to get himself a drink, how best to put it.

'*What*? Tell me what?' Charles really could be incredibly exasperating at times.

'That –' said Charles, bringing the words out slowly, one by one, '– I have been asked to go to the States to make a series of documentaries.' Rachel said nothing. 'As of September. The documentaries may be some time in the making. They're to be about the relationship between Britain and America down the centuries –'

'Don't bother with all that at the moment,' interrupted Rachel. 'How long will it take?'

'A year. Maybe eighteen months. Maybe more. I have to move out there to get it done. I can't go on flying backwards and forwards the way I have on this recent project. I want you and Oliver to move out there with me while I'm working.'

'But . . . Charles, there's my job . . . I'm a partner. What about my clients, my cases? I can't just suddenly go off and live in the United States.'

'There are always jobs. You're not tied to Nichols

for life. You're a good lawyer. You'll get work anywhere.'

'Not in the States I won't! I'm not qualified to practise there. And even if there was work I could do there, I'd have to find it first, and then go through all the rigmarole of getting a permit – it would all take a very long time.'

'Then don't work. Simply take a year or two out, and come and enjoy yourself in California.'

'Charles, it's not that simple . . . I like my work. I'm not good at doing nothing, especially in a place where I don't know anyone, or anything . . . Anyway, what about Leo?'

'That was why I said you should let him see as much of Oliver as possible until September, before we go to California. After that, he can come regularly and visit him. He's got enough money to do that.'

It wasn't that straightforward for Rachel. Although she was divorced from Leo, his presence in her life was necessary to her. To know that they moved in the same world, that work would occasionally bring them into contact, as well as those times when he came to pick up or drop off Oliver, was vital to her. She could tell Charles none of this.

'It seems so unfair. He's used to seeing Oliver every other week. It wouldn't be that easy for Leo to fly backwards and forwards to visit him in the States. You know yourself how tiring and time-consuming it is.'

'Rachel, you're the one who's preventing Leo from having Oliver at the moment, and suddenly you're telling me how vital it is that he sees him regularly.' Realizing that the conversation was in danger of becoming antagonistic,

Charles put his arms around Rachel and drew her against him. 'It'll work out fine, you know. And it's not as though it's for ever. Just look on it as a long holiday. When you come back here, you'll be able to find a partnership with some other firm, if not with Nichols. Anyway, you've always complained about what a bastion of chauvinism the place is. Maybe you need a change. Please say you'll come with me. It'll be bloody lonely without both of you.'

'What about permits? That all gets complicated, since I would only be going there as a visitor, not to work, and as I'm not a dependant –'

'Stop being such a lawyer about everything!' He kissed her forehead, then her nose, and looked into her eyes. 'Why don't you solve the problem by becoming a dependant, in that case? If we got married, there wouldn't be any problem.' Rachel said nothing, but her face was troubled. 'I know we've talked about it before, and you've always said it was too soon after Leo, but you have to get over that eventually.'

Rachel gave a sad, small smile. What Charles didn't realize was that, for her, there was no getting over Leo. She didn't think she would ever be able to marry anyone else, since she would never love anyone as she had when she married Leo, when she was carrying his child. Not even Charles came close. She did love him, but not enough. She wasn't even sure, at that moment, whether it was enough to go with him to the States.

'Let me think about it, Charles. Let me think about all of it.'

13

'Why is Leo always late for every chambers meeting?' murmured Michael, to no one in particular, as the tenants of 5 Caper Court assembled around the long, polished oval table in the room of the head of chambers, Roderick Hayter.

'I saw him talking to Felicity downstairs,' said David. 'Apparently, her boyfriend got sent down for manslaughter at the Old Bailey last week. Leo's always the one she goes to in times of distress.'

'Well, I hope she's not going to cry on his shoulder for long,' remarked Jeremy Vane, glancing at his watch. 'I'm going to the theatre this evening.' After Roderick, Jeremy was the most senior QC at 5 Caper Court, a blustering and self-important man, not a favourite with the junior tenants. He and Leo were often at loggerheads, largely because Jeremy disliked Leo's flippant wit and mistrusted his charm, particularly in court.

'What a very caring person you are, Jeremy,' said William, lounging back in his chair and crossing his legs.

Camilla wasn't listening to this exchange. She was covertly eyeing Anthony, who was leaning forward on the table on one elbow, doodling on the notebook in front of him. He looked awful – pale, with shadows under his eyes, and a grim, miserable expression. Very different from the boy he had been last year. She had imagined she had no feelings for him, after the way he had behaved, but as she looked at him now, she felt anxious and sad. You couldn't love someone for several months and then not care about their well-being. It was silly, thought Camilla, that they barely spoke to one another. Their love affair was well in the past now, so surely they should make some effort to get on in chambers. Or was it just being happily in love with Leo which made her feel so generous in spirit? She had no idea, but she hated to see anyone look so wretched.

At that moment, Leo came in and closed the door.

'Sorry to keep you all,' he said as he sat down. 'Felicity has a few problems at the moment.'

'Right, to business,' said Roderick.

For a while they discussed the delays to the annexe, and then Roderick brought up the matter of new tenants.

'Now,' he said, 'most of you will already have heard about the split in Maurice Faber's chambers. There's been a clash of personalities, and the upshot is that Faber, Ann Halliday, Roger Fry and Marcus Jacobs are all leaving. I've already spoken to a number of you about the possibility of them coming to 5 Caper Court, and the general consensus seems to be that while the juniors are all excellent people, Maurice Faber is perceived as something of a problem.'

'The man's a complete bastard, if you'll forgive me for saying so,' said Jeremy.

'We all have to work with the occasional bastard,' murmured William.

'He is notoriously arrogant,' observed David.

'And very unpleasant to juniors,' added Stephen.

'The thing is,' said Leo, 'we have here the possibility of taking on some very good people. We're in the process of expanding – Halliday and Fry bring in expertise in aviation, Jacobs in reinsurance, and whatever anyone may think about him personally, Faber himself is extremely good. Let's not demonize the man. He can be difficult, but I don't think he's likely to upset the chambers' dynamics. The point is, we need the talent, and that, for me, far outweighs any personal shortcomings Maurice Faber may have.'

'I wholeheartedly endorse that view,' said Michael.

Camilla, Anthony, Stephen and all the rest of the tenants murmured and nodded in agreement.

'I think Leo's right,' said Roderick. Jeremy said nothing, but glowered and sniffed. 'And I think it will help us to take on weight at a time when we need it most. We have expanded from ten to eighteen in the last two years, and with the new annexe we can increase our numbers to keep pace with other chambers.'

'In which case,' said David, 'we'll have to take on another clerk. Henry's been making noises for some time now.'

'Fine,' said Roderick. 'We can leave it to Henry to find a suitable candidate.'

When the remaining items of chambers business had been dealt with, the meeting broke up a little after six-thirty. It was as everyone was getting up to leave that Anthony caught the glance which Leo gave Camilla. It was slight, smiling, filled with expressiveness and directed solely at her. Anthony knew that smile of old, recognized the intimacy in the brief flash of those blue eyes. There was something going on between them. The certainty hit him with shock and panic. How could Leo do it? Since the night he had taken him to his bed, Leo had shown Anthony not an ounce of kindness or compassion. He had casually seduced him, had taken all the affection and trust and anxious love which Anthony had built up, and, after three weeks of torment for Anthony, had simply blown it all away with a few accomplished and cruel words. And now he had moved on to his next piece of prey.

They filed out of Roderick's room and Anthony watched carefully for any further signs of intimacy between Leo and Camilla. There were none. Each went off to their respective rooms. Anthony went slowly back to his own. He went to the window, staring down into Caper Court at the builders moving to and fro, seeing the summer light breaking through the clouds and suddenly illuminating the fresh young leaves of the trees in the courtyard. For the last ten weeks he had done nothing but try to drown his misery and confusion. Work helped, but the succession of girls whom he had taken to bed, hardly caring whether he liked them or not, had merely served to drag his spirits and his self-esteem lower and lower. He didn't seem to care about anyone, except Leo, and most of the time he hated him. There had been times when he had remembered the jaded way in which Leo had offered himself — *I'm always there if you want me*; words which should have meant everything, but, in fact, in Leo's terms, meant nothing beyond the most casual availability – and had been tempted to abandon every ounce of pride and simply go to him. Any contact was better than nothing. But he couldn't bring himself to that.

So now it was Camilla's turn. He watched the pattern of light through the leaves shifting on the flagstones, remembering himself and Camilla. He had thought he had loved her. Logic told him that he couldn't have, if he had been able to cheat on her so easily with Sarah, but Anthony knew that wasn't true. Sarah had simply been there, when Camilla wasn't. It didn't make the fact that he had loved Camilla any less true, just called into question the weakness of his own morals. Well, he was taking lessons from Leo there . . . He wondered what Leo would do to Camilla, how long it would be before she became another victim. The world must be littered with them, people whom Leo had picked up and discarded. He didn't really want to see Camilla added to the heap, but it was nothing to do with him. He couldn't interfere.

There was a knock at his door and Simon looked in. 'Are you coming?'

'Coming where?'

'The George. William's pre-nuptial booze-up, remember?' William had let it be known in chambers the previous week that he and his girlfriend of long standing were getting married in June, and had impulsively offered to buy everyone a drink after the chambers meeting by way of celebration.

'I don't know.' He didn't really feel in the mood for socializing.

'Oh, come on. Most people are going.'

It occurred to Anthony that Leo might be there. Maybe they would talk, and sort things out. Leo would be kind, and things would be as they had been before, and he wouldn't have to go around nursing this wretched, painful hurt any more. Maybe he had been entirely mistaken about the way Leo had looked when he smiled at Camilla. Maybe there was nothing going on there at all. Maybe . . .

So he went. Leo and Camilla were notably absent. In an attempt to cover up his dejection, Anthony proceeded to drink a good deal at William's expense, which enabled him, in a superficial and rather drunken fashion, to join in the general hilarity and banter.

Sarah was there, but Anthony, as usual, paid her little attention. Sarah, on the other hand, kept a careful eye on Anthony. She had noticed the change in his mood and manner over the past couple of months – he had always been pretty easy to read, not exactly a complex character, for all his brains – and had heard from mutual friends about his womanizing. She had observed, too, with her customary attention to detail, that the usual camaraderie no longer existed between Leo and Anthony. The two went through occasional patches of animosity, she knew that well enough, but never one characterized by such a change of behaviour on Anthony's part. She scented intrigue of some kind, and when Sarah scented intrigue, she liked to get to the bottom of it.

By nine o'clock, most people were heading for home. Anthony, Sarah and a few others hung on for another half-hour, but by the time William and David were leaving, only Sarah and Anthony remained. Anthony had stopped drinking some time earlier, and was now merely maudlin and morose. He decided to have one last drink to cheer himself up. He gave Sarah, who was spinning out a glass of wine, a hostile glance. Why was she still here? She disliked him as much as he disliked her, so why hadn't she left with the others? Sarah pretended to be lost in thought, and Anthony gave her another look. The worst thing about her was, she was so bloody attractive. That baby-blonde hair and innocent smile, like butter wouldn't melt between her legs . . . She had caused more problems for him than he cared to think about.

'So, Anthony,' said Sarah suddenly, 'are you going to buy me one last drink?'

He shrugged, nonplussed. 'If you like. What's that – dry white?'

Sarah nodded, and a few minutes later Anthony returned with the drinks. The pub, whose clientele normally consisted of City office workers and lawyers, was quiet now, with only a handful of people at the bar. Sarah and Anthony sat at their table in relative seclusion.

Partly because he could think of nothing he cared to talk about to Sarah, and partly because he felt in a vicious mood, Anthony found himself saying, 'Not seeing Leo tonight?'

Sarah was momentarily taken aback. Anthony couldn't possibly know that she had been sleeping with Leo on a fairly regular basis until recently – could he? Then she realized what he was getting at. 'Dear me, Anthony, you still haven't forgiven me for being there when you came round to talk to Leo, have you? Sorry to have spoiled whatever cosy little party you had planned.'

Good, thought Anthony. He was in a quarrelsome and spiteful mood, so she could have some of it in return for her drink. 'Frankly, it didn't surprise me in the least to find you there. If it moves, screw it – that's Leo's motto. Not exactly discriminating, is he?'

Sarah's eyes narrowed. 'You may have been fairly good at playing the rampant hetero, Anthony – but only up to a point. I think you want Leo all to yourself, don't you?'

Anthony said nothing for a moment. 'I've been there, Sarah, I've done that, and it's made me realize that Leo doesn't care about anyone. Not you, and not me.'

Sarah could not resist a faint smile; Anthony had just unwittingly laid his whole soul bare. So he and Leo had got it together, had they? Clearly it hadn't led to whatever Anthony had imagined it would. Anthony caught her smile, and misinterpreted it.

'You think you and he have something special, don't you?' he asked mockingly. 'Well, just about every other poor sod he comes across thinks that. They're all wrong. For your information, Camilla appears to be next on the list.'

Sarah gave a little laugh of disbelief. 'I hardly think so. She's not exactly Leo's type – not particularly sophisticated or worldly, our Miss Lawrence.'

'She doesn't have to be. She merely has to be available. I've seen the way they look at one another. Why d'you think neither of them was here this evening?'

An agonizing little current of jealousy jolted Sarah. It

had been obvious to her for some time that Camilla was completely drippy over Leo, but he couldn't seriously be bothered with someone like that, could he? All right, she had improved a lot since Oxford, she really was very pretty, if you liked that kind of dewy-eyed, natural niceness – but talk about boring. Brainy, yes, intellectual and so on, but how could Leo possibly find her interesting? Mind you, knowing Leo, that consideration was probably way down the list. If it was true, though – if that was why he'd given her the brush-off recently . . . Her mind revolted at the dire possibility that he had dropped her for Camilla – Camilla Lawrence, whom she'd regarded as her inferior in just about every way, the archetypal all-work, no-play, dull girl. And just when Sarah had thought she was making headway, that she was actually getting somewhere with making Leo her exclusive property . . . She was suddenly aware that Anthony was getting to his feet.

'I wish I could say I'm sorry if I've upset you. But it wouldn't be true. See you.'

Sarah sat over the remains of her white wine. What Anthony had said might be entirely without foundation. She had, as yet, no way of knowing. No point in letting it make her miserable. She leaned her head on her hand. She couldn't fool herself. Without meaning to, and for all her careful calculation and tactics, she now knew that her feelings for Leo were way beyond her own control. Her reaction to what Anthony had said had shown her that. For several minutes she was lost in her own unhappy thoughts. Then she sat up, as though mentally and physically bracing herself. Camilla, if she existed as an obstacle, was hardly daunting stuff. As Sarah recalled, it had been astonishingly easy to floor her with news of Anthony's infidelity. That was Camilla's weak spot. She was a moral innocent, the kind that never dealt well with harsh reality. A few facts would wipe her out. Anthony had already unwittingly supplied Sarah with some useful ammunition this evening. Camilla might have an almighty crush on dear Leo, but she couldn't have the first clue about his real character. And she wouldn't like it when she found out.

'Eight years, Peter. Just think about it. Eight years.' Felicity lay back in bed and sighed. 'By the time he comes out, he'll be thirty-six.'

Peter said nothing. He was a little tired of all this, had said as much as he wanted to say on the subject of Vince's incarceration. All of it sympathetic, of course, but he privately thought that the legendary Vince sounded like someone who needed locking up. He got out of bed and went to his jacket, hanging on the back of a chair, and took a little packet of white powder from it. Felicity watched as Peter carved the coke into neat little lines on the glass top of the bedside table, and then sniffed them up.

'Sure you don't want some?' he asked.

She shook her head, wishing he wouldn't do this in her flat, so casually and always without asking. He'd never asked if she minded. She and Vince had done a bit of dope in their time, but over the last couple of years she hadn't touched drugs. It somehow didn't seem the thing to be doing, in her job. Anyway, she found it vaguely boring. Peter thought it gave him some kind of edge, but often it just meant he wouldn't shut up, or wanted to go out and do stuff when she would rather stay in, or just go to bed. She didn't like to admit it, but the fact that he took so much coke made him – well, it lessened him in some odd way. Funny to think she'd thought he could do no wrong when she'd first met him. She stretched out a hand and drew it down his back. Still, he was undeniably gorgeous, and even if he seemed to take her a bit for granted these days, that always happened with relationships. It was natural.

He lay next to her, propping himself up on one elbow.

'I mean,' went on Felicity, 'what's he going to do at the end of it all? He's got nothing.'

Peter sighed. 'I thought you said he was going to appeal?'

'Yeah. Mr Davies in chambers has been really helpful. It was him who found Vince a good brief in the first place. And I don't mind helping Vince out with the money. I just don't think it's going to do much good. Mr Davies doesn't think so either.'

'Well, he's off your conscience, anyway. There is that.'

'No, he's not! That's just it – I feel so guilty. Being with you.' She turned to look into his eyes. 'Being so happy.'

'What I mean is, this way it dies a natural death. You don't have to drop any big bombshells.'

'What? Go on visiting him under false pretences for

the next eight years? What about you and me in all that time?'

Peter shrugged and looked away. 'Who knows?'

Felicity hated that, the way his voice and manner went all evasive whenever she mentioned the future. She wished she felt more certain of him, and saw him more often. He never saw her at the weekends, because he played so much sport, and liked to keep Saturday evenings for his friends. He said that was the way he'd always played his social life – girlfriends during the week, mates at weekends – and he wasn't about to change it. It was a situation which really irked Felicity, but since Peter could be quite unpleasant in an argument, she didn't nag him about it. Time would change things.

June drifted on, and Camilla saw as much of Leo as she could. She was oblivious to any idea that being so available might make Leo want her less. She didn't care. She had no time for manoeuvring or subtlety. She simply wanted to be with him.

'It's like not having a flatmate at all,' grumbled Jane. 'You're hardly ever here.' Camilla and Jane were having a rare supper together. Jane, who was a few years older than Camilla, was a criminal barrister with a rag-bag of a practice, chasing from one far-flung court to another in defence of petty thieves, small-time drug dealers and assorted no-hopers. She felt overworked, stressed from having to nag her clerk constantly about fees she was owed, and from the day that Camilla had moved in with her a year before, Jane had felt a growing resentment towards her younger flatmate. Last June, Camilla had been fresh out of pupillage, with hardly any experience, and Jane had been able to feel patronizing and generous towards her. But in those twelve months she had watched as Camilla's practice took off, her earnings far outstripping those of Jane, to the point where Jane almost felt moved to suggest that Camilla should pay more rent. And now, to cap it all, she had a man. Not just any man, not just the kind of common-or-garden hack whom Jane was used to dating, but the very desirable, glamorous, if slightly-on-the-old-side Leo Davies.

What genuinely irked Jane was that for the past two weeks Camilla had rarely been there. Jane's own social life was fairly dull, and she had been quite content when Camilla's had not been much livelier than her own. This new love affair meant that there was no one to moan to in the evenings about her caseload, and she always had to make her own supper and had no one to watch television with.

'Sorry,' murmured Camilla, which she wasn't in the least. She was far too happy to care whether Jane missed her company or not, and she certainly had no intention of feeling guilty about it. Jane was old enough to sort out her own social life.

'Why aren't you seeing him tonight?'

'He's playing cricket.' Camilla pushed her plate away and stretched her arms above her head. She really didn't feel hungry. 'I've never seen him play, but he must be very good. He was a cricket blue at Cambridge and he's a playing member of the MCC . . .' Jane, who had heard quite enough of the wonderful Leo to last her a lifetime, didn't listen to the rest of Camilla's eulogy, which lasted at least two minutes.

She waited until Camilla appeared to have finished and then observed, 'Don't you think he's a bit old for you?'

'You've said that before. I don't notice it. I think we like the same things, we have the same sense of humour, it's . . .' Camilla thought about being made love to by Leo, and went a little pink. 'It's quite amazing.'

'I know all that, but he can't have got to his age without having had loads of relationships. His marriage didn't last more than a few months. What makes you think he's serious about you?'

'I never said he was.'

'Well, the way you go on about him, it sounds as though you think you're both going to live happily ever after.'

'I do not.' Camilla was beginning to feel cross. 'I take it day by day. I don't expect anything.'

'Well, there's a difference between expecting and wanting. I hate to be blunt about it, but men of his age tend to get bored with younger women after a while. I just wouldn't invest too much in this relationship, if I were you.'

'I'm not investing anything. Now, let's leave the subject alone, please.' Camilla picked up their plates and took them to the sink. 'It's your turn to wash up, by the way.'

'I've done nothing but wash up every evening, as you're out all the time.'

Camilla gave a groan of exasperation and left the

kitchen. OK, Jane was jealous, but she didn't have to take every opportunity to remind Camilla that this relationship with Leo was bound to end sooner rather than later. She went to her room and lay on her bed and thought about what Jane had said. All of it was true, all of it was common sense. The way things were at the moment, the special way Leo made her feel, the pleasure he took in lying around just talking to her in the evenings, taking her to see things, enjoying making her laugh, making her want him, reducing her to helpless longing with just a few words and touches . . . all of that was simply because the affair was fresh and new. She'd only been seeing him for a couple of weeks, and the novelty hadn't yet worn off for him. But it would. Jane was right. She needn't think she was anything special. Oh, but the idea of Leo becoming indifferent towards her, his manner growing impatient and withering . . . that chilled her to the core. She had seen and heard that side of him in court with obtuse and exasperating witnesses, and in exchanges with incompetent solicitors. She couldn't bear the thought of him being like that to her, ever. She wanted everything to stay new and wonderful, to be safe and happy. Stupid, stupid . . . of course she was investing too much in this. She couldn't help it. Maybe she should back off a bit, spend less time with him, not make Leo the focus of her emotional life. The trouble was, she didn't know how to begin. She was deeply in love, and totally helpless.

For the first time in a long time, Leo felt that life was beginning to achieve some stability and harmony. The

Lloyd's litigation was running down, he had been granted his injunction against Melissa – who, either because of that or because of the little word Leo had dropped in her ear, appeared to have abandoned her harassment of him for the time being – and Rachel had agreed to let Oliver resume staying with him every other weekend. Added to which, he was very much enjoying possession of Camilla's unstinted affection and delightfully voluptuous young body. He found her gentle and amusing, ardent, and companionable, if occasionally somewhat naïve. For the time being, however, she was the perfect antidote to the world-weariness which he had been experiencing ever since his evening with Gideon two weeks before.

One morning, just before Leo was leaving for court, the phone rang, and the voice of Caspar II. Delaney III came on the line.

'Hey, Leo, I've just about finished all I came to do. How about that dinner we talked about?'

'Absolutely,' said Leo, reaching for his diary and leafing through it. 'When did you have in mind?'

'Well, hell, I'm catching a flight back tomorrow at noon, so that narrows it down a bit. How are you fixed for tonight?'

Leo had planned to spend the evening initiating Camilla into some rather more adventurous sexual practices, having spent a fortnight chipping away at her youthful inhibitions, but that could keep. She was a most obliging and understanding girl. 'No problem,' said Leo. 'In fact, before we have dinner, I'd like to take you on a quick visit to a new museum of modern art which I've been involved in for a year or so. I think it might interest you.'

'Sounds great. Want me to come to you?'

'Why don't you? Say around half-six.'

Leo rang Chay and told him about the projected visit. 'I know it's short notice and out of hours, but I think my friend would very much like to see the museum. He's a patron of a similar project in California, so he may be quite a useful contact.'

Chay promised to be there personally, to take Leo and his American friend on a tour. 'I think you'll like some of our new acquisitions,' Chay told Leo.

Caspar was most impressed by the Shoreditch museum, and wandered admiringly through the galleries. Chay recited to Leo the favourable notices which the gallery had received since its opening. 'Waldemar Januszczak in the *Sunday Times* was the best, in my opinion, because he went to such wonderful lengths to praise us and damn the Tate Modern at the same time. How did he put it? It was so brilliant I actually memorized it . . . "*The sense of purpose, cohesion of the themes and scrupulous dedication to sensible chronology puts to shame the imprecise, inchoate and thoroughly muddled articulation of the mess that is the Tate Modern.*" God bless the man.' He and Leo were making their way through the long rear gallery while Caspar was making a personal, close-up inspection of the massive Beckman installation. 'Come and see what we've done in the small end gallery,' said Chay.

Leo followed him through, and stopped in the doorway. He found himself gazing at a beautifully hung series of paintings by Germano Lehrman, the same pictures which had graced his own walls only a matter of months ago. He paced the room in thoughtful silence, which Chay took to be indicative of his admiration, trying to work out Gideon's role in this. The whole thing gave him a horribly uneasy feeling.

'Aren't they fantastic?' said Chay at last, keen for some sort of response. 'That delicate sense of abandonment, everything pared down to its essence . . .'

Leo nodded, saying nothing for the moment, while Chay wittered on. Eventually he turned and asked, 'How did you come by these?'

'That friend of yours, Gideon Smallwood – he happened to know the owner of the gallery which had recently acquired them. I'd already told him at the museum opening that we were interested in acquiring more, and – well, it was a piece of good fortune that you introduced me to him.'

Leo managed a smile. 'Yes . . . wasn't it? Can I ask how much the museum paid?'

Chay told him, and Leo nodded and glanced round at the pictures once more before they left.

If Chay was disappointed by Leo's lukewarm response to the new acquisitions, he tried not show it. They made their way back to the central hall, where Caspar was inspecting a Richard Long sculpture, and Chay invited them into the office for a drink. While Caspar and Chay chatted, Leo pondered what Gideon had done behind his back. He came to the conclusion that Gideon had worked a very tidy little scam here. Although he personally had made a decent profit on the sale of the Lehrmans through Gideon, it didn't take a genius to work out that Gideon himself was probably better off to the tune of several grand. Leo didn't much care about the money, but he disliked intensely the feeling that Gideon had deceived and manipulated him.

The more he thought about it, the angrier Leo became. While waiting for Caspar to emerge from the cloakroom at the restaurant where they were to dine, Leo rang Gideon's mobile, and left a voice-mail message asking Gideon to call him in chambers in the morning.

The matter of Gideon's sleight of hand, however, was totally eclipsed from Leo's mind by a chance remark of Caspar's over dinner later that evening. They were discussing, in a desultory fashion, the Lloyd's litigation and the die-hard motivation of the present group of Names, some of whom were American and known to Caspar.

'So what was behind this action? Why didn't they just settle like the other Names, instead of adopting this high-risk strategy?' asked Caspar.

Leo shrugged. 'Principle. The utter conviction that they are right. You know yourself how people deeply immersed in litigation can gradually cease to focus objectively. Lloyd's weren't fraudulent, just grossly incompetent, but they won't believe that.'

'And the guys that settled?'

'Their overall losses are marginal compared to what this lot stands to pay out by way of costs if they lose. Which, despite my polished advocacy, I suspect they will.

Anyone with any sense would have settled after the previous action.'

'You acted for that Charles Beecham guy, right? Wasn't he one of the Names?'

'Yes,' replied Leo, surprised at the mention of Charles' name. 'Why do you ask?' So far as Leo was aware, Caspar knew nothing about the significance of Charles Beecham in Leo's personal life. He had never met Rachel, had probably hardly registered the fact of Leo's brief marriage, and Leo, while he might have talked about Oliver to Caspar, had certainly never told him that his ex-wife was living with Beecham.

'I've seen him around our office a few times in the past couple of months. I didn't recognize him, but someone told me who he was. I remembered you mentioned his name a while back, said he was one of the people that got hit hard by Lloyd's. One of my colleagues, Dan Wiseman, is representing him in some deal for a big documentary series for NBC. Said Beecham's moving out to the West Coast, joining all the rest of the ex-pat talent. I guess they like the money and the climate . . .'

Leo hardly heard the rest of what Caspar was saying. He felt cold with shock. If Charles was moving to the States, Rachel must be going as well. And Oliver. How could it be that he had known nothing of this? Had Rachel been meaning to tell him and just not got round to it? He stared blankly at the tablecloth. They couldn't just take Oliver to the other side of the world, away from him. The thought of being unable to see Oliver for weeks, months on end, cut into his heart, acutely and unbearably.

He looked across at Caspar, who had ceased talking and was contentedly finishing his meal.

'Are you quite sure about that? That Beecham's leaving England, I mean.'

'Oh, yeah,' Caspar nodded. 'Dan's just about finalized the deal. He's gonna start work on the documentary series later this year.'

Leo tried to fight down his immediate sense of anger at Rachel. Now was not the time to think about this. It wasn't something he could burden Caspar with. He would just have to carry on normally for the rest of dinner and deal with it later, think the thing through. He had already decided, however, whatever the cost, that his son was not going to be arbitrarily taken away from him in the cause of enhancing Charles Beecham's worldwide celebrity.

After Caspar had gone back to his hotel, Leo went home, poured himself a drink, and sat brooding for a long time on what Caspar had told him. He felt a hollow sense of fear at the prospect of Oliver being taken away from him. He couldn't bear it. The boy was the most important thing in his life. If Rachel took him away, and he was to see him only every few months, what chance would there be of the kind of bond which Leo had always hoped for between them, which he knew was already developing?

He must find a way of preventing this, at any cost. Getting emotional about losing Oliver wasn't going to help. He must view the whole thing from a detached, logical perspective. If, as Caspar had said, the deal for Charles' documentary series was done, then Rachel must have known for some time about the impending move. Yet she had said nothing. Nothing. Perhaps, knowing how he would feel about the whole idea, she had been too afraid to tell him – was that it? No, whatever Rachel's feelings were, she wasn't a coward. She would have faced this from the earliest possible moment, tried to resolve things neatly and tidily. That was her way. She didn't like last-minute disputes and emotional trauma. Why, then, had she said nothing? The only possible answer, Leo reasoned, was that she herself had not yet made up her mind to go.

Leo rarely, if ever, dwelt on the dynamics of his relationship with his ex-wife. To the outward eye everything was amicable enough. They managed to work together, as they had on the Lloyd's case, and the arrangement they had reached regarding Oliver was, under normal circumstances, flexible and friendly. But Leo knew, too, that beneath her apparently platonic demeanour, Rachel still felt deeply about him. Perhaps not always kindly, but that was another matter. When they had married, she had been in love with him, not he with her, and if he had betrayed and hurt her, even if he had given her every reason to detest him, he suspected that it had only served to strengthen her feelings for him. Perhaps it was not a surprising response, in someone as damaged as Rachel.

He recalled how, last year, when his disastrous affair with Joshua had brought him to the edge of a breakdown, he and Rachel had had a critical conversation. She had offered to help, even suggested that she might leave

Charles and come back to him, if he wanted. Leo had turned her down flat, though he had put it in such terms as to suggest that he only did so to protect her from further pain. The poignancy of that recollected conversation, the look in her eyes and the tone of her voice, was something he did not normally care to contemplate. He contemplated it now.

He considered carefully from every angle the decision that Rachel was being asked to make. It was not just a question of going away with Charles, or even of taking Oliver away from his father. For Rachel, he suspected, there was the complex emotional problem of being asked by Charles, of whom she was very fond, but probably no more, to leave someone she deeply loved. And that someone was himself.

The solution to the problem, like the answer to some complicated legal question, came with rapid clarity. If Rachel didn't go, it followed that Oliver didn't go either. It was something which lay within Leo's power to ensure. He could always take the risk that Rachel would decide of her own volition to stay, to let Charles go off to the States alone. On the other hand, he could help to persuade her to make that decision. He lit a cigar and blew out the smoke. If last year he had said to Rachel, yes, leave Charles, she would have. Not that it had been what Leo wanted. He didn't love Rachel, and he certainly didn't want to spend his life with her. But the fact remained, she had been prepared to try again. Where did that leave poor old Charles? Loved, but not in quite the right way. Not enough.

Leo rose from his chair, crossed the room, and poured himself another drink. All he had to do was make her believe that he wanted her to stay, for himself. Simple enough. The hard part came afterwards when, having persuaded Rachel that he wanted to try again, she would have to be made to see that it simply wasn't working out . . . All right, she would be hurt, possibly badly, but hadn't she herself been prepared to take that risk when she offered to come back last year? He was simply taking her up on that offer, albeit a little late. As for her and Charles – well, that would be Rachel's decision. He might tilt the balance, of course, but it was still down to her. The point, above all, was that his son would not be taken away from him. Beyond that, he didn't care much about everyone else's feelings. They were all grown-ups.

It would mean, of course, that everything else in his life would have to be put on hold. Camilla would have to be sidelined, if he were to make this strategy work. Poor kid. He thought about her briefly, and a little sadly. He had no idea what he would do there. In many ways, he didn't want to lose her. In the meantime, though, he had to concentrate on Rachel. The thing would have to be handled with as much delicacy as he could muster.

Melissa had stayed at home for three days on end, going out only to buy groceries and cigarettes. The rest of the time she sat alone, wrapped in a dressing-gown, thinking and smoking. As the hours went by she could almost feel the world retreating. Sometimes, when she switched on the television, it would crowd in on her again, but then when things became silent again, the remoteness returned. She had written Leo several letters, and these lay scattered round the room. She was too afraid of him, and of the injunction, to post them. The buff folder full of clippings and photographs lay on her bed. She returned to it now and again, to look and touch. On the second day, she decided to write their story. She would do it by hand, so that she would have a real manuscript. She covered sheets of paper, starting at the beginning, when they had first met and fallen in love, moving through the rapturous early months of their affair, dwelling on their passion, and on their mutual tenderness. About that she wrote for hours, stopping only when she was too tired, and had to go to bed.

The next day, about to start again, she had been distracted by the phone. The real world pressing in, an editor reminding her of a deadline that afternoon for a piece on Tracey Emin. In a state of irascibility Melissa spent the morning working on that, faxed it through, and then returned to her beloved saga. The remainder of the story about the happy times took her well into the afternoon. Then she stopped. She ate some food, drank some coffee, and blanked out to the television for the rest of the evening. She couldn't face what came next.

But the next morning, on the third day, she had to. The words were hard to write, and she wept as she dug them into the paper. The tale of how his love had turned into indifference, how he had betrayed her – not just with other women, but men. That man, that pretty man he had picked up at the museum opening. Him, and others.

She poured the hatefulness of it on to the paper, sparing nothing in the description of her own misery, and of how her love had turned to hate . . .

What happened next? She lit a cigarette, staring into space for a long moment. Of course. It was obvious what came next. She picked up her pen and began to write again.

14

Thursday morning was sunny and pleasant, and Gideon was in a most agreeable mood as he walked down Whitehall to his office. He had already picked up Leo's voicemail, and could guess which particular topic Leo wanted to discuss with him. At his desk by eight o'clock as always, Gideon went through the post, drank his coffee, studied the papers with lightning thoroughness and, just before going into the inner sanctum to relieve the Minister of his red box at half past nine, rang Leo in chambers.

'Leo, old man – got your message. What did you want to talk about?'

'This isn't something I want to discuss on the phone,' said Leo. Gideon hadn't thought it would be. 'I suggest we talk about it over a drink after work this evening, if that's convenient.'

'That would be delightful,' said Gideon. 'Why don't we meet in the bar at Middle Temple, just like in the old days? We can have a stroll in the rose garden. See you about six.'

In the little intervals for free thought which arose throughout the day between Gideon's various duties, he reflected on how the conversation with Leo this evening might run. These things always had to be carefully handled, and with someone of Leo's intellect and tem-perament, special care was advisable. By the time half past five came, as Gideon set off from Westminster along the Embankment to the Temple, he thought he knew pretty well how he was going to play his hand.

Leo was kept late in chambers by a last-minute phone call, but when he arrived at the bar in Middle Temple at six-twenty there was no sign of Gideon. Leo bought himself a drink and went out of the doors leading to the rose garden. There in the evening sunshine he saw Gideon, taking his ease on one of the benches, a drink in his hand, gazing reflectively round the garden. Leo went down the steps towards him.

Gideon greeted Leo's approach with cheerful nonchalance. 'Good to see you, Leo. How's the case coming along? You know, it's a shame you had to dash off that night. You could have had a *most* enjoyable time.' He lifted his glass. 'I did. Cheers.'

'Gideon,' said Leo, sitting down on the bench next to him. 'I'll come straight to the point. I went to the Shoreditch museum last night. I think you know what I saw there.'

'Hmm. I think I do.'

'I'm not concerned about how much you made out of the deal, Gideon. What bothers me is that you went to some lengths to deceive me – and your gallery-owning friend, come to that.'

'Who's complaining? By my calculations, you must have netted something in the region of thirty-odd thousand on those paintings. You can't begrudge me my modest cut.'

'When you arranged for the purchase of those paintings, did you know just where they would end up?'

'Oh, Leo, if I'd known that . . . well, considering the embarrassment of your position, do you really think I'd have landed you in such a spot knowingly?'

'What d'you mean, the embarrassment of my position?'

Gideon gave a fastidious grimace. 'Well, as things stand, it does rather look as though you've been feathering your own nest. Of course, you and I know it's nothing like that, but anyone unaware of the true circumstances might suppose that you'd used your inside knowledge of the museum's collecting policy to sell on your private works at a profit. As a trustee, you're probably technically in breach of some code of practice or other . . . Well, it strikes *me* as embarrassing.' Gideon finished the remains of his drink, then added, 'I would never *dream* of putting you in that position, naturally.'

'But you have,' replied Leo, digesting this new and disturbing aspect of the matter. With Caspar's bombshell about Charles Beecham, Leo hadn't had a proper opportunity last night to think through the implications of finding paintings from his private collection in Chay's gallery.

'Yes, I have . . . I'm dreadfully sorry.' There was silence for a moment. 'The good thing is, you and I know exactly how this unhappy state of affairs came about, so no one's going to know unless I tell them.' Gideon paused again. 'The *bad* thing is . . . I'm rather strapped for cash at the moment.'

'What?'

'I know, I know, it's my own fault. Too many misspent evenings at Aspinall's. What can I say?'

'Exactly what are you suggesting?' asked Leo incredulously, although he already had a pretty good idea.

Gideon set his drink on the grass and leaned forward, clasping his hands between his knees. 'What am I suggesting, exactly? Let's see. Well, these embarrassing stories do have a tendency to get about – you know, they end up as malicious little titbits in some gossip column or other. Not good for the reputation – perhaps even rather damaging, depending on one's professional standing. I'm suggesting that, in return for a small loan, I'm prepared to ensure that nothing gets out.'

Both men waited as a couple of elderly benchers strolled by, drinks in hand, taking the evening air. Then Leo said, 'Are you actually blackmailing me, Gideon?' He smiled as he asked this, because Gideon's expression was so boyishly guileless, and because the thing seemed so farcical.

'Good heavens, no!' replied Gideon. He sat back on the bench. 'No,' he smiled, 'nothing like that.'

'Because I frankly don't see the need to pay money to prevent publicity about this unfortunate little transaction. Especially not to the likes of you. I should think, if I had to, that I could clear any misunderstanding up and conduct an efficient damage-limitation exercise where my reputation is concerned.'

'No doubt you could – if that was all there was to worry about.' Gideon sighed. He caught Leo's look of bafflement. 'Oh, I hate to bring up something so unpleasant on such a lovely evening. That place we went to after the Clermont Club . . . You remember? As I understand it,' said Gideon, 'someone there took photographs. Don't ask me who. I was merely told about it. Very regrettable. Of course, they only show you kissing the boy. But at the time, it turns out, he was supposedly in the care of the local authority. He's back in care now. Absolutely scandalous. That's the kind of thing I want to protect you from. You know how the Sunday tabloids love that sort of story. *Top QC in romp at boy brothel* . . . People will do anything for money.'

'Won't they just?' breathed Leo.

Gideon picked up his drink, drained his glass, and gave Leo a questioning smile. 'Well?'

Leo, appalled, could find nothing to say. 'Tell you what,' said Gideon, 'you think about it for a couple of weeks. I have to accompany the Minister on a cultural fact-finding mission to Tokyo. I'll be in touch with you when I get back.' He patted Leo on the knee, rose, and left.

Leo sat in the early-evening sunshine, working through the conversation of the last ten minutes. He knew, beyond any shadow of a doubt, that Gideon would not hesitate to expose him in the fullest way possible if Leo did not pay him off. He had the measure of Gideon now, and reckoned he was more than capable of it. If someone had photos of his encounter with the boy at that ghastly place Gideon had taken him to, he knew only too well that Gideon would be prepared to sell them to the highest bidder. How the papers would feast on it, how the story would be spread out over page after page, every corner of his life raked over and exposed, even as far as Rachel and Oliver. He shut his eyes. His life would be ruined, in more ways than one. He thought about all the times when he had feared this kind of thing might happen. He had never dreamed it might happen through the agency of the Principal Private Secretary to Her Majesty's Minister for Artistic and Cultural Development.

That evening, his head aching horribly, Leo lay on the sofa in his drawing-room, the windows flung wide, the tepid summer air hardly moving the curtains. He had meant to see Camilla tonight, but had rung her to say he wasn't feeling well enough. He couldn't see anyone, least of all her. His mind was weary of going over and over his problems. Why, when life had seemed to be turning a corner, had it decided to do these hideous things to him? Within the space of two days he had discovered that not only was his son likely to be taken off to another continent, where he could hardly ever expect to see him, and certainly not to feature in his life, but he was also being blackmailed for something he hadn't even done.

His first instinct, as a lawyer, was to turn Gideon over to the police. But Gideon was the slipperiest, most glib-tongued individual, and at present Leo had no evidence to show that Gideon was blackmailing him. Even if he had, even if he could nail him, Gideon would make sure that everything to Leo's discredit, fabricated or otherwise, came to light. God alone knew what other information about him was in that man's possession. He could see no way round this. What alternative was there but to pay him? Of course, it wouldn't stop there, Gideon would always come back for more. But the man wasn't a fool. He had probably already calculated that if his demands on Leo were modest – or at any rate not extortionate – he could do very nicely out of this on a long-term basis. Leo was wealthy enough to weather it, he supposed. Much depended on how much Gideon was after. Once that was established, he would just have to try to live with it. The idea was galling, but he couldn't see what else he could do.

He got to his feet, stretched, and groaned wearily. He would try to put it from his mind for the present. He had a more pressing problem to address, in the form of his ex-wife. Tomorrow he would speak to her, see how the land lay, and take it from there.

Leo strolled to the window and looked down. Dusk was beginning to fall and the air was growing cooler, thank God. He thought about Camilla in her Clapham flat, wondered what she was doing, whether she was wearing her silk pyjamas. He found himself smiling at the thought of her, that funny thing she did in bed of rolling over on to him, like a puppy, when she had something to ask him. Thoughts came to her so fast, sometimes eccentric notions, sometimes deep questions. She liked to lie for a long time after making love, asking him things. He found it amusing and odd. She always seemed to want to know so much about his childhood. No one else had ever wanted to know him so thoroughly, not Rachel, not Joshua, not anyone. Two nights ago he had talked about his father, something he rarely did, and she had lain patiently against his shoulder, listening, never saying a word. Then when he stopped, she just kissed his face, and held him, and let the space and silence spread out around them. There had been no need for either of them to speak again. They just fell asleep.

He found himself wondering sadly what Camilla might have become to him, if this problem with Rachel and Oliver had not thrust itself upon him with such pressing need. But it wasn't worth thinking about, he decided. Next to Oliver, it simply didn't matter.

Rachel was in court the following morning, going through the previous day's proceedings with Fred, when Leo approached her.

'Are you busy at lunchtime?' he asked.

'No,' she said. 'Why?'

'I just wanted to talk. Catch up on things. Personal things, you know.'

She nodded, and watched him as he made his way back to the table where Camilla was arranging the day's bundles. Although their divorce was several months old, his presence was still familiar and necessary to her. Even long days spent in court listening to hours of cross-examination, the way he stood, the sound of his voice, the movements of his hands and body as he turned, picked up papers, nodded . . . It was like having something brought home to her, time and time again. She tried once more to imagine being on the other side of the world, without the knowledge that she would see him soon – if not that day, then at some case conference, or the next weekend when he came to pick up Oliver. The prospect was barren, almost futile. Maybe that was a good reason to go away, if only for a year or so. Give her time to wean herself from the addictive habit of Leo. For if she didn't, what future was there? Over the last couple of months, time spent with Charles had become more and more guilt-ridden. Perhaps they needed to be together somewhere where there was no Leo, and where she could feel she belonged properly to Charles, without this ghost of her marriage haunting her.

It did not occur to Leo to say anything to Camilla when the court adjourned for lunch; he was already in another sphere, one where Camilla was discounted for the time being. She watched as he and Rachel left together, telling herself that of course they must have things they needed to talk about, but conscious, too, of a smarting disappointment. Leo had suddenly resumed that air of preoccupation of two or three weeks ago, and it was clearly something she was going to have to get used to. His brief phone call of the night before, his absent manner this morning . . . she tried not to read anything special into these, but it was hard, very hard.

Leo had no real notion of what he was going to say to Rachel. He took her to a wine bar a couple of streets away, and ordered sandwiches and mineral water for both of them.

'So,' he said, 'will it be OK for me to have Oliver next weekend?'

Rachel nodded. 'I don't see why not. Assuming the

madwoman doesn't breach the terms of the injunction. It seems to be having some effect, for the time being, at any rate.'

'Yes,' said Leo with a sigh, 'for the time being.'

Rachel was about to ask Leo exactly what had gone on between him and Melissa Angelicos to precipitate her harassment of him, but thought better of it. She had decided to make a deliberate effort not to be antagonistic, even though it seemed to be the only way of provoking Leo to respond to her emotionally. Instead she said, 'Things must have been pretty unpleasant for you over the past couple of months.'

'Surreal, is the way I'd put it. The kind of thing you read about, but never for one moment associate with yourself. Being stalked has a most peculiar . . . tainting effect. I can't think of any other way of describing it. A sense of everything in your life being defiled. Not just yourself, but people you love.'

'Oliver.'

'You and Oliver.' He spoke the words swiftly and naturally, almost as though stating the obvious.

Leo did not so much as glance at her; he knew the effect his words would have. 'So,' he said, changing tack, 'has Charles finished all his business in the States?' This, he thought, if ever, was her clear opportunity to tell him. He waited.

'No, as a matter of fact, he's away again just now. He won't be back until next Wednesday.'

She wasn't going to tell him. She saw no present need. She still hadn't made her mind up. Leo took a sandwich and pushed the plate towards her. She shook her head. Leo knew of old that whenever she was even lightly emotionally stressed, she could not eat. 'Well, look, why don't you bring Oliver down to Stanton a week on Saturday and stay for the day? It gets rather dull, just the two of us. I'm sure he'd like it.'

Rachel hesitated. 'Do you think that's a good idea?'

'Why?' Leo gave her a smile. 'Will it be so hard to spend a day with me?'

She smiled in return, a little sadly. 'No, of course not. I'd like it.'

'Good. Come as early as you can.'

They talked for a while about Oliver, and about matters peripheral to the case, then Leo's mobile phone rang and he spent ten minutes talking while Rachel ate half a sandwich and read the paper. By then it was time to go back to court.

By the end of that Friday afternoon, Leo's recent troubles, combined with a week spent cross-examining auditors and underwriters, had left him exhausted. He was unusually quiet on the way back to chambers.

'Are you feeling better than you did last night?' asked Camilla.

'Oh, so-so.'

'What do you think was wrong with you?'

'Old age. Problems getting me down. I'm sorry I put you off. I wouldn't have been very good company.'

'What about this evening? I could come round and cook some supper for us. My cooking's getting a bit better.'

'I'm driving down to my country place tonight. I intend to spend tomorrow relaxing and thinking about nothing, and on Sunday I'm playing in the village cricket match.' He glanced at her. She was trying so hard to look nonchalant and not disappointed. He found it painful to contemplate how it would be for her when he had to transfer his time and attention to Rachel. Until then, they might as well make each other happy. Come to think of it, he would rather not be on his own this weekend. How could he possibly spend it thinking about nothing? He would welcome a distraction. 'Why don't you come down with me? We can pick up some groceries on the way. I promise you can still cook supper.' They had reached the steps of 5 Caper Court.

'I'd love that,' said Camilla. A summer weekend with Leo at his country house was the most perfect thing she could imagine. Maybe it meant he was getting serious about her.

'Good. You go home and put some things together, and I'll pick you up around seven. It only takes about an hour and a half to get there.'

On the way down to Stanton they stopped in Oxford to buy food, and Camilla browsed in the video-rental section of the supermarket while Leo bought some wine.

Camilla appeared at his side as he was paying. 'Give me something with your address on it,' she said. 'Not your London address. The one down here.'

'I don't think I've got anything . . .' Leo searched in his wallet and drew out a receipt from the village-garage repair shop. 'Here you are. What do you want it for, anyway?'

'So that I can rent a video.'

As they put the groceries in the car, Leo glanced at the video she'd taken out. 'What did you get?'

'*Now Voyager*. It's an old Bette Davis film. I really like it.'

Leo shrugged. 'One way of passing a Friday evening, I suppose.' He hadn't watched a Bette Davis film since the days of Francis, an ex-lover, who'd been an ardent fan.

While supper was cooking, Leo took a long, hot bath and listened to some Mahler. As he was getting dressed afterwards, he glanced out into the garden and saw Camilla walking slowly round the garden. She was singing something under her breath, but he couldn't make it out. He watched her for a few moments. She was happy, he knew, but there was nothing to be done. When this weekend was over, she would have to learn to do without him.

After supper they sprawled together on the high-backed sofa, cushions piled around them, and watched *Now Voyager*, which Leo had never seen. As the film unfolded, he was by turns amused, intrigued but utterly unmoved. Camilla cried at the end, while Leo stroked her bare feet and tried not to laugh.

'What utter tosh,' he said.

'How can you say that? I think it's a wonderful film. I wanted you to see it. I saw it on television with my mother years ago, and we cried buckets.'

'You didn't expect me to cry buckets, did you?' asked Leo.

'No. I don't suppose so.' Camilla looked a little down-cast. 'You're not very romantic, are you?'

'Not a tender bone in my body.'

'Haven't you ever been in love?'

'Hmm. I might have been. I don't think that has much to do with romance. Real love, in my experience, is painful and gut-churning and very unromantic.'

This evening clearly didn't qualify, thought Camilla. Sitting around on sofas watching old movies. Whatever existed between herself and Leo, she thought despondently, it wasn't love. He was too matter-of-fact, he laughed at her too much, though in a nice way, and she had the feeling that, while he might like having her around, he wouldn't much care if she wasn't there.

'What a sweet, serious face,' said Leo. He kissed her affectionately, and got up and went through to the kitchen. Camilla lay on the sofa for a moment or two, then rose and crossed the room to the French windows which led to the garden. She opened them and stepped out into the warm night air. The grass was damp and chilly beneath her bare feet, and she could catch the drifting scent of the roses which grew by the windows, winding upwards through the trellis. Faint moonlight lit the garden, casting deep shadows and etching the tops of trees against the night sky. She walked across the dewy lawn to the dark, twisted shape of a lilac tree and leaned there, wishing that she could live with Leo in this beautiful house, that life could stop here, wishing above all that he felt about her as she did about him. She knew he never would.

Leo saw her from the kitchen window. She looked so

solitary in the moonlight with her thoughts. He left the house and crossed the lawn to where she stood.

She turned at the touch of his hand and in the fragrant dark he held her close, then kissed her. The kiss moved something in him, something that went beyond affection and habit. He began to undress her in the garden, tracing the soft nakedness of her stomach and breasts, marvelling at the pearliness of her skin in the moonlight, the translucence of her eyelids as she closed her eyes to his touch. Looking on her young loveliness in the summer night filled him with something that was both wistful and erotic at the same time. By the time he took her to his bed, Camilla was wordless, lost with longing. Every caress sent further ripples of desire through her body, jolting her with pleasure. For a long and tantalizing time Leo played with her, taking her to an exquisite threshold of need, until he himself could stand it no longer. It was an act of consummation such as he hadn't known before, his lust so mixed with tenderness that when he spoke to her, a rush of loving, agonized words, he had no recollection of having once play-acted in the same way at Sarah's request. He didn't even hear his own voice, so immersed was he in her looks, her sounds, taking her pleasure as his, drawing it out as long as he could. When at last she cried out, it went to his heart, and he buried his face in her shoulder, astonished by what he felt.

The urgency of their lovemaking slowed, she drew her breath in sighs, her body dropping away from his, warm with pleasure. He leaned on his elbows, watching her face, her closed eyes, the soft pulsing of her throat. He dropped a kiss on the flushed skin of her neck, and as she opened her eyes to smile at him, the gladness he felt was blotted out by an imminent sense of loss.

'Where are you going?' she asked, as Leo got up from the bed.

'Stay where you are,' was all he said, as he pulled on his trousers.

He went downstairs and through the French windows, which still stood open to the night air. From the climbing rose bush he broke off a stem, with one open rose and a bud, and took it back upstairs. He laid it on the pillow next to Camilla, who stared at it, touched it, and then laughed.

'I am not entirely without romance,' said Leo, and kissed her forehead. '"Roses for the flush of youth . . ."' He gazed at her for a moment and then said, 'I have to go downstairs and lock up.'

When he had gone, Camilla lay fingering the petals of the rose, and breathing in its scent, utterly happy.

'I can't see you all this week, I'm afraid,' said Leo on Sunday evening, as they drove through the London traffic.

'Why not?'

It tugged at his heart, the way she asked this. She never thought to behave as though she was indifferent, or pretend that she was similarly too busy to see him.

'I have a lot of things to attend to. The case is going to end soon, and I've got to start looking ahead to other work.'

She nodded. It was happening again. Despite the

perfect weekend, the lovemaking, the long conversations, the careless pleasure of two days spent together, here was that note of preoccupation in his voice again, that absent look that didn't include her. She was beginning to learn the pattern. Maybe by the time next weekend came it would be better. And she would still have his company throughout the long days in court. There was that.

Camilla told herself that Leo had enough to do with that week's final closing cross-examinations, and with preparations for the Names' reply submissions. No wonder he needed to spend the evenings working. There was really no perceptible change in his manner towards her – he still talked in the same close way, still passed her the odd jokey little note in court – but she couldn't help feeling as though he had closed some door on her. As the week went on, Jane said nothing, but Camilla was conscious of the significance of her glance when Camilla came home regularly each evening. She began to wish Jane would say something, so that she could have the reassurance of hearing her own voice say that there was nothing wrong, that Leo was merely working hard. As it was, there was an I-told-you-so quality about Jane's silence which only served to fuel Camilla's anxiety. She thought of what Jane had said about how men like Leo quickly grew bored with girls of her age. Maybe that had happened. Maybe work was just an excuse.

As the week drew to its close, she desperately hoped he would want to see her, that he would casually mention at the last minute that there was a film they should see, or ask her if she'd like to spend Saturday evening with him, maybe even the whole weekend. But when the court rose on Friday, Paul Rollason and his junior joined them on the short walk back to chambers, and so there was no opportunity for Leo to do or say anything, even if he had wanted to. She went to her room, and filled the time with work she didn't have to do, simply in the hope that Leo might look in, suggest a drink ... Every time she heard feet on the stairs, her pulse quickened, but it was only the various members of chambers leaving for the weekend, one by one. Eventually, when everything was silent, she put away the papers she had been working on, and locked up the room. She went slowly downstairs past Leo's room. She turned the handle and went in, but the room was empty.

'Looking for Leo?' Sarah's voice startled Camilla.

'Not really,' said Camilla, blushing a little, not exactly pleased to see Sarah.

'I think he went to Daley's with Michael and David. I'm on my way there myself. Want to join me? Oh, listen, I must tell you who I bumped into at a dinner party last weekend. Do you remember that very tall man, Roland, who used to hang around with Gus Guthrie and his friends at Oxford, and who edited that bizarre magazine ... ?'

Camilla went downstairs with Sarah, caught up by her gossip and cheerfulness. Camilla never quite knew where she stood with Sarah, who had done some pretty spiteful things in the past, but who could be very friendly when she chose. They had a shared past, having been to the same Oxford college, and that brought its own special comfort at a moment when Camilla was feeling particularly bereft and in need of company. Besides, there was the possibility that Leo might be in Daley's, and although she wouldn't have cared to go there alone, which would look too much like chasing after him, it was another thing to go in the company of someone else from chambers.

'How's the case coming along?' asked Sarah, as they crossed Fountain Court. 'You know, I'm sorry if I was ever stroppy when you asked me to do things for you. It was just a strange kind of situation.'

'Oh, don't worry about that,' said Camilla, thawed by Sarah's charm. 'It's hard to know how the case is going, really. Leo's cross-examination has been excellent, but some of the witnesses . . .'

Sarah only half-listened as they walked up Essex Street to the wine bar. She frankly couldn't care less about the rotten Lloyd's case, but it helped to get Camilla warmed up, and it also brought in Leo, a subject she intended to explore more fully later on.

When they reached the wine bar at the end of Essex Street, Sarah was quick to notice how Camilla scanned the place hopefully, and how crestfallen she looked when she realized Leo wasn't there. You could read this girl like a book. Which was what she'd been doing all week, taking careful note of the fact that Leo and Camilla hadn't left once together, unlike last week when, on two evenings in succession, and with a gut-churning sense of jealousy, she had seen them drive off together from King's Bench Walk. Well, if Camilla was stupid enough to expect some sort of consistency from Leo, it was about time someone put her straight about him.

'Oh, stay and have a drink, anyway,' said Sarah. Camilla glanced quickly at her. Was it so easy to tell that she had only come in hopes of seeing Leo?

'All right. I'll have a glass of white wine, thanks.'

Sarah bought a bottle, and they sat at a table outside on the pavement and talked. The conversation was entirely steered and manipulated by Sarah, and consisted of ephemeral, cosy gossip designed to create a secure, confiding sort of atmosphere. Camilla wasn't used to drinking more than the occasional glass of wine, and by the time the bottle was two-thirds empty and they had got on to the subject of men, her inhibitions had loosened a good deal, and she was beginning to feel a real womanly kind of bond with Sarah. In fact, thought Camilla, Sarah was much nicer than people supposed. She let Sarah fill her glass again. Sitting here in the dusty summer air, surrounded by other City girls on a Friday evening having similar heart-to-heart talks, made her feel better about everything. The wine made thoughts of Leo less painful. It wasn't anything to worry about. He would call her, and everything would be fine again. How could she doubt him, after the way things had been last weekend?

'Thinking about Leo?' asked Sarah, with a look of girlish sympathy. The surprise of this broke Camilla's train of thought. She felt instantly defensive, but before she could say anything, Sarah added, 'I wouldn't waste your thoughts on him, if I were you. He's as bad as all the rest. Worse, in fact.'

Camilla felt dormant fears come suddenly, horribly to life. This was surely just a glib remark, an all-men-are-bastards throw-away line – wasn't it? 'What do you mean?' she asked. She couldn't help herself. She could have deflected Sarah's remark, said something to turn the conversation away from Leo, but something made her pursue it.

'First of all, tell me – tell me honestly.' Sarah leaned confidingly across the table. 'Have you and Leo been having a bit of a fling recently?'

Without wanting to, Camilla replied, 'Yes.' She waited for a few seconds, then asked, 'Is it that obvious?'

Sarah smiled. 'We've all been there. We all know the signs.'

'What signs?' Camilla could feel her face burning up. She kept asking things she didn't want to hear the answers to. She couldn't help it. Everything which had been warm and summery and wine-filled had gone flinty and unpleasant.

Sarah leaned back and, with the air of someone reciting a well-worn story, said, 'I'll bet it's been three or four weeks of bliss. You feel unutterably special, you have his company and his attention, he's charming and funny, nobody ever made love to you the way he does, the best sex in the world . . . And suddenly it's all gone off the boil, and you feel lost and confused, and you don't understand what he's doing to you.' Camilla said nothing, stared at her glass. 'Am I right? Of course I am. You're just another of Leo's victims, and London is littered with them, male and female.'

'I don't believe that,' said Camilla, believing everything, wanting to get away, but rooted to the spot. She lifted her glass to her lips, but the wine tasted tepid and sour.

'What? Boys as well as girls?' Sarah laughed. Camilla no longer felt any kind of womanly bond with her at all, only a sick sense of mistrust. 'You don't know Leo as well as I do. Nobody does. Do you know, I've actually seen him when he's so overcome by some desirable young man that he can't help himself. Literally. That's how close I've been, darling. And if you don't believe what I say, ask Anthony. He's another one of Leo's cast-offs. You should start a club together.'

'Shut up. I don't believe any –'

'You know yourself how attractive Leo is, how hard to resist,' Sarah went on. 'Are you telling me you've never noticed what a *very* special relationship Leo and Anthony have? Or had, I should say. Leo finally got him into bed a couple of months ago, and then dumped him just like that. It's cracked poor old Anthony to pieces. Not that Leo cares. He just moved on to you.'

Camilla's mind scrabbled for self-possession. Had Sarah brought her here just to drop all this poison in her ear? Probably. It was pathetic how easily she'd let herself believe Sarah wasn't as bad as all that. Of course she was. Worse. All this horrible stuff about Leo . . . 'Sarah,' she said, keeping her voice as even as possible, 'whatever exists between myself and Leo is none of your business. If you're saying all this out of spite because you have some sort of a thing about Leo yourself –'

Sarah's laughter at this was so delighted, so genuine, that it stopped Camilla in mid-sentence. 'Some sort of thing about him? Oh, that's wonderful . . .' Sarah shook her head. 'Since we've been having such a wonderfully girly chat, tell me if this sounds familiar . . .' She began to describe sex with Leo — at any rate, a random interlude — in vivid and intimate detail. Everything that was being described, Camilla had experienced. Sarah went on and on, her voice low and charged with erotic detail, inexhaustible in her description, making Camilla feel as though Sarah had somehow witnessed everything she and Leo had done together. 'I know the kind of words he uses, the things he suggests . . . He's a practised old Casanova, if you'll forgive the cliché.'

'Even if all of that is true,' said Camilla, who had a feeling she might cry at any moment, 'you're only saying it because he doesn't want *you* any more.'

'Darling, I'm the only person he keeps coming back to,' replied Sarah, picking up the bottle and draining the remains into her glass, 'because I'm the only person who knows him for exactly what he is, and doesn't care. Not like you. You really *do* care. Well, I'm sorry if I've wrecked your romantic idyll, but from what I can gather, it was probably over, anyway. Don't fool yourself into imagining any of it was ever genuine. From the moment he takes a new lover, no matter how loving and sincere his behaviour, dear Leo already has one eye on the exit. You're no different. No doubt I'll hear all about it soon enough. He does like to tell me about his various conquests. I still haven't had the full details about Anthony, though.' She raised her glass to her lips and smiled. 'I'm looking forward to those.'

Camilla felt unable to take any more. 'I never realized until now what an out-and-out bitch you are, Sarah,' she said unsteadily. 'You enjoy hurting people, don't you?'

'You can look on it that way, if you like. Frankly, I think I'm doing you a favour. You're so naïve, you'd probably have gone on deluding yourself for months. At least this way you know now he's not worth making a fool of yourself over.'

Camilla got up and left. Sarah sat and finished her wine, contemplating the future, wondering how long it would be before she could reinstate herself in Leo's life, and remind him once more that they really made a good couple. They were the same kind of people, after all, as she had reminded him on more than one occasion. He had never disagreed.

Rachel arrived at Stanton at eleven on Saturday morning, and unloaded Oliver and his belongings from the car. She watched as Oliver trotted to his father for a hug, and then moved straight on into the house, a familiar piece of territory. She stood awkwardly by the car, unable to share Oliver's territorial feelings. This was not her home, never really had been.

'He knows where everything is,' said Leo, giving Rachel a smile. His glance lingered on her a few seconds longer than necessary, and she looked away self-consciously. She had chosen the simple blue linen sun-dress she was wearing with more care than she liked to admit.

'I thought we'd go out for lunch,' said Leo. 'There's a pub not far away with some swings and a slide, and rabbits and that kind of thing. Oliver likes it.'

'Fine,' said Rachel.

There was silence for a few seconds. 'Come in and have some coffee,' said Leo.

Oliver's presence diluted the initial awkwardness, and lunch was easier than Leo had thought it might be. He could see that Rachel was in a stilted, unhappy frame of mind. If this thing was going to work, he would have to do his best to unbend her, render her more pliant. She had always been a slow starter, with a delicate, frigid reserve which he had once found something of a turn-on. He would have to thaw her out, slowly and gradually, over the afternoon, so that he could take her right back to where they had begun, and thus render Charles Beecham a totally lost cause.

By the time they had finished lunch, he had made her laugh more than once, and he could sense the warmth creeping into her manner, in her body language and in the way she glanced at him now and then.

'Come on, let's get back,' said Leo, scooping Oliver on to his knee and tickling him. 'Shall we go and feed the horses?' Oliver nodded through his giggles. 'Let's ask Mummy if she'd like to come, too.'

They went back to the house and Leo chopped up potatoes and apples and carrots and put them in a bag which Oliver carried importantly on the way down the road to the field where the horses grazed. Rachel, walking a little way behind Oliver and Leo, was remembering a time during the first year of their marriage when things had seemed to be working, when Oliver was only a baby, and days had gone by quite happily. Was it so hard, she wondered, just to be a family? Did it take so much effort? These were the easy parts, though, walks in the country, days in the sun. Anyone could do that. The hard part, for someone like Leo, was being faithful, keeping your hands off the nanny, giving up casual affairs with young men. Things he wouldn't begin to try to do. But she had picked up certain remarks he had made over lunch, things which suggested he was slowing down, looking for more stability in his life . . . Was there a chance that someone like Leo

341

regretted what he had lost, perhaps even wanted to try again? She watched as he hoisted Oliver on to the top of the fence and the little boy gingerly held out his palmful of apple and potato to the horse's whiskery lips. It was stupid even to hope for such a thing, but a part of her couldn't help it.

Leo turned and looked at her for a moment, squinting a little against the sun. 'You look very pretty today, did you know that?' Then he turned away again.

By half past three Oliver was growing tired, and Leo carried him back to the house on his shoulders.

'Time for a nap, young man,' said Rachel. She took Oliver upstairs to change his nappy and put him into his cot. Leo moved slowly round the drawing-room, half-pulling the blinds so that the room was shaded from the afternoon sun. When Rachel came downstairs he was standing there, waiting, hands clasped behind his back.

Without the little boy's presence, the atmosphere once again settled into vague awkwardness. Rachel crossed the room to the fireplace and picked up a photo of Oliver from the mantelpiece.

'I haven't seen this,' she said.

'I took it at Easter,' said Leo.

She nodded. 'It's lovely.'

The seconds ticked by. 'So,' said Leo, 'you didn't finish telling me about Charles's work out in the States. Oliver was just about to decapitate a guinea-pig.'

She put the photograph back. Would she say something now? He needed to know in which direction to play this.

His gaze moved to the neck of her dress. It must button up the back, he reckoned, thinking ahead to the moment when he would undress her and lay her down on the sofa. The way she turned to glance at him, lips parted, expression open, told him he would encounter no problem. Unless, of course, he said the wrong thing. That was always possible.

'He has some long-term project. A big documentary series. It means a lot of money, which is good, of course, but he's away a lot.'

'You must miss him.'

A fly buzzed behind one of the blinds, then fell silent. 'I suppose so,' said Rachel.

She looked away, glancing round the room. That pale, tragic profile, thought Leo. How rarely she smiled, and even then it was never the full thing. He felt utterly unmoved by her loveliness, realized how little desire he had to kiss or touch her. She belonged to the past. But Oliver was the future, and she was not going to take that away from him. Just two slow paces towards her, a couple of soft words, the right look. That was all it needed.

Suddenly Rachel bent down to pick something up from beside the television.

'What on earth is this?' she asked. 'Don't tell me you like old Bette Davis films.' Leo saw what she was holding. It was the copy of *Now Voyager* which Camilla had rented. Typical of her to forget it. There must be at least a tenner owing on it. 'Or does it belong to some boyfriend of yours? She is something of a gay icon, I believe.'

How odd, thought Leo, having imagined it might be

he who would say the wrong thing. He watched as Rachel turned the video over in her slender hands. He thought about Camilla lying across him, dabbing her eyes with the edge of her T-shirt as she watched the film, while he stroked her warm, bare feet and laughed. He remembered taking her from the garden to his bed, and the incredible, perfect pleasure he had taken in their lovemaking, the tenderness she summoned up in him which he hadn't thought existed. It was not difficult to bring her to mind, the way she smiled, entirely and happily, her endless questing after the heart of him, looking for ways to know him and make him her own.

He put out his hand. 'May I have it please?' Something in his voice made Rachel glance at him in surprise. She gave him the video and he said, 'A friend of mine left it. A girl, as a matter of fact.'

Rachel lifted her head slightly, conscious that some delicate thread which had bound them all day had suddenly broken. 'I suppose I should be relieved it's a girl. I know how complicated your life can get.'

Leo looked down at the video. 'It's not really complicated at all. She's someone I happen to love very much.' The silence in the room took on a new dimension. 'Tell me,' said Leo at last, 'when are you and Charles planning to go to the States? I have to know.'

Rachel sat down in an armchair. 'How did you know anything about that?' She knew she shouldn't feel so astonished. Leo was always ahead of the game, his own and everyone else's.

'I heard about it through a friend, an American lawyer

who works with Charles' Californian attorney. It's a small world. You should know that by now.'

'Why didn't you say something before? Why did you wait until now?'

Leo paced around for a moment, then sat down on the sofa opposite. 'Surely that's something I should be asking you. But if you want an answer to your question, I'll give you one. When I found out, I tried to work out why you hadn't said anything. I thought at first that you were afraid of how upset I'd be about losing Oliver.' Rachel said nothing. Her eyes were fixed on Leo's face. 'Then I worked out that the reason you hadn't said anything was because you hadn't made your mind up yet whether to go or stay.' He looked down at the video, turning it over and over in his hands. 'I invited you here today because I thought I might be able to influence your decision.'

'How?'

Leo let out a short, sighing laugh. 'Believe it or not, I was going to make love to you. To make you stay. Keep Oliver here. I was going to tell you I thought we could try again.'

Rachel swallowed, her throat dry and constricted. 'That would have been a lie, of course.'

'Of course.'

'You would have let me believe that? You would have done that just to keep me here, so that you would be able to go on seeing Oliver?'

'Oh, yes.' Leo nodded. 'I had thought I would do anything just to prevent you taking him away. Only it doesn't work that way, I now realize.'

'Not because you've suddenly discovered some moral scruples, I take it,' said Rachel.

'That's not quite the discovery, no.'

They sat in silence for some time. One by one, pieces fell into place for Rachel. She saw very clearly that Leo could quite easily have done as he had intended, and she would have let him. She would have believed him, she would have thrown away everything she and Charles had for Leo's sake. For any lie, however flimsy. But Leo had been unable to carry it through. They had both found out certain truths in the past ten minutes.

'Well,' she said at last, 'you would have been wasting your time, anyway.'

Leo, who had simply been staring at the box and thinking about Camilla, glanced up. So she was going to take Oliver away. He had lost his nerve at the last moment, and this was the price. 'I see,' he said, and nodded.

'I'm not going to the States with Charles. I'm staying here.' Only now did she give in. She began to cry quietly. Leo crossed the room, fetched some tissues and handed them to her.

'Does Charles know?'

She shook her head. At last she blinked back her tears. 'Not yet.'

'I'm sorry. I mean, I'm glad you're not going away. I'm sorry about you and Charles,' said Leo.

'It wasn't your doing. Not quite.'

'No.'

'Look . . . I think I'll just go, if you don't mind. There's nothing more to talk about at the moment. I really don't want to stay here.' Rachel wiped her eyes and stood up. She took her car keys from the bookcase where they lay.

'Forgive me . . . for what I had in mind,' said Leo.

She nodded. 'It's not so much what you did, as what you didn't do.'

Leo didn't think he really understood this, and made no reply. Breaking the silence at last, he said, 'I'll bring Oliver back tomorrow at tea-time.'

Rachel nodded. 'Fine.'

He went to the door with her and watched as she got into her car and drove away.

When he dropped Oliver off the following evening, Charles was there, bleary-eyed from his flight, but cheerful. He even invited Leo in for a drink, but Leo declined. Clearly Rachel hadn't yet told Charles of her decision; she looked strained and spoke very little.

Leo got back into his car and sat for a moment before turning the key, trying to work out whether he was in any way to blame for the impending split between Charles and Rachel. He simply had no idea. Anyway, the important thing for him was to get hold of Camilla. He had rung her last night at her flat, only to be told by Jane that Camilla had gone to her parents in Kew for the weekend. He presumed she would be back in Clapham tonight. He needed to see her, to reassure himself that his casual behaviour of the past week hadn't had too bad an effect on her. It was as easy to wound her as to make her happy, the work of an instant. He now knew it was one of the things he loved most about her, and wondered how he could have been so utterly blind to it until yesterday.

Camilla had spent the weekend trying to come to terms with everything Sarah had told her about Leo. She had no doubt that all of it was genuine, that Leo was everything Sarah said he was. Sarah clearly knew so much about him, and what she said made sense. There had always been some instinct in Camilla that told her that a man like Leo – successful, wealthy, charismatic – was not on his own without good reason. Now she knew the answer. His ruthlessness in court, the charm which could turn to acerbity in seconds, the interest which could abruptly transform itself to indifference – those were the clues which should have told her their love affair would end as quickly as it had begun. Through the long hours of the weekend she thought it through, and it seemed pitiable that she should ever have imagined he really cared for her. Whatever the truth was, though, and even if she was to spend several wretched months getting over him, she would rather have kept certain beliefs intact. As it was, she was now left with the thought that every tender word, every gesture and idle, loving caress, had probably been a matter of calculation and fabrication. So she had nothing left at all.

The part that was truly beyond her understanding concerned Anthony. Her somewhat fuzzy liberal views about homosexuality, insofar as she ever thought deeply about the matter, told her that she should have no qualms about two men making love. But when she reduced it to real terms, and to Leo and Anthony, it was not so much that it offended her, as that it lay outside her comprehension. Given what she knew of both of them, she couldn't envisage it. She tried not to. It was no good telling herself that it didn't make Leo an immoral person. If what Sarah had said was true, and if Anthony's behaviour and apparent depression over the past months could be attributed to Leo's callousness, then he was guilty of far worse things. And now she herself was included. She had no idea of how she was going to face him in court on Monday.

Leo rang the Clapham flat on Sunday evening, but Camilla still wasn't back. He went to her room in chambers the following morning, but Simon said she hadn't been in. When he spoke to Felicity, she said that Camilla had rung in to say she was going straight to court.

Not since Joshua had Leo felt such an apprehensive build-up of feeling. With every hour that had passed since Rachel's departure, it had become clearer to him how much he had taken Camilla for granted. It now seemed to him unforgivable that he should have let her spend all last week thinking that he no longer wanted to see her. He had selfishly set his mind on achieving his own ends where Rachel and Oliver were concerned, and almost jeopardized everything.

His heart lifted when he came into the courtroom and saw Camilla sitting at the long table, leafing through documents. He sat down next to her, thought for a second, then said in a low voice, 'The first thing I have to say is that I have been a complete bastard this past week, and I want to apologize.' She lifted her head, which had been resting on one hand, and looked at him. Her eyes seemed large and luminous, and he found her expression difficult to read. 'The second thing –' He put a hand to her neck and adjusted her collar, '– is that your bands are on crooked. There.'

'Don't,' she said, raising her own hand in a defensive little gesture.

His smile, his touch, sent currents through her, as always. She had no idea what to say. His seductive charm should hold a new aspect now, in the light of what Sarah had told her, but it didn't. It was just Leo, and her feelings about him remained as strong as before. The thing that had changed for ever was that she now no longer trusted him. She had a powerful intellect, and a strong instinct for self-preservation, and in that moment she told herself that she mustn't let this go on, or she really would become another victim. Though she felt like one already.

Leo glanced round to make sure they weren't over-heard. 'Look, please don't sulk. I had some problems last week. I should have rung, or said something, I know. I'm sorry.'

'It has nothing to do with that,' she muttered, staring down at her papers.

'What hasn't anything to do with what?' He was aware of Rachel, who was standing talking to Caradog-Browne a few feet away, staring at them. 'Will you look at me? Please.' Camilla turned her face to him again, and he saw instantly that something was wrong, something had changed. At that moment the court usher intoned, 'Court rise,' and Mr Justice Olby's dignified figure bustled through the side door.

'I'll talk to you at lunchtime,' said Leo.

'I don't want to.'

'Oh, for God's sake,' muttered Leo in exasperation.

Mr Justice Olby, now seated, glanced in Leo's direction. 'A number of housekeeping points, Mr Davies, if you could assist me, please. First of all, in the documents that emanate from Mr Rider, could you remind me in which bundle I can find Mrs Lacey-Cameron's draft affidavit?'

Leo rose, hitching his gown. 'I believe it is in C2, my Lord.' The last thing he needed, in the closing week of the case, was to have an emotional trauma going on behind the scenes. He would take her to lunch and try to soothe her ruffled feathers. It wouldn't take any more than that, he was sure.

When the court adjourned for lunch, Leo said to Camilla, 'Let's go across the road to Cutler's, just the two of us, and have a talk.'

'I can't, Leo,' said Camilla, putting her papers together. 'I'm expecting a call from Rob Shaw in New York on a new case.'

Leo let out a sigh. 'Something's obviously up. I need to talk to you.'

'No, you don't.'

'Don't say that! I don't understand what's wrong, but I want to see you. What about this evening?'

She shrugged. There wasn't any point in putting it off.

She'd have to explain what had happened at some point. Better sooner rather than later. 'If you like.'

'Fine. I have a few things I've got to do in chambers after court, but I'll come to your room around half-five. And please,' he added, 'will you stop looking so damned miserable. You've nothing to be miserable about.'

Camilla didn't even look at him, just picked her papers up and left.

In the clerks' room, Henry slammed down the phone. 'Why do you suppose listing officers are such officious bastards?' he asked Felicity.

'They go to a special camp at weekends and learn to behave that way. Here,' Felicity handed him some papers, 'that's the fax from Holman's.'

'Ah,' said Henry, 'Mr Gibbon's been waiting for that. I'll take it up to him.'

Felicity looked at her watch and sighed. What a bugger of a morning. They hadn't arranged to see one another today, but maybe Peter could make lunch at short notice. They could buy some sandwiches and sit in the sun somewhere. She'd ring and see.

'I'm sorry,' said the receptionist, when Felicity rang Peter's chambers, 'Mr Weir's not here.' Recognizing Felicity as the clerk from 5 Caper Court, she added, 'He was in earlier, but his little boy was taken into hospital, so he had to dash off.'

'Oh, right,' said Felicity faintly. She felt as though her stomach had just dropped through the floor. The bastard. Married. With a kid. She should have known. She put the phone down. She should have bleeding known.

At that moment Henry came back in. He glanced across at Felicity, who was sitting at her desk, very still. Felicity never sat still, always had to be doing ten things at once.

'You all right?' he asked.

'Oh, fine,' replied Felicity. 'I'm just going to get some lunch.' She picked up her handbag and went out.

Henry returned to the problem of a new clerk, which he'd been toying with all morning. The trouble with bringing in this new lot, Maurice Faber and other assorted egos, was that to handle the extra volume of work, they'd need someone who wasn't wet behind the ears. What they wanted was someone middleweight, with maybe just a bit more experience than Fliss, but not someone who'd put her nose out of joint. Nor did Henry want someone who might regard himself as senior to Henry and start lording it about. A thought occurred to him. He hadn't heard of barristers bringing their own clerk with them, but there was just a possibility . . . These new tenants would need a lot of looking after, and who better than someone who knew them already? Henry smiled to himself. No time like the present. If he called now, maybe they could settle something over lunch. It was always worth a try.

Camilla was working at her desk, window open to the warmth of the late afternoon, when Leo came by. Camilla glanced up. 'I'll just be a second.' Just the sight of Leo, and the thought of what she had to tell him, made her heart start thudding horribly.

Simon, who was trying to sort out a shelf littered with briefs on the other side of the room, glanced over. 'You two going for a drink?' he asked. 'I might join you in a bit. Where are you off to?'

Leo couldn't exactly put him off. Naturally Simon assumed they were merely going for a friendly drink after work. 'Middle Temple, probably.'

'Right. Nice evening for sitting about outside. I'll see you there.'

'So,' said Leo, once he and Camilla were beyond the doors of 5 Caper Court, 'are you still in a bad mood?'

'It isn't anything to do with my mood.'

Leo thrust his hands into his trouser pockets. 'Right, then you're angry with me. Obviously it's something I've said or done.'

She shook her head.

'Would you rather go somewhere else, other than Middle Temple? I get the impression we could do without Simon.'

'No. What I have to say won't take very long.'

With a sense of foreboding, Leo decided to say nothing more until they got to Middle Temple, where he would buy them both a drink and try to sort this out.

They took their drinks to a secluded bench at one end of the garden.

'Now, no more prevarication, no sulking,' said Leo firmly. 'Just tell me what is upsetting you.'

He watched her closely as she sipped her drink. Whatever it was, she was finding some difficulty in saying it. At last Camilla said, 'I found out a few things. Please don't think I'm making judgements about you, Leo, but I really don't want to go on seeing you.'

He felt an icy sliver of fear in his insides, and wondered what he was about to learn. What she had learnt. 'Who exactly,' he asked, 'has been speaking to you?'

'Sarah.'

Leo nodded, his calm outward exterior belying the cold fury he felt. Not for the first time, that girl was making mischief on a grand scale, with consequences she neither foresaw nor cared about. He wondered how big a damage-limitation exercise he would have to perform. She might be a year older than Sarah, but Camilla was far younger in every way, and, despite the inhibitions which he had managed to lower over the past few weeks, still capable of being shocked and upset by the big, wide world.

'What did Sarah say?'

'It doesn't matter.'

'It does. Look, Camilla, you mean a great deal to me. I didn't know it until this weekend, but I can't let things Sarah has said damage our relationship.'

'It's not what she said that's done the damage. It's who and what you are. Things I never knew about you, that you were never going to tell me. For instance –' She turned to him and held his gaze, '– you never told me that you sleep with Sarah on a regular basis. That you have done for years.'

'That's not true. Sarah and I go back some time, but she is absolutely nothing to me. I haven't slept with her in –'

'In what? A month?'

Leo said nothing. So far as he could see, what he did a month ago shouldn't bloody well matter, but in Camilla's eyes it clearly did.

'And what about Anthony?'

'What about him? He has nothing to do with anything. All I care about is –'

Her voice was soft, and deadly in its condemnation. 'I know he's been your lover. I know all about it.'

'Oh, for Christ's sake . . .' Leo passed a hand over his face. How on earth had that bitch Sarah found out about Anthony? Was there nothing she didn't know, nothing she wasn't prepared to use against people? Gideon Smallwood could take lessons from that young woman any day. He took his hand away and met Camilla's gaze. He could see no point in being anything but frank. 'So what? So I'm bisexual. What difference does that make? Since I met you, I haven't looked at anyone else. I don't want anyone else. I'm forty-six, for God's sake. You can rake through my past and dig up any number of lovers, male and female. What are they to you?'

Her expression faltered slightly at his directness, but then she replied, 'I suppose it's because you're such a clever lawyer that you're evading the point, Leo. I don't care if you and Anthony were ever lovers. As you say, it's in the past and it's none of my business. But if what Sarah says is true, then you did something to him from which he's never going to recover. You've damaged him. You can see for yourself how he's been these past few weeks. But you don't care. Sarah told me how you manipulate people, make them think they matter to you, then just cast them off.' Leo said nothing. What could he say? What kind of protest could he make against the incontrovertible truth? Camilla went on, 'I'm not in a position to make any judgements about what you've done in the past. But as you said, you're forty-six. You're not going to change now. Why should you treat me differently? I just can't bear to be used by you. I don't know any other way to protect myself, except by not seeing you any more.'

Leo swirled the ice in his whisky, then looked across the garden, squinting his eyes against the evening sun. 'You're right, of course. I didn't want you to know the kind of person I am. Not to protect myself, but to protect you. But – may I say something in mitigation?'

'What?' Camilla met his gaze, wishing he didn't have this effect on her.

He leaned towards her and put his finger lightly against her cheek. 'I love you. I didn't know it till this weekend. Certain things happened. Things I don't want to go into. But from the moment I realized how much you mean to me, I've hardly been able to think about anything other than telling you that I love you. And here we are, in this mess. I imagine it doesn't really count for much now.'

'I wish it did.'

'Do you?'

'Of course,' said Camilla. She looked at him with large, miserable eyes. 'Don't you think I'd like to be able to believe you? For weeks I've wanted just to be able to look at you, and tell you how much I love you, and hear you say it back.'

Without thinking about it, Leo kissed her. Kissing in the formal surroundings of Middle Temple rose garden, so far as he knew, was not exactly protocol, but at that moment he didn't care which of his worthy fellow barristers happened to be looking on. The look in her eyes made it impossible for him not to, and he kissed her for several long, gentle seconds. 'How can I make you believe me?' he asked.

She was silent for a moment. 'If you really mean it,' said Camilla, 'marry me.'

Leo looked at her in mild astonishment and perplexity.

'You don't want to, do you?' said Camilla.

'No, it's not that. It's . . . it's . . .' He had no idea what he was meant to say.

'Of course you don't. It's not part of the plan. I said it partly to see how you'd react. The reason you won't, is because you actually don't intend this to last. You can't make anything last. I'm not saying that you don't mean what you say. I didn't believe it when Sarah said that you were never capable of being sincere. I think you were sincere last weekend. But it would all have to end in the long run, and I love you so much, I don't think I can bear that.'

For once, Leo felt entirely flummoxed. 'Can't we – can't we just enjoy the here and now?'

'I don't think so, no.'

A voice called across the garden, 'Hello, you two!' and

they looked up to see Simon approaching, holding a very full pint of beer.

Camilla drew away from Leo, and swallowed the remains of her drink.

'Simon,' said Leo, in tones of dismal enthusiasm, 'come and join us.'

'I could see you two were deep in conversation about that Lloyd's case,' said Simon, settling himself on the grass with his beer and stretching out his legs. 'I'll bet you never talk about anything else.' He held up his drink. 'Cheers.'

Camilla stood up. 'I have to be going,' she said.

Simon glanced at her in surprise. 'Oh. Right. I was just about to buy you both another drink. Oh, well.'

Camilla murmured goodbye to Leo, then picked up her jacket and walked away across the lawn.

'Is it me, d'you think?' asked Simon, watching as she went.

'I doubt it,' said Leo.

'I hope not. I'm beginning to get rather a thing about her, actually.'

Leo sighed and said, 'Simon, why don't you go and buy me that drink?'

Gideon, who had returned from Tokyo the day before, had been to check on the progress of his new house and was gratified to discover that he would be able to move in at the end of a fortnight. He told his mother the news that evening.

'Oh, darling, how lovely,' said Lady Henrietta. 'Though

I shall miss you. Will you come and visit me often? Good. And I shall visit you, of course. The evenings will be so dull without my boy, and it's nice to think I'll be able to drop by and see you when I like.'

Gideon merely raised his eyebrows at this. 'One thing I'm going to need,' he said, 'is some good furniture.'

'What about the things from your last place?'

Gideon wasn't about to tell his mother that he'd sold them some time ago. 'Well, of course, but this house is larger, you see, and I do need a few more things.'

Lady Henrietta waved a hand. 'The furniture from the house at Chesterton is still in storage. Most of it, that is. Take what you like. It's of no use to me any more.'

'Nonsense. What if we win against Lloyd's?'

Lady Henrietta gave a small, tremulous sigh. 'Your hopes are more sanguine than mine, Gideon. No, you take what you need. I'll ring the people tomorrow and give you an authorization.'

'That is so generous of you, Mummy.' Gideon dropped a kiss on her head. 'And now,' he added, 'I must go and make some phone calls.'

In his room, Gideon leafed through his personal mail, and then rang Leo.

Leo, who had been lying on the sofa in his Belgravia flat reflecting on his conversation with Camilla, was unpleasantly surprised to hear Gideon's voice.

'Got back yesterday, Leo. I had an idea you'd be waiting to hear from me.'

'In a manner of speaking.'

'Have you thought any more about my proposal?'

'I have to see the photos.'

'Of course, of course.' Gideon glanced at his watch. 'I can pop round later, if you're not busy.'

'Very well.'

'See you in an hour.'

The walk from his mother's house to Leo's place took Gideon a mere ten minutes. He had the photos carefully tucked into the inside pocket of his jacket. He had given some thought to the question of whether Leo was the kind of person to involve the police, but he had come to the conclusion that this was unlikely. All in all, Leo really had far too much to lose. It was now just a matter of fixing a price.

He rang the bell, and Leo let him in. Gideon sauntered through to the drawing-room, glancing round. 'Do you know, those Lehrmans really weren't right for this room. They look much better in the museum.' He indicated the whisky decanter. 'May I?'

'Go ahead,' said Leo.

'Such a good malt,' said Gideon, as he took a sip of his drink and replaced the stopper in the decanter. 'Now –' he reached into his inside pocket,' – here are the pictures. Just two.' He put his head on one side. 'Not very good of you, but certainly recognizable.'

He handed the pictures to Leo, who looked at them. They'd been taken from the right, he saw, and the inference was inescapable. Yes, he was recognizable, once identified, and yes, it looked every bit as bad as Gideon had suggested, despite the fleeting, relatively inconsequential nature of what had actually occurred.

'Not bad quality, are they?' said Gideon, glancing at them over Leo's shoulder. 'Considering they don't use a flash or anything.'

Had Leo had a knife in his hand, he might gladly have slipped it between Gideon's ribs. Gideon left his side and sauntered across the room with his drink to inspect a Whittaker print.

'You're really very trusting, coming here alone, Gideon,' said Leo quietly.

Gideon turned, and Leo saw from his face that he was immediately alert for sounds in the silent flat. Fear flickered in his dark eyes.

'No, Leo, that's not your style.' His voice, however, did not carry its customary note of assurance.

'What? Having you beaten senseless for my own satisfaction? Oh, I don't know . . .' Leo tossed the photos down on a table and sighed. 'No, don't worry. The idea is attractive, but I don't want to add to my troubles, no matter how much I'd like to make you suffer for this.'

Gideon swallowed his fear and relaxed. 'So, I take it you're agreeable to making me a modest loan?'

'That depends how modest it is.'

Gideon cocked his head on one side. 'I had in mind – say, a hundred thou.'

Leo had not expected this. 'I am a man of means, Gideon, and you are obviously in dire need of funds, but that's a very high price.'

'It's actually quite generous on my part, Leo. For that, I am prepared to throw in the negatives, and my assurance that this stops here.'

Leo gave a short laugh of disbelief. 'You expect me to believe that you won't be coming back for more?'

Gideon shrugged. 'Why should I? There's the future of our friendship to consider. I may need a good lawyer one day. As for believing me – well, you have my word as a gentleman.'

For some odd reason, Leo was inclined to believe him. 'I need some time.'

'You've had two weeks.'

'Apart from anything else, I have to move funds around. It's a great deal of money.'

'Isn't it just?' laughed Gideon, his eyes sparkling with a pleasure that was almost childlike. 'Tell you what, just pop a cheque in the post to reach me by the weekend. That'll do the trick. And I'll see to it that the negatives are sent to you. Don't worry,' he said, seeing Leo's face, 'you have my word. Oh,' he added, gesturing to the photos on the table, 'you can keep those – for your album.' He put his empty glass down. 'Thanks for the drink. I'll see myself out.'

When he had gone, Leo sank on to the sofa. Gideon had asked for far more than he had expected, but it was a small price to pay for peace of mind. Gideon would return the negatives. He had no idea why he was so certain. He just was. Whatever else Gideon might be, Leo suspected he prided himself on being a man of honour.

Gideon arranged to leave work early the next day, and went to inspect his mother's furniture at the warehouse where it was stored. He found enough furniture sufficiently to his taste to furnish most of his house, and in addition arranged for the removal to Christie's auction house of a very fine pair of George I walnut chests, an eighteenth-century longcase clock, a pair of early Victorian parcel-gilt pier glasses, a Victorian oak reading table, and an exquisite featherbanded bureau bookcase. His mother would never know. Over the years, and from beneath her very nose, Gideon had been responsible for the disappearance of eight pieces of Derby porcelain, two eighteenth-century Bilston enamel boxes, several items of Georgian silver, and an Alfred Glendining oil which he had found in the spare room.

Leaving the warehouse, Gideon made his way home to Pimlico, ringing the ministry *en route* to check with his secretary the progress of various matters. When he got home, he remembered that his mother was out at a bridge party. Gideon showered, changed, and watched the early evening news. He was deeply bored. He went through to his room and unlocked his desk, and took from a drawer a small dossier containing notes and a couple of photographs. He thumbed through these thoughtfully. If Leo came through with the money, as Gideon was certain he would, the little matter of the adulterous behaviour of Tony Gear, his lord and master, the country's cultural figurehead, could be postponed. He had never put the squeeze on a Cabinet Minister before, and even Gideon felt some qualms at the prospect. On the whole, he would rather not. Still, useful to keep the dossier for a rainy day. He had the feeling, however, that Tony Gear was not likely to last long in office, and the future value of the dossier's contents might sharply decline.

With the matter of the money from Leo at the forefront of his mind, Gideon decided to call Leo before he left chambers, and check that the thing was in hand. Gideon's finances were, as ever, in a precarious state, and even when Leo's cheque came through, it would take some days to clear. He wanted to make sure he got hold of the money as quickly as possible.

Leo told Gideon he had taken the necessary steps that afternoon, and that the money would be with him before the end of the week.

'While I think about it,' said Gideon, 'I'd rather you didn't send it here.' And he gave Leo the address of the flat in Ealing. He preferred to keep his most personal papers, together with a variety of intimate paraphernalia which would shock Lady Henrietta deeply were she to stumble across it in her occasional wanderings through his room, at his weekend retreat. The Tony Gear dossier was here only because it was an ongoing project, but as he intended to shelve it for the moment, Gideon decided to take it with him to Ealing this evening. This was a

Tuesday, and although Gideon was accustomed to devote only Friday and Saturday evenings to his various pleasures, he decided tonight to vary his routine. The prospect of the money coming his way had whetted his appetite for amusement, and he felt too restless to spend the evening in Pimlico. Besides, the following day Tony Gear was making an all-day visit to a performing-arts centre in Scunthorpe, which mercifully did not require Gideon's attendance, and he could afford to get in a little later than usual in the morning, and take it easy.

At a little after ten p.m., attired in an immaculate, blue pinstripe Kilgour French Stanbury suit, Armani shirt and tie, and Tim Little shoes, Gideon took a cab to Foxtrot Oscar on the Royal Hospital Road. His arrival at the restaurant was greeted with a happy cry of 'Gideon, you old piss artist!' Gideon always found a number of like-minded friends wherever he went in London. He consumed a plate of eggs benedict and a bottle of chilled red, chatted for a while, and then set off with a couple of friends for the Ritz club and a spot of gambling.

Even Gideon, however, knew how dangerously close to the limit his finances had gone, and despite the protestations of his friends he left after only an hour. He took a cab to Ealing, to a certain gay club which he liked to frequent, but he could find nothing there to interest him. At around two in the morning, still bored and frustrated, he went to the Ealing flat. He always had alternative ways to keep himself amused. Once there, he took off his shoes, jacket, trousers, shirt and tie, and made his preparations.

*

So Peter was married. He was married with a kid, he was a lying, cheating bastard, he had strung her along for weeks, and Felicity never wanted to see him again. That was her initial reaction to Monday's discovery. By the time Tuesday evening came, she'd had the chance to consider the possibilities. Maybe he was separated from his wife, maybe even divorced. Perhaps he wasn't even married. You never knew. The receptionist had said his little boy had been taken to hospital, and any father would rush off, wouldn't he? Only if that were the set-up, how come he'd never mentioned the fact that he had a son? Most blokes would, unless there was something else to conceal. No, Felicity thought miserably, everything fell into place. Never seeing her at weekends, only seeing her the odd night here and there . . . Though God alone knew what he told his wife the nights he was at Felicity's flat. She had been taken for the proverbial ride by a married man who wanted a bit on the side.

She felt gutted, sick with anger, and above all heart-broken. For she really thought she'd found someone special, had even begun to imagine the relationship could go somewhere. As of today, it was going absolutely nowhere. She felt like calling Peter up, giving him an earful, letting him know just what she thought of him. Only she didn't have a number for him, except in chambers. He always rang her, always. Now, what did that tell her? Bastard, bastard . . . She would just have to wait until she saw him at lunchtime next day. Part of her still hoped, though, that she'd got it all wrong.

*

They met in a coffee bar at Ludgate Circus. After ten minutes of listening to him come out with his usual glib, inconsequential patter, Felicity couldn't stand any more.

'How's your little boy?' she asked.

His reaction, while it confirmed everything she had suspected, was most gratifying. He stopped mid-sentence, mouth open, and stared at her. The change in his face was quite remarkable. The bright, good-looking features blanked, seeming to close up, and for a few seconds he didn't look handsome at all. He looked down at his coffee and stirred it slowly.

'I'm really interested – how is he?' asked Felicity.

Peter cast around for a few seconds, then said abruptly, 'He had an asthma attack. He's all right.'

Felicity nodded. 'When were you going to get round to telling me you were married?'

'Dunno.' Peter tried to shrug off his embarrassment by glancing out of the café window at the street. He couldn't meet Felicity's eye.

'Don't just say it like that, like it doesn't matter,' said Felicity angrily. 'You've taken me for a complete ride!'

Peter struggled to recover some of his aplomb, smoothing his hair back from his face and then looking her in the eye. 'Come on, Fliss. What's the big deal? We have a good time, don't we?'

'What's that got to do with it? You're married, with a kid! Weren't you ever going to tell me?'

He shrugged. 'I might have. I was worried it might put you off me.'

'Too bloody right it would! I don't go out with married men. I don't like the idea of busting up marriages.'

'Nothing to bust up. Anyway, how did you find out?'

'I tried to ring you in chambers yesterday. What do you mean, "nothing to bust up"?'

'Debbie and me, we do what we like. Free agents. We sort of agreed to keep it that way a couple of years ago. Only we're there for the kids, we keep it together for them, especially at weekends, holidays, all that.'

'Kids? There's more than one?'

'Yeah. Ricky, Paul and Leanne.' He looked down at his coffee once more; his embarrassment seemed to have returned.

'Oh, how bloody wonderful! And all this time you've been stringing me along, letting me think I really meant something to you.'

'You do mean something to me, Fliss.' The way he said it, the look on his face, reduced Felicity almost to tears. She so wanted to believe it.

'I actually thought we had something special, that our relationship might be going somewhere. You let me think that! But it's not going anywhere, is it?'

'I'm not leaving Debbie, if that's what you mean. Not while we've got the kids. They're everything to me.' It was the first time in the conversation that he had sounded anything like resolute. Felicity could think of nothing to say. She knew now exactly where she stood, her value to him, his order of priorities. He kept his domestic life ticking over, and she was his bit on the side, nothing more, never could be. If he and his wife, Debbie whoever, had decided to do their own thing two years ago, Peter must have been knocking girls off on a regular basis, not telling them, or stringing them along until they found out . . . She was probably one in a long line. The worst thing was the idea of him keeping it all from her. She didn't matter enough to know. She was just another bit of stuff.

'Well, that's it, then, isn't it?' Her voice was flat.

'Come on, Fliss, it doesn't have to stop, you know. OK, you feel I've deceived you. But you know the set-up now. Debbie doesn't care. Why can't we just go on as we are?' He essayed one of his smiles, the kind that crinkled the corners of his eyes.

'You don't get it, Peter, do you? I want more than just to be someone's mistress. What a word! What a stupid, poncy word! I don't want to be some furtive little thing you do when no one's looking, a sort of add-on extra to your real life. I'm not putting up with that!'

'Don't make it sound like that. You're really special –'

'Yeah, like I believe you. Your kids are special, you mean. You're special. I know just what I am to you.' She picked up her bag and stood up. 'I really don't ever want to see you again.'

'Look,' said Peter, putting out a hand, 'sit down again. It's not that simple. There's something that's come up –'

But Felicity was now too wound up and fizzing with righteous anger to listen. She should have seen from the beginning what a smarmy, lying git he was. She'd have liked to have called him that to his face, but since they'd had to conduct the entire conversation on a subdued level in a crowded café, she didn't feel she could. She stormed out of the café and up Fleet Street, heels clacking on the pavement, sniffing back her tears. Why did she always pick the wrong blokes? Why did she get taken in? First of all Vince, a waster and a loser who'd ended up in prison and still thought he had some rights over her, and now Peter, all smarm and charm and lies. At least she'd had the strength of mind to end it. It would have been easy, all too easy, just to let it go on, do as he suggested. That was the worst of it. For all that he was a two-faced liar, she really, really liked him. She didn't really want to stop seeing him. But there was no choice. It wasn't going anywhere, and she'd only have got hurt in the long run. As long as she never had to see him again, it would be all right. She would get over it eventually. People always did.

That didn't stop her locking herself in the loo and crying for twenty minutes when she got back to chambers.

Camilla had no idea what she expected from Leo when she saw him on Tuesday. He seemed, however, entirely normal, slightly preoccupied, talking about the case on the way to court, making no reference to anything that had happened the previous evening. It was as though everything had suddenly swung back three months, to the way things had been between them before their affair had started. As though it had never started. Camilla supposed she could expect nothing else. Hadn't she told him she didn't want to go on seeing him? She shouldn't, anyway. She shouldn't want to have anything more to do with him. He hadn't denied anything. Not sleeping with Sarah, not the business with Anthony . . . It was all so horrible that it was just as well he was behaving as he was. With indifference. Not studied, but genuine.

Counsel for Lloyd's was moaning about some letter or other which the Names' lawyers had failed to produce. Camilla didn't even pretend to concentrate. She could think about nothing but the conversation of the evening before. She hadn't been able to sleep because of it. She realized Paul Rollason had stopped talking. The judge glanced in their direction and murmured, 'Mr Davies?' At her side, Leo rose to his feet.

'My Lord, in view of what Mr Beddoes has said previously, we have sought to see if that letter is available. There is no reply among the Chairman's papers. As I indicated to the Court on a previous occasion, we are prepared to provide to the Court Mr Long's finality statement . . .'

Clearly it hadn't affected Leo's concentration in the slightest. As ever, he was focused entirely on the case, as though nothing had happened in the last twenty-four hours to disturb him. When he sat down, he didn't so much as look at her, hardly seemed aware of her existence. All day she had sat next to him in court, conscious of his every movement, tone and gesture, but he was on another plane, not thinking about her at all.

Which only went to prove that she had been right. He had simply shrugged her off. He must have been lying when he said he loved her. He must have. Look at the way he'd reacted when she'd said that stupid thing about marrying her. She curled her fists into her palms in embarrassment when she recalled that. What a mad thing to say. She'd only done it to show him, to show him how false everything he said was. And it had worked. Now they both knew it. Now he wasn't going to bother pretending anything any more.

When he got back to chambers, Leo went to the clerks' room to pick up his post and gather the latest news from Henry.

'All the new furniture's arriving next Thursday,' said Henry. 'Carpets in on Wednesday, so people can start moving in the week after. I'm still sorting the phone lines out, mind, but we should be ship-shape a week Monday.'

'Good,' said Leo. 'We want this transition to go smoothly.'

'Oh, while we're on the subject, Mr Davies, I think I've sorted out the matter of a new clerk.'

'Oh, really?'

'Yes,' said Henry, with a smile of satisfaction. 'I had lunch with Peter Weir yesterday, from 3 Wessex Street, and he's prepared to make the move with Maurice Faber and the rest. I reckon we're rather lucky, really. He's got a good style about him, should bring in the business. And the advantage is, he's used to looking after this new lot. Bit of a turn-up, eh, sir?'

'Yes, well done, Henry. Bringing on board someone who's already used to Maurice Faber's gentle ways is certainly a good thing. Doesn't Peter Weir work on a commission basis, though?'

'No, salary. So that should be straightforward enough.'

'Fine. What do Felicity and Robert think?'

'Haven't had the chance to tell them yet, sir. I think

they'll rub along nicely with him, though. He's quite a charming bloke, Peter.' It had occurred to Henry that Peter Weir might be a bit too charming where Felicity was concerned, but he wasn't much worried. The bloke was married with kids, after all.

Leo went up to his room and sorted out various papers for a while. After half an hour he knew he couldn't put it off any longer. The bank had confirmed that the funds were in place, all he had to do was write the cheque. He did so reluctantly, detesting having to write out Gideon's name, then the ghastly amount. It was worth it, though, if it would buy silence, and those wretched photos. For the thousandth time, Leo was plagued with misgivings. He should go to the police, he knew, expose everything that Gideon was doing – not just to him, but probably to nameless others as well. Yet he folded the cheque, slid it into an envelope, sealed it, and wrote Gideon's name and the Ealing address on the front. He sat back in his chair and stared at it, remembering Gideon as he had been at twenty. Bizarre, really, that it had come to this.

He glanced at his watch and saw that it was after six. It would just have to go with tomorrow's post. He was in no hurry to enrich Gideon Smallwood. He took the letter down to the clerks' room and dropped the envelope in the post tray, then went back upstairs. He closed the door to his room and went to the window. There he stood for a long time, thinking about something else entirely.

*

374

'Have you had a row?' asked Jane.

'No,' replied Camilla shortly. She was sitting on the window-sill in the kitchen, her back to the open window, her bare feet propped up on the table. The weather was sultry, and she had changed from her oppressive black suit into combat trousers and a crop top. She had eaten two bananas and a yoghurt in the hope of avoiding Jane's cross-examination over supper later, but Jane started to badger her as soon as she got in. Camilla's disappearance to her parents for the weekend, and Leo's phone calls, had put her into a state of greedy curiosity.

'So what *has* happened?'

'I told him I didn't want to see him any more. Not because we had a row, but because – well, just because.'

'There must be a reason why –'

'Jane! I don't want to discuss it any more! OK?'

'OK, don't get stressy. I just thought it might help to talk about it.'

The doorbell rang, and Jane went to answer it. She buzzed Leo up and waited at the door to let him in, because she wanted to get a good look at him up close. She'd only seen him around the Temple now and then from a distance.

'Is Camilla here?' asked Leo, who had hoped to find Camilla on her own.

Oh, yes, thought Jane, he was the business. Not very tall, but obviously in good shape for his age, fantastic bones, knockout eyes, and that silver hair . . . It took her a second to recover herself. 'Yes, go through. She's in the kitchen.'

Camilla was just scraping the last bits from her yoghurt pot when Leo appeared in the doorway of the kitchen. She could feel herself going pink, and could think of nothing at all to say.

Jane was hovering around in the living-room in the background, hoping to pick up snatches of what was clearly going to be an interesting conversation.

'I'd like to talk to you, if I may.' Leo's tone was quite businesslike, even a little stern.

'Right,' said Camilla uncertainly. She hadn't ever seen him look quite like this before.

'Let's go for a walk,' he said, glancing over his shoulder at Jane.

Camilla slid off the window-sill and slipped on some shoes. They went downstairs together and out into the street, leaving a disappointed Jane watching them from a window above.

They walked down the dusty street for fifty yards or so. Camilla wondered when Leo was going to say anything.

At last Leo stopped on the pavement and turned to her. 'The first thing I need to know is whether those things which Sarah told you have made it impossible for you to care for me.' It was blunt, almost awkward, and Camilla took a few seconds to answer.

'They made it – they made it seem like a bad idea, that's all.'

They walked on a little further, as Leo pondered this. 'You're right. I'm certainly not to be recommended . . .' He stopped again. 'If I said that I wanted to change

376

everything, that I wanted my life to become ordinary and – well, uncomplicated, whatever . . . Would you be prepared to love me?'

'I didn't say I didn't love you. I only said I thought it wasn't a good idea. I can't help what I feel. Leo, I love you anyway, whatever you are. I just don't want you to do me any harm.'

'Oh, dear God . . .' murmured Leo, and looked across at the sun dipping behind the roofs of Clapham. 'I have thought about nothing but this all day –'

'No, you haven't. You've spent all day ignoring me and worrying about Mr Long's finality statement and the letter that Beddoes claims went missing.'

'Well . . . Up to a point, obviously.' Leo frowned. 'I haven't *ignored* you. How can you say I've ignored you when I've been thinking all day about marrying you? When I haven't been worrying about Mr Long's finality statement, of course.'

Camilla stared at him. 'You don't mean that. You're just saying that because of what I said last night.'

'Well, of course that's why. I said, how can I make you believe I love you, and you said, marry me. So there we are. Marry me.'

'No.'

'Why not?'

'Because you don't mean it. Because it wouldn't have entered your head if I hadn't said it. And I wasn't being serious.'

'You might not have been. I am.' They were standing outside a greengrocer's and an elderly man had to inch past them on the pavement to get by. 'Sorry,' murmured Leo, stepping back.

'You love me enough to want me – for good?' asked Camilla, astonished by everything Leo had said.

'Well . . . It does sound rather extreme, doesn't it? No, no, don't look like that. I do mean it. If you're prepared to accept me as I am, which is all the things Sarah told you and far worse besides . . .' He stopped, because Camilla had offered her face up to be kissed, and he had to kiss her.

'You don't have to marry me, Leo,' said Camilla.

'I think I do. I don't much care for the idea of living without you, you see. Let me take you back to your flat. You can pack your things and come with me. It's as easy as that.'

'No, it's not. There's the rent and everything.'

'I will pay the rent a hundred times over. Tell Jane to send every damn bill to me.' And Leo kissed her again.

They talked late into the night.

'I don't think I've ever told anyone so much about myself,' said Leo at last. He turned to look at Camilla, who had been lying next to him, staring at the ceiling as she listened. He leaned across and kissed her. 'Was it all as bad as you expected?'

'I don't know . . . Not all of it. Not the bit about your aunts in Wales. I think I'd rather forget the rest.' Leo smiled. 'There was one thing you failed to explain,' added Camilla.

'What?'

'Motives. Everyone has motives for the way they behave.'

God, she was sharp, thought Leo. 'Not necessarily. Some people are just careless, thoughtless.'

She turned to look at him. 'I don't believe you're that kind of person. You do things for a reason.'

He was silent for a moment. 'No, well . . . I suppose if you investigated even the most irreproachable behaviour in the world, you might find unworthy motives. I'm not going to explain myself any more. Apart from anything else, I'm too tired. Too tired for talking.' He drew his fingers lightly across her lips, down over her throat and to her breasts, and she sighed and closed her eyes. 'So tell me – now that you know the very worst about me,' said Leo, moving close against her, 'do you still think you can love me?'

'Oh, I can love you,' replied Camilla. 'I don't know whether I can trust you. Are you sure there aren't any more horrible skeletons in your closet?'

Leo put thoughts of Gideon from his mind. He hadn't told her about that because it was too recent, and, anyway, he trusted that problem was solved. Or would be shortly. 'None I can think of,' he said.

'Promise me,' she murmured, as his hands moved down across her body, 'that nothing you do will ever hurt me.'

'I promise,' said Leo, without hesitation.

Melissa had taken great pains to ensure that every detail of her affair with Leo had been faithfully chronicled, from the initial rapture to the eventual abuse and cruelty. She dwelt on his infidelities, his neglectful treatment of his son, his jealous rages, his professional insecurity . . . The final document ran to twenty pages. She photocopied it, folded each copy up, put them in envelopes, and addressed them to the two newspapers which she thought would be most likely to use what she had written. It would be her vindication. Everyone would know the truth, the reason why she had come to this. It was all Leo's fault. If only he had loved her.

After she had walked to the postbox, she came back to her flat, had a bath, washed her hair, put on the robe she had been wearing on the night that Leo had so cruelly humiliated and rejected her, and settled down on the bed with three-quarters of a bottle of Smirnoff blue label, and a large quantity of prescription tranquillizers.

She was discovered by her cleaning lady at nine-thirty the following morning, apparently dead to the world. The paramedics took her to hospital in an ambulance, and it was found that the overdose she had taken had not been fatal. There was every reason to think that she would make a full recovery, and would be sitting up in no time. That was what the nurses told the reporter who dropped in at the hospital, on the off-chance of something news-worthy, a reporter who happened to work for one of the papers to whom Melissa had posted her missive the previous day.

When he went into chambers next morning, Leo was surprised to see Edward Choke in the reception area, deep in conversation with Anthony.

'What Chay needs to show, you see, is that the museum collection is of pre-eminent national importance,' Edward was saying. 'Then he has to present costings and architectural plans to the Museums, Libraries and Archives Commission, showing how they fit into the overall museum strategy – morning, Leo!'

Leo returned Edward's cheerful greeting, but noted how Anthony pointedly ignored him. He must do something to repair the relationship. Whatever Anthony might think, Leo needed Anthony's friendship. He sincerely regretted now that he had ever allowed certain things to happen. He had no idea how he was going to mend the damage, but it now seemed to him vital that he should. He couldn't let Anthony go on thinking he didn't care for him. Things just hadn't happened at the right time . . .

On the way upstairs, Leo met Sarah on the landing.

'Ah, the very person. A word, if I may,' said Leo, drawing her into his room. He closed the door and leaned against it, regarding her stonily. 'It may interest you to know that your attempt to wreck relations between Camilla and myself was unsuccessful. If you ever try to do anything like that again, however, I will personally make sure you never get work in any set of chambers, nor in any shipping office, nor any P&I club in London. You're not the only one who can go around damaging people's reputations.'

Sarah gave him a considering look. 'How lovely to think of you two as an item. Such a contrast. The worldly, libidinous QC and the sweet, innocent junior. Maybe you see in her some kind of redemption – is that it, Leo? Well, don't fool yourself. You can't change that easily. And when you find that out, you'll still need me. We talk the same kind of language, after all.'

He said nothing, but stepped aside and opened the door for her.

She carried on downstairs, her expression nonchalant, but inside she felt wretched with pain and anger. She'd tried not to let her feelings for Leo go as far as they had, but she'd been helpless to stop them. And now she'd failed entirely. It was something she'd just have to try to get over. After all, he wasn't the only man in the world. As for Leo's threats, the last thing in the world she cared about was getting a job anywhere. No, there had to be other eligible men around, with enough money . . .

She came to the foot of the stairs and saw Anthony talking to Edward Choke. She watched as they said goodbye to one another, and Anthony went off to the clerks' room. Just as Edward was about to go through the door, Sarah stepped forward.

'Edward!' she said, with a look of delight. Edward turned and beamed at her. 'I haven't seen you in ages! Don't you think it's time we got together for a drink?'

Leo and Camilla arrived at Chichester Rents half an hour later. As they went up in the lift together, Camilla scanned the front page of the morning paper.

'Oh, dear,' she murmured, as a story caught her eye, 'that would be funny if it wasn't so awful. Some civil servant has been found dead. *"Sources indicate that death was brought about through auto-erotic asphyxiation. The deceased was* dressed in a woman's corset, and items found near the body, including a bicycle pump and a dog lead, suggest that death was brought about accidentally during a sexual act. Detectives are also investigating allegations that Smallwood, who was known to frequent local gay haunts in Ealing, had blackmailed local gay Jewish youths and forced them into sexual encounters by threatening to reveal their sexuality to their parents." Wow . . .'

Leo, who was glancing through some notes, was hardly listening.

Camilla carried on reading. ' "Gideon Smallwood, Principal Private Secretary to Tony Gear, the Minister for Artistic and Cultural Development, was a flamboyant figure in Whitehall circles –" '

'Let me see that!' Leo grabbed the paper from her as the lift doors opened. He stood outside the courtroom, scanning the page for the story. Dear God . . . Gideon. He read it through quickly. Found in a flat in Ealing . . . What a squalid way to go, thought Leo. His emotions at the news of Gideon's death were mixed. On the one hand he was deeply sorry that a man of such charm, with a mind more brilliant than most, and an infinite capacity to amuse, had become so devious, so ruthlessly and criminally exploitative, and had died such a foolish death. He felt a touch of sadness as he remembered Gideon, the gilded youth of twenty, sitting for endless hours at the bridge table. Yet Leo was also conscious of immense relief at the knowledge that he had nothing more to fear from him. He glanced at the small photograph of Gideon. It didn't show him at his best. Gideon wouldn't have liked it.

He handed the paper back to Camilla. 'Come on. We're going to be late.'

Camilla glanced at him curiously. 'Did you know him?'

'Yes. Slightly.'

Camilla looked away, said nothing, and just as Leo was trying to read her thoughts, an awful realization came to him, like a cold blow to the solar plexus. The cheque he had sent to the flat where Gideon had died. Oh, Christ . . . What would anyone make of that when it was found? He could not in that instant formulate the nature of the scandal that might ensue, but a hundred thousand pounds paid by a prominent QC to a homosexual blackmailer . . .

He and Camilla went into their respective robing rooms adjacent to the court. Leo took off his tie and slipped on his gown, thinking feverishly. He had put the envelope into the post tray yesterday evening, he recalled. It would go this morning. He must ring chambers. Never had his hands fumbled over his wretched bands as they did now. He pulled his mobile phone from the pocket of his jacket and rang the number of the clerks' room. Robert answered.

'Robert, listen, has the post tray been emptied this morning?'

'Hold on a minute, sir, let me have a look . . .' The longest six seconds in the world elapsed, and then, before Robert could come back on the line, Leo's phone gave a little beep and went dead. The battery had gone. Leo had failed to recharge it the night before. He swore and thrust it back into his pocket. There was no time now to borrow anyone else's phone. He would have to go into court. Olby would be arriving any minute.

Leo slid into his seat next to Camilla just as the usher declared 'Court rise!' Mr Justice Olby trotted in, as he had done every day for the last sixty-four days, and the final couple of hours of the Lloyd's litigation got underway. As he glanced at the clock, Leo remembered the book which Fred Fenton had opened among all the lawyers on when the case would end, to the exact hour and minute. There had been some argument as to whether they would time it by their watches, or by the court clock, which was fast. Eventually they had agreed to go by the time which appeared on the court stenographer's transcript. Leo, when he had made his guess of twelve-twenty and put in his money, had had no idea he would find himself earnestly praying that Fred Fenton, who had made the earliest estimate at eleven-thirty, might win.

As the clock ticked towards twelve-fifteen, Conor Grimley was still wringing the final drops from some drearily confused issue concerning the relationship of various litigants-in-person. 'My Lord, the point I make, and obviously my learned friend has not taken it, is that unless and until there is evidence saying that Mrs Aldous is Mr Denman's sister, which I know not one way or the other, there is no evidence before your Lordship giving your Lordship that information . . .'

Come on, please, thought Leo. While Conor bumbled on, Robert could be emptying the post tray, consigning that letter to its fatal destination. Perhaps it had already gone . . .

Mr Justice Olby, however, was as anxious to conclude the proceedings as anyone else, as he had already arranged to be at Ascot that afternoon. He looked up wearily as Conor drifted to a halt.

'Mr Grimley, is that all you have to say on that matter?'

'My Lord, yes . . .'

'Right. Anybody want to say anything else?' No one stirred. Mr Justice Olby dived briskly into his closing address. 'This has been a long and difficult case. I express my gratitude to the teams who have worked tirelessly on the case for their support and assistance, to leading and junior counsel on both sides for their comprehensive presentations and submissions, to the stenographers for the efficient production of the transcript, and to the court staff and my clerk, who have had to put up with long hours. I direct that further communication with the Court must be through solicitors. No letter should be sent to me direct by a litigating or non-litigating Name. I will aim to deliver judgment by about the last week of October or the first week of November.' As the transcript time of twelve-twenty-one showed on every laptop throughout the courtroom, Mr Justice Olby rose.

Camilla, putting her papers together for the last time, was about to say something to Leo when he asked, 'Have you got your mobile?' Aware from the tone of his voice that it was urgent, she took her phone from her bag and switched it on, and handed it to Leo without a word. Leo went quickly out to the robing room and rang chambers again.

'Robert? My battery went dead earlier. Has the post gone?'

'No, sir,' replied Robert. 'Well, it would have gone half an hour ago, but from the way you sounded earlier I guessed there was something you wanted held back.'

God bless that boy, thought Leo, for his perspicacity and intelligence. 'Well done, absolutely right,' said Leo. 'There's a letter in there, my handwriting, with an Ealing address on it.'

After a couple of seconds, Robert said, 'Yeah, got it, Mr Davies. A Mr Smallwood, Dresden Road?'

Leo closed his eyes in relief. 'That's the one. Hold on to it for me till I get back. The rest can go.'

'Right you are, sir.'

Leo switched off the phone. He sat there in the robing room, feeling drained. Paul Rollason came in, tugging off his bands. 'Well done,' he said. 'The transcript time came in at twelve-twenty-one.'

'Did it?' said Leo. 'I wasn't paying attention.'

As they waited to cross at the traffic lights, Leo noticed that Camilla looked preoccupied. 'What's up with you?' he asked.

'How well did you know that man, the one who was found dead yesterday?'

'I told you. Hardly at all. He was one of the Names. He and his mother.' Poor Lady Henrietta; Gideon had been the light of her life. 'He never came to court, though, so you wouldn't have met him.'

'Good. He sounded a pretty dreadful person.' They

turned through the gate into Middle Temple Lane. 'I didn't like to think there were more awful things you hadn't told me.'

Leo felt suddenly weary. He shrugged. 'Maybe there's no end to them.' He stopped at the foot of the stairs leading up to chambers. 'If you feel it's all too much, that you really can't live with someone like me, I will understand.'

Camilla said nothing. At that moment Robert came out, on his way to lunch.

'Oh, Mr Davies, that letter you wanted kept back – it's on my desk in the clerks' room.'

'Thanks.' Leo turned to Camilla. 'Don't wait for me – I want to talk to Robert about a couple of things.'

Camilla went into chambers, thinking about what Leo had just said. She picked up her post from her pigeon hole in the clerks' room and, passing Robert's desk on the way out, she glanced down and saw the letter which Robert had mentioned to Leo a moment earlier. There on the envelope, in Leo's distinctive handwriting, was Gideon Smallwood's name, and his Ealing address. The address of the flat in which he had been found dead. She stared at it, realizing in those seconds how easily Leo had lied to her.

For five minutes, Leo and Robert stood outside chambers discussing bookshelf sizes. When they had finished, and Leo was about to go, Robert added, 'By the way, that's a shame about Mr Cross.'

Leo looked back at him quickly. 'What about him?'

'Apparently he's leaving.' Seeing Leo's expression, he added hastily. 'Sorry – I thought you knew.'

'No. No, I didn't.'

Leo went slowly up the steps and stood on the threshold. He could hardly imagine life in chambers without Anthony, without the daily sight of the boy, his smile, the sound of his voice. This was the damage he had done. By trying to play down Anthony's significance in his life, abusing and betraying his trust and affection, he had driven him to the point where he wanted to get away, never to have to see Leo again. Anthony's love, which he had taken for granted and squandered, was his no longer. What, wondered Leo, was the point of trying to give new direction to his life, in the face of that simple truth?

For several moments Leo stood motionless in the sunlight, working through his thoughts and emotions. He could not, would not let the worst crisis in their relationship pass without trying to undo the damage. He knew in his heart that the last thing Anthony wanted was to leave 5 Caper Court, to take his practice to another set of chambers. Whatever it took, he must try to dissuade him, to heal the injuries he had inflicted – if such a thing was possible. He simply knew that he could not bear the idea of Anthony leaving.

He turned and went into chambers. Camilla was coming out of the clerks' room, but Leo scarcely gave her a glance as he headed upstairs to Anthony's room.

A Measure of Trust

CARO FRASER

The next book in the Caper Court series is out
in Spring 2004. But if you can't wait that long,
here's a taste of what's to follow . . .

Chapter One

'You know what? I reckon you want to go for something more vibrant next time you have your colour done.'

Ann Halliday said nothing, merely glanced at Charmaine's reflection in the salon mirror. Charmaine stroked Ann's newly cut hair reflectively. Then she nodded. 'Yeah, go for something a bit more blonde.'

It was an effort for Ann to think of an appropriate response. Her hair didn't interest her a great deal. It had taken her over eighteen months to persuade Charmaine not to blow-dry it into some voluminous style that could not possibly be accommodated under her barrister's wig. She liked it to be cut neatly and sensibly, in a way that wouldn't attract any attention at all. When she was younger, when her light-brown hair had had a youthful sheen, she'd worn it long and sleek. But age had faded that lustre, and grey was creeping in. Better short and unobtrusive.

She gazed at her own reflection. Then again, maybe Charmaine was right. Perhaps blonde highlights would brighten things up a bit. But she didn't want to attract comment — and teasing comment, even if kindly meant, she would certainly get from her male-barrister colleagues, particularly the three she was about to have lunch with. She would hate anyone to think she had gone to trouble over her appearance. Such a thing was suggestive of vanity – and vanity, Ann Halliday thought, was strictly for the young.

Charmaine picked up a square mirror and wagged it back and forth behind Ann's head, as she always did, showing her a reflection of the cut. Ann could never see the point. It meant she had to smile and nod appreciatively, as though she cared what the back of her head looked like.

Charmaine put down the mirror and unfastened the Velcro on the gown, lifting it from Ann's shoulders. 'Off anywhere nice?'

Ann stood up and let Charmaine brush her down. It was a fair enough question, since she normally came in to have her hair cut on Saturday afternoons, rather than on a weekday, such as today. 'I'm meeting some friends for lunch.'

'Lovely. Nice way to cheer up a Monday. A girly get-together, is it?'

'No. Some male friends.' As soon as the words were out, she felt they sounded odd, not what she meant to imply at all. 'Colleagues,' she tried to add, but Charmaine was already off.

'More than one! Now, that's what I call greedy!'

'It's sort of a business lunch. Nothing very exciting.'

She paid the bill and tipped Charmaine, who fetched Ann's jacket and helped her into it. 'Well, you enjoy it, anyway.'

Ann left the salon with mild relief, stepping out into the summer air, focusing her thoughts on lunch. It seemed strangely dislocating, meeting up with Marcus, Roger and Maurice in this way. Like a bunch of outlaws. Last week they had been fellow tenants at 3 Wessex Street, a large and prosperous set of barristers' chambers, but now they were free agents. Well, for the time being. The departure from the chambers where she had always worked still held an air of unreality for Ann. Looking back over the past few months, it seemed now as though she had been swept along, a victim of forces not of her own creation. A set of barristers' chambers was not like a company, or even a partnership. It had no animus, but was a collection of individuals, each paying rent to occupy space in the same building, each in his own employment, answerable to no one, but all relying on the same group of clerks to organize their professional lives, bring in work and process fees. Just as the identity of any set of chambers depended on the personalities of the individual tenants, so it was that the stability and smooth running of chambers depended on the tenants' mutual dependency. Where personalities clashed, splits and factions were often the result. It had been Maurice who had started the whole thing. Maurice – ambitious, aggressive, piqued at not having been made head of chambers – had created the split almost as an act of reprisal at those who had opposed him, fomenting little rows and divisions within chambers. He had gradually brought others into his camp – Roger, who had been a protégé of Maurice's and who tended to take his side no matter what, and then Marcus and herself. She had had her own grievances, of course. She had felt for some time that she wasn't being clerked properly, not getting work of the quality she deserved, but without Maurice's per-suasion, she wondered if she might not have stuck it out. It had been a great leap, to leave the chambers where she had been a tenant for seventeen years. Maurice had flattered her, talked her into it one evening in a wine bar. 'The fact is, Ann,' he'd said, '5 Caper Court want to expand. They're too small. They need people of your calibre, your expertise.' She'd known then that his own vanity required that he take people with him when making his departure. But she'd agreed. Should she be grateful to him? Should Marcus and Roger, for that matter? Time would tell. By the end of the week they would be newly installed as tenants at 5 Caper Court – not as large in number as 3 Wessex Street, but no less prestigious. The word was that the head of chambers there, Roderick Hayter, was destined for the High Court bench in a few months' time. Did Maurice have his once-thwarted ambitions focused on that position in a new set of chambers? Very probably.

It was a five-minute walk to the restaurant in Gray's Inn from Bloomsbury, where Ann lived. Marcus and Roger were already there. Marcus, black, beautiful, and twenty-five, was lounging in his chair at a table by the window with an air of magnificent boredom, looking as immaculately turned out in chinos and an open-necked shirt as he ever did in his three-piece suit. Roger, on the other hand, who was sitting studying the menu through his round glasses, was dressed in a Gap T-shirt, scruffy jeans and trainers, and looked as dishevelled as he did in the eternal M&S suit and unironed shirt which he wore for work day in, day out. The attention paid by each to his appearance, Ann always thought, was symptomatic of their peculiarly different, though formidable, intellects. As a lawyer, Marcus was fastidious, hard-working, and somewhat haughty, fiercely proud of his ability to deliver snap opinions on complex legal problems. Roger Fry was another character altogether. Sweet-natured, kind-faced, with a donnish air which belied his twenty-eight years, Roger conducted his social and his working life in an erratic and eccentric fashion, but seemed somehow to bring both off. His appearance was a matter of general indifference to him, so too his surroundings. Conferences with well-heeled and powerful clients in his room at 3 Wessex Street were generally conducted amid a clutter of books, papers, and cardboard boxes stacked with documents. It was as though Roger was too focused on law, on the case and the facts before him, to pay much attention to his immediate surroundings, unless those surroundings happened to be a pub or a wine bar. But both Roger and Marcus were successful and well regarded in their profession, and each attracted a different kind of client. Like Ann, however, they had begun to feel that the best cases at 3 Wessex Street were being diverted by certain clerks to other, less deserving members of chambers. So here they sat today, waiting for Maurice Faber, bound together by their new destiny.

'Hello,' said Roger, glancing up at Ann. Marcus, with his customary impeccable good manners, half rose from his chair. Ann smiled and sat down, and Marcus subsided.

'It's a strange sort of day,' said Ann, taking off her

jacket. 'I should be used to working from home, but for some reason I couldn't get down to anything this morning. I went to the hairdresser's instead.'

'I know what you mean,' said Marcus. 'It's odd not having chambers there in the background. Briefs to pick up, mail to open, coffee to drink, people to chat to.'

'Office syndrome,' said Roger. 'It's a security blanket.'

'You think that's why Maurice arranged this lunch?' said Marcus. 'Give us a sense of security?'

'Identity, more like. He thinks this is his show, and he's running it.'

'I find it rather exciting, joining a new set of chambers,' said Ann. 'Like a new school term.'

'You found those exciting?' Roger put down the menu, took off his glasses and rubbed his eyes. 'It honestly doesn't make much odds to me, so long as I've got a desk and a telephone.'

'You look very tired,' said Ann, glancing at Roger with motherly concern. 'Have you been working late on that shipbuilding case?'

Roger laughed and replaced his glasses. 'No, Ann. Kind of you to think so. I went on a pub crawl round South Ken last night with some friends.' He gave an enormous yawn. 'Sorry. Only got out of bed an hour ago.'

'New surroundings are one thing,' said Marcus. 'What about the people?'

'You met them all at that chambers tea a month ago,' remarked Ann.

'Yes, but I can't honestly say I know anyone well. Except Anthony Cross.'

'I'm fairly friendly with David Liphook,' said Roger, 'and Will Cooper, Simon Barron. They're a decent bunch. And Leo Davies, of course – didn't you have a case against him a couple of months ago?'

Marcus winced inwardly. He didn't care to remember his one and only courtroom encounter with Leo, in a dispute concerning the personal liability of freight forwarders. He hadn't exactly come off best. He had to admit to a grudging admiration for Leo Davies' skills of advocacy – not to mention his taste in clothes. Marcus was always prepared to respect anyone who dressed as well as Leo did.

'Ah, yes – Leo Davies. Every woman in the Temple is supposed to be madly in love with him – isn't that right, Ann?' Marcus glanced at her.

'Something of an exaggeration,' said Ann dryly, turning her attention to the menu. She and Leo went back many years, having been at Bar School together. She didn't run across him much nowadays, though she heard a good deal about him. Without being flamboyant, Leo had managed to cultivate a reputation which was unusual in the staid world of the Temple. He was renowned for his brilliant mind and acute professionalism as a barrister, and was regarded as witty and amusing company, but there were always darker rumours circulating about him which, everyone assumed, must have some foundation in truth. Ann harboured a certain curiosity as to whether or not he merited his libidinous reputation – it certainly wasn't the way she remembered him at twenty-one, even though she had always found something both provocative and beguiling about those sharp, blue eyes and his gently modulated Welsh voice. Not that she would have admitted that to the likes of Marcus and Roger. Besides, she regarded herself as a hardened, professional woman, not given to weaknesses where other members of the Bar were concerned.

Marcus nodded in the direction of the door. 'Here's Maurice.'

Maurice Faber was in his early forties, tall, with thick, very dark hair and heavy eyebrows, which gave him an Italianate look. His movements, bodily and facial, were brisk and energetic, his glance and smile quick and keen. Unlike Roger and Marcus, he was dressed in a suit and tie. He held up a folded copy of the *Sun* as he came towards their table, grinning.

'Any of you seen this?'

Ann, who was strictly a *Guardian* reader, shook her head.

'There certainly wasn't anything in *The Times* that got me going,' said Marcus.

'I haven't been up long enough to look at the papers,' said Roger. 'What's the scandal?'

'Hah! Scandal is just the word.' Maurice sat down. Ann could tell from his eyes that whatever it was that had Maurice so excited was bound to involve downfall or humiliation for someone else. Such things invariably turned Maurice on. She felt an anticipatory compassion for whoever the unfortunate person might be.

Maurice held up the front page for them to see. 'MY LOVE HELL MADE ME WANT TO END IT AT ALL,' read the headline, and below that, '*TV's Melissa tells how top QC lover drove her to suicide bid*.' There was a large, glamorous picture of a blonde woman, familiar to those present as Melissa Angelicos, presenter of a Channel Four arts programme. Below that was a somewhat smaller photograph of the very man they had just been discussing: Leo Davies.

'Bloody hell,' said Roger. He reached out for the paper, and Maurice handed it to him, then sat back, relishing the moment.

'What on earth is that all about?' asked Ann incredulously, as Roger and Marcus huddled together, devouring the story.

'It seems,' said Maurice, 'that Leo Davies was having some intense relationship with this television-presenter woman, and it all began to go off the rails. He was knocking her about, having affairs with other women–'

'Other *men* as well, according to this,' said Roger, without looking up.

'– it began to affect her work, she lost her job in television because of it, and in the long run she got so unhappy over him that she wanted to top herself. But before doing so, she decided to tell the world what a shit Davies was by penning a lengthy suicide note, giving intimate insights into their affair and detailing his many failings. Which –' Maurice indicated the paper '– is what you're reading. She posted it off to the *Sun*, then swallowed a large quantity of pills and vodka. Not quite enough, however, because she woke up in hospital the next day.'

'And they've printed it?' marvelled Ann.

'Well, not in its entirety, apparently. But the good bits.'

Marcus shook his head. 'He'll have them. This is pretty strong stuff. He has to sue.'

'If he can. Not much point, really. The damage is done.'

'Listen to this – '*But love rat Leo claims he hardly knew Melissa. "I have never been romantically involved with Melissa Angelicos," said Leo Davies, when our reporter spoke to him on the phone at his chambers in the Temple, from where he conducts his one-and-a-half-million-a-year commercial practice –*'

'Ha, ha. He wishes.'

'"*She is a neurotic woman who has been pestering me and my family for some months, and her story is a pathetic, delusional fantasy." He declined to comment further.*'

'They must be mad to publish it,' said Ann.

'Oh, come on. Think of the increase in circulation. Even if this woman is completely nuts and has made it all up, they hardly lose out.'

'I'd be straight round to Carter-Ruck, if I were Davies,' said Marcus, still poring over the juicier bits of the story.

'Let's have a look.'

Marcus passed the paper to Ann. She scanned the contents, which were admittedly pretty bad, and glanced across at Maurice.

'You and I both know Leo,' she said. 'None of this sounds remotely true.'

Maurice shrugged, but said reluctantly, 'I have to say I agree with you. Much as the story adds to the gaiety of our nation, I suspect that, reading between the lines, most of it is fabricated. There may be some basis to it – perhaps they did have an affair – but certain things don't ring true. I don't believe he's the type to behave violently towards anyone. More to the point, all that stuff she comes out with about his professional insecurity is so much crap. He's one of the best lawyers around. And one thing they fail to mention in that article is that Davies obtained an injunction against her a couple of months beforehand because she'd been harassing him.'

Ann gave a small smile. Maurice had certainly done his homework. He'd probably been ferreting away at this all morning.

'So you believe him when he says that he was never involved with her?'

Maurice grinned. 'Well, to quote another unreliable female – he would say that, wouldn't he?'

While the four of them sat discussing the scandal over lunch, the same topic had been exercising the members of the clerks' room at 5 Caper Court. The *Sun* was not a newspaper which any of the barristers in that august set of chambers would deign to purchase, but everybody, on their way in and out of the clerks' room, normally paused for a few moments to glance at the copy belonging to Robert, the junior clerk. On this particular morning, however, Robert had been at the House of Lords, and didn't come into chambers until ten-forty-five, until which time the inhabitants of 5 Caper Court remained blissfully unaware of the events which were about to overtake them. When Robert did finally come in, newspaper in hand, he was agog.

'Have you heard?' he asked Henry, the senior clerk.

Henry, a harassed man in his early thirties, with thinning hair and an expression of almost permanent dejection, looked round from where he sat at his computer screen in his shirtsleeves.

'What?'

Robert dropped his copy of the *Sun* on to Henry's keyboard. Henry glanced down at it, smoothing it out. He gazed at the headline, then at the photograph of Leo, in disbelief.

'I would have thought plenty of people in the Temple would have been on the phone to you about it,' said Robert.

Henry shook his head slowly as he read the story.

'Then again,' said Robert, 'it's so bad they probably didn't like to.'

Oh, Mr Davies, thought Henry – oh, Mr Davies, what have you gone and done? His heart sank as he digested the details. As though this bunch didn't give him enough grief. It was bad enough trying to keep their work in order, without them getting their sodding love lives all over the papers. *Continued on pages 5, 6, 7 and 8 . . .* He couldn't bear to look. What would this do to business? A scandal like this was bad publicity, whichever way you looked at it. The work was bound to suffer. Clients didn't like see ing their barristers' faces in the papers, especially not a story like this, beating up his girlfriend, driving her to suicide . . . He glanced back at the picture of Melissa Angelicos. No, not Mr Davies. Not his style. Mind you, whether it was true or not was completely beside the point. Henry groaned aloud.

'Pretty bad, isn't it?' said Robert, agreeably thrilled. This was about the most exciting thing that had ever happened in chambers. By and large, barristers were a boring bunch, not given to all the stuff this woman claimed Leo got up to. Bunking off with blokes, for instance – mind you, Robert had always thought there was something a bit fruity about Mr Davies.

A third clerk, Felicity Waller, came through the swing doors at that moment and caught Robert's last remark.

'What's bad?' she asked.

Felicity was a buxom and very pretty twenty-three-year-old, with a cheeky, brisk manner which endeared her to most, if not all, of the barristers at 5 Caper Court. Even those who didn't entirely approve of Felicity's plunging necklines and thigh-skimming skirts were appreciative of the fees she negotiated for them, a skill which Felicity put down to genes inherited from her South London market-trader father.

Henry had long nursed a silent, hopeless and unrequited passion for Felicity, and would normally have given her his full attention, particularly as she was wearing a figure-hugging summer dress of some brevity, but today he didn't even look up. He just shook his head and stared despondently at the paper.

Felicity put her cup of coffee down on her desk and came over.

Robert indicated the paper and endeavoured to mask

his excitement with a tone of regret. 'Mr Davies has got himself into a bit of trouble.'

'Let's have a look.'

Henry's phone began to ring. He answered it, handing the paper to Felicity, who took it over to her desk.

'Bloody hell . . .' She took in the headline, the picture of Leo, and sank slowly into her seat. She looked long and hard at the picture of the faded blonde which dominated the page, then began to read through the sordid list of her allegations against Leo. That he'd hit her. That he'd had affairs with other people during their relationship, men as well as women. That he'd neglected his son by his ex-wife, failing to turn up on access visits. That his professional life was a mess. That he drank. That he rubbished colleagues. She glanced up at Robert, who'd sidled over to assess her reaction.

'This is crap', said Felicity. 'It's total and utter crap. Mr Davies isn't like that.'

'Not the point, though, is it?' Robert shook his head sorrowfully.

'He's a lovely man. He wouldn't do any of this.' Felicity's view of Leo was somewhat coloured by the fact that when her erstwhile boyfriend, Vince, had been up on a manslaughter charge two months ago – through no fault of his own, Felicity always averred – Leo had spared no effort to help her and advise her. Not that it had been of much use, since Vince had gone down for eight years. Still, Mr Davies was her champion, he'd got her this job in the first place, and he was bloody lovely to look at as well, so she would hear no ill of him. Like Henry, she knew in her heart that this was not Mr Davies' style at all. 'Poor bloke. Not going to do his practice much good, is it?'

'Is he in?' asked Robert.

'No, I haven't seen him all morning – thank God,' said Felicity. 'He's probably got wind of this and is steering well clear. Can you imagine having to walk around the Temple, knowing everyone's seen this and is talking about you? He'll probably lie low for a couple of days.'

Henry, engrossed in morose speculation about the way in which this scandal was likely to tarnish the reputation of 5 Caper Court, clicked on his computer screen, and brought up, out of curiosity, the list of tenants who were in chambers that morning, witnessed by the swiping of their electronic tags as they came into the building. There was Leo's name.

'He's in,' said Henry, puzzled.

The fact was that at five-thirty that morning, as dawn light pearled the eastern sky and crept across the silent cobbles of the lanes and courtyards of the Temple, Leo had come into chambers to do some work on a skeleton argument on one of his cases. He had parked his Aston Martin in the deserted car park at the bottom of King's Bench Walk and, apologizing to the dosser in the doorway of 5 Caper Court for disturbing his slumber, had come into chambers to enjoy a few hours of steady, uninterrupted work before the telephones began to ring and feet and voices to sound on the stairs. Since no one was aware of his presence, no one had troubled him all morning.

Now, at ten to eleven, fatigued even by his own industrious standards, Leo Davies closed his books, rose, stretched and yawned. His lean figure was trim and athletic for a man in his late forties, his features clean-cut and handsome, his blue eyes sharp and intelligent. The premature silvery-grey of his thick hair, in the eyes of Felicity and other admirers, only added to his attractiveness. He stood now at his window, gazing down at the figures hurrying to and fro across Caper Court, his mind paused in a rare state of idleness, and decided to have a coffee and go downstairs to collect his mail and catch up on the gossip.

Down in the clerks' room, speculation was rife.

'D'you think he knows about it?' asked Felicity.

'Dunno,' said Robert. 'Depends. What a way to start the week.'

The door of the clerks' room opened at that moment, and all three clerks turned as Leo came in. They looked at him in horrified uncertainty. The cheerful expression on his face suggested that he knew nothing of this calamity.

'Morning, troops,' said Leo mildly, going to his pigeon hole to extract the bundle of letters which lay there. Then he glanced round at them in puzzlement, surveying their silent faces. 'Some problem?'

Henry took it upon himself to deliver the blow. He rose from his desk. 'Robert's just brought the paper in, sir. You'd better have a look at it.' He picked up the newspaper from Felicity's desk and handed it to Leo, who took it wonderingly.

They stood in stricken fascination as Leo scanned the

front page carefully. His expression didn't falter, except for one moment when he raised a brief and quizzical eyebrow. He might as well have been digesting the contents of an interesting, but not very remarkable, brief. They waited.

Leo tossed the paper on to Robert's desk and passed a hand across his brow. He looked up at Henry. 'That's a bit of a nuisance, isn't it?'

'Yes, sir,' replied Henry, somewhat nonplussed by Leo's reaction.

'It's a complete load of balls, of course. Some journalist rang me up a week ago and asked me about the contents of this suicide note, whatever it is, that she'd written, and I told them then. I didn't expect them to print it.' As though the import of it had only just hit him, Leo sat down. 'Holy Christ.'

'It's not good, Mr Davies,' said Henry.

'I knew it was rubbish when I read it,' said Felicity. 'I said, none of this is Mr Davies' style.' She glanced at Robert for support. 'Didn't I?'

Leo gave a wan smile. 'Thank you, Felicity.' He drew the paper towards him again and studied the photograph of Melissa Angelicos. That vindictive bitch. It was like being pursued to the very depths of hell by a madwoman. She'd seemed innocuous enough on their first meeting, as co-trustees of a recently opened museum of modern art, but what had seemed like a mild crush on her part had turned, over the course of a few months, into a full-blown obsession. She had stalked him, lain in wait for him outside his flat at night, pestered him with letters and gifts, followed him in her car to his country home, turned up during court proceedings . . . The thing had become a nightmare. It was when she began to harass his ex-wife and their baby son that Leo had taken legal steps to obtain an injunction against her. He had thought that that, plus a few quiet threats, had done the trick. But no. A failed suicide attempt, this farrago of lies and fantasy committed to paper and sent off to a daily newspaper who were stupid and evil enough to print it, and she was succeeding in wrecking his life once more.

He flicked through to the pages where the story continued, embellished by another picture of himself emerging from the law courts, and glanced through the contents. That they had actually had the gall . . . Didn't they have any respect for privacy, or decency, let alone the truth? He felt a hot surge of anger. He would make those bastards, and Melissa Angelicos, pay for every lying word printed here. He'd have a writ issued before the day was out.

The phone rang, and Robert went to answer it. Leo folded the paper up and rose. 'I'm sorry,' he said to Felicity and Henry. 'This isn't going to make life very easy for you people.'

'We'll cope, sir,' said Henry. 'Not the first damage-limitation exercise we've had to carry out.'

'What will you do?' Felicity gazed at Leo with big, anxious eyes.

'The first thing I'm going to do,' said Leo, 'is to go home and consider my options. Field my calls. Don't tell anyone where I am.'

As he left the clerks' room, he passed Simon Barron, a

junior tenant, without saying a word. Simon, who had heard about the scandal from friends on his way back from a con in Paper Buildings, gazed after him.

'I hadn't expected to see Leo in chambers today. Not after the news.' He glanced at the clerks. 'I take it you've all heard?'

Henry nodded grimly. 'Mr Davies has only just found out himself. He's going home.'

'Best place for him,' sighed Felicity.

Leo drove back to his flat in Belgravia. The summer air was heavy with the threat of thunder, and the first drops of rain were pattering on the leaves of the plane trees in the quiet garden square as he parked his car in the mews garage. In the flat he opened one of the long windows in the drawing room and let the scent of rain, now splashing heavily on to the pavements and parks, fill the room. He stood there, watching, listening, thinking.

He turned from the window, loosened his tie, and sat down in an armchair. The room was large, high-ceilinged, expensively furnished in a restrained, minimalist fashion, the walls hung with works of modern art from Leo's own collection – and to Leo at that moment it felt nothing like home. The place never had. Only Stanton, his house in Oxfordshire, felt like a safe haven. Even in the house where he and Rachel had lived, during the brief months of their marriage, he had never properly felt any sense of belonging. Not to the house, nor to Rachel. And now, in this moment of isolation and humiliation, with a hungry world outside feasting on fabricated stories of his licentious doings, he badly wanted to be somewhere safe and far away. He closed his eyes, trying to work his way through his anger to thoughts of how best to deal with the situation. The phone rang several times, but he ignored it.

After twenty minutes, the buzzer to his flat sounded. With a sigh, Leo rose and crossed the room and went to the intercom. 'Yes?'

'Leo, it's me – Camilla.' The voice was light and young, charged with anxiety.

'Come up.' He pressed the buzzer to let her in, and went to the front door.

She appeared at the top of the stairs, breathless, rain-soaked, and came into his arms, unquestioning and loving, and hugged him. Touched, he passed his hand lightly over her auburn hair.

'You're very wet.'

'It's stopping now. I ran all the way from the Tube.' She took off her raincoat and Leo hung it up.

'Aren't you meant to be in court today?'

'I am. But when I rang chambers and Felicity said you were here, I had to come. I can't stay long. I've got to be back in court at two.' She hugged him again, then looked at him, eyes wide and sad. 'Oh, Leo . . .'

He essayed a smile. 'Not much fun, is it?'

'There was a copy of the paper in the robing room at the Law Courts. I couldn't believe it . . . I still can't.'

'What does that mean? You don't believe it? Or you don't want to?' Leo turned and went into the kitchen. Camilla followed him.

'Of course I don't believe it! No one who knows anything about it possibly could. You told me all about her, the way she was harassing you. I was in court with you that day she showed up with her camera – remember? I just don't want other people to believe it.'

'Yes, well . . . there's not a lot you can do about that, unfortunately.'

'But you can.'

'Issue proceedings, you mean? It's not something I ever advise anyone to do lightly. Litigation is a mug's game, as well you know, which is why the mugs pay people like you and me so handsomely to conduct it.' He opened the fridge. 'Can I make you a sandwich, or something? Can't sit around in the Court of Appeal on an empty stomach.'

'No, thanks. I'll get something on the way back.' She came over, closed the fridge, and hugged him again.

He sighed and put his arms round her, giving himself up to her ardour and sympathy. 'You are the sweetest thing in the world. I'm glad you came.'

'I called you on my mobile. Why didn't you answer?'

'I assumed it might be some journalist.'

'How would they get your number? Henry wouldn't give it out.'

'True,' he sighed. 'I'm getting paranoid, fairly understandably. Come on –' He took her hand and led her from the kitchen. '– I want to sit down and hold you.'

He stretched out on the sofa, Camilla nestling against him. They talked for a while about the newspaper article, about what Leo could do about it. 'The trouble is,' said

Leo, 'I still feel rather numb. It's hard to think properly. The best thing for me right now is you.' He kissed her. 'It seems absurd that you still haven't moved in. I could do with a bit of domestic security.'

'Leo, it's not that easy. I can't just pack up and leave. Jane has to find a new flatmate, and that takes time.'

'I've told you that I'll happily pay dear Jane as much rent as –'

'It's not just that. It's not just money. And it's not just Jane. There are my parents to think about.'

'Oh, God.'

'Leo, look at it from their point of view. How will it sound if I tell them I'm shacking up with some forty-seven-year-old? I'm twenty-two. You're older than my mother, for heaven's sake.'

'You could point out to them that I'm a perfectly respectable commercial lawyer, who's –' He paused. 'No, I suppose the respectable bit is shot to pieces, isn't it?' Leo ran his fingers through his silver hair in exasperation. 'Christ, if a libel action is what it takes, then so be it. But you're grown-up, for God's sake. Why worry about what you parents think?'

'Because they are my parents! And I love them. I don't want to upset them.' Leo gazed at her. Twenty-two. From a parental point of view, still not much more than a child. She kissed him. 'I do love you – you know that?'

Leo returned her kiss gently. 'Yes, I believe you do.'

She got up. 'I have to get back to court. Sorry it's such a fleeting visit. I'll see you this evening.'

He lay on the sofa, listening to the sound of the front

door closing. He thought about the evening a week ago when he had gone round to her flat. He'd been afraid that he'd lost her, fearful that all the things she'd heard – about his bisexuality, his fling with Anthony, and God knows what else – had estranged her from him for good. Did he now regret the impulse which had prompted him to propose marriage to her? It wasn't a question of not loving her enough. God knows he did . . . But if anyone had told him, a few years ago, that at forty-seven he would be on the point of marrying for a second time, he would have laughed in disbelief. Someone whose sexual appetite ran to men as well as women wasn't exactly ideal husband material. He had spent twenty years cultivating for himself a private life utterly detached from his professional existence, one in which he enjoyed spending the considerable sums he earned in his practice at the Bar, by indulging his tastes in clothing, works of art, wine and ridiculously expensive cars. Being tied to someone, unable to do exactly as he pleased, with whomever he pleased, was not his style at all. Which, naturally, was why his marriage to Rachel had come unstuck. One homosexual affair and a fling with the nanny was probably more than most wives would tolerate in their husbands. Not that his marriage to Rachel had ever been more than one of convenience – his own, at any rate – something to scotch the rumours about his sexuality which had, at the time, threatened to harm his professional reputation. And she'd been pregnant. Oliver, his two-year-old son, was the one good thing to have come out of that mess. He had never thought it possible to love another being as much as he did Oliver . . . Beyond Oliver and his own mother, Leo didn't care much for the idea of family.

At least with Rachel he hadn't had to contend with anything more than her mother, and those encounters, while she'd been alive, had been mercifully few. With Camilla, however, he was going to get the full works, he could see that. He rubbed his hands across his face. Parents. He was going to have to meet them. Oh, Lord . . . he really wasn't up for this. It was already beginning to feel oppressive. Not Camilla herself, who was delightful, clever, astonishingly sensuous, and touchingly young, but the set-up, the encroaching involvement of other people. A wedding. Relations. She would want babies, eventually. Shades of the family prison-house begin to close upon the ageing rake, thought Leo – and a lot of people would doubtless say it served him bloody well right.

He shouldn't have asked her to marry him. Just to move in. But in thinking that, wasn't he admitting that the thing wasn't necessarily going to be long-term? It was possible that she would grow tired first, feel the need of someone younger, closer to her own age, but in all honesty, the doubts lay with him. He knew himself too well. How long until his notoriously restless gaze fell upon someone – male or female – and he found himself unable to resist the temptation? He loved Camilla, but he didn't trust himself. Just a couple of months ago certain episodes with that departed wretch, Gideon, had forced Leo to the decision that some clean, respectable living was what he needed at his age. For Oliver's sake, if not his own. Camilla had seemed like the key to that. Marry her, settle down, live quietly . . . Now, as the reality of what it all involved began to dawn on him, he felt less certain.

With a groan of exasperation, he stood up and paced around the room. Forget Camilla for the moment. Forget about marrying anybody. That could wait. The pressing issue right now was what he should do about this hellish thing in the papers, and limiting the damage it was bound to cause. The one person to whom he very much wanted to talk was Anthony. There was no one closer to him. But he had succeeded in damaging that precious relationship through his own irresponsible behaviour. The mistake had been to sleep with him, to let Anthony think there was something more to it than . . . What? Friendship? He doubted if there was any of that left. A week ago Anthony had been ready to leave chambers just to get away from Leo, so hurt and disillusioned was he, and Leo, having spoken to him only once since then – a brief, unhappy exchange which had resolved nothing – had no idea if that was still his firm intention.

He needed to speak to him, to sound him out, to help him decide what to do. He had never gone to Anthony in that way before. Maybe it would help to resolve more than one troublesome issue. He went to the phone, picked it up, and rang chambers, asking to speak to Anthony.

As good as Joanna Trollope, or your money back

We hope you've enjoyed *A Perfect Obsession* by Caro Fraser, and are looking forward to reading the next instalment in the lives of the partners at Caper Court. What will the enigmatic and sexy Leo Davis QC do next? What will happen to Melissa? And will Camilla get her man...?

If you don't agree with our suggestion that Caro Fraser is as good as Joanna Trollope, we'll refund you the price you paid for this book. To claim your money back, please return the book, along with the till receipt, giving us the reasons why you didn't enjoy it, to:

> The Marketing Dept
> Penguin
> 8th Floor
> 80 Strand
> London WC2R 0RL

Filling in the following details:

NAME ....
(PLEASE NOTE cheque will be made payable to this name)

ADDRESS ....

....

....

CONTACT NUMBER ....

NB This offer is valid for six months from publication date (05.6.03). Offer ends 05.12.03. Full refunds for the purchase price of *A Perfect Obsession* will be issued within 28 days of receipt of returned book. Postage and packing cost of returned book will not be refunded. Replacement books will not be issued. This offer is open to UK and ROI residents only.